Under
THE
Avalanche

Annen Cabe

Copyright © Anne McCabe, 2011
The author has asserted her moral rights.

ISBN: 978-1-908417-10-7

Published in 2011 by **Shackleton Publishing**
an imprint of **The Universal Publishing Group**

www.theuniversalpublishinggroup.com

A CIP Catalogue record for this book is available from
The British Library and the Irish Copyright Libraries.

Designed, typeset, printed and bound in Ireland by **The Book Producers Ltd.**

www.thebookproducers.ie

Under
THE
Avalanche

ANNE MCCABE

To the memory of Jerome

«The seed that bears my soul will fly and I shall live forever.»

CONTENTS

Prologue

My grandmother was born under the avalanche, the only one ever to have happened in this valley, or indeed any valley anywhere in Ireland. It left a place of deep shadows and sadness so that even the birds didn't sing there anymore, on the side of that lonely hill in Wicklow. But that is how Gertrude, my maternal grandmother, remembers and marks her birth, as if her life hasn't cast enough shadows of its own.

The avalanche was unusual, for the snow never fell so deep nor were the mountains so high that such snowfalls and landslides could occur here, as they did in the Alps. It was a combination of sleet and high winds that forced the snow ever higher into mounting banks until a raging gust tipped it down the valley side of the mountain. It slid, gathering pace, until it unleashed the rocks of the earth to roar downwards on top of a little hut which housed a young family of a couple and six children asleep in their beds. When they awoke it was all too late to stop the tidal wave descending down out of the darkness. Not one of them survived. The baby was newborn, one day old.

A mass of rubble, boulders and ice covered the dwelling. The neighbours spent the next day digging and dragging out the bodies before the frost at nightfall could harden, imprisoning them in an icy tomb forever. Then they laid them out side by side on a makeshift stretcher and carted the bodies down through the debris one by one, while a cold wind blew capricious and cruel. It took some days to bury them as the ground was hard and unyielding. The snow glittered cruelly on the mountain to mock them. The family had been cottagers tending a few sheep high up on the side of the mountain. They were waked below at the nearest house, which was half a mile away.

No wonder it is a place of silences. Only a simple cross now marks the spot. A Mass used to be said there once a year but even this custom, of late, is dying away. Most snows stay on top of the mountain in January now, covering the earth with a hard frost that glistens but never betrays movement.

Granny was born Gertrude Cullen, 'born after the avalanche,' she always said, although it was probably years afterwards, but that doesn't really matter. It's part of the telling of the tale.

She heard the story in the kitchen from Bridie when she was a little girl, over and over again. 'That baby will get you if you roam too far,' Bridie would scold.

So in the child's imagination the avalanche towered over Gertrude's youth even while she romped freely in the hills and valleys before adult life took over. The one part of the story that stuck in her mind to haunt her was this: the newborn baby had no coffin, but was buried alongside its mother, only one day old. It was said the spirit of that little baby was still abroad in the forest crying in the wind.

I didn't know my grandmother when I was growing up on a sheep farm further down the valley under the avalanche hill, close to the bend in the river that leads off up an avenue to the big house. But at the end of my teenage years, while still as innocent as the day is long, I was thrown together with her in unusual circumstances.

It started in 1984, the year they found the baby's body on the beach. It had been stabbed twenty-seven times. That was down in County Kerry. Terrible things began to happen here too that year in the shadow of the avalanche. Mammy's nerves began to get at her because Master Cullen, her beloved grandfather, was dying. Then she was going on end-lessly about her mother Gertrude and how she shouldn't have been living up in the schoolhouse with him. She never liked her mother.

And then me. God I was so innocent. Me and Simon.

I didn't mean any harm, or ever to kill. No I didn't. But I was so mithered and confused and I had no one to talk to, only a house full of kids, with Helen gone to Carlow for the hairdressing course.

It was a long nine months in that very cold winter of 1984 going into 1985, when I often wished I hadn't been born Catherine Mulhall, with relatives up in the big house – or a cousin called Simon.

And so I came to know Gertrude; Granny.

I had hardly known Granny at all growing up and in fact I was very afraid of her, especially that time when I went up to the schoolhouse with my shame.

After a time though we became quite close, in a distant sort of way. Maybe she was glad she had someone to talk to after all those years – someone who would listen, sort it out in her head.

As the weeks went by it came flooding out, all the secrets lurking in the shadows. She told me her story, but in her own way. She even pretended most of the time it wasn't her but some other person whom she hardly knew.

She took no notice of me. Maybe she didn't want to see.

But that was then. I was only seventeen. And blind, blindly in love with Simon. Fool.

Still, in a funny way, I don't regret any of it. The thrills of the previous summer lit me up in flames and sustained me in my imprisonment for most of the final three months. There are certain memories that remain vivid, a fire in the heart, long after the love goes cold. I only have to shut my eyes and think about it to warm up inside. It was late August, around the time of the Annual Show. Simon had come down for the holidays and somehow, magically, I managed to be with him for hours, roaming on the hillside. We seemed to be drawn to the twinkling stones on the mountain, shining in the sun.

One day we headed towards the forest. The river tinkled through soft brown earth highlighting the silence of the woods, sated in a dead heat. Flies buzzed. Not a breath of air. My talking, our flow of chatter, just dried up. My head swam. The oak tree on the opposite bank seemed alive, its arms suppliant, watchful.

Then, light on my eyes. Red inside my lids. Black spots swimming. I look up.

Leaves against the sky. Very blue. Light off the water shimmering on the leaves. Dazzling when you looked at the water, millions of tiny diamonds. All those water drops.

Running river, lighting up the tree from underneath. The water-tree dance. The tree dancing and waving its branches, saying hello to the river.

'Friends, great friends,' Simon's voice somewhere murmurs.

Music. Tinkling like the shimmers. The tinkles shake the leaves. The tree sighs.

'We're friends,' says Simon.

'Can I see?'

His hand on my breast, oh the leaves danced some more.

Water runs warm. Water in my mouth, drinking his. A finger in my pants. The sky red, redder behind my eyes. Hands, more dancing, tussling, twisting, the tree waves and the river laughs and was wet, so wet.

'We're good friends, aren't we?' he says.

'Yes, yes,' I say, and more I don't say, more more more.

'No, don't. Can't.'

'OK, OK.'

'Now, yes.'

River singing, eyes red closed. Grass in my nose. River mud on my mouth. A green smell. Wet. Fresh. Like him. River mud smell in Simon's trousers. In my jeans. My pants wet.

The river swims away with the tree in it.

Snap. A twig breaks. It stops the river as it lands, then sails away. The sky darkens suddenly.

Simon stands up. Pulls up his zip. Dressed suddenly.

I feel stupid. All muddy. I don't look up.

'Friends, right?' he says.

'OK OK.'

No more word. Or words.

He leaves first. Just goes.

I sit in the mud on the riverbank. The tree waves and nods.

I am mud and soft swell, sore. I see his face in the tree shimmering from the river. It is smiling. I smile back. It is our secret.

'Friends,' he said.

Friendly river, smiling tree.

That is the moment when my story begins. But really it goes far far back, way back to a time when I was not yet born, but the impetus of genes, life's longing for itself, had already begun to stir in my ancestral blood.

This is Granny's story as told to me then.

Gertrude, 1943

Gertrude was grandmother's name, Gertie to her intimates of whom she had very few, apart from her immediate family. Gertie Cullen, the schoolmaster's daughter from Moyne. She too was destined for the schoolroom, and so after consistently being the best in the class she went off to Dublin to teacher training college. That was in the 1940s when Ireland was a censorious dark place. From old photographs Gertie was very pretty, and always well turned out: flowery dresses, belted at the waist, with neat hats, matching gloves and bags, and a fine pair of legs in seamed stockings which were finished in court shoes. She was the only daughter of Master Cullen, his pride and joy. To be able to afford to educate a girl was his dream. All Jim Cullen's life savings went into that masterplan which he had mapped out for Gertie when she was only three and already had every nursery rhyme under the sun off by heart in her high sing-song voice. By six she was reading the children's classics, *Black Beauty*, *Treasure Island* and *What Katy Did*. In Master Cullen's mind she was set to make a good match, and from an early age he encouraged frequent visits to the big house at the head of the valley where the Hawthorn Thwaites lived.

Little William Hawthorn Thwaite was being groomed to be Master of the Hunt as was his father before him. Gertie would disappear for hours down the valley on her bicycle from the time she was twelve, and Jim was quietly confident in the knowledge that she was romping innocently in the surrounding hills with the Thwaite boy. She always came back with stories of what they'd had for afternoon tea at Glenview House where Evie the housekeeper made scones with butter and home-made blackberry jam. But what Jim hadn't counted on was Gertie's longing to increase her experience of the world, and her body, an inner territory with oceans to discover.

Nor had he reckoned on Tommie Mulhall, Tommie the blacksmith's son, big brawny Tommie with eyes of cornflower blue whose twinkle would send a shiver to your toes. That was how Gertie experienced him anyway, when she'd skip, breathless, off her bicycle and run to meet him at the bend in the road by the river. He always stood in her way with a long slow grin that crinkled his eyes, and stared her into laughing out loud. She felt free with Tommie, and stared back unashamed. The chat would tumble out of them, valley lore and the tales of daily disasters, minor and major, that kept the wheel of social intercourse whirring and the valley tongues well oiled. Gertie loved his words, and the way he had with them, and the things he was always up to. One day it was a fox he was snaring, another day a catapult he had made for pegging stones at rabbits, or later an old gun he had fixed to go after deer on the mountain at night. He never stopped, he was always roaming and busy, and great with his hands, like his father. He'll never want with a pair of hands like that, they said. The forge was busy then, all the shoeing that had to be done for the hunt in winter and the shows in summer. The people in the big houses on the good land down near the village were horsey people, had beautiful hunters and jumpers and show horses, mares and foals, some even had stallions for breeding.

Gertie loved the valley and felt truly part of it when she was with Tommie. But even in her joy and freedom, before puberty properly set in and her studies took over, she sensed it was borrowed time, on holiday from her real life. Her real life, she imagined, would bring her back, one day in the future, to the valley as the schoolmistress of Moyne. It was known she was great with Tommie but when she was eighteen it all stopped suddenly. Gertie had grown up and her childish past was behind her. Gertie the schoolmaster's daughter had a secret, one that was hidden deep within her soul, battened down to keep its cancerous rays from leaking into the light. But its tentacled shadow seeped out from down below and crept along the valley, into her descendant's blood, like blight.

In the summer of 1944 Gertrude Cullen left school, among promises of undying friendship from her group of classmates who, like her, thought schooldays were to be the best years of their lives. They walked in groups of three or four round the hockey pitch, all tingling with the knowledge that this phase of their lives was at an end. They talked excitedly of their new lives in the autumn, if they all, as expected of this group, got good enough results in the Leaving Certificate to go into further education.

Gertie and her friend Maire were lucky enough to have fathers to support them in their ambitions. Some girls with good results could look forward to a glamorous job in Aer Lingus or the bank, but most found some secretarial work to put in the few years before they would be married and stay at home to have children, five or six being the norm.

Now in these last few days of May they were filled with anticipation, feeling they were on the brink of importance. Neat and clean in their gabardine school uniforms they walked sedately, the seniors of the school now, to give good example. They were about to be released into the adult world and they all felt grave with the responsibility of it, owing so much to parents who had sent them to this good school whose academic achievements with young women was renowned.

'Will you go home for the summer, Gertie?' asked Mags Kiernan, a Dubliner.

Gertie nodded and smiled. She hadn't dreamt of doing anything else. With her mother dead and her father nearly sixty, she knew she would light up his life for the few months until she would go again to Dublin to teacher training college, if she got her results.

'Isn't your chap there that you're doing a line with?' pursued Mags.

Gertie blushed scarlet. 'I am not,' she squealed. 'He's only a friend.' She pushed her classmate playfully.

'Ooh, what colour's red Gertie?' teased Maire, and they all laughed.

And so ended the last day of the first part of Gertrude's life, as she boarded the bus that would deposit her in Arklow where her father would be waiting in the old Ford.

The valley was sunlit and Gertrude filled up with joy when she saw the old stone house standing up on the hill in its embrace of copper beech trees. It sat in the lee of the avalanche mountain, modest but imposing with cut granite window and door frames. The sun glanced off the quartz in the stone making the house twinkle in welcome. She climbed out of the Ford stretching her arms high over her head and breathing big gulps of fresh mountain air. 'Oh it's so great to see it all again,' she sighed to her father. He beamed his pleasure.

Just then the front door opened and out charged a barking dog.

'Spot, Spotty,' she called excitedly, 'come here to me my old segotia.'

She fell to her knees to hug the wagging little brown terrier that nuzzled into her lap. Behind in the doorway was Bridie in a navy apron.

'Hello Gertrude,' she said, and even she was smiling on this sunny event; cold old Bridie who came in to 'do' for her father these last years.

'Hi Bridie, are you well?' she shouted, spinning off down the front lawn and over the ditch with Spot to run into the field beyond, whirling in a downward descent of skirts and hair and cardigan flying in the wind.

Master Cullen, Jim, stood with a lump in his throat watching his beautiful daughter, her reddish brown hair golden today in the sunshine, as her long strong legs ran and jumped with the dog, a swirl of grey and blue and gold against the green of the valley. It was to make a picture postcard in his brain, a sepia image engraved in his mind's eye, already tinted with nostalgia for that moment of innocence and freedom.

That summer was a long hot one, unusual for Ireland. As the days grew hotter the summer seemed endless. Gertrude was suspended in a lethargy of heat and helplessness, as she waited the long wait for her exam results. She slept late into mid-morning, then sat in a stuffed chair in the parlour devouring *Anna Karenina* and *Madame Bovary*. She would go dazed and blinking into the afternoon to help Mikey and Paddy, the farmhands, round up the sheep or she'd talk to her father while he chopped up logs for the winter from the trees that had fallen across the driveway in the big storm of the previous February. She kept out of Bridie's way in the house, while Bridie scolded and goaded that she would never make anyone a good wife; she was so lazy and couldn't lift a finger even to put away the breakfast delph after she had washed and dried it.

'What's the point?' Gertrude would argue, 'we'll only be taking it out again later.'

She had never liked Bridie, her red fingers and her crude ways, like slurping her tea off the saucer – 'to cool it', she said. But her father needed somebody to keep the house clean and the beds changed and the clothes washed and ironed. Bridie came from down near the village and was a good worker. By three o'clock Bridie would get exasperated with Gertrude's lassitude.

'Can you not go out and get some fresh air for yourself, and go and help your poor father or make yourself useful?' she'd scold.

Gertrude would put on her flowery skirt and plimsolls, tie her hair back in a bow, and walk the two miles down the valley to the shop to buy an ice-pop or an orange squash. The road was high with hedgerows on either side and in the heat midges buzzed in clouds. Underfoot was stony and dry. Tall grasses bent and swayed, sweet-smelling in the fecund air, thick with scent and summer silences.

This day, Gertrude's pace quickened as she neared the shop. It was at the crossroads where the creamery was, and people often came to sit on the low wall outside for a chat or a cigarette. She felt her skirt brush her thighs and her thighs rub a little together at the top as she walked. She was wet in the heat down there. She might meet Tommie.

Sure enough he ambled out of the shop, pulling on a cigarette. His eyes crinkled in greeting and narrowed under his cap as he inhaled swiftly.

'How'ye?' was all he said, and she fell into step beside him on the road. Her heart began to hammer in the heat. Her throat was dry. As she walked she noticed his behind swinging in brown serge trousers, pulled in at the waist with string. His buttocks were hard. His arms swung by his side, tanned and scored with sinews under the skin. A lock of black hair fell over his collar. Gertrude longed to lick it from his neck, as once she had licked her own hair held between her fingers in a school day-dream. He cocked his hat at her to indicate a gateway, then leapt up and over the gate. Gertrude gave him her hand. His palm felt hard under hers as she stepped up on the wooden bars, held both his shoulders as she jumped down on the other side. Her skirt swung out high and her hair fell loose from its bow as she landed with a thud. They were in a large meadow with high grass. Purple and white flowers swayed in a lit-tle breeze. Gertrude felt a bead of sweat drip down into her eye from her forehead, and she almost stumbled in the shimmering heat. There was a hawthorn tree on a fairy mound on the far side of the field, hidden among high ferns. Tommie pushed his way through the stalks and she followed. They sat, side by side in silence in the pungent green fronds.

Gertrude's head swam as the blood pounded in her ears. Her palms and under her arms were wet. She was swollen with heat. Tommie turned to her, about to start a sentence, saw her stricken eyes, blue and dilated. He stopped, then reached out to touch her breast, hard under cotton. She gasped and opened her mouth. His lips were on hers and they smothered in saliva as they tongued their longing. Gertrude's was like a thirst now that wouldn't be slaked. Her body strained against him and a point of desire like pain somewhere between her legs raged to be satisfied. As Tommie's hand reached in under cotton to release her breast she swooned again. Touch me, touch me, she wanted to cry, more, more, that feels so good. Then her blouse was open and she clung to him, pushing to alleviate the pain, hard against his leg, rubbing and pushing to feel the point make contact against something hard within him. His hand slid down under her skirt and he got there, a finger slipping into her pants. She moaned and in flooded more heat. The hammering in her head rushed backwards like the tide going out. All was suddenly still. Then a shadow loomed over her. She looked up to see Tommie begin to pull down his trousers.

'What are you doing?' she gasped, startled.

'No more than you,' he smiled, and pulled the last cuff off over his shoe.

'Oh no,' she stuttered, 'we can't. No, don't.' Her voice rose in panic.

Tommie sat back on his hunkers. A silence fell between them. Somewhere quite close by a cricket cackled in the hot field. Gertrude choked on her words. She didn't know what to say. She pulled her blouse to her breast for safety and sat up.

'Tommie, we can't,' she mumbled.

He looked at her again quizzically, and slowly pulled back on his trousers, not saying a word.

As July dragged on towards August Gertrude's lassitude and longing increased, not helped by her avid readings of classic love stories. In this limbo her imagination raged and soared. Her surroundings were somewhere out there on the other side of a tinted glass, and she, untouchable, within. But she knew that on the day when the letter would fall through the door with the state insignia on it, that this dream of a summer would be over. Then she would have to kick back into being Gertrude Cullen, the schoolmaster's daughter going on for the teaching. Her father tried to tease her and cheer her up, attributing to this lethargy nervousness about her exam results.

'You'll see, brainy, how well you'll do. Sure how could you not with all those years up at the Mercy nuns.'

When she didn't reply the Master would continue. 'Sure it'll be no time at all and you'll be on the bus up to St Pat's. I remember the day I left, it was the first day of the rest of my life, and Mam waving at me behind the bus with her white handkerchief.'

Then he'd be off on a train of reminiscences which the farm lads got a great laugh out of, and which left Gertrude off the hook.

During this time Gertrude went nearly every day to the shop, hoping to see Tommie, the voice in her head saying she only wanted to talk to him like she used to. If he wasn't there she would drag herself home in a lather of anxiety: he doesn't love me anymore, he doesn't care because I wouldn't do it. If he was there, she would fall into step with him as usual and the chat was easy between them, but he never again brought her over the gate into the field that summer.

'So,' he said, 'will you be off up to the big smoke soon?'

'Oh, I don't know, I don't know if I'll get my honours. It's very hard to get in.'

'Sure the Master's daughter was born with brains,' he said, and tweaked her hair fondly. 'You'll soon be too good for the likes of us.'

'That's not true Tommie, I love the valley, you know that.'

'Oh,' says he, 'I bet there'll be no talking to you at Christmas. Your nose will be stuck up into the air with notions from Dublin.'

'Tommie,' she protested, genuinely hurt, 'you know me better than that. I don't see any difference between us.'

He stopped smiling. 'Gertie me darling, it's only the way of the world and I won't blame you.'

'But I won't change,' she said earnestly, 'I love this place and the people in it.' She nearly said 'I love *you*' but didn't dare. But that is what she thought and felt that summer before she went to Dublin, just as she had sworn eternal friendship two months earlier to the girls in school.

'Gertie, you're a grand girl,' was all he would give her in return, a squeeze around the waist his only reassurance.

August came and with it the long-awaited letter. Gertrude Cullen got six honours in her Leaving Certificate and the Master was as proud as punch. Gertrude herself was a little surprised that her intellectual achievements could cause so much jubilation in the household when her main concern was somewhere else entirely. The workings of her head, all the scholarship of the previous winter were distant memories now, while her blood pounded passionately through her veins daily and gave her fevered dreams at night.

Then as if to close the summer season there was to be a dance after the Annual Agricultural Show. The next thing she knew William Hawthorne Thwaite from Glenview House at the head of the valley came knocking on the door.

'Come in William,' she said surprised, 'how are you?'

'Great, great altogether thanks,' he mumbled. 'Great weather we're having. I'm roasting actually. Do you have anything to drink? I'm after walking all the way up the hill in this heat.'

So they sat down and chatted and William said he had heard about her great results and how she was going off to Dublin and then, clearing his throat, he said all in a rush, 'I would be honoured if you would accompany me to the ball.'

Gertrude stopped her tea preparations, surprised. She hadn't been to the dance before, it was a grown up thing every year. She turned and smiled. 'I'd love to but I'll have to ask Daddy, and oh my God what'll I wear?' She clapped a hand to her mouth.

'I'm sure you'll look splendid,' he said gallantly.

Splendid. Now where did William get this confidence and charm, she wondered. Probably that posh school he went to in Waterford that cost a fortune. He had grown up into a proper young gentleman who wore a checked sports jacket and Crombie hat just like his father. His face had a fair reddish complexion, his eyes a weak blue under gingery eyebrows.

She was pleased and flattered by his attentions and got excited about the dance. It helped that Master Cullen was equally enthusiastic and would attend it too, with his sister-in-law Maisie, also widowed. They went off to Arklow in the Ford to buy Gertrude a ballgown. She loved trying on the dresses and finally chose a simple one in white broderie anglaise with a pink sash, which fell almost to her ankles and accentuated her height. She would wear her hair up, dressed with little white flowers on the night. Even Bridie was smiling and proud when Gertrude came down the stairs made-up and powdered wearing high heels and gloves up to her elbow on the night of the ball. It was the end of August and the following week she would leave for Dublin.

The marquée was crowded and loud, full of men in good suits and women in nice frocks with high heels. The smell of cheap perfume mingled with sweat as the couples waltzed around the smoke-filled dance floor, bodies bumping and touching in the low light. There was an air of gaiety that night as the band played the latest Glen Miller number and people let loose and swung and jived. Gertrude was elated. She loved the music and found she was free in her movements. She also noticed the looks she was getting from men of all ages. This spurred her on into wilder movements and she laughed out loud in joy and abandonment. Her body felt free and she was sure of herself, as if the ugly duckling had come out from years of slinking around in a long grey gaberdine uniform and had arched into a swan, graceful and proud. She caught her father's eye and he winked at her as he trotted round the hall with Aunty Maisie. She saw old Mick from the creamery, and also Major Hawthorn Thwaite who commented to his wife as she passed. Yes, Gertie Cullen has grown up, their looks said.

On the last dance of the night, 'In the Mood', Gertrude flung herself into William's arms and they danced wildly round the floor, round and round in a big exuberant arc of happiness. When the music stopped William leaned in to kiss her cheek, and slid his hot mouth towards hers. She kissed him back with the gusto of the evening. Then the music stopped and the lights were switched on full. As Gertrude opened her eyes to come to in the white lights of the tent, she saw a figure watching her from the doorway. It was Tommie Mulhall. His eyes burned into hers like a warning and then he was gone. Gertrude felt stung as if slapped. Then William grabbed her around the waist and she allowed herself to be lead out in the other direction. A stone dropped down to the pit of her stomach, its fall sounding deep like a gong.

September came and with it crisp air and cool evenings bearing the scent of turf smoke. Gertrude Cullen set off for her new life in Dublin on the bus from Arklow, with a small group of family and friends to wave her on her way. Tommie Mulhall was not among them. William had bade his farewells some days earlier to go off to Britain to join in the war effort; 'to make a man of him', he said.

Gertrude arrived at her digs in Drumcondra on a wet day and was instantly dismayed by the seemingly endless rows of houses and grey streets. The landlady Mrs Linden was brisk and led her to a single bedroom on the first landing. It smelled musty and contained a small bed covered in a fluffy pink candlewick spread, a mahogany wardrobe and a small table for studying. On the chimneybreast hung a paltry one-bar electric fire for heat. That was extra and so the students, all girls, made do with big woolly cardigans and blankets to get them through the books on a cold winter's night.

The college was an imposing granite building set around a quadrangle, which was crisscrossed hourly with lines of students rushing to lectures. Gertrude put her head down and attended to her books, enjoying the new challenges of learning her profession. Her friend Maire from school was there also so she let herself be led along in a group of mainly Dublin girls into social nights at the debating society and week-end walks with the hiking club. These activities filled the weeks and months of her first term. She dared not think of Tommie: he was part of her past life, her girlhood. William sent a card with greetings from England. The boys in college were in the main pimply youths, earnest behind glasses, the swotty types, with few exceptions.

Then the Christmas lights began to appear on Henry Street and the girls packed up to go home for the two-week break. Gertrude was excited when she saw the familiar rolling hills again, but was also appre-hensive about the festive period. There were so many social obligations, so much expected of her in the family. Still, when she came in to the baking smells of home, to be greeted by a blazing fire and the Christmas tree already up, she burst uncharacteristically into tears. She didn't know how much she had missed home, even though in boarding school she had also been away most of the time. But this was like being a child of eight again, and she wanted to nestle right back in as if she were still in school uniform.

The days passed in a flurry of preparation for the Christmas, clean-ing the silver, washing the linen tablecloths and icing the cakes and puddings. These activities always brought a lump to her throat as she remembered washing the currants, raisins and mixed peel with her mother, now ten years dead.

Then it was Christmas Eve. The morrow would bring an early start, six o'clock rising for the first Mass. At around five in the afternoon Gertrude escaped into the fields with the dog to get some fresh air and a little time to herself. It was frosty and night was falling as she reached the river. She always liked this spot, a small stream with brown trout in it in summer, which they used to try and catch as children. She stood in the twilight leaning against an oak tree, and sighed. She was growing up and away from childish things. Suddenly she heard a twig crack. Her heart hammered as she saw a tall figure crunch his way through the dead leaves underfoot. She flushed in recognition. It was Tommie. He stopped. No one spoke.

'Tommie?' she queried softly, and he came to her and took her by the shoulders, looking deep into her eyes. His gaze was intense and she shiv-ered and looked away.

'You'll catch your death here, Gertie, in this cold,' he said simply.

At the sound of his gravelly voice in the lilting tones of Wicklow, she started to shake and abruptly laid her head against his shoulder. 'Oh Tommie, keep me warm, please,' she pleaded.

As his arms enfolded her she swayed as if in sleep, maybe for a minute, or some more, but it seemed to last for much longer. Gertrude felt a great peace welling up inside her. Now she was really home. Tommie lifted her chin and examined her in the quick-falling darkness.

'Well the Lord be, it's prettier you've got, but a bit thin and pale. It must be the bad air up there.'

He smiled his wonderful smile and she smiled back, reaching up to kiss him quickly on the cheek. He turned his head away. She stepped back, puzzled and confused.

'Gertie, I don't play second fiddle to no one,' he said, sounding harsh.

She was stung by his tone. 'What are you talking about?'

'You and William,' he snapped, and turned to go.

'But Tommie, you've got it all wrong. There's nothing between me and William.'

It was too late. He had swung around to step smartly away up the hill through the trees and was gone.

Christmas continued with its homely familiarity and set routines, the Mass-going, the present-giving, the neighbours in for a pre-dinner drink on Christmas morning, the glass of sherry to the farmers in their Sunday suits, with neat little wives. They stood around smiling like cats and nodding to please Master Cullen. It was his day. He had taught two generations of valley children, and was well-liked.

Gertrude went on through the motions but a strange humming ran in her veins. She couldn't get Tommie Mulhall out of her mind. His face in the dark in the woods appeared in front of her when she lay down to sleep at night. She blinked him away but his tone seared her. The words 'second fiddle' played in her lower abdomen to sicken her. Then she would get angry and tell herself he had no right to claim her like that, she wasn't officially his girlfriend and anyway, everyone knew, and Gertie herself if she would admit it, that the likes of Tommie could never marry the schoolmaster's daughter. She wouldn't ever say such words but she thought he knew too the unwritten rules of the valley. It was like with the animals, each breed and seed to his own. So she told herself each night but then the summer sensation of heat would rise to haunt her and she would moan in the bed with stifled longing, for green ferns and crickets and the blue blue sky.

One day, maybe three days after Christmas when they were all fat with feasting, Gertrude took the dog out to go for a long hike. She couldn't stand anymore the rounds of relatives and afternoon teas, and turned her back on Bridie's loud protests of 'what about your Aunt Maisie?' as she slammed the door. She needed to walk off this high-wire energy that came both from being cooped up in the house with the same people all day every day with no escape, and the fever in her head about Tommie. Only out in the open could she let herself think about him in peace. He had assumed the stature of a spurned lover and romantic hero in her mind, perhaps far away from the real flesh and blood young blacksmith's son that he was. She walked and walked over fields and hills, crossing the river above the schoolhouse in Moyne, and continued on down narrow lanes until she was at the edge of the forest on the far side that clothed the famous mountain.

She shivered with excitement for here truly was a fairytale. This was the place where they used to frighten themselves as children tormenting the old woman who lived here and hoping she would come out and chase them away. She was a relative of the family who had been lost in the snow and people said she could talk to ghosts. Now Gertrude noticed her hut was derelict. No smoke snaked out of the chimney any-more. Here was the place of the avalanche and it had always given her vicarious thrills as she imagined the terrible slide that had engulfed those poor people. Now in these last few days of the year's end, the place was flat and melancholy in the last light of the December day. She won-dered what they had been so scared of as children. Just a mountain, overhanging and ominous granted, with a growing coniferous forest scenting its slopes. She heard the dog growl and hoped it was Tommie, there to come upon her again by accident, as in all the black and white pictures, to sweep her up off her feet and over the threshold into the hut. But there was no one there, only a barn owl out hunting early in the year's end.

The following day she made a resolution. She walked the two miles to the shop at the crossroads, knowing that at some point Tommie would be in for the messages for his mother, as there was no other shop in the village that was open on these Holy days. Her wait was rewarded and she stood in his way on the road.

'Tommie, I want to talk to you,' she said. 'Meet me at the hut.'

He looked puzzled but said nothing. She knew he understood what that meant.

'At four o'clock,' she whispered, then ran jubilantly down the road home. She had done it. He would come.

And so apparently he did. My grandmother and Tommie Mulhall met in secret for the ten remaining days of that Christmas period and nobody ever knew. But Gertrude danced around in the best of moods for the next few days, and was so charming and disinterested in William when he came calling that he fell hopelessly in love with her and became a persistent suitor. What went on in that hut we can only guess at, but Gertrude blossomed into a ripe young woman not suspecting that her life was to change course again soon afterwards.

Gertrude was in Drumcondra in her digs. It was a miserable day in the middle of January and she had come home wet to the bone at four-thirty. She had tried to dry out by the electric fire in her room but by six was hungry and still cold. The dinner of boiled bacon and marrowfat peas did little to cheer her up, even though the bread and butter pudding was sweet and comforting. By seven she was back in her room reluctantly opening her maths book. She had to grapple with theorems even though they wouldn't be taught in primary school. But there they were, impenetrable on the page. Gertrude was limp with a strange longing, not especially for Tommie Mulhall, but for some kind of warm thing that would take away this cold feeling she now lived with every day. It was loneliness and it resided in her stomach like a rat. She couldn't shake it off, not by studying or chats over coffee with the girls, or even a day out shopping in Grafton Street in Dublin on a Saturday. Whatever it was it gnawed at her innards and left her hollow and tired. By four o'clock every day all she wanted to do was crawl home and sleep. If she got an hour lying down before dinner she would fall into a sleep that was as deep as a bottomless well, from which she would rouse herself with increasing difficulty. Then, dazed and confused, she would sit at the tea table with the four other lodgers, and pick vaguely at mounds of mashed potatoes, trying to mimic and nod her feigned interest in the babble and chat around her. Mrs Linden said she looked peaky, she must be working too hard, a dose of fresh mountain air was all she needed. Gertrude didn't argue, longing only to escape again to her room and take a book with her to read in bed. She slept deeply until the dim light of early morning when the rat would creep back inside her to gnaw and tug.

Maire tackled her. 'Hey Gertie, have you done your essay on Milton yet?'

'No,' she muttered, 'I'll do it tonight. I was reading for it though.'

'You know it's going to be counted in the exam marks and Mr Pierce wants two thousand words. I'm on my last five hundred, I didn't know how much work this was,' Maire persisted.

'That's how many pages?' asked Gertrude.

'About twenty,' said her friend.

'Goodness,' breathed Gertrude, 'I had no idea.'

'Gertie,' said Maire, 'is there something bothering you? You've been awfully quiet lately.'

'No, just a little tired, that's all thanks.'

'Are you missing Tommie?' she asked gently.

'No, no, not at all,' said Gertrude, but she turned away suddenly to hide the tears that had filled her eyes. She just felt wretched these days. She couldn't concentrate and no longer saw the point of all this book learning. She opened her books now with real distaste where once she had torn into them, a model student.

One evening she was sitting hunched up in the bed with the pink candlewick bedspread around her shoulders when there was a knock on her door.

'Visitor for you,' called Mrs Linden.

Gertrude sat up in fright, but it was only Mags Kiernan, big bright Mags from Fairview.

'How are you?' she exclaimed, sweeping into the room to hug her friend. 'My goodness you've changed, got thinner or something. Are they not feeding you at all?'

Gertrude looked back from under lank hair and attempted to smile. 'Sorry, I was sitting here trying to keep warm, they don't heat this place very well, I'm always freezing. Here, have a seat,' she said, jumping up to pull over the Bentwood chair from the small table where her books lay unopened. 'Well Mags, tell us how's the nursing going?'

They hadn't seen each other since the last day of school seven months previously. Mags had been accepted into the Mater Hospital in Eccles Street and was delighted with herself.

'Well we're only paid skivvies of course, and the nuns would drive you mad, but you meet so many people and it's really great to be able to help the patients.'

'What about the doctors?' Gertrude ventured.

'Mostly stuck-up but there's one or two junior doctors who are quite dishy and treat us like people. We go on the rounds with them and have to stay quiet, but there's one of them who always gives me a wink on the way out of the ward.'

The two continued chatting away for an hour or so, then went down to the parlour where Mrs Linden had set out tea for the visitor and the other students. When it was time to leave Mags hugged her friend at the hall door and told her to write to her at the Mater. Gertrude closed the door to her room awash with relief. Something wasn't the same anymore and even she couldn't say why. Gertrude Cullen was like a visitor in her own body so out of kilter with herself did she feel.

It wasn't until a month or so later that Gertrude began to suspect the worst. She had missed a period, her 'aunty' as the girls called this monthly inconvenience, and now she was due again. She had never paid much attention to it before, grateful that she could avoid the messiness for as long as possible when as often was the case her period was late or irregular.

Gertrude thought she felt period pains once but nothing happened only this hollow feeling and constant tiredness, and a hunger that couldn't be assuaged by eating. The smell of food at mealtimes made her retch. She closed a door in her head and shut it tight to keep away the vision of horror on the other side. At the same time she couldn't quite shake off the image that crept into her brain, crawling in at the edge of consciousness to seek her attention.

That last time with Tommie: the day of the storm that had brought little swirls of snow tapping on the window in gusts. They had been curled up on a cushion watching the last embers of the fire they lit early every afternoon in the hut, until it died in the gathering darkness that was the signal for them to hurry home. Tommie had shivered and pulled her close. 'Come in my snowbird,' he said. They both remembered then the myth of the mighty snow, and without speaking she touched his cheek to trace it with her finger. She found it infinitely precious in the chilly silence as the snow shrouded the window in a bluish light. Gertrude had wanted that moment to freeze in time forever, she felt so fragile and light, there with Tommie as their breaths wreathed and froze like wraiths in the so still air: every nerve end on her skin prickled with apprehension, as if they were on a precipice and might soon topple over into a perilous place. She clung to Tommie, feeling the steady beat of his heart, and nuzzled against his warmth. He was the only bastion against such a landslide, and she felt herself in mortal danger. This feeling was so intense that it overwhelmed her and silent tears poured out of her eyes and down her cheeks to land on his wrist with a warm splosh.

'Gertie,' he murmured concerned, but she just released her sobs into his chest and let go, unable to articulate the wave of grief that swept over her, for lost innocence, for childish summer things, and for her mother, in great tangled heaves of sadness.

Finally she stopped shuddering and mumbled through a swollen nose, 'it must be this place, it always makes me so sad,' and then this time it really had happened, their coupling, as she clung to him in a defiance of all that might engulf them.

Gertrude let this scene play once more in her head before she sealed it in a vault forever.

At the beginning of March she had a show, a rush of fresh red blood that frightened her as well as relieved her anxiety. Was the nightmare over? She tamped the blood with towels and cried off college for two days. That was it. But Gertrude didn't feel any better. The hollow feeling persisted and she still felt weakened as if a layer of skin had been removed. She was easily slighted and had withdrawn into herself, so sensitive was she to female teasing. She couldn't take the tea table gossip and laughter about who was doing a line with whom, and shrank into herself to avoid comment. Her breasts grew tender and to her horror seemed to swell, and then about a month after the bleeding she felt a hard lump like a grapefruit incline out from under her navel. She knew. She had no real knowledge of such things but she knew. Her mind would not, could not, dare not articulate the horror. On the other side of that door in her brain her life was laid stretched out in a wasteland of devastation. In the far corner, her father was hunched over and huddled in agony, a man old before his time. She could not allow this vision to reign. That door must never be opened. Never.

As the second term in Teacher Training College came to a close, the Easter holidays loomed. How would she face them at home? Gertrude remained in a limbo. The gnawing fatigue had given way to permanent anxiety and sleeplessness. She looked dreadful. If she slept it was to be haunted by the spectre of her father, crumbling before the giant shadow of her sin, his shoulders hunched in shame. No, she could not inflict that pain on him, her kind old father who had been both mother and father to her since the untimely death of her beloved mother. To shame him – she, Gertrude Cullen, the schoolmaster's daughter from Moyne – no, that would be a crime worse than murder.

Gertrude acted then with precision and lucidity. No one must ever know, but she did need help. She was not going to become one of those girls of whom it was whispered 'she went to England', or of whom people spoke in hushed tones because although they came back to the village they had been away for a period of unexplained absence. She was not going to live with her head hanging in shame over a secret that everyone knew about but never dared bring out into the open. She was not going into one of those homes for fallen girls run by nuns as laundries where the poor and unfortunate women often ended up in servitude for life, never to be allowed forget their original sin. She was not the kind of girl made for this. She was not to be like an older cousin on her mother's side who had taken refuge in the valley from another village, and then had given up her baby for adoption, so that from then on every baby brought home by a childless couple fell under suspicion of being her bastard. No, that was never to be Gertrude Cullen's lot.

This was not meant to be. It was not in the scheme of things. Above all, Tommie Mulhall must never know. It was truly none of his business. There was the little matter of how. Gertrude took pen to paper and wrote to Mags Kiernan in the Mater Hospital. She would have to take one chance and trust somebody. Mags would know the right person. It was, after all, an ancient art. She also wrote to her father saying she wouldn't be home for the holidays as she had an invitation to spend it with Maire in Roscrea, and could she count on his kindness to send her some money as she fancied a new dress and hat for Easter. Master Cullen wrote back promptly with a postal order wishing Gertrude a happy Easter and said she would be greatly missed.

When Gertrude met Mags she came straight to the point.

'Mags, I'm in trouble,' she said briskly, and as the other went to embrace her with a loud cry of sympathy Gertrude put up her hands in a gesture of defence or denial and said, 'I'm fine, really, really I am, I just need some advice.'

And so, one week later, Gertrude Cullen went down the steps of a basement flat in Harcourt Street on a spring evening having sworn her friend to secrecy until her dying day. She was curiously cold, steeling herself on the inside and folding and unfolding a sprig of lilac in her gloved hand. She had the money in her handbag. Inside a short stout woman, a retired nurse, led her to a sitting room stuffed with a nylon-covered sofa and a chintz bucket chair. There were magazines and newspapers on every chair and occasional table. The air was dank. Nurse Rooney sat across on one of the stuffed chairs.

'I won't ask you your reasons dearie,' she said, 'but I have to get a few details on your state of health. Oh, and then that'll be £25 please.'

Gertrude answered a few questions about her dates, and then nodded her assent. She just wanted it all to be over.

Nurse Rooney brought Gertrude into an inner room, which smelled strongly of disinfectant, and asked her to remove her shoes, stockings and skirt and lie on the bed. She took a blue hatbox from the top of the wardrobe, opened it to take out two metal instruments, a syringe and a piece of tubing. Then she erected a screen and asked Gertrude to open her legs. She poked around for a bit with a cold metal instrument.

'Fine, I think we can manage to bring it on, but you mustn't feel the pain dear,' she said in her slightly English accent.

She put a cotton pad soaked in formaldehyde over Gertrude's face and asked her to breathe deeply. Gertrude went woozy and as Nurse Rooney poked around down below she felt a sharp jab, followed by a rush of hot liquid from between her legs.

After that Gertrude was in and out of consciousness as the labour pains commenced. She felt like throwing up, so to steady herself she concentrated on that one little snowflake that had hit the window that December day, and had taken forever to slide in a white eternity down the glass pane. Gertrude saw its every arm of intricate lace open in a dance of supplication as again and again it landed and slid, landed and slid, over and over into white glass light. Melt and fade into nothing.

The pains came rushing like boulders down a mountain to land with deadened thuds on the borders of Gertrude's mind, as the blood and matter and water all gushed out together in a hot liquid torrent and she slid through it into oblivion.

Throughout this Gertrude did not flinch or once think of the tiny fish inside her. She only wanted her life to continue as before on its ordained track. However the lingering scent of lilac on her gloves made her gag for a long time afterwards.

In the last week of May Gertrude along with three hundred of her classmates from First Year were sitting in the Aula Maxima to take their examinations. It was the English paper, Gertrude's favourite subject. She was normally well-prepared for exams and looked forward to the challenge of writing down all her knowledge in neat blue ink in the three hours allotted. She grasped the pink exam paper nervously as the supervisor handed it to her, tore open the pages to see if the questions were the ones she had prepared, and started to write.

She wrote swiftly for ten minutes or so, and then stopped to think up her next paragraphs. It was an essay about Jonathan Swift, on his satirical piece, 'A Modest Proposal' to control the peasant population. The essay asked the students to discuss the irony of his proposition: 'There is likewise another great advantage in my Scheme, that it will prevent those voluntary Abortions, and that horrid practice of Women murdering their Bastard Children; alas! too frequent among us, sacrificing the poor innocent Babes ...'

Gertrude wanted to use the quotes she had memorised and started to write out the words 'I have been assured ... that a young healthy Child, well nursed at a Year old, a most delicious, nourishing and wholesome Food; whether Stewed, Roasted, Baked or Boiled.'

Although meant satirically, a lump rose in Gertrude's throat and stuck there. She gagged out loud and then, as heads turned, beads of sweat broke out on her forehead. Her eyes swam and she saw double. In a panic now, she had to get out to go to the toilet. Her hand shot up and the supervisor came down to her desk along the rows in the hall, his heels clacking all the way on the wooden floorboards. She half stood and had to be led out, where a female teacher put an arm around her and accompanied her outside. In the fresh air her legs buckled under her.

'I have to go back in there,' she gasped. 'I have to finish the paper.'

The teacher was a kindly middle-aged person.

'Gertrude, take your time there now, you can go back in a few minutes.'

'But my exam,' she wailed, 'I'll fail it.'

The teacher rubbed her back kindly. 'Look Gertrude, we know you are a good student and that you have great ability. Your work seems to have slipped a little in this last term, but maybe you were nervous about the exams. Anyway, don't worry about it now, if you don't pass you can always repeat in the autumn.'

'Repeat?' asked Gertrude shocked. 'But I can't fail, I never fail, what'll my father think?'

'Look, I'll get you a drink of water and when you feel better you can go back in there and finish the paper.'

Gertrude found herself sitting again in the large hall in a wet fit of anxiety. Why hadn't she worked harder? She should have pushed herself to get up earlier in the last month to do some cramming, as she always had. But she had been so tired, and was bleeding all the time, on and off. Her legs constantly felt like lead. She was just so weighed down somehow. But fail? Never. The more she scolded herself the worse it got, and the words just would not come out onto the paper which stayed blank and virginal in front of her. She sat paralysed in the chair, sweating profusely, as a summer of disgrace rose up before her eyes. What would she tell her father? Then she started to shake and the tears came, as she sat there at the small desk among the hundreds of others in the crowded hall.

Outside the chatter was eager and excited. 'What questions did you do? What essays did you chose?' Gertrude hung her head and avoided giving answers. Later that day she went to see Matron.

'I can't go on with these exams,' she said. 'Can you give me a sick cert. so I can repeat in the autumn?'

Some of Gertrude's old resoluteness was back. Matron looked sceptical.

'I normally advise girls to continue and make a shot at passing some of the papers. It doesn't look good to give up so soon.'

'I got news of a death in the family,' lied Gertrude, 'an old aunt I was close to, and I'd rather go now and attend the funeral. I've been too upset to sleep.'

'Right then,' said Matron, 'but I'll have to examine you.'

Matron found Gertrude's blood pressure to be low, and was concerned by the girl's tale of heavy periods. She recommended a tonic and agreed to sign the sick cert.

Gertrude ended up going home to the valley a little earlier than planned, bracing herself for the barrage of questions that would follow. But she had her story ready. If she could keep them all at bay she might have enough peace in the holidays to clear her head and study for the autumn repeats.

So Master Cullen found a new reserve in his daughter, a reluctance to answer questions that was completely at variance with her sunny character of before. Moreover, there was the little matter of the letter, which had come for her over Easter with a postmark stamped Roscrea. "Wasn't she staying in Roscrea?" He queried gently.

'Oh yes,' she shrugged, 'Maire and I thought it would be fun to send each other letters anyway.'

The Master noticed a pink flush rise to her cheeks, which in his long experience of teaching eleven year olds told him she was surely lying. She gave him a sudden peck on the cheek then that so disarmed him he was prepared to forgive her anything. A minor slip-up, that was all. Gertrude learned to give back answers that were assured, plausible and without the slightest giveaway colour on her cheeks. She stayed indoors and whenever she was asked to go for a message to the shop, or help outside to fetch the sheep, or even help Bridie change the beds, she said she was studying. It became her standard answer for every request.

Gertrude took to wearing a long skirt whose flowery pattern was worn and faded, a loose blouse and no stockings. She let her hair fall loose and washed it rarely, so that it hung in limp lifeless strands over her face. She got spots which had never happened to her as a teenager, but it was probably from all the fried food she ate. At about eleven o'clock when she rose every morning she would get out the frying pan and put on sausages and a fried egg; for her energy, for her brain to work, she said. She would finish off with several thick slices of homemade brown bread smeared thickly with butter, swilling tea until about twelve. And so she thickened a little around the waist. Master Cullen often watched her when she wasn't looking, and a little sigh of regret would escape him, as he thought of his beautiful daughter of the previous summer who was lithe and spirited. It was not the spots, nor the rolls of fat over her waistband which bothered him, it was her heaviness, as if she carried the weight of the world now on her stooping shoulders. Her sparkle was gone. 'What had Dublin done to her?' he wondered. He even asked himself if the pressure of studying was all too much, a high price to pay for the loss of his daughter's smile.

The summer wore on as Gertrude maintained a semblance of studying, while becoming more and more bored and unmotivated. She had however discovered some new personal talents: the ability to lie without blushing, a quick answer for everything, and a whole library of strategies for avoiding tasks. By succeeding in her pretences she perfected the art of manipulation. This was to serve her well in the not-so-distant future.

Late that summer when William came home for good at the end of the war, he found Gertrude as charming as ever. He was glad to have a girl waiting for him back home after all the tension of living in siren-filled London. By now Gertrude's devotion to the books had outlived its usefulness. She had decided not to repeat the exams this time. However by August she was ready to come out of her lair and show herself again, which is how she came to be seen for the second year in a row at the Annual Agricultural Ball with William Hawthorn Thwaite.

Gertrude wore a blue ball gown this time, one cut down from her dead mother's dress. It was midnight blue with a dropped waist, so it flattered her tall figure and disguised the thickness. The blue also set off her eyes, and she wore little diamanté earrings that sparkled. Master Cullen was proud, and relieved it must be said, to see her blossom again. Gertrude moved with confidence on William's arm as if she had been born to this ascendancy class, and enjoyed the repartee with William's father, old grisly Major Hawthorn Thwaite. It was obvious that he found her a grand girl altogether and he beamed in her company. Gertrude had learned also how to scan a room and find the most important people to talk to. She enjoyed this part of her feminine power, and basked in the glory of their attentions.

On the night of the ball the band played on as the air thickened with smoke and sweat. Later, when the dance floor thinned and there were paper cups and sandwich crusts scattered underfoot, the lights went on and the populace stood to the strains of the National Anthem. Then the older couples collected their coats from the cloakroom, and the younger people stood about in groups hoping they would find time to be alone with their paramours, for a kiss and a court on the way home.

This year as Gertrude Cullen left the tent on the slightly tipsy William's arm, she saw again in the shadows of the gateway the long tall figure of Tommie Mulhall. She put her nose in the air and faced towards William, signalling clearly to the onlooker that that was the end of that. All anyone saw, had they been looking, was the red tip of the cigarette glow angrily in the dark, as its owner stiffened and inhaled sharply.

In September they made the announcement: Gertrude and William were to be engaged. Master Cullen was not as delighted as he thought he might be, because although it was the fairytale ending to his dreams and a good match, some of the magic of the romance had been lost. It was over too suddenly and with it his daughter's childhood. She would no longer take his place in the schoolroom in Moyne. She had told him very clearly that her book learning would not be needed when she became lady of the manor. Her tone had been light and mocking, but there was no changing her mind about the exams.

And so Gertrude Cullen was to be married to William Hawthorn Thwaite, pending the application to the bishop. Meanwhile William was sent to Dublin by his father to do an apprenticeship in a solicitor's office. Gertrude was to stay at home, for what would be the point of repeating first year if she would never finish? She had anyway to organise the wedding, book the hotel, send out invitations and have the dresses made. Gertrude told William she did not want a very long engagement, tantalising him by licking his ear and nestling against him as a promise of sensual things to come.

So William bought his fiancée a diamond ring and they celebrated their engagement with a quiet family gathering. They set a wedding date for the following autumn, one year later.

Master Cullen stood uneasily in the draughty drawing-room of Glenview House while Major Hawthorn Thwaite poured copious amounts of the sherry he had squirreled away during the war years for such an occasion. Matilda, the Major's wife, was a kindly sort who lived very much in her husband's shadow as if she were still apologising to the natives for being English. She adopted Gertrude under a motherly wing and for this Master Cullen was grateful. He was trying to see the good side in all of this and keep up with Gertie's enthusiasm for the arrangements, while disappointment gnawed his heart over her lost academic ambition.

'Well Master, in no time at all you'll have your grandchildren in the classroom. They'd better not be long about it so that the little ones can have the benefit of being taught by their grandfather before he retires,' chortled the Major.

Master Cullen shifted uncomfortably. While offspring would one day be a source of pride and joy, for now he had to get used to the idea of Gertie becoming a bride, never mind becoming a mother. As for retiring, the thought hadn't entered his head. Who would take over from him now anyway with his hopes of Gertie's career dashed? His spirits slumped even further and it was with great difficulty that he could find any suitable repartee.

'I'm sure it will be nice to see the Hawthorn Thwaite stable being used again by children,' he replied bravely.

'Ah yes, the horses, young William was a great little horseman,' the Major beamed fondly across the room where the now not-so-little William was holding up the fireplace. His cheeks were crimson as he helped himself liberally to more sherry.

'Good stuff this, Gertrude my girl, we'll have to make sure Pa liberates some more of his supplies for the big day.'

William barely took the trouble to move his mouth when he spoke, so giving the impression that he was bored by the world, or just sneering at it. It was an affected mannerism he had picked up in England, this attempting-to-be-sophisticated drawl. Gertrude didn't know then just how grating she would come to find it, or how his fondness for the juice would irritate her. Just now she enjoyed the status that being his fiancée conferred on her, and she rose to the occasion with grace and assurance. She was so relieved that she wouldn't see that small bedroom in Drumcondra again, or have to go through the ordeal of exams. She heard a note of envy in Maire's voice when she told her the news and saw the light of admiration in her eyes. Imagine achieving the status of married woman, and you not yet twenty, her eyes said. Gertrude wrote to Mags Kiernan as well to announce her engagement, knowing the other would be pleased and relieved, and that the other matter would never be referred to again.

This was the time then that people noticed the distinct cooling off in the acquaintanceship of Gertrude Cullen and Tommie Mulhall, how they didn't even give each other the courtesy of a civilised greeting when the social occasion so required. It was said Tommie became moody and sometimes went on the batter for days, getting into fights outside Byrne's hotel in the village. Gertrude once saw him talking outside the shop with Kitty Murphy and her heart flipped for a moment as she saw those blue eyes stare for a little longer at someone else. She looked away clicking her heels haughtily as she passed on into the shop with her basket on her arm.

Gertrude focused all her attention on her new life, until one day Tommie came calling.

It was a late October day at the end of a hot spell, an Indian summer they called it. The sky was blood red and flushed, sending out low rays the colour of ripe apples. Gertrude opened the door in a flurry of flour and apron as she had been baking the brown bread, learning at last some culinary skills. Her father and the farm boys had gone to the mart in

Knockananna, and it was Bridie's day off. She stood back in shock, as Tommie loomed large in the doorway. She had to ask him in, as he had no appearance of stepping back to leave.

'Come in,' she said. 'Is it my father you want?'

'No,' says he, 'I'm here to see you. I wanted to see the bride-to-be for myself.'

He smiled his long slow smile, and took off his cap, almost swaggering down the hall into the kitchen.

'Well, do I get a cup of tea, missus,' says he.

Gertrude picked up the slight mocking tone as he slowed his intonation on the 'tea.' She noted the extra emphasis on 'missus.' She moved carefully to fill the kettle at the sink in the scullery. She flushed with annoyance. What was he doing here? Her father could come back at any minute, and he had no right to barge his way into her house, sure he had never wanted to set foot in the door before, despite being asked often when they were younger.

She resumed her politeness. 'And how are you doing Tommie?' she asked, 'I heard you might be going working on the buildings in England.'

'That's right, you heard right. Sure what is there here for me now?' and he left a pause.

Gertrude felt very uncomfortable. She blushed.

'Tommie, you don't understand,' she rushed on, although he had not sought an explanation.

'I only know that we had something special,' he said evenly, 'and that some little runt with an English accent came wiggling his weaselly way into your heart, God above only knows why.' His gravelly voice rose and the lilt was emphatic. 'Why Gertie?' He stood suddenly to put his arms around her from behind. 'Why?' he murmured, nuzzling her neck.

Gertrude filled up with such longing that she thought she would burst. Her heart hammered and she longed to turn to him, let his arms enfold her as before, and melt into him, to make everything all right. Just for an endless moment. Instead, she stiffened and let out a long breath, pulling herself loose from his grasp.

'I am to be another man's wife. I don't think this is right. You'd better go.'

As she said it she swallowed, especially when she saw the look on his face at her tone. His eyes were pools of blue, and in them was a deep hurt and longing, so that he looked like a little boy about to cry. She wanted then to rush to him, to throw her arms around him, to pull him to her breast, to make it better, but the new Gertrude took control and she turned away from those eyes to mutter, 'I'm sorry Tommie, it was never meant to be.'

At this he cursed under his breath and stalked back down the hall, slamming the door as he went. In the silence after the reverberation Gertrude's legs went from under her and she sat down shaking. She fought back tears of frustration and anger that he should have dared do this to her, to disturb her like this. Then she lifted her apron and burst into tears, glad there was no one in the house to hear her animal cries of pain. Behind her eyes was a swirl of red like the sky.

About a month later Gertrude heard there was to be a going-away party for Tommie in his house, a real old-fashioned American wake although it was only to England he was going. But it was said his mother was heartbroken and didn't want him to leave like his brothers before him, who came back less and less frequently as the years went by. Christmas was the pinnacle of the year and when the sons started not appearing on the last train from Dun Laoghaire off the mailboat on Christmas Eve, Mrs Mulhall's heart would quietly crack further in two. She knew they too had succumbed to the way of the Irish in London and were probably in some Salvation Army hostel having a charity dinner, glad for it and knowing no one would complain if they opened another bottle of whiskey or two since the season was provident. So, to wake her last son Mrs Mulhall wanted to send him off with a good spread, baking for days on end with all the love in her heart and putting it into apple tarts and fairy cakes and jam sponges with whipped cream, and a boiled porter cake with mixed fruit and a drop of Guinness in it.

The house was a thatched cottage at the edge of the FitzWilliam estate where once the groomsmen of the Earl lived. For two generations now, it had been occupied by Mulhall, the blacksmith. When the day came, Mrs Mulhall lit a log fire in the open chimney so it would flicker and flame through the evening as the fiddler fiddled and the dancers danced. Tommie was mortally embarrassed by it all as he had meant to slip away quietly, not anticipating the ferocity of his mother's reaction or the fuss it might cause. He only knew that there was nothing much left in the valley for him and he wanted to stretch his wings and seek new horizons, sow his wild oats as they say. He wanted to make his money in England and return a rich man in a number of years to build a fine house near the village. He meant to come back not as an old man, but with enough life left in him to enjoy his wealth and look after his mother who deserved a comfortable end to her days. This was his intention, and he couldn't see what all the fuss was about.

And so the time came for the farewell. It was the night of the party, more of an open house really, with neighbours and relatives and cousins dropping in from far and wide to say their goodbyes. It was festive in the way of a good wake, with a kind of manic abandon that grief often brings. Tommie was flushed with the heat from the chimney and allowed his uncles to pour him liberal doses of whiskey. He also had a pain to kill which he couldn't speak of to anyone. Maybe it was this his mother had picked up on somehow, this note of melancholy which had crept into her son's blue eyes, dulling the twinkle that had always resided there.

Over in the stone house under the avalanche hill, Gertrude Cullen watched and waited in an agony of indecision. She had heard about the farewell hoolie in the village and wondered if she should appear there. Her father had asked her if she would drop in on the family to pay her dues.

'It's not a funeral Daddy,' she had snapped. 'Sure you'll do for us Cullens.'

She drove herself demented with reasons as to why and why not she should appear there, as her place in the valley and her status as the schoolmaster's daughter would normally require. She gave herself very good reasons too why she should go, by imagining her entrance. She would sweep in wearing her best blue winter coat and black suede gloves. Would she also wear a hat? Then Tommie would cross the room and greet her to take her by the shoulder. No, rather his eyes would meet hers and no one would see the mutual shiver of recognition, and in his eyes would be understanding and forgiveness, and then she would cross the room and magnanimously kiss his cheek as a gesture of farewell.

Instead, Gertrude refused the final offer from her father to accompany him as he was leaving, and said that really with so much to do for the wedding she needed a night's sleep, and anyway she wouldn't be missed. When the door shut after Jim Cullen Gertrude felt very alone. Bridie was dozing by the range in the kitchen and would soon go to bed. Gertrude was fidgety, on edge. No matter how often she replayed these scenes in her mind could she actually imagine carrying them off. Other images, more rabid, jumped in to invade her, where the room went dim as soon as she entered and the only two people left in the world were herself and Tommie Mulhall. He would cross the room, his eyes locked into hers, to sweep her off her feet and lift her to a place of swooning darkness where her imagination was no longer necessary. As she spoke to herself like this, Gertrude's senses raced ahead to betray her.

Struggling with this inner war she opened the front door to stand on the step and inhale the November frost. Somewhere down below in the valley and beyond the village deep in the woods, a little house was lit up with candlelight and firelight where shadows danced in the windows and sounds of revelry and wild singing travelled into the dark country-side all around, sending out cries of merriment, like lost souls wandering in the firmament. She, Gertrude, was the outsider looking in, standing enviously like the little match girl, left out and lonely. She sighed. Tommie was going and that was that. There was no need to make an extra effort to wear nice shoes and stockings on little trips into the vil-lage on the off-chance she might see him, hoping he would still notice her and that she was somehow a woman in his eyes. Recently she had seen no sign of him and she felt the want of that approval badly. She did-n't want to sit up on the hill in a stone house with William away and no man to take her in his arms. She needed also William's approval, liked it very much when he complimented her gallantly on his infrequent visits home.

Before she noticed she was moving Gertrude's legs had already taken her as far as the gate, and out into the chilly dark. Luckily it was a still night well-lit by stars and moonlight. She hurried along the road impelled by forces that were not part of her rational mind. It was the blood pounding in her veins that rushed to her feet and kept her going, her only goal a vision of Tommie's eyes as they lit up with pleasure on seeing her. The thrill this caused in her belly was enough to propel her down all the miles of cold dark road on that November night long ago. Why, she never knew later, but the urge was unbearable and the longing intense. Only when Gertrude reached the cottage did she falter, and then only to keep herself hidden in the shadows lest she be seen. All her senses were fixed on one goal only, to see Tommie one last time. She would watch and wait until morning if necessary such was the rage in her heart.

The fiddle was still playing Gertrude crept around to the back of the house to get a better view of the kitchen window. She recognised many of the neighbours and shrank back in shame at the thought she might be seen. No, she must wait until they had all stumbled away into the night before she would act. Even then she had no idea of what she would do, only that she would somehow look into Tommie's eyes again. She shivered in the night air, and pulled her cardigan around her. It was woollen but besides that she had no coat, and was still in her slippers. She allowed herself a small smile at the absurdity of it all. Nevertheless she would wait there undeterred. It was only now, as if she had come home to herself in these dark and extreme circumstances, that Gertrude Cullen could admit the truth to herself: she was hopelessly in love with Tommie Mulhall, and she would tell him so even if he took that declaration with him to the grave.

At about four o'clock in the morning the house had cleared, and the lights inside were dim. Soon there were no shadows left around the fire, save one. It was unmistakably him. She opened the door and tiptoed up behind him where he was slumped in a chair asleep. She touched the back of his neck, stroked the hair that curled over his collar, and leant to kiss it. He stirred and mumbled in his sleep. Gertrude gently brought her palm over his eyes and down his cheek and touched her lips to his. Tommie's eyes opened wide in amazement. Then he sat up straight to exclaim loudly. She clapped a hand over his mouth.

'Shush, shush, my love,' she said.

Tommie's eyes and mouth opened wider still, as he struggled to make sense of this vision before him. 'What? What's going on? Is something wrong? Is there somebody dead?' he babbled.

Gertrude knelt before him. This wasn't quite so easy, and Tommie's breath smelled strongly of whiskey. She looked him full in the eyes and said, 'I just had to see you one more time Tommie.'

He woke up sharply then and rushed her out of the house cursing under his breath to the shed out the back. It smelled of hens and cats and in it they found a bed of hay. Tommie took her hungrily, angrily maybe, like revenge. She melted into him and claimed him urgently in return.

When it was over light was breaking through onto a sorry scene, where she was frozen and sore and he was lying drunk and snoring on the hay. Gertrude scurried home along the road, triumphant with a kind of righteousness that left a dry sour taste in her mouth.

It was the week before Christmas and William was due home. Gertrude wrote him a letter to his digs in Dublin, saying she was coming up on a Christmas shopping trip and couldn't they meet up for tea in Wynn's Hotel? William wrote back by the next post, saying how he would be delighted because he was so fed up with the long boring days in a solicitor's office, and that he would like to take her out on a proper date to the pictures in the Savoy cinema.

So Gertrude found herself at Westland Row station on a frosty December day, filled with large measures of excitement and apprehension in equal doses. She had taken care to wear her good grey suit, with a well-cut skirt to just below the knee. Three big black buttons on the jacket emphasised its narrow waistline, which had a peplum, flaring out over her hips. The skirt had a kick pleat to the back that allowed her knees to be seen intermittently as she walked. Her legs were clad in her best silk stockings with a flattering seam running in a straight line up her calves from her patent leather court shoes. She held a black clutch bag and wore long matching gloves. A neat airman style hat from which protruded a cocky feather sat smartly on her head. Her hair was tied back in a French chignon, her lips and cheeks were rouged. She might have walked out of a Hollywood movie.

The effect on William was the desired one. He ran over to her at the appointed place under Clery's clock at five, and stood back in awe and open admiration.

'Gertrude, you look absolutely splendid,' he exclaimed. 'My goodness my girl, but you're a right young woman now and I'm proud to have you on my arm.' He offered his arm gallantly and whisked her off down O'Connell Street.

As he chatted happily in her presence about his work and life in Dublin, Gertrude stole several glances sideways to appraise him also. William had filled out around the jaw line, and wore a bristly ginger moustache. It sat there under his round eyes as a permanent exclamation of surprise, so that he looked slightly comical, but also endearing. She found his taste in clothing excellent: his crisp clean shirt contrasted with his brown tweed sports jacket under an expensive cashmere coat. He walked with confidence through the streets crowded with festive shoppers, and gave off an air of bonhomie. He patted Gertrude's hand in proprietary affection every few moments to express his pleasure at holding her so, as he continued his animated monologue. He was slightly taller than she, maybe half a head, and for this she was glad. She had remembered him as smaller and rounder when he was a boy in the valley. Under his cashmere coat his shoulders were large and reassuring, so she began to relax and let herself be guided.

She had been desperately tense all the way up on the train, afraid of him not finding her pleasing to look at anymore or, if she was honest, the other way round. Gertrude Cullen was afraid she might not find William Hawthorne Thwaite attractive to her and then she would have a little more difficulty in carrying out her plan. Plan was probably too big a word for the intention that had been forming in her mind now for the past few weeks, as she felt her body begin to form itself into new shapes once again beyond her control.

At tea in Wynn's Hotel seated on hardback red velvet chairs, Gertrude listened with her full attention to William's stories of daily trials and tribulations working in a dingy solicitor's office in Rathmines. She then turned her face, fresh from the Wicklow air, eagerly to his as she recounted her stories, funny tales of Bridie or old Mrs Murphy in the shop, or her father's anecdotes of childish pranks that he brought home daily from the classroom. She spoke in her pure ringing tones, using her voice as a storyteller might, varying its pitch, raising and lowering the volume, pausing every so often to gauge the effect on her listener.

There was a grace about her, the way she inclined her head or used her hands, and a sparkling energy in her large clear eyes, which completely captivated William. His eyes grew misty with love as something in his lower regions woke up and stirred, and his heart was hers for the asking. She knew too how to take it, for later in the smoky seats of the Savoy cinema, she laid her head innocently, trustingly, on his shoulder, and allowed a delicate white hand, with its long long fingers, to lie on her lap, defenceless, and then to trail against his knee, so that he couldn't resist the urge to grasp it and hold it and knead it with all the urgency of his sweaty longing. By the time the picture was over, he was limp with desire. In the chilly street under a lamp-post she turned her face to his, which was exquisitely etched under her hat and bathed in a halo of gaslight. It appeared to him as an icon of virginal innocence hanging whitely in the darkness. This image was to sustain William for many years, and then come back to haunt him. But at that moment, on the twenty-first of December 1945, he leaned over to touch his hot lips to her cool ones and almost imploded in a ricochet of rising lust.

When it was time to put Gertrude back on the train, as it was still only nine o'clock, he implored her to stay. He had a cousin in Dublin who wouldn't mind putting her up and they could go there on a tram. William was ready to ignore all observances that social decorum might require, such was his need to keep Gertrude within his grasp. But Gertrude, poised and sensible, said sweetly, 'but William darling, you'll be back home to Wicklow in two days' time,' and smiled such a smile of pure innocence and suggestion that he spent days afterwards feeling himself up to relieve the terrible demon of desire that had risen up in him.

It was a particularly festive Christmas with real oranges in the stockings now that the war was over, and fresh produce on the tables including the latest invention, the white sliced pan. Amid all this abundance the Cullen household was more cheerful than it had been in years. Gertrude's engagement seemed to be the talk of the valley, and this alliance of two families was discussed with a mixture of pride and envy. There were the usual rounds of tea parties and relatives calling, and Gertrude was kept busy practising her newfound skills of baking tarts and buns. Brown bread was her speciality and Bridie was proud that she could carry on the tradition of a good kitchen like her mother before her. Master Cullen was more relaxed too at the idea of the wedding. Those in his care seemed happy. He attributed Gertrude's blooming figure to a womanly contentment at the prospect of marriage.

William came calling frequently and made every social event his excuse to be in the same room as his intended. Jim Cullen learned to talk horsey talk as they sat in the afternoons in the parlour of the stone house while the women served afternoon tea. He had to admit it was how he had always imagined it to be, his future son-in-law an able companion and well-up on the ways of the valley. Even Jim began to forget the great academic promise once shown by his daughter.

Finally by New Year's Eve William had a chance to be alone with Gertrude. The adults were off to the dance at the hall to ring in the New Year. William was to keep Gertrude company, along with the farmhands, but he had arranged a little deal with Paddy and Mikey, slipping them a couple of pound notes to go and buy a few pints for themselves down in Black Tom's Tavern below in the village.

When nine o'clock came and Jim Cullen went off to collect Aunt Maisie in the Ford, William sat down at the fire in his adopted sitting room with a large sigh, and poured himself a brandy. Gertrude came in to find him in her father's armchair by the fire, smiling like the cat that got the cream and smoking a cigarette.

'Darling, at last, come in and sit down.'

Gertrude was a little taken aback at his proprietary air, but moved to perch on the edge of the big old sofa. She smiled a half smile, and then lapsed into a silent trance watching the flames flare and dance around the turf in the fireplace.

'Penny for them,' said William gently.

Gertrude sighed. 'Oh, nothing special,' she said, and sat back dreamily on the sofa. In the flickering firelight William beheld his future bride, face flushed from the fire, gazing as if into the future with a strange sadness in her eyes.

'Gertie my love, you're so quiet. What is it? Is there anything wrong?'

At his kind tone Gertrude brushed away a little tear. It was genuine, for the strain of the past few weeks and the effort to keep up the merriment of the season was proving too much. She was tired and felt heavy all the time, but kept herself going morning noon and night. It was not the physical work that tired her, but the huge energy involved in keeping her secret. She was weighed down by a burden she could speak of to no one. Of Tommie Mulhall there was no news, except that he didn't appear home from England on Christmas morning and everyone knew that Mrs Mulhall's heart would be broken again.

William came and sat on the couch beside Gertrude. He put his arm around her. 'Cheer up my girl,' he said, 'don't we have such a lot to look forward to in this coming year.'

Gertrude, mastering her feelings, turned to him with her sweet practised smile and said, 'We do William, we do, it's just that sometimes I feel we are so grown up. It seems like yesterday when I would cycle over to your house and we would go catching frogs in the long grass out the back, and then Evie would make us tea with her currant buns.'

William beamed back at her, his eyes misty with nostalgia.

'Come here you silly billy,' he said, and pulled her head in against his shoulder. He held her out to take her chin and examine her face. 'Have I told you how beautiful you are, and how much I've longed for this moment. I thought they'd never leave,' he added with an impish smile.

Of course Gertrude let him kiss her then, and found it warm and good. She let herself melt a little, and then more, hoping as her senses raced that they would blot out those other feelings of loneliness and anguish that threatened to overflow and fall down her face in torrents. She kissed him back with a fierceness that surprised them both, and before long William's hand was rooting under her velvet skirt, and rubbing round and round her upper leg quite beside himself with passion. His eyes rolled unseeing in his head as she helped him ease down his trousers. His mouth was drooling as he licked her neck and face. His breath came in quicker and quicker gasps. She was clear now, and pushed herself against him. He fumbled awkwardly trying to find the place, but slipped out again and again. He was almost tearful in shame and raging desire when she took him in her hand and inserted him into her. He looked up once in shock before giving vent to large cries of satisfaction and relief. She put her hand over his face to stifle the sounds and then pulled his head into her breasts so that he wouldn't see the tears glittering there.

Afterwards she was mute as he jumped around collecting his socks and underpants amid the jumble of clothes on the floor, muttering apologies and avoiding her eyes. Eventually he said, 'Gertrude, forgive me. You're too good for me.'

She had a choice then to make him feel better, or to let him feel sorry for her. She pulled her skirt back down over her knees and sat with her arms around them in a hunched up position on the couch, staring again at the flames. William came to kneel beside her.

'Gertrude, I love you and I respect you,' he declared.

'Yes William,' she said quietly, 'but what'll we do?'

'Of course I'll still marry you, if that's what you're worried about.'

She started. Anything else hadn't occurred to her. She leaned over to touch his head, and said in a small voice, 'William, I'm afraid.'

His male ego swelled and he rose to fold her in his arms. 'My darling, my darling girl, don't be afraid, I'll look after you. I'll love you forever.'

She continued to stroke his head and then kissed him softly on the lips, and said with wide eyes, 'Do we have to wait until the summer to be together like this?'

William sat back in the seat and exclaimed. 'What a marvellous idea! Will you, would you, marry me as soon as possible? Oh Gertie,' and he pulled her into a huge bear hug.

Her reply was a coy 'certainly my darling' which concealed another smile of triumph, tinged with huge relief that her ploy had paid off.

And so it was that Gertrude Cullen and William Hawthorn Thwaite were married on St Valentine's Day 1946, just six months before baby Elizabeth Mary was born. Maybe because in her mind it would be, now, William's child, and maybe because the act itself had been awkward and loveless, this first child born to Gertrude was to be forever associated in her mind with the odour of dying embers, sea salt and shame. The child Elizabeth Mary would grow up feeling unwanted and unloved.

February came and with it the big day.

On the morning of the wedding, Gertrude went into a panic about her corset. She couldn't close the fasteners at the back as the bump below her belly button refused to disappear when she sucked in and clenched her muscles.

Bridie came to the bedroom to assist her into the bridal gown, but Gertrude shooed her away crossly. She could manage by herself thank you. She was in tears of frustration cursing through clenched teeth as she tried to pull the elastic garment over her tummy. Finally she succeeded with one last breath in. Gertrude exhaled in relief and hoped the corset would last the day.

The dress she had chosen in Clery's of Dublin was empire line, dropping from below the breasts, so at least it would not hug her waist. The neckline was low, deliberately so, to keep attention focused on her face. The fabric was a pearly white, simple satin with embroidered cuffs. The same lace edging trimmed the neckline. Gertrude wore two drop pearl earrings to match, set off against a pearl pendant which nestled on the soft skin just before her breasts bloomed. Over it all and around her head she would wear a flimsy mantilla-like veil, to cover the bare flesh of her bosom and neck. Because it would likely be cold, she had a fur stole made of grey squirrel, loaned to her for the day by Matilda, her future mother-in-law. When her hair was finished, piled up in glossy rolls on top of her head, Gertrude gazed long and hard at herself in the mirror. Her look was one of serious intent, with a flicker of admiration for the fine woman before her. She set her face in a resolute smile to prevent the pricking of tears behind her eyeballs.

'Gertie, you look magnificent,' beamed Master Cullen as she stepped sedately down the stairs, Bridie trying in vain to keep the veil from trailing along the ground behind her.

The church was packed with curious locals who streamed up from the village in their numbers to see the spectacle of one of the Hawthorn Thwaites getting married at the local altar. The organ played and the priest said the Mass in Latin with his back to the congregation, until he came to the wedding vows.

Gertrude gave her assent in a clear voice. William was almost exuberant now that the time had come. Father Murphy then solemnly slipped on the rings and declared Gertrude Cullen and William Hawthorn Thwaite to be man and wife.

In the wedding photograph, only someone who knew Gertrude intimately would have spotted that the smile was fixed on her face and that telltale lines of strain played about her mouth. If Master Cullen did notice it, then he pushed it down into the box of his heart to lock away his doubt with his dreams.

The wedding breakfast took place in the Wooden Bridge Hotel where over a hundred guests sat down to be served a fine meal of turkey and ham.

After the speeches there was dancing and some singing, although it would have to be said that the Protestant presence, from Matilda's English relatives, imposed a certain restraint on the extended Cullen family.

It was shortly before six that Gertrude and William drove off in the Austin to a hotel in Wexford where they would spend two days alone on their honeymoon. Truth to tell they had rarely if ever found themselves totally alone, apart from that one night by the fire on New Year's Eve. Since then Gertrude had found ingenious ways not to be alone in William's company, was always busy or tired or 'observing proper decorum', or so she said. She would just give him enough of a peck on the cheek for him to be satisfied, devotedly knocking again at the door the following Sunday when he came home from the solicitor's office in Dublin for the day.

So now here they were driving to Wexford town on their own. Gertrude had changed into her bride's going-away outfit of blue tweed. The suit's jacket was styled wide enough to bypass her waist. Night had fallen as they approached the hotel. It was nearly 9pm. They checked in and William tipped the porter who brought their luggage. Gertrude nodded approvingly, feeling very grown-up. Alone in the room William put his hand on her gloved one.

'Darling, I'm so glad we can be together at last. To tell you the truth this wedding business was beginning to bother me. Now we can just be ourselves.'

Gertrude smiled a tired smile, 'William dearest, would you mind if I lay down for a few moments?'

William the gallant went off to get a nightcap for himself in the hotel bar, and when he came back to the room he found his new wife fast asleep tucked up in bed still in her slip and corset. She slept the sleep of the dead.

So William got himself several more whiskeys, and drank them, looking longingly at her beautiful face so disarmed now in sleep.

Finally all he could do was crawl in beside her warm body to die of desire.

When morning came Gertrude opened her eyes wide, stunned for a moment in the unfamiliar surroundings. William snored beside her. She turned away in distaste at the stale smell of cigarettes and whiskey. Gingerly she stepped out of bed to get her dressing gown and crept down the corridor to the toilet. Then she gathered the good suit with all the money spent on it, and tried to dress herself back up into her new life. 'You are married with wifely duties,' she admonished herself. She did let her fingers linger for a moment on the satiny bridal nightdress still packed in her suitcase, then banished all thoughts of longing or self-pity.

When William woke up Gertrude was kind, and ministered to him a cup of tea and some aspirin, which she had ordered from reception. William was the one who was shamefaced and apologetic.

That whole next day as they drove around sightseeing, William had a sore head, a spot of perplexity burning over his nose between his brows. He couldn't quite shake it off and didn't feel as elated or happy as he thought he should. Gertrude was back to herself, impeccable as usual, and working hard at conversation. Too much of the damned sauce, he said to himself. He felt he was seeing the world from inside a bubble, his young wife unreachable on the other side of some invisible glass membrane.

The second night, Gertrude made an effort. She donned the satiny nightdress with its low cut neckline and thin straps, and sat at the dressing table to brush out her hair. In the lamplight she encouraged William to come and touch her bronze tresses. He had had a nightcap for Dutch courage. Soon he was beside himself with desire, as he slid his hand

down into his wife's now ample cleavage. Gertrude acquiesced grace-
fully, and it could be said that their coupling was adequate rather than
fully satisfactory. Gertrude was relieved enough the following morning
however to drive back to Wicklow where they would take up residence
in Glenview House under the roof of Major and Matilda Hawthorn
Thwaite.

By April it was becoming harder for Gertrude to conceal the round
orb that was her stomach. She took to lounging around the house wearing long skirts and billowing blouses, leaving her hair loose to complete
the appearance of a woman in negligée.

Glenview House had many large but draughty rooms, boasting four
reception rooms on either side of a grand front door, which rested on a
granite porch with three steps. The drawing-room at the front was
where Matilda entertained her friends for card parties, and where in the
afternoon she had Evie serve tea with a light snack: fingers of cucumber
sandwiches, followed by scones with clotted Devon cream. Then there
was the library on the other side of the entrance hall, where the Major
kept track of his estate and dealt with the mounds of bills and letters to
do with being Master of the Gleneevin Hunt. That left a spacious dining room and a small back parlour, which was used as a morning room.
It was to the latter that Gertrude retired in the afternoons with a book,
asking Evie to put down a fire for her. It was small and stuffy, with a hard
sofa and Victorian chairs, adorned with embroidered armrests. There
was one chintz-covered bucket chair under the window, reminiscent of
one in a dank basement in Dublin long ago in another life. It made
Gertrude's stomach muscles heave. She avoided it, and chose instead a
Chesterfield by the fire. She was happy to escape to this corner of the
rattling house for a few hours every day.

William still worked in Dublin during the week. Gertrude was a visitor in the house, on good behaviour, trying hard to remember the rules
and obligations of a dutiful wife. Sometimes it felt as if the part she must
play would soon be over, and she could return to the stone house under
the avalanche hill and be Gertrude Cullen the schoolmaster's daughter
once more. But the baby growing inside had decided her fate and very
shortly she had to own up to its now lively presence, the little kicks and
twirls nudging her into admitting its existence.

Gertrude joined Matilda for tea on a crisp afternoon in April with
the wind whistling under the doors and rattling at the windows. By now

of course she was blooming with good health but had to pretend to be poorly.

'Mother, I have some news for you,' she began.

'Oh,' Matilda exclaimed, clapping her hands for joy, 'so soon! I am so pleased. I have been longing for a grandson. Is William delighted?'

Gertrude interrupted. 'Mother dear, you are the first person I've told. It feels a little strange, and so I would like to tell William in my own time.'

'Yes of course dear,' said Matilda. 'Oh what wonderful news. Let me see ... an autumn child?'

'Yes,' muttered Gertrude flushing, leaning over suddenly to pour more tea. 'I'm not really sure about these things.'

'Then you shall have to see a doctor,' said Matilda.

'No, no,' said Gertrude hastily, 'I mean, maybe I'll wait just a little until I get used to the idea.'

'You'll be a wonderful mother Gertrude, but you must rest now and take very good care. I have an excellent gynaecologist in Dublin. I shall write to him to make an appointment.'

Gertrude wished she could share her mother-in-law's enthusiasm. Maybe babies were wonderful, as Matilda had repeated so often, but Gertrude's only recollection of them when Bridie's sister's children were little was whingeing and wailing and buckets of wet nappies steeping in Milton solution in the scullery, and their mother bent over the sink scrubbing and wringing them endlessly.

No, at the tender age of twenty-one, Gertrude Hawthorn Thwaite, née Cullen, did not find the prospect of impending motherhood remotely appealing. Still, this was the role she had been given to play, and play it she would.

When William came on Saturday after lunch from Dublin, Gertrude met him in her best blue coat and muffler. She greeted him with an unusually warm hug. 'Darling it's such a lovely day. Shall we go for a walk along the valley?'

'Certainly Gertie, but let me have some lunch first, I'm ravenous.' But he beamed with pleasure at this unexpected initiative; Gertrude had been so lethargic and disinterested in everything all through Easter.

They set off down the drive of Glenview House where the bluebells peeped out from under the carpet of fallen oak leaves, and marched on down to the bend in the river. From here they headed across country towards the mountain. Gertrude was confident in her stride, elated to be out in the fresh air and feeling like a young girl again. William was pleased at her exuberance, and they laughed a lot as they remembered their childhood adventures played out on these very fields and hills. All along the way Gertrude was taut with finding the courage to tell William her news. It was therefore not until they were upon it that Gertrude noticed her hurrying feet had brought her back to the hut at the base of the hill, under the avalanche. The April sun played about its gutted windows, falling in shafts to cleanse the dust within, and so it looked small and ordinary, just a mountain shack, without any of its magical connotations. As if she had never before darkened its door, Gertrude beckoned William to look. The fireplace held the charred remains of a fire lit by woodcutters many weeks before. Some scraps of newspaper scuttled across the floor in the wind. Gertrude shivered. Before a cold snowflake might land on the window of her mind and plead to be let in, she exclaimed, 'Oh what a silly little place, let's go before the ghost comes to shout us away.'

William hugged her fondly. 'We've come a long way from here my girl. Come on home before we miss tea.'

So it wasn't until evening that Gertrude found herself alone with William again. They sat at the fire in the drawing-room and finally she said quietly, 'William, I'm expecting.'

He started, and she could see that he was deeply shocked, but he recovered well enough to say, 'well, do I say congratulations, and well done Gertrude.'

'William,' she said sharply, 'you are going to be a father. It's yours too.'

Then she blushed violently, got up and turned to poke the fire. Because she had her back turned, William jumped up to put his arms around her, saying in his voice of forced joviality that he used in his men's club in Dublin, 'That's jolly good news darling. I'll bet Mummy will be pleased.'

Gertrude's cheeks were flaming now from the fire, or otherwise, as he continued. 'I'm sure you'll be a splendid mother.'

Well, thought Gertrude, 'at least it's out.' She turned to him. 'I'll have to see a doctor you know. It's all very new to me and it's a little bit strange.'

William patted her tummy. 'Well well I didn't like to say it but you were getting a little plump around the waist. When might it be born?' He poured himself a large whiskey, which glowed yellow in the firelight.

'Let's drink to health, wealth and happiness, and to our baby's future.' He slugged it back in one go, and looked at Gertrude a little tipsily. 'Do you suppose it's a honeymoon baby then?'

It was fortunate for Gertrude that his questions were not more precise, nor his knowledge greater, as they had seldom slept together in the previous months. You could count on one hand the number of times they had actually made love. There had been some fumbling and groping yes, but Gertrude was no longer inclined to guide William and lead him to the correct parts of her body. If he remembered their first encounter by the fire on New Year's Eve, he did not allude to it – that is, not until later.

Telling her father would be the hardest of all. She feigned embarrassment to avoid any conversation surrounding the progress of her pregnancy. She had been sent off to Matilda's doctor in Dublin, who knew quite well, despite Gertrude's stammered protestations, that the baby was well on its way and would be born by early August. If Gertrude was lucky she might go until the middle or end of that month.

'Well,' said the doctor sternly, 'I see we have a case here of a premature birth, am I right? Let me see. You were married in February, so the baby, shall we say, will be at least two if not three months premature.'

Blushing furiously Gertrude thanked the doctor and resolved to use the word 'premature' frequently from now on.

Gertrude felt unwell. It had been a peculiar weekend with William, one where she had been snappy and irritable one minute, and weeping for no apparent reason, the next. Before he left for Dublin on Monday morning she had clung to him in bed, shutting her eyes against his chest. She wanted to curl up like a baby, but the baby inside her came between them. William had had to extricate himself finally from her clutching embrace or he would have missed the train from Arklow.

After he left, Gertrude wandered moodily around the house. Her lower back was giving her trouble, twingeing and aching so that she couldn't sit still in any one chair for long. She had no appetite at dinner, and Matilda advised her to go to bed early. She escaped gratefully and Evie lit a fire to warm her room. She sank onto the bed lying spread out on the cover, relieved that she could be alone. Recently her dreams had been vivid and luscious, swelling her with a lust so torrid that she thought she might burst with it.

This night however a dull ache throbbed in her lower belly. It moved to attack her back, like severe constipation. Gertrude lay in the large gloomy bedroom tossing and turning, watching the flames spring up the walls to lick the ceiling in a hypnotic shadow play. This lulled her into relaxing for some moments between the twinges and twitches in her back and belly. The room had high ceilings with faded rose velvet drapes at the windows that didn't quite meet and allowed a chink of moonlight through. A faded Persian rug covered only the middle of the polished timber floor and the wind came whistling up through the rest of the bare floorboards. By midnight the fire was almost out, apart from a few remaining cinders that clinked and fell, so that when the wind howled a cloud of soot filled the room with the smell of acrid smouldering. She would always remember that peculiar dead smell of cold fire.

Sometime after midnight the pain in Gertrude's back became acute. She crawled around the bed on all fours, bending over a pillow to ease it. She had gone ice-cold yet sweat rolled off her forehead onto the sheets. She was fearful. Then a great wetness flooded out of her, so that she thought with amazement she must have gone to the toilet. Wearily she rolled up the wet sheet soaked through with the hot liquid then lay on her side holding the wooden frame of the bed, as pain writhed and coiled in her belly. Soon she was in the grip of great waves of it washing over her, leaving her gasping, beached on the other side, waiting for the next onslaught. Her mind at this point could no longer push away the horrible realisation that the baby was trying to be born. It can't be, she muttered, grinding her teeth through the cramps. No. Not yet. It is too soon. Perhaps that's why Gertrude did not call out or seek help. She buried her head in a pillow, gasping into it when the waves of pain rose and peaked, then clutched the bed frame hard with clenched fists.

It was now about 3am. The moon had risen and stared down through the curtains mercilessly. The room was ice-cold. Then there came an overwhelming urge to push. Instinctively she slid out of bed still holding on to the posts to squat on the floor. She was beyond reason now, her body straining and heaving with the spasms. A strangled groan escaped her on each one and she held on tight, biting the mattress, her mind still disbelieving. Finally she cried out, a long groan of release, as the baby slid out in a gush of blood onto the floor. Gertrude came to suddenly, out of her trance, heard the echo of her cry in the room, a sound that horrified her. Who might have heard? Then the wail started, cat-like from the tiny throat. Without thinking she put her hand on the child's face to stop the sound, but still it wailed.

'Don't, please,' she whispered as tears spilled over her newborn infant. 'Don't, stop it, there there, shush,' she spat.

Terrified now she went to place her hands on its neck. God knows what might have happened next.

Just then a hand touched her shoulder.

'Gertrude,' said Matilda, her voice stern. 'I'll do it.'

She knelt by the infant, took the blue-black cord and wrenched it between her fingers. Where it would not break she bit it speedily, then tied it into a knot on the baby's belly. Gertrude stayed frozen in her pieta-like position, petrified from cold and shock. She watched Matilda's hands, those disembodied white gloves of satiny flesh, turn the baby over, slap it on the back, take a sheet to wipe off the clots and slime, then wrap it up tight in a sheet. When that was done she laid it on the bed.

Thankfully the child was now silent, opening its inky blue eyes to stare at Gertrude. She looked away and trembled as aftershock overtook her, shuddering tremors racked her body. She was frozen cold, kneeling in a mass of body fluids, all dignity gone. She cried out once more as another spasm shot through her. Matilda said only 'push' and out slid the afterbirth, a black sack of slime. Gertrude leaned over and vomited, sobbing for her life into the side of the bed.

'I'll fetch some water,' said Matilda, and left.

Gertrude looked up from her weeping and saw the child wrapped in a stained sheet. A dart of hatred shot through her heart. It had come too soon. What could she do? What would she say? She didn't want it, never wanted it. Had she had an ounce of energy left she might have taken a pillow and squashed the life out of it forever.

But Matilda came back. She put down a basin of water and some towels. She didn't touch Gertrude or help her up. She said only, 'I'll take care of this,' picking up the baby as if it were a doll or a bag of old rubbish, and left. Gertrude managed to climb out of her soiled nightdress to wash down her legs. Then she wrapped herself in a towel and lay on the good side of the bed, the side where the sheet was still dry. She pulled the covers over her head, numb beyond cold, empty of all feeling.

A great silence seemed to descend on the room. Minutes passed, or maybe hours. Into the ashen light of early morning came the call of the first bird. It pierced Gertrude's heart opening it up to icy draughts of horror and shame. She was naked and exposed. Everyone would know her secret. What would Daddy say? The thought of it crushed her innards and tightened her throat. She rolled herself into a tight ball scrunching her eyes shut against the cruel light of day and slept fitfully.

At eight o'clock Matilda shook her awake with a cup of tea. 'I have taken care of everything. The baby is gone.'

Gertrude sat up in shock and let out a cry of innate protest. Matilda continued.

'You'll get it back in due course. From now on you will stay here in bed until your time comes. Then I will make arrangements for you to go to the National Maternity Hospital in Dublin, where you will have your baby on the due date. Is that clear?'

Matilda sounded as if she was planning a dinner menu and Gertrude reeled at her efficiency, her competence. But she felt somehow safe. Maybe Matilda could make it all right. The older woman stepped smartly away, turning when she reached the door.

'There will not be a word about this. Do you understand?'

'But William ...' Gertrude ventured.

It was the first loosening of the mask of Matilda's facial muscles. 'You'll tell him in time,' she said as she hurried out of the room.

The door closed with a final click. Her mother-in-law had left a clean nightdress on the bed, with a small cushion in a pillowcase. It took Gertrude several moments before she understood its purpose, then she almost smiled with relief: her secret was safe for the time being.

This was the fifteenth of August 1946, the Feast of the Assumption of Our Lady into Heaven. Gertrude would lie up in this room until mid November, when her baby would officially be born.

On the twelfth of November Gertrude arrived in the National Maternity Hospital at Holles Street in Dublin to begin the charade. The attending gynaecologist, in a voice luscious with contempt, said, 'Welcome to Holles Street. We have a fine child here, isn't that right Nurse?'

The nurses presented Gertrude with a pink bundle, all beaming smiles.

'Now Mrs Hawthorn Thwaite, congratulations, you have a lovely little baby girl.'

A bulb pops. There is a white flash. Click. In the photograph, William puts his arm carefully around Gertrude's shoulders. His fingers alight above her left breast. They look as if they never quite touched down there. The baby in her arms actually glances to camera, a small hand raised as if to wave a greeting, believing naively that the world will be a benign place. And Gertrude. Tall, statuesque, her head slightly inclined in a graceful curve, interrogative, wearing a starched frilly nightgown and a soft bed jacket. Her hair is freshly brushed and cascades over one shoulder; it has been carefully arranged by the photographer. The colours are probably baby pink because, after all, the child is a baby girl. But the photograph is black and white. Right in the centre are the pools of Gertrude's eyes. Despite the Holy Trinity pose, despite William's colluding grin, they reflect nothing. Even the photographer's best efforts to illuminate this corner of his portrait are doomed to failure, because Gertrude's eyes reflect no light. They are dead. Closed lenses, as if months later the still eager photographer had airbrushed the pupils out.

What did she go through as she lay in waiting during those three months? What did she do about menorrhoea, abdominal cramps, breasts swollen with unused milk, high fevers, and an unacknowledged primitive anguish.

It is another hiatus, an unwritten history, the gory bodily bits, shameful and inglorious. And how was she afterwards towards her baby? One can only guess, because the portrait reveals nothing.

I came to see this photograph only when I went to stay with Gertrude, and she was a changed woman by then. Softer, or cynical, I'm not sure which. Any of my previous ideas about her were filtered through Mammy, who could be vicious behind her seeming frailty and her bad eyesight. Mammy had her reasons, forty odd years of them. But I run ahead with my tale.

Elizabeth, 1945–55

In the interminable tyranny of daily life, the child Elizabeth Mary cried a lot.

Of its black head of hair, the doctors assured Gertrude it was likely to be shed within months, just baby hair, and who knows what the next colour would be.

'It looks like a red Indian,' said William, 'I suppose my mother had some Spanish blood in her. How else did the Catholics come to England.'

Gertrude laughed and shoved the tightly-wrapped bundle into his arms. He held it out gingerly between outstretched fingers and quickly gave it back before he dropped it. He had never seen an infant before. 'Reminds me of a puppy,' he said, and left hastily. His father bred hunting dogs. The smell of disinfectant and all the matrons in white flapping about chilled him. It was no place for a man.

Gertrude lay in a hospital ward the night after the supposed birth staring up at the ceiling. She had recoiled in alarm at the sight of the little mouth opening red and wailing. The nurses took the child away and bottle-fed it at four-hourly intervals, as had probably been the case during its early furtive beginning. The little creature was still so small, wrapped up tightly with its eyes closed and its tiny fists clenched. Gertrude felt immense pity for it afloat in the universe, but she had no feelings that came close to being maternal. She felt only a terrible tiredness and a kind of amazement that this little thing should be the outcome of many months of strain and pretence. For Gertrude none of the previous nine months had been joyous. She had managed to survive the three months in hiding. She had told William about the birth.

'I think we got caught,' she said sheepishly as he came to see her in the sick room at home.

'What do you mean darling?' he had asked anxiously.

She hesitated. 'The baby came early,' she said in a rush, flushing hot.

'What?' William jumped up. 'Where is it?'

'It's all right,' Gertrude soothed, 'your mother has made arrangements, sent it away for the time being.'

'Jesus. Good God in heaven, why didn't you say?' His eyes darted helplessly around the room, as if expecting to see a baby bundled up in the corner.

'William,' Gertrude was calm, collecting herself. 'Remember New Year's Eve?' She lowered her eyes. 'Well it must have been then. I'm sorry, I just didn't realise what was happening to me.'

'Jesus.' William swore again. 'Our first child. Does that make it illegitimate? A bastard?'

'William,' said Gertrude, calmer than ever, 'your mother is looking after everything. No one will ever know. I'm not telling. Are you?'

Her eyes bore into his, pleading.

He looked away. 'No,' he said defeated. 'Of course not.' He went on with his life tight-lipped and withdrawn, and they had not spoken about it again.

As to what had happened prior to New Year's Eve, in a barn in late November, Gertrude had blotted that out completely. Now in hospital she just accepted whatever medication the matron offered and sank into a sleep that she wanted to last forever.

After a stay of two weeks in a private nursing home in Dublin paid for by Major Hawthorn Thwaite, Gertrude came home to Glenview House. In the cold nights of early winter she rose several times to the sound of insistent wailing, a sound that drilled right through her head setting her nerves jangling. She dragged her exhausted body downstairs to warm the bottle, not caring that the wailing got louder and louder and could wake the whole household.

After the first week of this William removed himself to a spare room on his visits home. Gertrude lay alone wishing she could run out of the house in her nightdress to disappear into the velvet arms of the night sky and not come back. Often the blackness overwhelmed her so that she lay face down and sobbed from the pit of her stomach into the pillow, then fell asleep with swollen eyes but little relief, knowing that the wailing would start again at any minute. She longed for home, her home, for her mother's arms around her. Such thoughts sent more spasms of grief through her and she collapsed in floods of tears. By daylight she could barely rouse herself to the baby's crying. So concerned was Matilda about Gertrude's mothering abilities that she sent for Bridie to come every morning and take the child to nurse it.

One day when the child was four weeks old (but really four months) Master Cullen entered Gertrude's bedroom on an unexpected visit. He found his daughter slumped against pillows, her nightdress stained and her hair lank.

'Oh Daddy,' she said. Her voice trembled as tears slid down her cheeks. Jim Cullen patted her on the arm not knowing what to say. Mothers were supposed to be happy, he thought.

'Oh Daddy, I don't know what to do,' she wailed, and lay her head on his shoulder. He could not console her; this was not how it was meant to be. The remaining embers of his dreams for his daughter collapsed into wet cinders to the bottom of his heart. From that day on Master Cullen was a stooped old man.

Gertrude's disinterest in life and the baby turned into weeks and weeks of her lying in bed, staring at the wall; the baby girl was nursed by Bridie and Matilda between them. Gertrude's eyes barely flickered with interest when they brought the baby in to see her mother, dressed up in a frilly bonnet and pink home-knitted cardigan.

'See,' said Matilda, 'she's trying to talk to you. She coos and gurgles so wonderfully. If you hold her maybe you'll get a smile.'

But Bridie would snatch the baby away an instant later from Gertrude's lethargic stare, as if from the evil eye. Bridie took to walking the baby every day at dinnertime down the driveway of Glenview and up the road to the stone house at the top of the valley, where she had at least one grandfather who took an interest in her. Master Cullen played with the child in the afternoons, and became quite fond of her, but though he tried to find resemblances to Gertrude, either in appearance or aptitude, it was all in vain. There were almost none. Elizabeth Mary's hair remained a resolute mop of black curls, unwieldy and suspicious for most family members. They avoided comment.

In all this time William was a stranger in his own house. His wife had become inaccessible to everyone, including him. He found himself on yet another Saturday night on his return from Dublin in the drawing-room with his parents. For a man of twenty-two it was all becoming a strain. It was not what he had expected of young married love.

This night Gertrude heard raised voices coming up through the floorboards as she lay restlessly tossing and turning. She knew the household custom was for the men to start drinking once the genteel Matilda retired to bed. It had rarely cost her a raised eyebrow. The Major had a good supply of hard liquor and fine wines, and William was developing quite a taste for them.

Major Hawthorn Thwaite liked to tell stories, and usually repeated some of the stock tales from his time as a First World War soldier serving in Egypt. Gertrude strained to hear.

'Those people down in Luxor have whole tribes of children, all of them exactly the same, can't tell one from another. Fine heads of black hair on them all the same. Speaking of which, your Elizabeth, no sign of the old red-blonde in hers then, is there?'

'What do you mean?' William's voice rose suddenly. 'What are you saying Pa? That my child is Egyptian?' William's tone was tight in aggression. Father and son were drawn up, voices escalating.

'I merely allude to the quality and texture of your child's hair, but if all comes to all, she's more of the African variety than Arab perhaps.'

'Are you trying to imply my daughter is a nig-nog, you bastard!'

'Who's a bastard William?' his father snorted.

'Bastard?' William shouted. 'How dare you. Gertrude is my wife.'

'And a fine big child she was too, bless her.' He helped himself to more whiskey. 'I do not intend to insult you or your lady wife.'

Did William pick up the slightest pause on 'lady'? Puce in the face he pulled himself up to his full height of five foot eight inches. 'If you must know Gertrude and I became man and wife long before the wedding day.'

Even as he said it William's eyes were opened. Of course the dates didn't tally, but December to August did, didn't they? Once he had admitted this transgression to his father, the shadow of another, grosser transgression rose up before him and danced tauntingly in front of his eyes.

'No,' he roared, knocking his glass against the marble fireplace where it broke into smithereens. 'Gertrude is my wife. You will not sully her reputation. Take it back Father.'

'I meant nothing more by it son. Now pour another drink for yourself or you'll wake up the women.'

'You're the only bastard around here,' William muttered as he knelt to sweep up the broken shards of crystal littering the grate. They twinkled like his love for his wife and wounded him, drawing blood.

Upstairs in the room above the drawing-room, Gertrude heard the muffled 'Gertrude' and the shouted 'bastard'. She sat up rigid in fear, cold sweat on her palms. Instantly her old resoluteness came back. She had a mission once more. She held her peace that night, judging wisely that an inebriated man would seek outlets for his anger. So she waited.

Next morning Gertrude woke early and asked Evie to run her a hot bath. By breakfast time she had put on a clean blouse and grey skirt, and tied her freshly washed hair loosely in a scarf. She made up her face to hide the pasty complexion after four months of being indoors. She even went to the baby's room and took the child on her lap for a few minutes and, yes, the little thing cooed up at her, all innocence and trusting. Then she appeared at breakfast.

William was very surprised to see her. He sat holding his head to steady the hammering at his temples. Gertrude was kind and stroked his brow, suggesting an outing that afternoon, it being Sunday, if the weather was fine. William numbly allowed himself to be pampered. She nuzzled against him, pressing his sore head to her breast, and he forgave her everything: the months of rejection, the suspicion. No, here was the old Gertrude, his Gertrude. He flooded with warmth and was grateful. And so Gertrude slowly began to thaw and grow into her new life.

Since it was soon Christmas she suggested a shopping trip to Dublin. She was sure a re-enactment of the previous year's dinner in Wynn's Hotel was just the romantic boost they needed. So, in the bustling crowds of merrymakers before Christmas they found stars in their eyes again, and William filled up with an old familiar longing. Gertrude welcomed him back into her bed, so that within the next six months she was expecting again. Less than two years after Elizabeth's birth, Gertrude would bear William a son.

This time her confinement was relatively easy, with none of the pretence or strain of the first one. She was pampered and fussed over, and lay back accepting her status as mother-to-be. Consequently she grew plumper and with it, a lot more contented. She had her hair cut to just above the shoulder, and put in a permanent wave, so that she looked the picture of the perfect housewife of that post-war era, when women found themselves back in the home.

Gertrude had obtained in Dublin some of the glossy housekeeping magazines from America and, liking what she saw, made strenuous efforts to improve herself in her new position. She became what we might now call a career housewife. What had been once her intellectual prowess was transformed into pragmatic applications of common sense. She was determined to be more than a rural drudge. She wanted to excel, to have style. Nor was she content, like Matilda, to live in the shadow of her husband and merely continue traditions of Big House hospitality. She learned from this, but Ireland was modernising, albeit slowly, and she did not wish to be left behind.

Electricity came to the valley in the late 1940s, for those who chose to have it, and with it such delightful appliances as the cake mixer and the vacuum cleaner, apart from light, heat and hot water. Not that Gertrude actually cleaned the house herself, she had a girl to do that, but she did continue to improve her baking skills, first learned from her mother all those years ago, and then from Bridie before her marriage. She learned to make light sponges and cupcakes, tea scones and chocolate fudge cake, very American, and of course puff pastry for the apple tart on a Sunday. For these rituals she donned flowery aprons with scalloped edges and pockets. It was as if she had been preparing for baby James William's arrival, finishing an apprenticeship that meant she was now ready to be a mother. This child would be welcomed into a modern and efficient home. Elizabeth had been a prologue, whose premature appearance was merely a shaky rehearsal for the play proper. Now she had graduated and could proudly call herself Mrs William Hawthorn Thwaite.

But had something else motivated this transformation from girl to woman? Perhaps it was news whispered in the valley.

Gertrude wasn't in the habit of going down to the village much anymore. Sometimes, if it was a fine day and Bridie was off, she would put Elizabeth in the big pram and walk down the valley to Murphy's shop. There she might buy her weekly stamps and post some letters.

One day in late February when Elizabeth was officially three months old she heard Kitty Murphy say to Minnie Byrne, 'did you hear about young Mulhall? Getting married in England he is.'

Gertrude studied the rows of sliced pan with sudden intent while she strained to hear.

'Herself is going over, so they say. She bought a new outfit in Arklow. She's delighted at the news, he might give her a grandson at last.'

Gertrude's cheeks burned. She went to pay, scolding Elizabeth as she left, although the baby hadn't done anything. She forgot her penny change.

Gertrude walked home pushing the pram furiously. No, she didn't care. But Tommie a father? She couldn't imagine it. Tommie Mulhall who would never grow up? Huge figures of Tommie Mulhall clambered and slid down hills towards her, marched across the sky in seven league boots, waited for her at the bend in the road by the river, suspending in the air a Cheshire-cat grin. Tommie whose presence filled the valley. Tommie who had never really left. Tommie who would now never come back, stuck over in England.

Gertrude looked at her own child seated sagely in the pram, staring out at the hedgerows. Elizabeth's eyes often burned darkly as if looking backwards and deep into herself. Her daughter's eyes didn't reflect her back, Gertrude thought, not in any sense. She didn't see herself there, and she couldn't penetrate beyond the surface. Elizabeth's look was opaque, clouded internally: a child too young to be in turmoil, a child who might be in trouble one day herself.

But what Gertrude never did was to look for similarities to Tommie – never. She had convinced herself long ago that Elizabeth's dark blue-black eyes came from William's mother's people, unknown and far away in England. And now in England a little Mulhall would be born, surely soon, nine months after the wedding. She couldn't bear it. She shook inwardly and drove her feet faster and faster up the hill for home.

There at the bend she saw the river, a gushing stream now after the rains. The smell of rotting earth cut into her nostrils where the oak leaves had festered throughout the winter. The tinkling water broke over rocks, rinsed her brain, made her breath catch. It was crystal clear, uncompromising, and it tumbled on, revealing nothing. With a pang of emptiness searing her insides Gertrude trod resolutely the road home.

It was after this that Gertrude Cullen put away girlish things, and made a firm and conscious decision to become, not just a good home-maker, but a very good wife and mother as well. Perhaps it was to allay suspicion after the shouting she had heard that night several weeks after Elizabeth's arrival. Perhaps it was a mature reflection that told her the bridges were all burned behind her and that now, the practical, the sensible, indeed the intelligent thing was to take stock and regroup, before the war was lost.

She had stumbled and almost fallen in the initial battle, but a wilfulness, nay survival instinct, led her to pick herself up again and go on, using all the gifts God had given her, not the least of which was her physical power and presence. For Gertrude Cullen at twenty-one was a fine young woman, the kind of understatement used in the valley to mean a woman of ample yet graceful proportions, with a proud bearing, commanding stature, and a fine head of hair. Mostly they meant her face was beautiful, but such compliments could not be made publicly about another man's wife. Gertrude at some level knew this, so she took on the role she had not quite chosen, grew into it, made it fit, and acted it out supremely well.

Needless to say William was delighted and periodically besotted, especially when she would dress up in one of her stylish new outfits. She had found a very good dressmaker in Arklow, and chose her patterns from the best design books in Arnott's of Grafton Street, Dublin. She knew what suited her figure and so rang the changes and variations on those themes. She always had the best of accessories, and was never seen anywhere without her hat and gloves. William knew that when Gertrude appeared all dressed up to be taken out for the day, or even for a drive, that he would be teasingly seduced, and all he had to do was play along, be gallant and flirtatious, and that later, his reward would be great. In this way she kept herself pleased and William well satisfied.

In material matters also William generally gave in to all Gertrude's wishes in order to bask in her reflected happiness. Nothing pleased her more than to make plans, find new schemes, and then to see them unfold in accordance with her will. If her tastes and ambitions cost quite a lot of money, then she was fortunate she had the backing of the Hawthorn Thwaites, or at least William's access to his share of their assets. William himself would soon be a qualified solicitor and could leave Dublin to come back and buy into an established practice in Arklow. He would eventually set up a district office for the partners Jones, Patterson and Thwaite in the valley.

For now, as newlyweds, considering the parsimonious 1950s, life was good to them. It meant that Gertrude could persuade William to refurbish certain rooms of Glenview House, add on an extension to give them separate quarters, and Gertrude her own entrance porch. A further step of building their own house William opposed, on the grounds of being the Major's only son, and anyway, wouldn't it be nicer for the children to live with their grandparents, and vice versa.

James William, so called after both grandfathers, was born in March 1948, a year and a half after Elizabeth. Gertrude fell in love instantly with the tiny blonde baby. He was a sunny little boy, of easy and cheerful disposition, and had a shock of thick red-blonde hair that was unmistakably Gertrude's. He had William's short nose and pale blue eyes, which made him irresistible, a laughing cherub. Elizabeth hated him from the first moment. She often pinched his arm or bit his finger as soon as Gertrude's back was turned, but still he wouldn't go away.

Master Cullen had always worried about Elizabeth. One year when Elizabeth Mary was three years old, Gertrude brought back a china doll from the annual Christmas outing to Dublin. It was splendid, with a pale porcelain face, light blue eyes that could open and shut, and a painted red mouth with a felt tongue, resting on the tiniest teeth of white pearl. The doll's dress was made of crimson water silk, pulled in at the waist with a green sash. She had frilly pantaloons of real lace, and black leather booties. Under the doll's straw bonnet fell tresses of thick black shiny hair. Gertrude bought it because the name tag said 'Elizabeth.' It was also a beautiful object, one which Gertrude herself desired: a model child, acquiescent, its blue eyes sweet and vacant, its mouth silent, undemanding. Elizabeth was a difficult toddler, especially coming up to age two, after baby brother James was born. Gertrude found her flash rages and persistent tantrums unnerving. At age twenty-two she had neither the nerves nor the resources to cope. Elizabeth was relentless and even if on rare occasions Gertrude did try to appease and placate her, she remained sulky and unforgiving. It was hard to love such a child. Somehow Gertrude thought the doll would help, a pleasing present for the jealous Elizabeth, always afraid, rightly, that her little brother would get more attention. And Baby James naturally did. All the female hearts in the Hawthorn Thwaite and Cullen households melted around him. One could forgive that child anything.

So out of compensation for lack of warm feelings Gertrude invested a fortune in this doll which was truly handmade and finely crafted. She presented the box wrapped in tissue paper to her daughter. Elizabeth's eyes opened wide in anticipation, then narrowed in suspicion.

'Is it mine? All mine?'

Yes, she was reassured. She tore open the package casting aside great wads of tissue paper and grasped the doll to her chest. The doll became known as Dolly, and went everywhere with Elizabeth. She ate with her, slept with her, and God forbid anyone touch that doll or change its clothes.

One day Elizabeth was spending the afternoon at Master Cullen's house. Grandad Jim was Elizabeth's favourite grown-up, seeing as he was the only one who seemed to have time for her, especially since young Jimmy was born. The doll accompanied Elizabeth as usual, reclining in a small doll-size baby's pram. Jim Cullen was reading his newspaper by the fire in the sitting room when he heard raised voices. He got up and stood to watch Elizabeth while she played in the kitchen.

'Bold baby,' she scolded, 'bold.'

She took the doll out of the pram and put her over her knee.

'Now bend over,' she admonished, and proceeded to whack the doll with a large wooden spoon.

'Bold dolly, bold. Don't do that. I don't like it.'

The voice was stern now, posh like Matilda's, but the inflections were unmistakably Gertrude's. Then Elizabeth mimicked the doll's voice.

'Boo hoo, boo hoo. Sorry Mummy I won't do it again, I'm sorry boo hoo hoo hoo,' and sniffed loudly.

'All right, come here, there's a darling. Be a good girl now and wipe your nose.'

Elizabeth sat the doll up to face her on her lap.

'Boo hoo,' said the doll, 'boo hoo, you hurt me Mummy.'

'Stop crying, come on, stop that crying now.'

'Boo hoo,' continued the doll.

'Stop it. I said, stop it. I don't like crying. Stop it.'

'Boo hoo hoo,' said the doll in a high pitch, alarmed now.

'I said, stop it.'

With that Elizabeth took the doll by the shoulders, and shook her, deliberately, slowly, on each word.

'Stop that now. Stop that now. I said, stop it stop it stop it stop it stop it.'

She finally screamed and started to shake the doll so hard that its head wobbled back and forth as if it would fall off. Then she threw it down and away from her, in a gesture of total rejection, as for some distasteful thing, making a face, a grimace of contempt.

'Oh stop crying you crybaby. Big girls don't cry.'

The doll whimpered, and whimpered, sobbing softly.

The child Elizabeth let out a sigh of frustration, then crossed the kitchen tiles to pick up the doll.

'There now, it's all right, come to Mummy, there now, come,' and she lifted it and held it to her, tight, tighter. 'Come, Mummy loves you, I do, I do, really,' squeezing the doll desperately. 'I do, Mummy didn't mean it, you're my lovely baby dolly.'

A moment later, she held the doll away from her, the pitch of her voice rising again in adult anger, chilling.

'All right, be like that then. You'll never learn.' She cast the doll down in disgust.

'Stupid child, stupid stupid stupid.' She shook her head from side to side, then sat back on her hunkers.

As if a trance had passed over her, Elizabeth looked up. The Master caught her eye. In it glinted satisfaction, like cruelty.

Then, a little girl once more, she scrambled up when she saw her grandfather.

She fetched the doll and was about to put it back in the pram when she saw its teeth. They had slipped right back inside her mouth, as if she'd been punched there, the mouth now a round O of red surprise. Her left eye was squinting where the upper lid had jammed and got stuck on the eyeball.

'Oh look Grandad,' she said, 'bold dolly broke her teeth. What will Mummy say?'

Master Cullen bent down to try and retrieve the tiny pearl teeth inside the doll's mouth. He held the china body, fiddling with too thick fingers in the tiny mouth, to rescue it, make it better. He didn't succeed. He felt cold in his head, like the shadow of a dead person had brushed his cheek with icy fingers. It left him saddened and mute.

Later, Master Cullen drove his granddaughter and her doll home to Glenview House. Night had fallen for it was still winter. Gertrude was in the drawing-room by the fireside with James William. Together they made the perfect picture of mother and baby bliss. The flames flickered, Jimmy cooed in the playpen and built bricks, while Gertrude sewed by lamplight.

Whooshing in on a draught of cold air came Elizabeth and Jim Cullen. Gertrude shivered perceptibly as she looked up from her task.

'Shut the door please, it's freezing,' was her irritable greeting. Her jaw tensed slightly as she said to Elizabeth, 'Take your coat off Lizzie, why didn't you leave it outside. Here, give me dolly.'

Elizabeth sullenly held onto dolly while she struggled to open her coat buttons.

'My goodness, what have you done to your good doll?' Gertrude exclaimed.

'Her teeth fell down,' said Elizabeth.

'She dropped her,' said Jim Cullen at the same moment.

'Her teeth fell down? Really Lizzie you'll have to be more careful. Show me.'

Gertrude took the doll. 'Look at her eye, this doll looks like it was beaten up.'

'She was bold Mummy, a bold dolly, I smacked her,' said Elizabeth.

'This child is impossible,' Gertrude muttered to her father. 'Mummy will fix it,' she said to Elizabeth. 'I don't understand you. How could you? Do you know how much money this doll cost? It's made of china and came all the way from Dublin.'

Gertrude sat the doll up on the mantelpiece. Just then baby James threw a brick out of the playpen. It landed on the grate in front of the fire.

'Jimmy that's bold,' Gertrude admonished, but her tone was warm. 'Are you fed up in that playpen? Come here to Mummy.' She lifted the toddler up and over the bars and onto her knee.

'My dolly Mummy,' wailed Elizabeth.

'Stop that now. You're a bold girl. Breaking your good dolly.'

'She's my dolly. I want her. I want my dolly.'

Gertrude turned to her father, who stood helplessly by, still halfway across the room.

'Can you not take her down to the kitchen? Evie has her tea ready.'

Gertrude was nearing exasperation. Elizabeth let out a loud wail.

'I want my dolly. Give me my dolly.' She rushed to the fireplace to reach up for the doll perched on the end.

'Give me my dolly, give her to me.'

Elizabeth's dress hung perilously close to the fire. As she stretched up Jim saw a flame begin to lick it and whip around the hem.

'Gertrude,' he warned.

'Give her the stupid doll then, here, be done with it,' said Gertrude snatching the doll off the mantelpiece, not noticing the fire.

'Elizabeth!' roared Jim, springing forward now as the flame caught hold of the child's dress to creep up her back. He grabbed Elizabeth and rolled her on the ground. The flames sputtered out in smoke.

Gertrude shouted in shock, 'Now look what you've done, you bold bold girl. Come here.' She pulled Elizabeth roughly to her with one hand, holding Jimmy with the other, saying all the while, 'bold bold bold Elizabeth' first hugging her tightly, then pushing her away again.

'Look at your poor dress.' She hugged her daughter tight into her neck with a kind of fierce despair. 'Bold bold,' she murmured.

Master Cullen caught sight of Elizabeth's eyes as her head lay on her mother's shoulder. There was a glimmer of happiness there even as Gertrude scolded, because she was in her mother's arms. Jimmy had been set down for once.

Elizabeth looked up into Gertrude's face. 'I'm sorry Mummy.'

Gertrude kissed her smartly and let her go. 'That doll was a present from your Mummy and it was very dear, all the way from Dublin, so you better take care of her, all right?'

'Can I have my dolly now Mummy?'

'Say please.'

'Please Mummy.'

'All right then. We'll ask Grandad to fix it. Now, run along down to the kitchen. I have to change James.'

So after that brief and fractious encounter Elizabeth was sent away again while Jimmy regained his seat. Is it any wonder that Jim Cullen feared in his heart for the girl?

When some years later Gertrude proposed that Elizabeth be sent away to boarding school, for her own good, William agreed almost instantly. When Master Cullen heard the news however he flinched inwardly. Elizabeth was less than ten years old.

Master Cullen was the one who brought Elizabeth away. He lifted her trunk into the back of the Ford Cortina to take her to Dalkey, a small village on the south side of Dublin where the convent was situated on the coast. It was an old stone building set high on a cliff above the sea, with views of Dublin Bay in one direction, and Killiney Bay towards Bray in the other. For Elizabeth it was an adventure to go with her grandfather to Dublin, like going on holidays, except she wouldn't be coming back until Christmas. She had by now spent almost six years in the school in Moyne, in Jim Cullen's own classroom. She was shy in school, not inclined to join in or play games or put her hand up or volunteer answers, content to mouth the rhymes or singsong the tables, while Jim made efforts not to single her out or bestow any favours on her just because she was his granddaughter. But Jim Cullen was approaching his seventieth year, and the extension of his contract that the department had given him since he was sixty-five would soon run out, with no possibility of renewal.

Master Jim Cullen had said his final farewells to three generations of valley children and let a new and younger teacher, Miss Madden, step into his shoes. Gertrude wasn't keen on Elizabeth going to school there any longer, for she said she was mixing with the children from down the valley, and picking up a very flat Wicklow accent. It was time to send her up to the nuns and make a young lady out of her, to focus her mind on her studies so that she might make something of herself. Jim Cullen had no case to make, since he knew that sooner or later Elizabeth would have to go away to boarding school to get a secondary education. And so Jim Cullen stepped down as schoolmaster in Moyne and handed on the education of his granddaughter Elizabeth.

On this September day, 1955, Jim Cullen slid the trunk with metal clasps into the boot of the car. Gertrude had packed it carefully, with the regulation numbers of woollen socks, winter vests, big bloomers, three grey shirts, a serge pinafore and a woollen cardigan. All the garments had nametags of indelible black Indian ink sewn on, a task that had kept Evie mumbling and complaining until late into the night for the previous week. The tags were neat and stark: Elizabeth Hawthorn Thwaite. The girl Elizabeth did not look like the name suggested, someone of proud bearing with the blood of Anglo-Irish stock. She was still small for her age, and thin, her presence apologetic as if she were excusing herself permanently, shrinking back into herself between hunched shoulders. Her blue-black eyes glanced up shyly only when spoken to. Most of the time they were cast down watching her fingers fiddle with small things or staring into some middle distance, as vague and opaque as ever. She would soon wear spectacles. It was only the child's hair that stood out as anyway different in a crowd, springy, untameable and jet-black. If on the very rare occasion she did smile, as Jim Cullen teased her about some familiar thing, her face lit up and broke open into quite an endearing grin, happy to be seen and noticed, eager to please.

So after all the fussing and preparations Elizabeth was actually quite glad to climb aboard with Grandad and set off on her journey away from Glenview House. In the distance Gertrude and William stood waving, soon to be distracted by James William who came chasing after the dog with a big stick. So even the group shot of Elizabeth's departure was disrupted in her memory, riven through by a streaking Jimmy, tossing a nonchalant 'bye Lizzie' into the air as he ran off.

Elizabeth sat high in the front seat and in two hours they turned in through the wrought-iron gates of Loreto Abbey convent school for girls. She marvelled at the grand driveway, gasped at the building perched above the sea with gulls cawing and screeching around the hockey pitch.

'It looks like a castle,' she exclaimed.

'I hope you'll enjoy yourself here Lizzie girl. It'll be no time at all until Christmas, and I'll be here to bring you back.'

'I'll be fine thanks Grandad,' said Elizabeth, her voice tight and high with nerves and excitement. She was suddenly a grown-up little girl, her face set to meet whatever new world was here behind the massive wooden door. She was the one who pushed the bell. Ding dong, ding dong, a deep gong sounded within. A scuffling sound and the door was heaved back to reveal a tiny rolypoly nun, covered from head to toe in black. Her sparrow-like face peered out from under a white wimple.

'Ah. Come in, come,' she piped, 'I'll fetch Reverend Mother,' and she rolled away moving as if on castors.

Elizabeth's heart began to pound inside her chest as she stood in the entrance hall, pungent with polish and candle wax. The floor shone like a mirror. The entrance area was wooden from floor to ceiling where large oil portraits of nuns and noble people hung to stare down disapprovingly. A door led away onto a shadowy corridor. From within came sibilance and whispers, sudden gongs, scurrying feet. Elizabeth's hand tightened on her grandfather's. He could feel the sweat slippery on her palm, and he clenched it with a reassurance firmer than he felt.

Soon a boisterous masculine woman, dressed in a nun's habit but somehow not limited by it, swept into the room. What hit Elizabeth first was the stench of body odour and onions. She beamed at Elizabeth and took her hand.

'So this is our new scholar, is it, Miss Elizabeth Hawthorn Thwaite? You are very welcome,' she said. Then turning in a flurry of robes to Jim Cullen she added, 'Has she much luggage? A trunk, good. I'll have Tom the porter come round straight away to give you a hand. Come on Elizabeth, I'll show you to your dormitory.'

Elizabeth had little choice but to give up her arm and be whisked along down the dim corridor with Reverend Mother. She turned to wave to Grandad who stood cap in hand in the entrance hall. His hair was now snow white and thinning, and he looked quite bent with age, or sadness, as he half raised a hand in farewell. 'Bye,' she mouthed, disappearing into a doorway.

Elizabeth's new home was a lofty dormitory, where thirty girls slept in small cubicles, separated only by curtains. In each was a high window, a narrow bed with an iron bedstead, and a bedside locker. The wardrobes were lined up along the middle of the room, forming a partition. Here she was allocated a locker-type wardrobe for hanging up her spare uniform and keeping her outdoor shoes. The girls took a bath once a week, and changed their socks and underwear then, or maybe twice, so in the room there settled an animal aroma of dried sweat, greasy scalps, old wool cardigans and of course the smell of blood, stale in the darkness of clotting undergarments.

Elizabeth spent the first few weeks walking around feeling like she had landed from outer space. She didn't know the rules: a bell for waking, a gong for eating, another for getting in line. Rules that said walk left along the corridor for assembly, or right in the afternoons (to save the nuns' wooden floor), no talking in the corridors, stand up for prayers, endless prayers, in the morning, before class, before break, after break. There was the visit to the chapel after dinner, the vigil in the evening, prayer and more prayers; rules for when to sit, when to genuflect, when to keep the eyes down in an attitude of fervent piety, when to stand: all governed by bells and gongs, a strict regime. But gradually the girl child came to learn and adapt, and not flush with concern when she was left standing if the others were kneeling, or eyes down when they had already lifted theirs to adore the raised Eucharist, or the Host at Benediction.

At a quarter to two every day the bell rang for chapel. The girls would rise from the long tables in the refectory, where the remains of the dinner lay, and file line by line, by table and class year, out into the corridor. They would have eaten boiled bacon and cabbage, cooked in the bacon water so it was swimming with grease, boiled potatoes, a little on the hard side, and already half cold, probably prepared since eleven o'clock. They would have eaten custard with bread and butter pudding for sweet, or tapioca, or rice pudding boiled in milk with raisins. That would be one of the better menus, served twice a week, in between stews full of grisly lumps of beef or lamb. The whole lot would be served and then cleaned by the kitchen nuns, a lower order of beings, not in terms of their religious commitment or vocation, but because their families couldn't afford to send them with a dowry.

When the bell rang after dinner, the girls stood promptly to join their class file. On the way they had to pick up their teacups and place them on a tray where they would be washed and used later for tea break at four o'clock. Then one girl at each table would be assigned the job of wiping the tabletop clean, with some fou-smelling rags from the kitchen. When all that was accomplished the lines of girls would move off, down the stairs, along endless high passages into the old stone chapel in the west wing of the building. They had to move smartly and in silence. At the end of the longest passage, which ended abruptly at a window was a sharp turn left for the chapel.

This day Elizabeth was on table duty, and was so eager to be proficient at this menial task that by the time she had left her dish cloth down in the scullery sink, the line of girls had already gone. Alarmed, she raced along after them, taking care to tread softly on tiptoe, and to alternate her run with a few fast-walking steps for fear of being caught running. By the time she reached the start of the long passageway she was quite out of breath. The girls must already be seated, she thought. She slid along quickly in her leather indoor slip-ons and saw the high window ahead loom large like a full stop. Nearly there. Elizabeth was relieved. She was about to turn the corner when a shadow appeared out of nowhere, silhouetted black against the great window at the end of the passage. She gasped in shock. A hand reached towards her, its bony fingers sank into her arm. An elderly nun, nay, ancient beneath an extraordinarily large wimple and veil, pulled her close. The face was yellow leather, the eyes rheumy, cold dots in bloodshot white. Elizabeth was rigid with fear.

'Come here my child,' a trembling voice rasped. Elizabeth was already very near, yet the nun clawed her closer, the bony fingers boring into Elizabeth's forearm in a skeletal clutch. The nun dragged her downwards to peer into her face.

'You're a new girl I see. Good. Good.' The reptilian eyes were fixed, the tongue licked old lips dryly. 'Say a prayer for me now, good girl, good,' the voice rasped. 'Say your prayers. There is nothing else.'

The claw released Elizabeth's forearm. Elizabeth, who had felt the blood drain from her face, flushed with relief.

'I will Mother,' she stuttered, and as a reflex, curtseyed swiftly and ran into the chapel.

The hymns had begun and she didn't dare walk up the centre aisle to find her class pew. She sat down suddenly on the last bench, her legs trembling both from running and shock. She had never met anyone so old, nor so ugly. The creature was terrifying. She was not like a person, no longer resembled anything Elizabeth had ever known as human.

While she sat there gasping for breath, the prayers started. She knelt gingerly, searching the chapel for her classmates. She was late, she was sitting in the wrong place, she didn't know what to do. She sank her head onto her clasped hands to join in the prayers. When she opened her mouth to speak only a croak came out. Her mouth was parched dry. Then suddenly, for no reason, she started to laugh, a dry cackling sound, like cracking twigs. She shuddered all over, and couldn't stop. She could see a few heads turning to scold and shush, but she couldn't help herself. Her body trembled and the sound just kept coming, like gunfire. A clockwork metal bear, wound up to clatter.

Just then a hand pinched her arm hard above the elbow. Reverend Mother was beside her somehow, holding her in a vice grip that hurt. Elizabeth smelled the onions off her breath as she hissed, 'Pull yourself together. You are in the Lord's house.'

The order was issued in a voice so commanding it could only pull one up short. Coming so soon after the first shock it had the desired effect. Elizabeth's cackling stopped. Her body however continued to quiver and shake, and her teeth chattered. Reverend Mother held her tighter. The grip on Elizabeth's flesh bored deeper, hurting her. There would be blue-black bruises on the morrow.

Reverend Mother hissed again, 'Stop that now child. Stop it.'

At this new command Elizabeth burst into tears, which bubbled noisily through her nose as the prayers continued, rising and falling in incantations, female voices pleading for mercy until the release into song of the last hymn, culminating with the final Amen. All through this ritual, the daily afternoon prayer, Elizabeth shook and sobbed. Each time she tried to open her mouth to sing, a gurgle escaped, the notes choking on hot liquid in her throat. Reverend Mother hissed again, 'Stop it child. Stop this nonsense. Sing now.'

Somehow it was all in vain. Elizabeth had gone to pieces. Reverend Mother marched her out ahead of the hundreds of uniformed girls, and asked her what class she had next.

'Latin with Mrs Mulvey,' Elizabeth managed to wail.

Reverend Mother marched her through the chapel door, out along the corridor. As they reached the corner to the long passageway, Elizabeth searched frantically for the old nun, but like an apparition she had vanished back into the wall, just as she had appeared out of nothing and nowhere. Reverend Mother threatened and entreated to make Elizabeth stop shaking. They finally reached the First Year classroom where Reverend Mother sat her down at her desk. When the class filed in they looked over her way but kept a wide berth, repelled by a whiff of madness, shamed by the outcast, the one who broke the rules.

Mrs Mulvey came in and started the class with the usual quick 'Hail Mary' mumbled to an end with the clatter of desk lids and books slamming open. Halfway through Virgil's *Aeneid* she glanced at Elizabeth Hawthorn Thwaite, head down on her arms on the desk, staring glumly into space. She went to her, puzzled and concerned. 'Elizabeth, what is it, are you ill?' she asked.

Elizabeth shook her head mutely. She couldn't reply to any of the subsequent questions. Every so often a tremor came over her, which she would stifle by blowing her nose. Mrs Mulvey sent Catherine Clarke to sit by her side. Even this minimum level of human warmth helped to calm Elizabeth down. She had no idea why she was so upset. But whenever she tried to concentrate the image of the ancient nun came popping into her head before her eyes. Reverend Mother's crisp commands to 'stop it' rattled through her head, making her shake again. Then she would blink and think she had imagined the whole thing, so she did not speak of it to anyone.

Hallowe'en came and with it the anticipated visits from families on the Sunday of the long weekend. Elizabeth looked forward to seeing her parents and little brother Jimmy just like anyone else, but at the same time had something wriggling in her stomach at the thought of their arrival. It was a mixture of excitement tinged with an early cautionary disappointment. It would let her imagine running into her mother's arms with a great shout of greeting, only to be offered a cold cheek to kiss politely instead. That was how her tummy felt: longing and the self-censure of that feeling. It left her confused.

On the Friday of the long weekend, the last day of classes and schoolwork for some days, Elizabeth was called into the Purser's office. The Purser, Mother Carmel, was a short stout nun, wearing thick black glasses over a stubby nose and blotchy skin. You could imagine her being hairy, with bristles sprouting out of her armpits. She was a cheerful practical sort, and welcomed Elizabeth into the office.

'Here Miss Thwaite, a parcel has just arrived for you in the afternoon post. Must be a tuck box,' she chuckled, seeking amiability. Elizabeth grasped the box and went to tear it open. 'You may bring it to the Common Room child, and then leave the contents with Sister Kathleen in the kitchen.'

So Elizabeth carried the cardboard box wrapped in brown paper and string down shadowy corridors to the Common Room. Since she knew hardly anyone as yet, she sat quietly at a corner table. She tore the paper open to reveal pots of jam, homemade by Evie, and smiled. Then a letter fell out, a white envelope etched in blue ink by her mother's perfect handwriting. Its contents were as crisp as the fine white paper they were written on.

Dear Elizabeth,

We hope and trust that you are well, and that you are attending to your studies with diligence. All is well here. Your father is busy as usual, helping the Major out with the Hunt every Wednesday and Saturday. I have quite taken to it myself. I have to tell you I am very proud of Jimmy. He managed a three-bar jump yesterday at the riding school, and so Daddy has given him permission to follow the Hunt on Saturday next as far as Avoca. I should accompany him, so I'm afraid this means we shan't be able to visit this weekend. I'm sending some tuck from Bridie. We'll see you at Christmas, D.V. (Deo Volente). In the meantime, be a good girl, be polite to the nuns and say your prayers.

With my affection,

Your Mother.

Elizabeth stared at the letter. The wriggly feeling became a knife. They weren't coming. No one was, because of Jimmy. Her mind tamped down the tide of rage that rose in bile to her throat.

'Oh well who cares. I got my tuck box anyway,' she said lightly. She pierced the greaseproof membrane, which covered a pot of blackberry jam, stuck her finger in fiercely, pulled it out covered in a big black blob, and stuffed it into her mouth. In this manner she had the pot of jam eaten in five minutes flat, her face sated and sugary, until she felt better. The knife had dissolved away into a jelly-warm mass inside. It was in this condition that Mary Dunleavy found her, when the girls seated at the large centre table had finished their card game.

'Oh look, look what Elizabeth Hawthorn Thwaite has done,' she squealed.

Teresa Moore and Goretti Kelly came running.

'Oops, you better tidy up quick before Mother Carmel sees you. Eating tuck in the Common Room is not allowed,' said Mary Dunleavy.

'Only in the refectory at break-time,' Goretti chirped.

A tall, older girl intervened.

'I'll help you with this,' she said kindly, packing up the tuck box and handing Elizabeth a handkerchief. 'How was she to know? She's only new,' she tossed over her shoulder to the other First Years as they watched open-mouthed while the tall girl led Elizabeth away.

'Ooh, that's the Fourth Year prefect, isn't it?' breathed Teresa Moore.

'Yes that's the girl from Donegal, Angela O'Donnell.'

'Lucky Lizzie,' said Goretti, and they giggled.

Elizabeth followed Angela all the way to the kitchen, watching the older girl stride with confidence down dark passageways, her red-gold hair swinging in tresses down her back. She was flooded with gratitude.

From that day on Elizabeth swore eternal devotion to Angela O'Donnell. She used to run after her and offer to carry her books at every opportunity. She would strain her neck at Assembly to catch sight of her, light up and flush if Angela's eyes caught hers in greeting across the hall. Her heart would swell if she saw the red-gold hair glinting on the hockey pitch after school. For Angela she would sit for a whole extra hour in the study classroom, hoping that Angela's Fourth Year French class would just be finishing around the corner when the bell went. She waited and watched.

Once Angela saw her peeking through the door of an open classroom, and she winked. Elizabeth nearly died of embarrassment and pleasure, and she nursed that one snapshot for months and months, seeing it in her mind's eye as she went to sleep at night. She told no one.

During this first year of boarding school life she became friendly with Catherine Clarke, who had been so nice to her that day after the incident with the ancient nun. Catherine was a large girl, slow and kind, and used to sit beside Elizabeth and lend her ink and pencils. They helped each other out with the homework which they both found difficult, as they laboured over theorems together. Since Elizabeth was not someone who had ever put herself forward or willingly joined in, she was not part of the gang of popular girls, preferring to sit away quietly to the side and let others shine.

Maybe because of her timidity she also attracted unkindness. Mary Dunleavy teased her for a long time about the tuck, asking, 'has anyone seen my jam? Don't leave it around, a certain person might polish it off.' Elizabeth used to flinch at her sarcastic tone, and would shrink back into herself to nurse her wounds, not inclined to fight or talk back. This would egg Mary Dunleavy on even more, who liked to mimic Elizabeth and say, 'Have you lost your pony have you?' in a thick country accent. 'Or was it a donkey, hee-haw, hee-haw?' and then she and her cronies would snort with laughter. Elizabeth had never done anything to Mary Dunleavy, and she found such treatment unfair. But, as she was used to doing in her life before now, she didn't question it, and merely shrank back out of sight so as not to attract attention.

One of the best days she had in First Year was the day she was asked to carry a letter to the Fourth Year classroom. She couldn't believe her luck as she hadn't put her hand up to volunteer because she always went so red. But Mother Carmel called her up and gave her the letter. 'It's for the prefect,' she said. So, heart pounding, Elizabeth slipped along the corridor, silent now as all the girls were in class, and paused outside the door. She could hear the murmur of recitation within. She knocked timidly. Someone pulled open the door. She saw a sea of faces and halted. The few feet between the door and the teacher's rostrum had become a huge expanse, an ocean in which she might drown. Mrs Mulvey stopped the class and looked, querying her, then nodded to the seated class. Just then Angela O'Donnell stood up and walked over to her, confident and assured.

'Oh hi, it's Elizabeth Thwaite from First Year, come in, we won't bite you.' She took the proffered letter and smiled at Elizabeth. 'Oh, it's for me anyway, thanks.'

Elizabeth was rooted to the spot, so that Mrs Mulvey had to dismiss her, saying 'you can go now.' She raced back out along the corridor dancing with glee and relief that she had survived the ordeal. And Angela had smiled at her. She felt warm and special. So much so that some months later she sat beside Angela at recreation, and asked her a question that had been bothering her for some time.

'Have you ever seen the old nun?' she whispered in a rush.

A fat girl sitting beside Angela laughed out loud. 'She means Mother Augustine, that old bat, tee-hee.'

Angela turned to Elizabeth's serious little face and said in her soft Donegal lilt, 'Yes, I have. She won't hurt you, she's harmless, a "duine le

Dia", which means in Irish 'a person with God', that's all,' which was a nice way of saying that Mother Augustine was gone in the head.

Elizabeth was again grateful, and much relieved, for she had spent many restless nights tossing and turning, then waking up suddenly with a sensation of someone gripping her forearm. She hadn't dared mention it to anyone for fear she was imagining it, but the dreams had swelled during the day and formed a big question in her head that only Angela could answer. She knew Angela wouldn't think her strange, if and when she found the courage to ask her. The wonderful thing was that Angela didn't, on that day when she finally dared. She had patted her arm in reassurance, and Elizabeth had smiled one of her rare smiles.

Catherine's Diary

By the time my part in the story begins I had just gone seventeen and Elizabeth, my mammy, seemed like an old woman. She was probably only forty and a bit. She was stooped and careworn, with her hair pulled into a bun at the back. Her dress code was still strict and grey, but her hair always struggled to escape in unruly little curls which played at her neck. My diary of that time shows how the whole country was obsessed with the Kerry Babies case – even us.

29 December 1984

Had the last of the turkey today – in sandwiches. And the Lemon's boiled sweets have run out. Thank God the Christmas is nearly over and Daddy will ease off going to Black Tom's.

The six o'clock news on the radio was about that terrible thing in Kerry, where they found a baby's body on a beach. Someone had stabbed it twenty-seven times. Only just born.

Then on the telly tonight they were saying they found the woman who stabbed the baby. But she said she didn't do it. She did have a baby that died all right.

She said how she had her baby out in the barn. She felt her pains coming on and started praying to Our Lady. Then the baby came out and she dropped it in the hay. She left it there because she didn't want anyone to know. When she came back in the morning it was dead. She said that looking straight down the telly at us, and didn't cry. Then she took the baby – it was still warm, she said – put it in a plastic bag and buried it in a hole in the ditch, and just went back to bed.

'God love her,' said Mammy. 'God love her, that's shocking.'

'Sure what else was she to do?' said Daddy. 'You heard the girl, no one wanted the babby. She couldn't keep it. She was rearing one already in that house. What were the brothers going to say? They didn't want another one, sure weren't they good enough to keep her the first time.'

'God love her,' said Mammy. 'The poor baby. I'll pray to the Sacred Heart tonight for the repose of its soul. It will go to limbo.'

'What's limbo?' said John Paul.

'It's where the souls of babies go when they're not baptised. All she had to do was pour water on its head, but she didn't. She didn't baptise it. I'll say a prayer for her too.'

'That won't do no good,' said Daddy, 'wasn't it her own fault, and she off cavorting all around the country?'

I was thinking later, they never said if the baby was a boy or a girl. They're still saying though that she is the one who murdered the baby on the beach. Only now she says she had the baby in a barn. Very confusing.

1 January 1985

I spent all day yesterday alone on New Year's Eve. God I hate it when everyone says Happy New Year all the time, they don't mean it. I am so lonely. I wanted to get Helen on her own to tell her. There's no sign of a period and now there's a hard lump in my stomach, like an orange there below my belly button. So we went for a walk, in the afternoon, up to the avalanche.

'Helen, can I ask you a question, but it's a secret, you're not to tell anyone, Daddy'd kill me.'

She had her mouth open with delight.

'It's not funny. I think I'm pregnant. I'm not sure but me periods didn't come yet.'

'Jesus, Kitty, what are you going to do? Are you sure?'

'I am, but I don't know what to do.

'Jes Kitty, how could you be pregnant?'

'Well I think I am because I went with this fellow in Arklow.'

'You mean that time before Christmas?'

'He had a car and he was giving me a lift home. He said if I didn't he wouldn't go out with me again. He said all the girls did it like. I didn't want him to think I was cheap or too easy but then he just did it anyway.'

'Kitty, did you not stop him?' she said.

'No, I didn't say anything.'

'Christ.'

'It hurt too but I knew that because I heard the girls talking about it and they said it could hurt the first time.'

'So it was your first time?'

'Yes, it was.'

'You fucking eejit, why didn't you say no?'

'Well I didn't say no because he said he wouldn't go with me again if I didn't.'

'Why on earth didn't you stay with the girls?'

'They all live in town and can walk home together but no one lives up this way.'

'That was so stupid.'

'And I wanted to get out again next Friday night. You were let out at sixteen.'

'Did I not tell you not to let the boys touch you? Who was it?'

I blushed then but I wouldn't say. I couldn't let on to Helen. If I told her the truth she'd blab it out all over the valley. Especially now she's doing hair. She'd think it was great gossip.

'But do you think I could be pregnant Helen?'

She made a face. Like, she didn't believe me.

'I don't want a baby. I want to be married,' I mumbled.

'So you've gone and got yourself into trouble?'

She sounded cross like an older sister. She's not; she's ten months younger.

'Daddy said he'd kill me and whip me first if I ever did anything like that to the family. Helen, what'll I do?' I was getting scared.

'There's always England.'

'Yeah I suppose that'd be a good idea. I could say I'm going over to Uncle Mattie. He'd help me, wouldn't he Helen?'

'Why the hell did you do it?'

She patted my head. She thinks I'm not the full shilling, I know she does.

'Kitty you poor poor thing.'

Tears came up in me. I was sad for what really happened.

'Yeah I was a bit sore. I went to the bathroom and washed.'

'Kitty, promise me you won't let it happen again.'

'No, I won't. I'll say no. You're right.'

'I want you to promise me if it ever happens again ...'

'Yeah, I'll say no. Helen, what'll I do if I'm pregnant?'

She stopped walking to pull on a fag.

'You could have an abortion.'

'Do you mean kill it? That's a sin. I've seen those babies in buckets. No. I'd never do that, that's murder.'

And we left it at that. But she was looking at me over the tea. I wished she'd stop.

3 January

Simon never came to wish us Happy New Year. I don't know how I got the courage but I had to tell him. This feeling came up in me and I couldn't get him out of my mind, every night and every morning. That's why I was so quiet, going in on myself thinking about him. He'd know what to do. This feeling like wanting to burst made me hop around the place, hopping and fidgeting. Maybe I was picking it up off Mam, the way she hops around the kitchen touching all the plugs all the time, with her nerves. There were two of us nearly bumping into each other, so I says I'm going out for a walk. I pulled on the big anorak, and off with me up to Glenview House. I knew he'd still be there before the holidays were over at Little Christmas.

So I ring the door. There are big steps in granite going up to it. It's very heavy and dark brown. Simon answers, and thanks be to God Aunty Linda and Uncle Jimmy are out visiting somewhere. He is surprised.

'Hi. Er, come in Catherine,' he says and leaves me sitting in the big drawing-room. It's ages before he comes back with a glass of red lemonade. Does he think we're still children? Anyway I look at him.

'Simon I'm in trouble.'

'What do you mean?'

'You know ... What we did. At the river.'

'What? Ah now Catherine, that's mad. You're making it up. That's ages ago and nothing happened.'

He saw the tears in my eyes.

'It wasn't nothing,' I mumble.

He comes to sit beside me and for a minute he was the old Simon.

I look at him. 'Simon, we can get married.'

He shoots up again out of the seat. 'Catherine, stop it. You're imagining it. I can't get married- I've just started college. Catherine, you know that.'

Then he asks all sorts of questions like, 'are you sure?' and, 'did you see a doctor?'

'Are you cracked?' says I, 'nobody knows. And you're not to tell Daddy.'

'Jesus no,' he says, 'we've got to get rid of it.'

'What?'

'Well you don't want it, it's all a big mistake, and I don't want it, if it is mine, which I doubt very much.'

'It is,' I say, going very red. 'I never did it with anyone else. I wouldn't. Unless I loved them.'

And then I'm so red and hot, and can't look at him. I put my head down, with my arms around it, the blood pounding and hammering. I don't want to look up.

'This is terrible, I want to die.'

Simon comes and touches my sleeve.

'Catherine, stop it now, come on, we'll figure something out.'

He pulls my face up to look in my eyes.

'Promise me one thing, promise or I'll never ever speak to you again. You are not to tell anyone. Not anyone.'

'I told Helen.'

He goes white.

'What did you tell her?'

'Just that I missed my periods and I must be pregnant.'

He is awful relieved.

'So you don't know in fact if you really are?'

He is nearly cheerful.

'No Simon,' I says, 'I do know. I don't want it, and I didn't want this to happen to me, but I am. I'm very very sorry.'

'Catherine, never, never say what you said. That it's me. Anyway it isn't. So we'll sort something out. The main thing is that nobody knows. Then we can get rid of the baby somehow.'

I was in floods on my way back. It was dark, I had no torch and the avenue down from Glenview was awful long and dark.

There were two things he said made me go cold, very cold. 'It isn't mine,' he'd said.

He's sure it's not his. That's terrible. It must be. How could he forget that day?

And 'Get rid of the baby,' he said.

When he said 'baby' I got a shock. I suppose it is. A baby.

There was only me and my breath and my footsteps on the mud of the track, and it was frosty. I saw the first stars out and that's when I started to cry, and cry, I couldn't stop. I think Simon doesn't really love me. I don't want this, this ... baby. Oh God.

6 January

I wasn't able to write in my diary all week with all that's been going on here. Helen didn't go back to Carlow yet so she's hanging around looking at me all the time. She keeps asking am I OK and then I tell her to shut up, somebody will notice. She was never that nice to me before. I'm the one who brings milk out to the calves and brings in the logs and cleans the stove and peels the spuds. She sits there all day putting on the telly trying to get the picture better, and doing her nails and talking away about everyone. Mammy likes that, she laughs and is in much better form. I think it got all too much for her when she had all the kids, and the ones that died in between. Maybe if she only had one daughter like Helen she'd be all right. The rest of us are a worry to her. Mammy does get the dinner and washes up. It keeps her busy.

Daddy said, 'you're awful quiet Catherine, did the cat get your tongue?'

Well I don't say much anyway but now that Helen's home they notice more. It's true I am very quiet. I get through the day and do me work. I don't think about what's happening. I want it all to go away.

That's a bit hard with Helen at me. She comes to bed and starts talking, lighting up her cigarette.

'Catherine, you're going to have to do something.'

'I won't,' says I, 'and stop smoking in the room, the blankets'll catch fire and Daddy'll smell it when he comes home.'

'Never mind him.'

She's not afraid of him.

'Take me away then with you.'

'There's no room in the digs in Carlow, and everyone would find out.'

'Then we'll go to England,' says I.

'You've no money, Catherine. I can't leave the hairdressing and you can't go on your own. But you can't stay here. You're right, Daddy would beat you stupid, and the baby. But Kitty, you have to tell me whose it is.'

'I told you already Helen, a chap from Arklow.'

'I know who. That fecker Mossie Dollard,' she says, 'I'm not letting him away with it.'

'Don't,' I say real fast, 'don't say anything. It'll do no good. What can he do about it, it'd make it worse.'

'You could marry him,' she says, 'Daddy wouldn't mind that, he plays for Enniscorthy now.'

'I don't want to get married, I'm not in love with him.'

'Love?' she says. 'It's a bit late for that now. Catherine, stop pretending, you have to do something, your tummy is beginning to show.'

I don't know why but with Helen I feel so stupid. She doesn't understand.

7 January

The next day who was at the door only Simon. I got an awful shock. It was teatime and Mammy was putting out the beans for the kids. I was wetting the tea and Helen was stuck in the armchair at the telly. The news was on with Charles Mitchell and that Kerry Baby stuff. They're having a national tribunal of investigation now. Dragging it all out on the telly all over again. Everybody talking about getting up the pole, and how many times, and where, treating that girl like a criminal.

Lucky Daddy wasn't at home, he'd gone off up the back to get the sheep down.

I nearly scalded myself.

'Hello everyone,' he says coming in very tall at the door, 'Happy New Year. How's Helen?' he says, 'and Catherine?' as if he's never laid eyes on me.

The kids all stood up and started asking him questions and teasing him.

'How's Dublin?'

'We heard you're getting a car from Uncle Jimmy.'

'Were you at the match?'

Danny says, 'did you hear the one about the man who fell off of a tractor?'

Then he sat himself down in the middle of them all at the table, and Mammy asked him if he wanted tea, put down a plate of toast and a sausage in front of him. It was her plate. She didn't lose her manners, that's from her good school. I was shaking so I stayed at the sink.

'Well,' said Helen, 'long time no see stranger,' and I'd swear she was going to light up and offer him one. But she didn't. You could see she was thrilled with the company. She talked all about Carlow and the hairdressing, never shut up she didn't, and I sat over by the fire while they ate. Even Mammy cheered up and asked how's Jimmy? When he said he and Aunty Linda were off up to see Granny she stopped.

'Is she never coming out of there, is she?'

Kind of aggressive like, so Simon just smiled and said, 'oh well, she says she has a lot to do up there, nursing the Master.'

'Poking her nose in,' she said. 'I hope she's not thinking of selling the house when he dies, God forbid.'

'Oh no,' said Simon, charming as ever.

Mammy gave a kind of a sniff and took a big sup of tea that steamed up her glasses.

Next thing Helen says, 'we were just going out down the village, will you come Simon?'

And he says, 'I will.'

I was astonished and looked at Helen. 'Come on Catherine, old slowcoach, you too.'

I don't know how it happened but as we were walking the two miles down the road, Simon says, cool as you like, 'so poor Catherine here's in trouble.'

'What?' says Helen shocked, 'Jes how do you know?'

'She told me herself,' says Simon.

'I met him,' I said, 'when I was out for a walk yesterday.'

'You never said, Catherine,' she accused me.

'Well,' says Simon, 'it is a serious situation. Maybe I can help, we can all help.'

So we're sitting down in Dolan's at the corner, and there's Helen and Simon discussing between them what they're going to do. The upshot of it all was Helen had a great idea.

'We can hide her, where they'll never think of looking.'

'Do you not think she should see a doctor all the same?' said Simon.

'No, no way, he'd tell Mammy and Daddy,' I said.

Simon stopped drinking then and said, real slow, 'she can go up to the schoolhouse.'

'Oh my God no,' I said, 'with Granny?'

'But she's not talking to anyone anymore,' said Helen.

'And you could be keeping her company, and keeping house for her. Helping with the Master.'

'Mother would love it,' added Simon, 'because she wouldn't have to call there anymore either.'

'Brilliant,' said Helen.

'Wait a minute,' says I, 'what about the baby?'

'I'll make arrangements,' said Simon.

'In Dublin,' said Helen.

I don't know. I don't know what I think. I suppose they're right. I have to go away somewhere.

Afterwards on the way home, Simon put his arm around my waist and held me tight.

'Everything's going to be fine, Kitty,' he said in his old voice, and gave me a big hug. 'Just do as I say, and keep our secret, not a word, not even to Helen remember?'

He put his hand on my face. It was hot. I wanted to fall asleep on it. But when we said goodbye he was the big Simon again, all Dublin and sensible.

'I'll give you a ring,' he says. To me? Or to Helen?

Now that's the end of all that week. I'm in a spin. But at least I don't feel sick anymore. I feel perfectly normal. As if nothing was happening.

I'm sort of happy now. Simon hugged me. I think he loves me.

20 January

It's been awful cold and snowy. The snow is piled up outside the kitchen door, it's nearly as high as my wellies, it slides down inside the legs and makes my socks wet. Daddy got the tractor out and brought a bale of hay up to the top field for the lambs. One of them died already. We have another one in by the stove. He's sucking away from a baby's bottle.

Helen's been gone two weeks and can't get home again because of the snow. It's very bad everywhere, the roads are blocked. They had to bring in helicopters from the army to drop in hay and food parcels up above Knockananna. I made it down as far as Murphy's yesterday. It took me and Danny three hours, and when we got there we got the last loaf of bread, three days old it was, stale, but it does for the toast. We had great sport going down while it was sunny and we slid on an old tray, like we used to. On the way back it got dark very fast, and was very very cold, my feet were like ice. Lucky we still have logs to keep the kitchen warm; the rest of the house is freezing.

I don't mind the snow at all. There's even talk of an avalanche. I love them old stories, Daddy is great at telling them. They say it'll never happen again, it's only the way the wind was that one time. The snow had piled up on the crest of the mountain, frozen hard for weeks with no thaw. Then one morning the sun shone in a blue sky, just for the time the sun ran over the hill, and then in the dark the frost glittered again. Nobody knew that under the crust the snow had started to shift. Bridie's mother had been a girl at the time, and so she took her cloak and went up the hill to visit the new baby, born that very day.

'You'd want to see where the hut was,' says Daddy, 'high up on the side of that mountain where only the sheep go.'

'I know,' I said, 'we used to play there.'

'Cottagers they were, that's what they called them then. The river ran below the hut cutting into the side of the hill with the fir trees on it, slicing its way down to the bottom. Anyway during the visit that night the wind blew up again, and more snow threatened, so they asked Bridie's mother to stay the night.'

Daddy sat back to cough and swallow his spit, then on into his story.

'"I won't" says she, "I'm expected at home." She pulled the big hood of her cloak up around her and set out for home. Wasn't she the lucky lass? For not one hour later they heard a roar like the wind, and thought a tree had come down. It was the mountain beginning to move, and it shifted and slid until there was a torrent of snow and rocks chasing down the slope above the cottager's hut, covering them in a river of snow and brown mud. They were all killed outright. The father and mother, and all the children: the eldest was a boy of ten, then there was a girl of eight, another of six, and two little ones besides the baby. Imagine, only one day old in the world.'

Daddy looked around proudly, for it was his party piece, and said, 'I seen the death certificate myself once. And do you know what's written on it? "Died in their beds smothered by an avalanche". Do youse know it was the only avalanche ever to come to Ireland?'

'Yes Daddy,' we say.

We always have to say that, because every time he tells it we have to let on it's the first time we ever heard it. But I love listening to him tell that story, the way he's proud as punch.

'What were their names anyway?' I asked.

'Mulhalls,' he said.

'You're not serious,' I said. 'Are they belonging to us?'

'Maybe way back, but it's as true as God,' says he, 'I seen it for meself on the death certificate.'

'Was the baby a girl or a boy?'

'Do you know, that I cannot tell you, for it had no name yet,' he said, 'seen as how it was not baptised. By the way, is that babby still abroad on the hill?'

He starts saying 'woow, woow' and trying to frighten us. I laugh so he won't notice anything.

That was after breakfast.

I cleaned up and went for a walk before dinner, about twelve. The trees looked beautiful with the snow on the branches. The sky was blue, and I was warm in the sun. I went towards the mountain. I don't know why but I wanted to pray to that baby. I'd say it was a girl. Maybe she's a guardian angel now, and she's up there floating around the hill and over the valley. I could ask her what to do. Be my guardian angel. So she was flying alongside me as I went across the fields. There was the old hut hanging off the side of the hill, all lit up in the sun.

Me and the angel went over to it, and I went in and sat inside on an old stone that was in under the chimney. It was very quiet. The snow seems to do that, hushes it all up and makes it so silent you can hear your head think. If I coughed it was too loud. I said 'sorry,' and shushed myself. I sat there for ages, dreaming away.

Then I felt something in my stomach. Weird, like something flipping over, butterflies. Oh, the baby's doing a somersault, are you baby? I said. Oops, up and over, it did it again. I'd say it was talking to the angel baby.

Catherine, stop being stupid, I said to myself. You're daydreaming. And anyway, this baby is going away. You're to go away, do you hear me, I don't want you, go back to where you came from and stop annoying me. I'm not your mother. I don't want to be a mammy, go away.

Anyway I'm only making it all up, it didn't happen. So I couldn't be pregnant, and tomorrow me periods will come and I can stop this raving.

That's what I said in the hut.

Lucky no one could hear me, I wouldn't even say those things in me head in the house, for fear someone would hear me thinking. It's terrible, I keep me head down and the big jeans on me, and an old shirt and jumper of Daddy's saying I'm too cold to take them off. I sleep in them. I didn't have a bath for weeks. I'm afraid they'll see, anyway I've nothing else to wear. I'm manky by now. But it didn't matter in the hut. I was just myself. Quiet.

There was sunlight coming in the window across the floor, with dust swirling and playing in it. That's where she was, twirling away and dancing.

Are you happy? I said, and I smiled. That's how it was. If anyone'd seen me they'd say, she's flipped now, that Mulhall one, talking to herself and seeing things. But they wouldn't be surprised, after Mammy I do hear them saying she's not the full shilling, too highly strung. That's not true, she wasn't always like this because I remember when I was little and she told me great stories about St Teresa of the Little Flower.

Mammy loves being clean, she's always washing herself. I can't, it's too cold.

Then with all my mad thoughts something flipped in my tummy again and a big lump came in my throat. I said, poor poor babba, but you're not mine and I don't want you. Please go back to God.

That pair didn't come back with all their big ideas. Helen wrote once saying she couldn't get home in the snow.

But she couldn't write anything else to me. I suppose Simon's gone off with himself back to college. I'm sitting there in a hut thinking it was all like a film, it never happened.

My face was wet. I said, 'thank you angel,' to the little dead baby and went home.

Elizabeth, 1956–58

Elizabeth was panic-stricken when she saw the blood. She was alone in the chapel at about seven o'clock on a dark November night.

First she felt wet between her legs. Then something hot trickled down her inner thigh onto her stocking. Her fingers reached down to touch it and came away red. She gasped and looked around. She hadn't cut herself. She felt no pain. Maybe the miracle was happening, maybe St Teresa had answered her prayers, and was now taking her away to God. She would bleed silently to death and they would find her in the morning early, turned to white marble forever as she knelt in holy prayer. But nothing happened, no heavenly chorus sang her exit. Elizabeth sat still and felt hot again on her leg. She flushed with an awful realisation. She wasn't being taken, she was being punished. God was warning her, telling her he had found out about the bracelet.

In an agony of guilt now she fretted and fidgeted. She shouldn't have taken it, shouldn't have told lies. But it had been so pretty, and she had wanted to make Angela happy. She could never have bought such a beautiful thing herself. It was two Sundays ago, and there was a long wet afternoon in the Common Room while the girls played cards and then were allowed to dance. Someone wound up the gramophone and they paired off to the sound of the Blue Danube, learning to waltz. Mother Anthony, the Maths and PE teacher, was supervising.

'Girls girls,' she had trilled, 'this is the one you need to know on your wedding day, so take your partners and off we go. One two three, one two three ...'

Elizabeth had danced with Catherine Clarke, and they stumbled and shoved their way round the room tittering and embarrassed. As she was checking her feet for the umpteenth time, Elizabeth spotted something shiny on the floor. Next time as they twirled she looked closer, and saw it was a silver chain strung with little white pearls. She couldn't think who might have owned such a pretty thing, as jewellery was not allowed in uniform, but on Sundays especially the girls often put on trinkets and these were tolerated. However she had never seen this object before, so as she came dancing round the floor for the third time, she shoved out her shoe and swished the bracelet in under a chair by the wall. She would retrieve it later in peace, to marvel over it. Finders keepers, after all.

But by the end of Sunday afternoon recreation a Third Year girl was in hysterics, saying her rich uncle had bought her a very precious bracelet from Arabia and that she had had it since her First Holy Communion. There was a clatter of Third Years in a circle around her, trying to comfort her saying, 'are you sure you were wearing it?' and such other cries of consolation. While this was going on, Elizabeth hung back to make sure she could no longer see the bracelet. Only she knew where it was. She pushed the chair it was lying under further against the wall, so the chain lay along the skirting board. It would not be visible to searching eyes.

'Poor Helen Burke,' Catherine Clarke said to her on the way to the refectory for tea, 'she's so upset. I bet she didn't have it on at all, she's only looking for attention and an excuse to tell us she has a rich uncle.'

Elizabeth agreed, nodding sagely. All through tea though she wriggled inside with excitement, imagining holding the wonderful chain in her palm, and then flushing with pleasure at how Angela would smile at her, take her hand and kiss it, and tell her how much she valued her friendship. Later, Elizabeth scurried back to the Hall on the way to chapel, tiptoed swiftly over its polished boards to retrieve the chain, terrified it would no longer be there and that she would not receive her cherished prize: Angela's smile of gratitude.

The bracelet was there however, lying tight against the wall. Elizabeth tucked it into the top of her wool stocking, under the rib where it was held up with elastic. She was late for evensong but flew along the passages on winged feet, elated by her success. Her heart had poured out praise and thanks that evening, as she basked in the warmth of Angela O'Donnell's smile, imagined over and over again. She almost forgot to plan the details. How on earth was she to get close enough to give it to her? She tossed and turned all that night until she came up with a plan. In the downstairs cloakroom was a row of coat hangers, under which were shoe racks for holding the indoor shoes when the girls went outdoors, for hockey or walks to the village. She would put the bracelet in Angela's shoe, and although the gift would come anonymously, she would smile at Angela in the refectory, try to pass her by and look into her eyes for a second longer than usual, and Angela would know. Then she would smile. And Elizabeth would be blissful.

However, by the following morning her plan was already being sabotaged. At Assembly Reverend Mother announced that a valuable object had been lost, and that whoever came across it, or whoever knew anything about it, was to report at once to her office. Elizabeth's insides turned over in terror. How was she to get the gift to Angela? For she was still determined that she should have it. Her palms began to sweat and her heart beat faster. She would not calm down until she had delivered that bracelet.

By mid-afternoon she had managed to slip it into Angela's shoe rack, right into the toe of her indoor shoes. Elizabeth flushed with a private triumph, cosy in her fantasy of Angela's attention. Somehow she missed the whispering in the corridors, missed the rumours that the bracelet had been stolen and that the culprit was a girl from this very school, a thief and an impostor amongst them.

When Elizabeth surfaced from her trance and the deed was done, it was too late. Angela O'Donnell was standing red-faced in front of the whole school, in the refectory at six o'clock, stuttering her excuses. She burned with shame, saying she had found the bracelet in her shoe, stammering and protesting her innocence. Whispers ran along the benches as all the faces were turned towards Reverend Mother, part anxiety, part thrilling to this spectator sport: a prefect in disgrace. Angela spoke in a sad low voice.

'I apologise for the distress caused, but I am telling the truth, I did not take the bracelet and I have really no idea how it came to be in my shoe,' she said.

Her humility was impressive and the girls shifted visibly in sympathy and forgiveness. Elizabeth was inwardly aghast. Did she not know? Did she not appreciate what lengths she, Elizabeth, had gone to to show her devotion? Why, oh why had Angela said anything? Could she not have taken it and treasured it and kept it under her pillow to dream on?

Elizabeth went into some inner fog, feeling abandoned and rejected. Unloved. She barely heard Reverend Mother say, 'Angela, since you are normally a trustworthy person and have been a very good prefect, I accept your apology. However, until this matter has been satisfactorily cleared up, I shall ask you to step down as Fourth Year prefect for an undefined period.'

Angela gasped in shock, and went white. Her friends led her away to a table, where she crumpled in tears. Elizabeth could see her shoulders heaving with silent sobs. She was shamed and humiliated and worse still, she was entirely innocent. Elizabeth did not enjoy seeing her idol suffer so, indeed she allowed herself a small smile of pity, but her lip almost curled in contempt. Angela looked younger and smaller, her red-gold hair lank and greasy. Elizabeth was shot through with a moment of triumph, like cruelty, like her doll, all those years ago. It was weakness, this show of emotion. She would never tolerate it, preferring later in life to sing it all away, pour all her feelings into soaring liturgical arias. But now, in this moment, cruelty was just a momentary glint, light glancing off steel as the knife turns. Then it was over, to be buried deep in her emotions, waiting to affect her future.

Angela was heard to say when she surfaced for air amid her sobs, 'Whoever did this to me is going to pay, they are not going to get away with it.'

If she heard, Elizabeth took no notice. She was gone beyond hurting.

Now she was in chapel and God was punishing her severely, reprimanding her for her thoughtlessness and stupidity. She would bleed to death from some inner wound. Her soul was pierced, like the Sacred Heart. Then Angela's words came back, about the person not getting away with it, and she saw the finger of God pointing at her above the altar, blaming her, telling her she was wrong. She shivered and blanched as waves of remorse washed over her. How could she have done this to the girl she loved, got her into so much trouble. Oh Lord God, dear sweet Jesus, what can I do? How can I make reparation? And then she knew. She must accept her punishment, pray and fast and tell no one of her grave deed.

So on this dark November evening, Elizabeth sat in the side chapel, stock still on the wooden bench, as the candle flickered and the lights grew dim. Prayers were long over, so when one of the kitchen nuns came to put out all the lights, Elizabeth went unobserved, a statue frozen in agony or ecstasy. She did not dare to move, for fear the blood would gush down her legs in a big stream on the polished floor killing her on the spot. So she prayed, fervent heartfelt prayers, where she made atonement for all the wrong she had done in her life: disobeying her mother, biting Jimmy, answering back her father, and now, letting Angela O'Donnell down, bringing her into disgrace.

The chapel grew ice-cold, and there would be no one there until the next morning at six, for Matins. Soon Elizabeth could no longer feel her fingers and toes, frozen into lumps of ice, her back was rigid, and still she did not move. The sudden gushes of wet heat between her legs soon cooled down, and congealed there. But she deserved it. If God took her now she would welcome it: to lie back and sink into eternity, most of all to be forgiven in His eternal light, to be held close, in warmth. This would be fine, preferable to having to go on the next day, with her insides bleeding out, preferable to having to explain, confess or atone. If only he would take her.

Elizabeth must have nodded off, for she woke with a jerk to her neck. The candle had burned out, leaving an acrid aroma, like hell. What if demons or the devil were coming to get her, for her sins? Still she could not move but her heart was in her mouth with terror. It was so dark she couldn't even see her hands, resting upturned on her lap. There was only her soul and the darkness. Maybe she had already died and this was limbo, where she was waiting to be sent into heaven or hell.

She heard an owl shriek and a volt went through her, sending beads of cold sweat running down her forehead. She swallowed. "God, God, forgive me, I'll do anything you ask, I'll be your devoted servant forever, I will serve you as a nun within these walls and never leave, only save me now, at the hour of my death." She pulled her arms around herself and started to whimper in terror. "Please God, please," she whispered. Then she keeled over in the pew, pulled up her frozen feet and lay in a ball.

That is how she was found the next morning early, when there was sudden shouting and lights and the flurry and scurry of flapping nuns hovering over her. She blinked open her eyes and went to rise, but none of her limbs obeyed her orders, and she lay there until she was lifted, a rug around her shoulders, away off into the sick bay. She was mute under questioning, couldn't admit to her terrible shame, this thing that was happening inside her. She began to have cramps too, and was sure that the end was near. Because of her obduracy, added to by her habitual vagueness, that opaque non-reflective look in her dark eyes, Sister Vincent in the infirmary decided that she had had visions, and that she must not be disturbed. So the rumours started, and it was said about Elizabeth Hawthorn Thwaite that she was blessed by God, and that one day she would make a very fine nun, such was her devotion to Saint Teresa.

As for the period, the onset of menstruation, the same Sister Vincent found the stale blood on the sheets three days later, and told Elizabeth the facts of life, giving her towels and an elastic contraption for around her waist.

Elizabeth, if she admitted it, was much relieved. She was freed from the certain knowledge that she was dying, but was still unshakeable in her faith and devotion, preserving forever the pure image of the candle in the chapel that night, along with her agony. She felt she had been absolved, and had made her pact with God in return: she would devote her life to Him.

Never a moment passed from that day on that Elizabeth didn't sit in the chapel and thank St Teresa for sparing her. She learned all her Latin hymns and sang beautifully in the choir, becoming one of the leading sopranos, often being given solo parts at the most important liturgical functions. In this roundabout way she was recognised as a talent for the first time in her life, and became known as an ascetic, singled out at an early age for a vocation of service to God. Yet her heart still throbbed with longing, a secret longing for her loved one. For love.

In Third Year of Loreto Abbey convent school for girls, Elizabeth Hawthorn Thwaite was a bespectacled and pimply young adolescent of fourteen. She wore her springy black hair tied tightly back in a ponytail, scraped high off her face to reveal a white oval with a high forehead. The unruly hair sprung untamed out of the back of her head, but from the front was an air of chaste studiousness. Her black-rimmed glasses sat permanently on her nose, enlarging her eyes to make them owlish.

Over the two years she had managed to find herself fairly frequently in Angela's company, sometimes at a card game in the Common Room, or at tennis lessons in the spring. Then she would be extra helpful, run to pick up all the stray balls and give them back to Angela herself, presenting them shyly. Mostly she got a smile. She didn't mind now that other girls had noticed her infatuation, for that is what it was, and a relatively normal occurrence too at this age and in these circumstances. Catherine Clarke would puck her in the ribs at Assembly, and whisper loudly, 'here she comes, her Majesty.' Elizabeth would mumble, 'shut up you,' puck her back and blush. She couldn't help it, she always blushed when she saw Angela, always warmed up in her presence, and was unwavering in this devotion.

As a First Year she could offer to carry her books or her bag, but such offerings were only for the Freshers and were frowned upon after that. Now she was a Third Year and Angela was in Sixth, about to do her Leaving Cert.

One early spring morning, which would always remain in her mind, Elizabeth wandered at breaktime into the orchard where the cherry blossoms waved and danced in the light breeze. There, spread out on the ground, was Angela side by side with another Sixth Year. They lay there, lazily watching the petals fall, talking in intimate murmurs about secret desires. Elizabeth stopped, keen to watch her Angela, savouring the way the light played on her long hair, burnished gold against the grass. Her body too was long and lean, with brown legs showing above rolled down knee-socks, extending all the way up to the hem of her skirt, which was pulled up to her thigh.

Elizabeth breathed quietly, wanting to stay invisible. She was dying to know what they were saying, and so crept closer through the escallonia.

The other girl, Rosemary, teased her.

'So Angie, did you let him?' at which Angela rolled over lazily and squinted at her confidante.

'Well, above the waist is allowed, just a little, and I kept my blouse closed.'

'Did you enjoy it, come on, tell us, what was it like?' persisted Rosemary, both relishing the details that were to follow.

'First he kissed me, here, and put his tongue into my mouth.'

'Ugh,' said the other, 'what was that like?'

'Well,' she said again, 'it was a bit yucky and wet, but then I sort of melted and forgot all about it because then ...' and she paused for effect, 'his hand slipped down my gym slip and he sort of slowly rolled his palm over my nipples, like this,' and she demonstrated. Rosemary laughed and leaned over to kiss her on the cheek. They both blushed and giggled, and pushed each other a bit around on the grass, whooping with a shared glee.

In the bushes Elizabeth was boiling. She wasn't sure if it was the mention of boys, or that kiss. Really, the way Rosemary leaned over and just did it. She was astounded. 'How dare she,' she thought, and waited for Angela to push Rosemary away. But all Angela had done was laugh, and then kiss her back. Elizabeth was raging, burning with jealousy and betrayal. Her Angela, a kiss meant for her, long dreamed of and never realised. She felt like throwing herself on the ground and howling in protest like a two-year-old, but bit her lip instead, and sneaked off to nurse her wound.

Then to make matters worse there was all the talk of the Leaving Certificate and the summer holidays, and how all the Sixth Years would be leaving to find jobs or go to secretarial college. Some of the brainy ones would go on to university. Angela O'Donnell would be one of them, leaving to go out into the big world, probably to be a teacher, as she had the brains.

After the Easter holidays there was another shock. Angela O'Donnell didn't come back to school. They said she had a chance to go to university in England, a place with a big reputation, and Angela couldn't turn down a chance like that. 'But what about the Leaving Certificate?' thought Elizabeth. Surely she would need that at least. But no, she was gone. She would sit her Leaving Certificate examinations privately.

For Elizabeth, the thought of coming back to school the following September with no Angela there was devastating. What would be the point? Anyway, she hated most of her school subjects and if she was going to be a nun, why couldn't she just enter and forget about the big exams, she wouldn't need them anyway in the convent.

It was this reasoning that she presented to Gertrude when she was home in Glenview House for the summer holidays that year. She didn't want to go back to school. Gertrude was incensed, pulling herself up to her full height, magnificent in her fury.

'Elizabeth, do you know what you are saying? Throwing away the chance of a good education, to make something of yourself in life. What on earth did your father and I spend all that money for sending you to one of the best schools in the country? After all you could just as well have stayed in the valley and gone out to work at fourteen, skivvying for one of the other big houses.'

Gertrude paused for breath, far from having sufficiently expelled her rage.

Elizabeth hung her head and waited. She had nothing to say, and anyway, wouldn't be heard. Gertrude continued, 'I am so disappointed in you. I thought you might want to make something of yourself. After all, let's face it Lizzie, you are no Elizabeth Taylor are you? Who do you think is going to marry you or look after you? A girl needs a profession. Why wouldn't you go on for teaching, make your grandfather proud of you? As for this nonsense of becoming a nun, now there's a waste. I'm not saying they don't have their place, do a good job, but the best ones all have an education too you know. No, Elizabeth, I won't tolerate this nonsense for a minute. Look at Jimmy. He's doing so well up at Newtown, he'll be well able to take over your father's practice one day, someone to be proud of.'

Gertrude paused for breath. Elizabeth never reacted, never fought back, just stood there looking blank. There was hardly any point having a row with her, because she didn't defend herself. Gertrude gave up. She'd have to talk to the nuns about it. But Elizabeth had learned so well to hide her feelings that she stayed silent, a tiny red spot on her cheeks, and resolved somehow to defy her. She hated her at that moment, hated the tall handsome woman who called herself her mother. She had known more kindness from Mother Carmel or indeed Catherine Clarke. And Angela had shown her love, in small hidden signs. She was convinced of that. There was no point in going back to school with Angela gone.

So for now, Elizabeth stuck in her heels, and said that unless she could enter the convent she wasn't going back up to Dublin. Stubborn as a mule, she achieved an inner satisfaction from seeing her mother so upset. Served her right. Served her right too when she got off with Mathew Mulhall during the next Christmas holidays. Served her right when she let him put his tongue down her throat, just to see what it was like, same as Angela.

Catherine's Diary

28 January 1985

Master Cullen died today.

Mammy was at the cooker getting the dinner when the knock came. 'Get that Catherine, will you?' she said lifting the potatoes without looking at me, or the door.

I didn't have to because the door opened all by itself. It was Uncle Jimmy. Mammy went white. Jimmy never set foot in our house, so she knew straight away.

He started to say, 'I'm afraid I have some bad news' but Mammy set the plate down with a clatter and went running out the door with her apron still on, wiping her hands in it.

The boys all stopped eating and looked at Uncle Jimmy. 'He's gone I'm afraid,' he said.

'Master Cullen, is it?' said Danny, chirpy because he knew the name.

'That's right, your mother's grandfather,' said Jimmy.

'That's our great grandad,' piped up Liamey, not to be outdone. 'Sure he was ancient anyways.'

I jumped up then when I realised, and ran out after Mammy without giving Uncle Jimmy a cup of tea. She was already up around the bend.

'Mammy, wait for me.'

She had her head down and was rubbing her hands on the apron the whole time. 'Oh the Lord have mercy on his soul,' she was muttering, over and over.

Up she went along the road and up the hill, with the wind whistling by us. It was cold only we were so hot from running. Up around the corner until we seen the avalanche hill over beyond, and then the school-house under it where the Master lived all his life.

We must have got there in ten minutes, the fastest ever. We could see the door open and the nurse coming out.

'I'm sorry for your troubles Mrs Mulhall,' she says to Mammy. Mammy brushed right past her and went into the hall calling for him. Up the stairs with her – I nearly didn't dare follow – her feet clacking on the steps, and into the bedroom.

I got an awful shock then. I'd never seen a dead person. He was lying under the covers but his head was sticking out. It was tied up with a bandage below the chin. His mouth was tight shut and there were pennies on his eyes. The smell was sickly. I couldn't go in anymore, so I stayed at the door. Mammy fell on her knees with her head on the side of the bed.

'Oh oh oh, oh God,' she said, and started her Holy Marys. The room was gloomy but I swear his face was yellow, a horrible colour.

Something moved in the corner by the window. I jumped. It was Granny Gertrude. She was there all along and I hadn't seen her. She was quiet like a statue with her back to us, looking out the crack in the curtains down the valley. Mammy got up.

'Why didn't you send for me?' she attacked.

'He went peacefully, at about eleven this morning,' Granny said in a very tired voice.

'Sure he's not yet cold,' Mammy was wailing. 'You could've got me, but you didn't want to, did you?'

God I was mortified. Her shouting over a corpse.

'Mammy,' I whispered loudly.

'Oh hello Catherine,' said Granny. She came over to me at the door. 'Jimmy is making the arrangements. We bury him on Friday.' She left.

Mammy just looked at her with one of her stares, and then when she was gone she went back over to the bed and touched the Master's cheek. She let out a big long breath and in it I heard, 'oh God have mercy on us all, he's warm still, God help him.' She kissed his forehead. I was disgusted. He was dead.

I had to go home to clear the dishes. Mammy said she was going to wash him and lay him out. Daddy was there when I got home.

'I hear His Lordship was here,' he says, meaning Uncle Jimmy. 'Lucky for him I missed him, even on his mission of mercy.'

'Does Helen know?' I said. 'Will you go and bring her home from the salon, because Mammy's staying up above? Mrs Nolan expects me in the shop at four, and there's no one to mind the kids.'

'We'll mind ourselves so,' says John Paul.

'I'm minding me calves meself,' says Danny.

'Lookit,' says Daddy, 'there's a funeral to be organised and we can't leave it to that crowd to do it all. Our side will have to be told, and we've to send for Mattie and the relatives beyond in England.'

'Who's them?' says Liamey.

'Your cousins,' says Danny. 'In England, stupid.'

'There's me father for starters,' says Daddy. 'We haven't seen sight nor light of him for a good number of years. But by the hokey none of them would want to miss Master Cullen's hoolie. Wasn't every child that was born in this valley and under that hill there educated by him? Every last child until he could no longer stand in the classroom. Sure wasn't I there myself? And he gave us all the reading, writing and 'rithmatic. It'll be a great funeral.'

I decided to go up and get her myself when Mammy didn't come home by teatime. So before it got too dark I set off up the hill. Helen was home minding the lads with the telly on. It was scary in the dark, with only a torch for light for fear I'd get knocked down. The avalanche mountain was very high and black against the sky up ahead. I normally wouldn't be out on my own but I was getting worried about Mammy. That old hill is full of ghosts. I heard her. I did, the avalanche baby crying in the wind. Howling she was.

When I got there the house was all glowing with a candle in every window, like Christmas. It cheered me up. There were shadows moving inside. I heard the murmuring of the Hail Marys first, coming out of the parlour door. Inside there was people sitting on chairs along the walls, and in the middle was a long table with the Master laid out on it. He looked so different, with a suit on and the beads entwined round his fingers. In the light from the candles he looked asleep. There was a big white candle on a stand at one end of the table. The room smelled of burning wax. It was wonderful in a way, the shadows and the light, like a fairytale.

I just stayed standing in the door watching. Everyone was very quiet except for the mumble of the prayers. Nurse Mahoney was leading and whining out the 'Hail Mary full of grace', and then they'd all mumble the rest, 'Holy Mary Mother of God'. It was nice not to have to be in it, to just stay watching. Mammy had us on our knees for years in the kitchen doing the Rosary every night, until the boys gave out – they wanted to watch the telly and Daddy let them. I know the poor man was dead but you felt there was something really happening and going on in the house, more than for many years. An occasion.

I heard a noise. A floorboard creaked over my head, then footsteps started to come down the stairs.

'Mammy,' I said, my heart hammering with relief when I saw it was only her, 'what are you doing?' She was nearly falling under a cardboard box she was lifting down the stairs.

'Ah, Catherine, can you help me with this? There's a good girl. I have to get it home.'

'Mammy, it's far too heavy. Daddy can bring it on the tractor.'

'Shush, now Catherine, do what you're told.'

'Mammy, they're saying their prayers, you'll be disturbing them.'

'There's no disturbing the poor Master. He's in a lovely sleep God bless him. Didn't I do a good job on him now, didn't I?'

She had the box at the bottom of the stairs and was huffing and puffing with her eyes gleaming.

'Mammy don't strain yourself,' I said.

'Come on quick and get it outside, we won't be long getting it home,' she said.

What could I do, I couldn't talk any louder. We had it down at the bottom step of the front door when a big black shadow fell over us.

'Elizabeth,' said the voice. It was Granny Gertrude. 'What has possessed you?' She was whispering loudly. 'I'll do all that.'

She hissed so loud I felt the spit.

'Come on Catherine,' is all Mammy said, getting me to lift the box with her and off down the road with us. Granny was left standing in the doorway. I didn't look back but I suppose she just went in again. What could she do? Mammy is very stubborn.

'It's not right so it's not Catherine, it's not right,' is all she kept saying all the way home, and it was a long way home that night.

'Mammy what's in the box anyway?' I asked.

'My things, and she's not getting them.'

'What things?'

'Old things, mine, from when I was small.' She stopped suddenly in the road. The box was so heavy we let it drop in front of us. 'She's a right old B. so she is.'

'Mammy, that's an awful thing to say about your own mother.'

'But it's true Catherine.' Mammy looked at me with her two glasses pointing at me. 'She wants the house.'

I couldn't see her eyes in the dark, but I could see her mouth moving and her teeth spitting.

'I spent more time with him than she did this last forty years. Sure didn't I bring you up there as babbies every day, wheeled you up in the big pram. That was my home Catherine, and the Master was a father and a mother to me. She's an old bitch.'

Mammy picked up the box herself and off with her, I don't know where she got the strength for dragging and trundling.

'But Mammy, she is your mother.'

She muttered something as she was running.

'How would you feel if your own mother didn't come to your wedding?' she said, sounding as if she was coughing.

'God, Mammy, that's terrible. Is that true?'

'Catherine, you don't know the half of it.'

She was walking so fast I had to nearly fight with her to get a hold of the box before she'd do damage to her back. Then she dumped it in the barn and went into bed without saying a word.

And do you know what was on top of the box under the flap? A doll. Just an old doll with a cracked china face on it. Mammy's funny.

29 January

Today Mammy slept late. I told Helen about the box and we went to look.

There were a few school copybooks inside with Mammy's name on them: Elizabeth Hawthorn Thwaite. Very posh altogether. It's hard to imagine Mammy at school, being a young lady, though I have to say she is fussy about manners and certain things. Like she is very particular about changing your knickers. She always says if you get knocked down and were brought to hospital you'd want your knickers to be clean. That's how she is.

I picked up one of the old copybooks: 'Geography. Third Year Loreto Abbey Dalkey'. Inside it she had drawn some maps and written some essays. Her handwriting was very small and neat, done with a fountain pen in blue ink. On the last page and all across the inside of the red cover was a name: Angela O'Donnell. Written again and again, in big letters, small letters, joined writing, print, and in capital letters outlined in ink until the paper was torn with all the ink going into it where the nib had pressed down. Just one name all over: Angela. The last one had a squiggle around it, like a decoration.

'Ah for God's sake Kitty it's only old schoolbooks, not even love letters!' said Helen. We laughed.

At four o'clock we all got dressed up in whatever black clothes we could find for the removal. I told Mrs Nolan I wouldn't be in work again until Monday. I put on a black jumper over a navy skirt and wore a beret with my hair up. The boys had on their grey school jumpers. Helen was done up in a new coat. She lent me her black tights. Anyway, Mammy went on ahead of us so I walked up with Helen. Daddy brought the boys on the back of the tractor but he was going to park it well out of sight before the house.

I couldn't believe it when we came around the bend. There was a line of people there stretching back out of the front door, all the way down the hill by the side of the ditch, standing waiting to go in. We had to push past them because we're family. The doorway was jammed and the house was stuffy with all the wool suits wet from the drizzle.

I followed Helen into the front room. In daylight you could see the Master dressed up in the good black Sunday suit, looking like he was going off to Mass or something. And his face, he was so rosy cheeked. I don't know what Mammy had done to him but I swear he looked alive again.

Helen let out a big cough, which turned into 'oh my God' with her hand up to her mouth, and she grabbed me.

'Jesus Kitty, I've never seen a dead body.'

'He's lovely isn't he?' I said.

She looked at me.

Mammy was sitting on the other side of the coffin minding him. The people all came in and touched his cheek or made the sign of the cross on his forehead. Mammy was looking pleased with herself. She had a black hat on with her good coat and gloves – oh, and her shiny handbag. We all had to push in by the wall and stand and let our hands be shook by the neighbours. They all whispered 'sorry for your troubles' and took their hats off, the men that is.

So we stood there watching for what seemed like ages while they came from all over.

Granny Gertrude was at the head of the coffin with her black coat and veil, and lipstick. Red lipstick. No red eyes even. Just perfect looking, with her gold hair in a bun, like a film star. She gives me the creeps. Grandad William was with her, with his big red face and bushy moustache. He's nice really, so he is, he came up to me on the way out and patted my head and said, 'How's Kitty then? You're so like your grandmother when she was your age.'

Well it's nice of him but I don't think so, except my hair is long but more strawberry than blonde.

Then there was a wheelchair in the corner. In it was Grandad William's English mother, Matilda. She's very very old. She's like a corpse herself, all shrivelled under a blanket with two black holes looking out for eyes. She just stared straight ahead and didn't seem to see anybody at all. She'd be ninety-something like the Master himself, ninety-four he is now he's dead.

Uncle Jimmy came in then huffing and coughing, with a smell of perfume off him from Aunty Linda, who followed after with her hair-sprayed blonde hair; I nearly got sick the smell was so strong. She rattled and jangled her bracelets and pulled out a lacy hanky to blow into. Mammy just looked daggers at her and Jimmy. I'd say Aunt Linda didn't notice.

The priest then started to say prayers before they put the lid on the coffin.

Daddy came in at the last minute with the boys, and insisted on having a look before the lid was closed. He had his cap in his hands and his curls were greased down. Uncle Jimmy kind of moved over and out of his way.

I'm going to sleep now. I'm too tired from all the people to write about the rest. Oh. Simon. I forgot. He wasn't there. I wonder will he come tomorrow?

30 January

Today was an awful wet day for the funeral. We were all up early. Mammy was very cheerful.

'Are you sure he's coming home?' she said to Daddy.

Helen looked up. 'Who? What are you on about?'

'Your Uncle Mattie,' says Daddy. 'Sure she would'a married him only I got her first, isn't that right Mammy?' he says, pucking her in the ribs.

She was smiling behind her glasses, for a change, because she was doing a lot of sniffling and coughing yesterday evening.

'Great,' says Helen, 'I love funerals, it's the only time I get to see my cousins in England.'

'What are you talking about?' says Danny. 'It's the only time you get to see the snobs too.'

'Will Simon be there too?' asks John Paul. He likes Simon because Simon tells him jokes.

'Simon's not so snobby,' says Liamey.

'He can't help it,' says Daddy, 'sure isn't his mother a Protestant? Still and all he's your only cousin this side of the water.'

'Ah, Aunty Linda does her best,' said Helen. 'She gave me a nice scarf for Christmas. But that Simon thinks he's God's gift to the girls.'

'Ye shouldn't all be fighting at a funeral,' I say.

'And it hasn't even started,' adds Daddy with a big guffaw out of him. 'It'll be a good day out, we'll give the Master the send-off he deserves.'

We all rushed out then not to be late. I didn't feel sad like I was going to a funeral, for my heart was thumping in case I'd see him. You know.

The church was packed. The front row was supposed to be for all of us, but Granny Gertrude got there first with her family – fair enough, she's his only daughter. Well, Mammy's her family but ... So I was very disappointed when their bench only had Granny Gertrude, Grandad William, Uncle Jimmy and Aunty Linda. No sign of Simon. I let myself cry at the singing. Very sad and low. May he rest in peace, the Master was a good man, and nobody ever had a bad word to say about him.

After all the prayers and blessings, the coffin waited on a stand in front of the altar. On a nod from the priest, Daddy went and stood at the front corner of the coffin waiting for to carry it down the church. Then Jimmy got up, dragging Grandad William with him, and they stood on the other side. Jimmy started to wave, and who came walking up the side aisle only Simon, up to carry the last corner of the coffin. When Daddy seen this, he went over and pulled Uncle Mattie out of his seat so when Simon got to the coffin the four corners were filled. He stood there with his mouth open looking at his father, the whole church now standing up to sing, while Daddy gave the signal to Uncle Mattie.

Uncle Jimmy just stared back at Simon and screwed up his mouth, because the music started and the men all hooshed the coffin up on their shoulders and started to shuffle slowly down the aisle. Simon was left standing. He saw me looking. I kind of smiled to show him I understood. He just turned away. I felt terrible. I didn't do anything. Maybe he thought I was laughing at him.

I spent the whole day trying to talk to him. But it was so crowded. We were all in a big bunch in the graveyard, with our feet sinking into the clay all around the hole and trying not to slip. The priest said the prayers and then there was a whole decade of the Sorrowful Mysteries. It was very sad, I have to say, when they threw the clay down on the coffin and that was the end of Master Cullen.

Mammy was howling. Daddy was trying to stop her and kept handing her his handkerchief. Granny Gertrude threw down a red rose, I thought they only did that in films. I couldn't see if she was crying with that veil on her.

I was looking for Simon but I couldn't keep twisting around or Helen would've noticed. Anyway I had to keep a hold of John Paul, he's a slippery little divil and I didn't want him falling in.

Back at the house there were tons of sandwiches, I don't know where they all came from, the neighbours I suppose. Uncle Mattie pulled a bottle of Jameson out of his tweed jacket and was soon singing. Mammy sat beside him with a big pink face on her. I'd swear she was at a party, I never saw her enjoy herself so much.

My hands were sweating I was so worried I wouldn't get to talk to Simon, so I went out and around the house in case I might have missed him.

And there he was, under a tree with a cigarette.

'I ...' my face went into a silly smile.

'Oh. Catherine.' He pulled on the fag for the longest time and didn't look at me.

'Sorry about what happened in the church,' I said.

'Oh. That.' And he threw down the cigarette.

'I know he's me father but he shouldn't have done that Simon.'

'Family stuff, I hate it. It's humiliating. I hate them all.'

'Simon! They're not all bad.'

'Ah fuck it,' he said. 'I'm glad I'll be gone out of here soon. College starts next month.'

'So you're going back to Dublin are you?'

'Yep,' he said. 'And then I'm out of here for good.'

My heart was in my mouth. I didn't know what to say.

'Would you like to go for a walk?'

He looked at me funny and nearly smiled, and I could feel myself bubbling up inside, when God Almighty what happened only Helen came out to the back door shouting, 'Catherine. Oh Kitty-yyy, you're needed to wet the tea. I can't keep up with the lot of them.'

Simon laughed his head off, a big snort, and holy Jesus I swear his eyes were gorgeous, like a film star's. So brown. I love it when he laughs.

I forgot the best bit. When he was going, with Uncle Jimmy and Aunty Linda, he squeezed my arm and said 'see ya Kitty', with a wink, kind of.

Then when they were all gone out the front door, a knock came that nobody heard because of the singing. I was the only one in the hall so I opened the door. There was a fine tall man and he said, 'Am I in the right place?'

He took my hand to shake it.

'You're definitely a Cullen,' he said, 'you have the look of Gertie about you. Mulhall, Tom,' he said, raising his cap to go in past me.

Just then Granny Gertrude came out of the kitchen. She stopped in her tracks as if she had seen a ghost.

There was a bit of a commotion then because she didn't feel well and everyone had to run around her, as usual. Maybe she does see ghosts.

6 February

Mammy has been in an awful state ever since the funeral, so much so that I haven't time to be thinking about myself. Or Simon. So it was a big surprise when down he arrives from Dublin at six o'clock one evening out of the blue in a new car, saying, 'hop in girls'.

It was getting dark when we knocked. You could hear a squeaking noise within and then the door opened a small bit. She looked out at us and you could see her jaw drop. She didn't open the door either. 'What are you doing here?' she said to us, and then, 'Simon, is it you?'

He said, 'it's me Grandma, let me in,' so she opened the door a bit more. I got a shock when I seen her. Her hair was all hanging down like straw and her face was fallen in on itself with no mouth. There was no red lipstick anyway. She let the door open a little bit more, with Simon talking all the time.

'How are you Gran? Are you keeping well?'

She stood back to let us in. I didn't say a word, with that pair talking so much, I wouldn't have been able to anyway, I was too scared. I had the old anorak on so she wouldn't notice anything.

She took us down the hall to the kitchen. She had an old tilly lamp on the table, beside a pile of newspapers and a loaf of bread. It smelled oily and cold, with black smoke rising up out of it.

'Grandma,' said Simon, 'are you looking after yourself at all?'

'Watch those papers,' said Helen, 'they might burn.'

'Don't touch them,' says Granny, coming to life.

'And I'm very well thank you Simon. And who have we here? Helen, I hardly knew you, did you change your hair?'

Helen's hair is bright red now, and a little bit short, like one of those punks. Daddy went mad when he saw it.

Then she turns to me, and says, 'How are you Catherine? My my you've grown so much.'

I'm sure I blushed scarlet.

She wasn't so bad then, wetting the tea and giving us some biscuits, only stale Marietta. I nearly wasn't drinking out of the teacup it was so chipped, a flowery china one.

'Haven't seen your father in a week, Simon, is he well?'

Simon sucked up to her some more, saying Uncle Jimmy was very busy and with all the snow you couldn't take out the car. Helen was yapping away but I noticed Granny didn't ask about Mammy.

They went on talking so I looked all around. The kitchen was very dark, with curtains hanging off the windows. The trees were waving outside, making shadows and squeaking against the pane, scratching them. It was very chilly because there was no fire in the range.

When I was very small Mammy would bring me and Helen to see the Master long before he got sick. He was an old man then with white hair but I wasn't afraid of him like Helen was because he was kind, and once gave me an apple. That was before he started calling me Gertrude when he was in bed all the time. So I didn't remember the house being so cold and dark, with no life in it. There was always old Bridie who kept the kitchen, but she went into a nursing home in Bray.

Anyway my stomach was sinking. I had goose pimples on my legs and shivers up my back. It wasn't only the house being cold; it was Granny. She kind of looks at you with bright eyes, but they have a black dot in the middle that stares at you very hard. I know they said she was beautiful once but I can't see it.

Well, I thought out of there I'd never get. Simon was driving his new car and we went down to Dolan's for a drink after. I had a hot whiskey. I didn't care what Daddy would say, I was freezing to death after the schoolhouse.

'No way lads,' I say. 'I can't go up there.'

'Catherine, don't be silly. It's going to be fine. Sure it'll be over in no time,' says Helen.

'I'll talk to her,' says Simon.

'You didn't say anything did you?

'No, no, we'll work on it. I'll go and see her again next weekend, and mention it to her. The plan I mean, not the, the ...' and he didn't know what to say, so he looked away to order another round.

I was looking at him real hard trying to make him look at me back, but he kept chatting and yapping. I wanted to say 'Simon, please, maybe I can go to Dublin with you, and then everything will be all right.' But they were laughing and skitting and making great plans. I'm all confused tonight. You'd swear it was a party they were planning.

'You buy the food,' says he, 'and then I'll come on a Sunday with the turf, and we'll cook a chicken,' and so on.

Helen says, 'what is it Kitty? You're awful quiet.'

'You don't know what it's like,' I mumble.

'You have no choice, no choice, do you not see that Kitty?' she says. 'You're lucky Simon is taking all this trouble to help you, he doesn't have to, you know.'

'Right,' says he, 'I'll call to see Gran next weekend, and we should get you in around the end of the month.'

'What are you having?' he says to Helen. 'Sorry Catherine, what would you like?'

'A double brandy,' says I. Feck it.

8 February

That Kerry Babies tribunal is on the news morning noon and night. You'd think there were never any babies born illegitimate in Ireland.

Now they're saying the Kerry girl killed her baby. Put her hands on its neck. Not the baby on the beach but her own baby, the one in the barn.

'But I saw her on the television,' said Mammy, 'and she said she had the baby out in the hay barn, and that she prayed to Our Lady and then in the morning the baby was dead.'

'Yeah, that's what I thought too,' I agreed.

'Catherine, we'll have to get down on our knees and say a Rosary for all that's going on in this country.'

Lucky for Mammy, Daddy was out. She got Liamey and John Paul on their knees too, in front of the stove and between the table and the door, in a circle.

Mammy took the lead, calling out the Sorrowful Mysteries. She went into a kind of trance with her eyes looking up at the Sacred Heart on the wall. She has his light lit every day now since the Master died.

The boys were skitting and shoving and so I had to be shushing them and giving them filthy looks. Danny burst in right in the middle of 'Jesus Falls the Third Time', and gave a big snort. 'Here, I'm off again,' and he slammed the door.

Mammy didn't stop. Then she said the Hail Holy Queen. The kids didn't know the words to that one. I remembered it from school, at May time.

Then in a high holy voice Mammy says, 'bless this house and keep us all from harm.'

I made a cup of tea and gave the boys some digestive biscuits before they went to bed.

Mammy is still sitting there looking holy.

'Catherine, we have to remember to pray. It's the only way. I'm worried about Helen, we don't know anymore where she is or who she's with.'

I coughed.

'But sure she's only doing her course,' I say. 'She'll be back soon to get a job in the village. Then she'll be at home again.'

Mammy looked off out the window at the dark, folding her hands.

'Bridie told me a story once about a girl working on a farm. Not here but in another village over the hill a long time ago. Mary was her name. She was a serving girl who lived with a farmer and his wife on a big farm. Mary was no spring chicken mind, being in her late twenties. Anyway, she was a great worker who helped inside and out, harvesting and pulling and weeding and doing all the kitchen chores as well. Every day she rose at dawn and went to milk the cows, then put down the fire and cooked the breakfast for the whole family. Out she went to the fields again, then in to cook a big dinner for all the other farm hands, and so on: never a moment's rest and she never complained.

'One day, during potato harvest, as they were digging out the potatoes and saving them for the winter, Mary said to the lady of the house, "I have a headache and would like an hour off to lie down."

'So the lady said yes. After two hours had gone by she began to wonder, so she went into the house and up to the attic room where Mary slept. The door was locked. Inside she heard an infant's cry. She knocked at the door but Mary didn't open it. She went for help and they came and broke down the door. Mary was inside sitting on the bed.

'"I heard an infant cry," said the lady of the house.

'"I heard nothing," said Mary.

'So they searched the room, and under the bed they found an old suitcase. Inside it was the body of a newborn baby, still warm. There was a stocking tied around its neck.

'Mary's father was sent for, and she went walking home down the road behind him, carrying the suitcase. No mention was ever made of the baby.

'Three days later Mary was back, working away as before. After another two weeks she collapsed out in the field with a high fever and was taken to hospital. They said her breasts were nearly rotted off her with the unused milk.

'But she got well, and came back, and nothing more was said ever again.'

When Mammy finished I nearly got sick. I was sweating and stayed quiet. I had my hair hanging over my face staring into the fire. Then after a while she says, 'it was a big farmer a few miles away, but wasn't he married with nine of his own? "Silly girl – Bridie said that – silly girl, ruining her life."

My hands were sweating. Mammy lay back with her head against the armchair with her eyes looking very sad. The Master I suppose. She cries quietly all the time these days.

I didn't know what to say so I went to bed, thinking about the schoolgirl in County Longford who died in the grotto, giving birth all by herself in the cold. Nobody even noticed she was pregnant, or so they said. Her baby died with her. Maybe Our Lady took them all to herself. I'll be saying more Rosaries again tonight. I'm asking Our Lady to help me too, she's the only one who can.

15 February

I forgot it was Valentine's Day last week but then I never get any valentines. Helen always does. She'd make you sick. She got three, says she has no notion who they're from.

Last evening there was a dance on in Arklow for teenagers, a social run by the youth club. Helen said I should go, that it would do me good to get out of the house and meet fellas. She's terrible what she gets away with. I don't know how Daddy doesn't find out she's smoking and drinking.

We all went off in Mossie Dollard's car to the Bay Hotel for the disco. I'm a bit shy and my jeans are a bit hicky looking. I had Helen's flowery top on but it was too tight over my breasts. So I was standing in the back looking at the lights flashing, and everyone looking purple with very white teeth. Then I was afraid to go out and dance because the lights would show up my bra all white too. I was watching a couple who were on the floor by the wall, really going at it. I couldn't take my eyes off them – he nearly had her skirt off. God that's disgusting I was thinking. I moved over to the bar. There were only minerals for sale but the girls had brought in some vodka in a bottle of 7Up. I took a slug to see what it was like. Well it was bad enough standing there looking so hicky, I didn't want to make it worse for meself.

Mossie comes along anyways and starts chatting to me, didn't ask me to dance mind, but then he sort of had me back against the wall kissing me. He looks at me with those yellow dog eyes of his and I knew he was mad for me.

Feck it, I think, I don't care. Maybe I'll have a go, just in case. I'm feeling so down in myself it won't make any difference.

I can't say it was nice at first, he was smelling of Guinness, but then he put his hand up my back under my top and was pushing against me. His hand came round onto my breast and he slipped his finger in and I felt very warm all over. My mouth watered and so did his. I'd say I was getting carried away when somebody came and pulled him off me.

'Hey none of that, break it up there,' the sacristan from the parish said.

I felt so embarrassed then, just looking at him with my mouth all wet like an eejit. He just said 'sorry babe' and walked off. I was sore sorry too and wouldn't have minded if he'd kept on doing it. It was nice. Not anywhere as nice as that other time except that was broad daylight. Though it's different when you love somebody. Then it isn't a sin, is it? Later Mossie gave us a lift home. He never looked at me but had his hand groping under my skirt all the way.

Daddy was asleep by the fire in the kitchen, He just opened one eye and said 'ah Catherine, you're back, good girl,' and fell asleep again. What was I worrying about?

16 February

Yesterday I was thinking about whether I should've gone or not. That flowery top was miles too tight. My breasts are so big, I feel like a cow, so heavy. I can't stop them growing. Can't stop any of it, all the widdling at night. How do they think that Granny won't notice? I'm so sick when I think of it.

Mammy is going on again about her. Tonight when Daddy was gone she pulled out some old photographs and held one up very close, examining it.

'Look at that Catherine,' she pointed to the middle of the picture. Well it was black and white and very crumpled but I saw it- and Mammy peeping out from behind it.

'Well be the hokey,' I said, 'what in the Lord's name is that?'

'An elephant,' she said, very proud.

'The one you told me about? And was that you?'

'It was. That was the day the circus left the village in 1960, after the winter. We all went down to wave them off on their all-Ireland tour.'

'And did you touch the elephant? Do they bite?'

Mammy smiled a big smile from ear to ear.

'No, they don't. They're very gentle and very nice. And see,' she said, 'that's your father there, standing on the left.'

'That's Daddy?' I was amazed, he was so good looking in a long coat with a hat on him.

'And that,' she said, pointing again, 'is your Uncle Mattie. Wasn't he a fine cut of a man all the same?'

'Janey Mac, Mammy, I wouldn't know him at all. And you look lovely too,' I said, because she did. She had a summer dress on and her hair was all out, thick and curly at the sides.

Mammy was so happy thinking about it all.

'And here's my wedding photograph,' she said, holding out a bigger one.

A small group stood looking out at the camera, all dickied up in their good suits and hats: Mammy in the middle, very thin and like a little girl, in white without her glasses, Daddy, Mattie, and in the back row of relatives there's a tall man towering over them all, boldly smiling at the camera.

I pointed. 'I know him.'

'That's Tommie Mulhall. I'd never seen him either before that day because he was off in England.'

'That's the man who came back from England after all those years the night of the funeral?'

'He did,' said Mammy.

'And then Granny took her little turn.'

'She did, didn't she? Always looking for attention, and your Daddy delighted that his father had come all the way. Mattie came too, of course,' she said, lighting up. She sat smiling to herself and I didn't get any more chat out of her tonight so I went to bed. It's great when Mammy smiles.

An elephant in the village. That's a good one.

Elizabeth, 1958–60

It started in church. Village lads hanging round outside the door, lounging on walls. Elderly farmers alighting from red tractors and donkeys and carts to walk, stooped in reverence, or bent against the wind, up the path to the massive wooden door. Inside it is hushed and dark, musty with disuse during the week, damp because the roof leaks.

A well-dressed family sits in the second pew, not quite arrogant enough to push forward to the front; the last shall be first, first shall be last. They are the Hawthorn Thwaites: Gertrude, well turned-out in a crisp black and white check two-piece, wearing a hat of course, perched up on top of a tight bun, the once abundant tresses severely in check; next, we have James William, called Jimmy at home, tucked up to the neck in a blue blazer and tie, every bit the bored snob, wearing a pout that says 'I shouldn't be here, I am not one of you', with rubber lips and golden hair, fair rather than white gold, but thick, to back up this petulant assertion; next, Elizabeth, now fifteen, demure, serious, thin, in a grey frock coat a little too small which pulls in her bony frame so she looks almost bent, still tilting slightly to the side in her apologetic way; lastly, old Jim Cullen, now seventy-five, hair snow white, frail and bent, but inclined kindly towards Elizabeth. They hold missals bound in black with red and yellow ribbons marking the Mass for the day. At the back of the books are the Latin hymns. It is 1959, pre-Second Vatican Council, so the priest stands with his back to the public and raises his outstretched hands to implore heaven for their sins – in Latin. His vestments are a glorious green, emerald like Ireland at the time.

The Mass is sung, for it is the Feast of the Assumption, and Father Murphy croaks and gasps his way through the liturgy. Elizabeth Hawthorn Thwaite cannot restrain herself. When he begins the 'Tantum Ergo' she opens her mouth and emits a high pure note, which has been hammering at her vocal chords to escape: years of habit. It slips out of her mouth and carves a path up over the altar into the stained glass of St Mary and St Joseph. Her notes continue, equally pure and thrilling, until the Latin hymn comes to an end. Amen.

Father Murphy dares not look around, for the liturgy is inexorable and must be finished. He is its captive. At that time, voices of the lay congregation did not join in the singing, not unless by prior arrangement, and not unless invited, like a choir of nuns from the convent in Kiltegan. Elizabeth must not have been aware of this. She sang her praises to the Lord, oblivious. Oblivious to the startled looks exchanged between parishioners, oblivious to the grimace of consternation growing on her mother's face, oblivious to Jimmy's smirk of suppressed mirth. She sang on, as always, innocent and oblivious. And there was nothing anyone could say or do – until afterwards. As the congregation streams out, sniffling and shuffling, murmuring among themselves, Gertrude squeezes Elizabeth's arm very hard, smiling through gritted teeth as she greets neighbours.

'What?' snaps Elizabeth silently, giving her mother one of her looks, sullen and surly.

Did she know she had transgressed certain social mores, broken unstated boundaries?

Two village kids, brothers, hang about down the back of the church by the baptismal font. They raise their hands to their foreheads in a cursory blessing by touching their caps. They have heard the silver tones shimmer across the stones of the nave and they have looked at each other and grinned. They puck each other when they see the Hawthorn Thwaite family bless themselves at the water font in the porch, and saunter over.

'That was lovely so it was,' ventures Mattie, cocking his head and winking with an impish grin.

Elizabeth blushes madly and her mother shoves her on keeping hold of her arm as Johnny mouths 'beautiful' to her as she leaves. She doesn't hear their laughter as they snort and chuckle with the other kids. She is too busy remembering their faces, Mattie's cheeky good looks and Johnny's sideways smile. She hardly hears Gertrude's remonstrations: 'Really Elizabeth, have you no sense at all? Singing like that, making a show of us.' Doesn't notice the two fingers the kids give James as he turns to threaten their laughter with a supercilious stare. No, Elizabeth was inured in her walls of self-absorption, captive to the stirrings of fantasy. Who would have thought that love stories begin in church?

Elizabeth went back to school the following September, after a summer of the usual routine and obligations of Glenview House: travelling to shows to see James compete in local gymkhanas; hanging about in beer tents while her father got merry and told endless stories of how he got one over on Jones, his partner in practice; and listening to her grandfather, the Major, recounting his horsey tales. Her mother would always be immaculately dressed and playing personal maid to James. Elizabeth was mightily sick of it all by the end of the holidays. It had been one of those dreary Irish summers when the rain is habitual and unyielding, the skies relentlessly grey, day after monotonous day.

Despite her earlier protests, Elizabeth found herself back at the door of the convent, glad to rediscover the narrow bed of her cubicle and the predictability of the bells. She drifted along in a drill of daily order, now and again loosening her heart to sing as the rituals demanded, or finding a way to slip into chapel as before for a private chat with Himself, the man above. Now however her mind filled with images other than the purity of female saints, flowers fresh at their feet. Rather, there intruded into these private spaces some ragamuffin articles of clothing, mud-smeared hands, and a gap-toothed grin, all swirling around in a carousel of circus music. She couldn't get it out of her head, the oom pah pah of the tuba and the dramatic roll of the drums. That was the night the circus had come to town in the last week of August.

It was to be a treat for Elizabeth before she went back to school. 'Farinelli's Circus', the posters proclaimed, in the wide white smile of a clown with red curls. Elizabeth was only going along to please her father, whose idea it was. She found the prospect childish and the notion that she would still like such infantile pleasures condescending. She was not prepared for the fun, the sheer exuberance of the performers, the energy of the acrobats, the antics of the clowns. Most of all she marvelled at the animal acts, the puppies trained to beg and dance wearing pointy hats, the ponies trotting and rearing waving feathers on their heads, and the final act, the elephants. In they came after an impressive drum roll and build-up from the ringmaster, one big she-elephant and her baby. They lumbered in with their trunks waving, the little one holding his mother's tail in his trunk, on their big tree trunk legs. Elizabeth laughed out loud as they placed their toes on upturned drums and seemed to bow to the crowd. She found them so sweet, so old and wrinkly. And who was there helping to hurry them along, as the elephant boy? Mattie Mulhall, prancing round in an old dinner jacket with a red bow tie, snapping a stick into their sides and for once looking deadly serious at his task. When the crowd applauded as the elephants reared up on their hind legs to sit, his face broke into a grin of relief and then he relaxed into sharing the adulation. The ringmaster even thanked him by name.

'And our thanks this evening to Nellie's helper, Mathew Mulhall.'

Over on the other side of the ring there was a whistle, followed by a few catcalls and whoops. You could see Mattie was pleased. Elizabeth kept smiling too, for she had caught his eye and was sure he had winked at her. Or was it a trick of the light? Or the mass euphoria? Anyway, she begged afterwards to be let go out the back to visit the animals, as Gertrude went off to the refreshment tent to buy orange squash.

Outside the great tent there were coloured circus wagons, parked in a line, and a container-like construct which housed the elephants. Along the way were barred cages, where the dogs and ponies were being rubbed down and fed. She could hear the calls of men, several of them, as they rounded up the elephants and enticed them back behind bars. Elizabeth looked in, curiosity pulling her forward, until she saw Mattie. He was heaving and puffing at the great grey flank, earnest at his task. She waited until he had closed the cage door and the other men had left, before stepping forward into the entrance. Mattie was startled as he was caught unawares.

'Oh, it's yourself, did you enjoy that?' he said, suddenly cocky, still sweating from the exertion and reeking an animal smell of hide and muck.

Elizabeth nodded shyly, lost now for words. 'It was great ... thanks,' she added, as if he were totally responsible for the show.

'Massive, aren't they,' said another voice, and there was Johnny, the brother, sidling over to her.

'Oh yes,' breathed Elizabeth, 'I've never seen anything so big.'

Mattie looked at Johnny and guffawed. Elizabeth went puce, she didn't know why. Johnny turned to her kindly and said, 'you'd feel sorry for them all the same, locked up like that, a wild beast.'

Elizabeth smiled gratefully, then ran swiftly away.

Jimmy teased her in the tea tent. 'Off seeing your new boyfriend, are you Lizzie?'

She blushed furiously. 'I saw the elephant, it's so big, it's amazing,' she mumbled.

'Where were you Lizzie? I got you an orange,' Gertrude interrupted. 'What's this about boyfriends? Leave her alone Jimmy darling, she's far too young for all that nonsense. As for those Mulhalls, well ...'

She rolled her eyes and clicked her tongue, leaving one of those pauses that condemn a man or his family forever. Elizabeth didn't satisfy her by asking what she meant, and filled up with some kind of churlish feeling instead. This is how she went back to school, mute and incommunicative as always.

'Really,' said Gertrude, 'anyone would think she preferred the nuns' company to ours. Maybe she should enter after all,' she taunted, as if Elizabeth were not present.

Now back at school in the chapel, Elizabeth relived every second of that circus night. Nothing had happened, but to a fifteen-year-old imagination starved of colour and experience, the smells and sounds of that night infused her senses and peppered her imaginings. Mattie had come towards her, and smiled. Or Johnny had put his hand on her shoulder, touching her kindly, sending hot shivers into her stomach. Or Mattie, mostly Mattie, had stared hard into her eyes, and had stepped forward swiftly to chuck her under the chin, catching sight of the dark pools of her eyes. Why oh why was she still wearing glasses? Big bottle ends, enlarging her irises, making her look imbecilic. Next time there wouldn't be any.

Elizabeth plotted and planned during the months at school, and when she was home at Christmas, she went off for a walk up to Ballybeg, where Farinelli's Circus wintered out in the outhouses and gardens.

Ballybeg House was an imposing building going to rack and ruin, standing at the end of a curving driveway of copper beeches on fine parkland behind the mountain. For several years now the circus had stopped there and Lady Guthrie had even built an extra high shed to accommodate the elephants. Elephants had been coming to stay in the valley since nearly as long ago as the avalanche. Nobody who lived there realised what a privilege this was. The circus people were mainly Irish, for Farinelli had arrived on Irish soil after the Great War and stayed, marrying an O'Toole from Knockananna, a great niece of the Guthries; hence the invitation to winter there. The circus people rested up in peace and let their children go to school in Aughrim for a few months until spring when they would take to the road again for their all-Ireland tour. The house and grounds were busy with people coming and going, preparing meals, cleaning and exercising the animals. Mathew and Johnny Mulhall were allowed to do this for a small payment. For them, it was better than being in school.

Now it is Christmas 1961. Elizabeth is sixteen and home for the holidays. She makes her way down the road from Glenview House, past the bend by the river, on a mile towards the village, and turns in down the length of curving drive to Ballybeg House. Even though she is without her glasses, in the distance she sees coloured shapes moving among caravans, hears thin cries in the crisp cold, and smells the smoke of campfires. Her heart starts to pound. Her mouth is dry as she reaches the main house. Her feet bring her round the back to the tall outhouse where she hopes he will be. The elephant? Mattie Mulhall, of course.

She hears trumpeting and stops still in fright. The sound breaks across the fields, loud as African jazz, and rips the Wicklow hills apart. She laughs out loud. This is how she feels too, like shaking up the hills from their centuries' old sleep. The roars spur her on to the iron door of the elephant shed. She looks in and sees the mother elephant dip her trunk into a basin of muddy water and spray it out with the roar of her trumpet. There under her trunk holding a yard brush is Mattie Mulhall, covered in mud and cursing out loud.

'Blast you, you bloody animal, come here to me,' he cries as he tries to scrub her sides.

'Hello,' Elizabeth grins with amusement.

Mattie turns around, again caught by surprise, and lets out an expletive. 'What are you doing here?'

'I just came over to see the elephants. I thought about them all the time when I was up at school.'

'Did you now?' says Mattie. 'Ah would you hold your wisht now Nellie. Sorry eh, Elizabeth, isn't that right, give me a minute till I put this lady to bed, are ye right now, come on, come on, Missie, good girl.'

Elizabeth isn't quite sure what to do but feels bolder now that she is here, actually here with the elephants and Mattie. The air is dense with animal dung and rich fleshy hide.

'I'll wait outside so,' says she, feeling brave.

Mattie emerges eventually covered in mud.

'Jees but I'd say now there's a bit of a whiff off of me, so there is.'

'I don't mind,' she says simply.

'So you liked the circus that time did you?' he continues, steering her away down a muddy laneway. They reach a gate. He stops and pulls out a packet of Sweet Afton.

'Do you?' he queries, as he strikes a match.

'Oh no, no, thank you,' she rushes.

'So how did you get on over the Christmas?' says he.

'Grand, thanks.'

'And how are they all up at the Big House?'

He pauses on the last two words and she almost hears the ghost of a sneer.

'It's not that big,' she says, then realises for the first time in her life that that is how the Hawthorn Thwaites are seen down in the village, so she rushes on to say, 'but I'm not like that you know.'

'Like what?' he asks, teasing.

'You know, like my mother. She's a bit snobby,' she apologises.

'It's far from Glenview House and the Hawthorn Thwaites she was dragged up' says he.

'What do you mean?' asks Elizabeth.

'Sure everyone knows how great she was with me father Tommie before he went to England, so he says anyways.'

'I never heard that,' says Elizabeth, 'I only mean I'm not snobby, if that's what you think.'

'Oh no, now I didn't say that, you're different all right.'

Elizabeth blushes then, not knowing if he is teasing her or not. But she glows inside, and does feel different. Special even. For the first time.

'They'll be looking for me, the ponies is next for feeding.'

'Right-o,' says Elizabeth, suddenly feeling dismissed.

'Can I come and see the elephants again?' she asks, and goes even redder.

'You can,' says he and he cocks his head and winks, taking her arm momentarily to lead her back up the path. 'I'll see you so,' says he, as she goes.

She holds this exchange in her head to dream about at night, adding and subtracting looks that are meaningful, breaths that are whispered, until she's almost sick with excitement.

Elizabeth went back to the circus encampment the next day and the next to see Mattie. On the third day as she turned to speak his mouth was upon hers, bumping her nose, and his tongue was wiggling its way round her mouth. She found it wet and uncomfortable, a bit embarrassing really, but she allowed her tongue to explore back, just so she would know what Angela had been on about. By the end of the week she couldn't wait to get her lips all bruised and her mouth full of saliva. It felt like conquest. It must mean at last that she wasn't so bad-looking either. She felt good, a little bit loved, and so it wouldn't matter what her mother said.

'Those Mulhalls are no good, not our sort,' she'd say, if ever they were mentioned in Glenview House.

Back at school after the Christmas holidays it was her turn to boast to Catherine Clarke.

'I've met a boy,' she announced.

'Ooh, sweet sixteen and never been kissed,' sang Catherine.

'No I'm not, I mean, yes I have,' she reddened. 'It's quite nice really, once you get used to it. It's a bit sloppy at first.'

Elizabeth nursed all these scenes at the circus shed to herself until the following summer, by which time she was bursting to get home from school to see Mattie, who had assumed massive proportions in her head. She couldn't wait to be let go to the first social event of the summer, on the June bank holiday, in the function room of Byrne's Hotel. It was a farewell party from the circus to thank the townspeople for their hospitality. She was dying with anticipation. She had to drop it into conversation without making it obvious.

'What can I wear Mummy?'

'I'll buy you a new dress in Arklow,' said Gertrude, glad that Elizabeth was at last showing some interest in her appearance.

The night of the party Elizabeth walked in wearing a new velvet dress with a white collar. It was a deep scarlet, feminine at the waist with a little black belt, but tight and virginal at the collar. She looked like the overgrown schoolgirl she was. Her hair was brushed back into a hairband and curled at the bottom, kept in check for the moment. It was the new fashion of the time, like Jacqueline Bouvier Kennedy. It shone black against the deep red of her dress, setting off her pale skin. She had left off her glasses, which made her look both simple and vulnerable. She was ready to come out of her burrow.

The ballroom was crowded with brightly-coloured people, dressed in spangles and silver and feathers. Elizabeth shrank back against the wall to watch, and wait. The band played pop songs, all the latest ones from Buddy Holly and Cliff Richard. The older people tried to waltz and were awkward with the new rhythms, until some of the younger women from the circus, the acrobats and dancers, started to jive and twirl, laughing freely. Elizabeth felt uncomfortable. 'They're only showing off', she thought, feeling prim, disturbed by their exuberance, but not daring to join in.

Then there he was, Mattie, strutting in to the centre of the dance floor, wiggling his hips as he walked. She rose with a cry of greeting to go and meet him. He was carrying a drink and swerved when he saw her, as if to go the other way. But it was too late.

'Howye Elizabeth, home again are you?' he asked, before continuing on his way.

Elizabeth was rooted to the spot. Her greeting, and her heart, stuck in her throat, as she blinked in the coloured lights, mouthing disbelief. He didn't talk to her. She couldn't believe it. 'Mattie,' she had said clearly, and the wave of her feeling had risen out to meet him on a crest of hope and joy, to freeze there in mid-air, and turn and curl and flood all over her in icy trickles. She sat down by the wall, drowning in disappointment and embarrassment. She was such a fool. A silly little girl, a stupid stupid worm. Well, she had been right. This kind of life was pointless. Better to serve God and have visions and be assumed into heaven, than live with little peasant people like that. The music played on and the dancers danced, Gertrude and William among them, her mother laughing like a young girl and swirling with joy. She was revolting.

Elizabeth sat on the wooden bench and ate ice-pops. One, two, three, she sucked on the sweet orange sticks and rolled them round and round in her mouth. When each was finished she took the wrapper and tore it into little pieces, then rolled it into a ball and chewed it slowly before spitting it out on the floor in front of her. She sucked and rolled and bit and chewed and spat, disconnecting from the spectacle in front of her, the bodies and flesh and sweat and clamour, feeling supercilious, almost contemptuous. The mountain of little paper balls gathered round her feet, like her fantasies, grimy, dried up and squeezed tight. How silly people were, what a boring way to spend one's life, year after year, pathetic really, no point to it, she mused and frowned, her face curdled in a surly stupor like a large china doll whose mouth had been put on upside down.

She could see Mattie Mulhall in the other corner of the ballroom, leaning on the bar, a pint glass of beer in his hand, smoking and laughing with a woman from the circus. She had red hair and also smoked, a loose type. It was not done here in the village that a woman smoked and stood so provocatively, sticking her bosom into Mattie's face.

'Well let him put his tongue down her throat then, ugh, it makes me sick to think of it,' was what she said to his brother Johnny Mulhall when he came to sit beside her. He looked at her strangely and said, 'yeah I know what you mean.'

Johnny was wearing a suit, probably one of his father's because it was loose and the sleeves were too long. He looked as if he had had a bath.

'I'm getting a drink. Will you have one with me?' he asked.

She almost declined. What was the point in this whole charade? Then she said, 'an ice-pop please' and he laughed and said, 'if I'd wanted to get you an ice-pop I'd go to the seaside.'

'All right then, an orange. I've taken the pledge, not like your brother there,' she said petulantly as she looked over once more at Mattie. Yet she was somehow pleased. All right, it was only Johnny, but at least he came and talked to her.

'You're a headcase,' he said smiling.

They talked while the music played in the smoky hall. Elizabeth told him that night that the way people behaved like animals was disgusting, she didn't see what good anyone could do with their lives. She had found her vocation and was entering the convent next year when she was seventeen, and as for marriage, she found it utterly stupid.

The next day she put away the red velvet dress in its tissue paper and never wore it again, associating it in her mind with sin, although she hadn't done anything, not ever, not really, with Mattie, but maybe the intention had been there. It had all been a lesson from God about what happens when she wanted her own way, the way of the flesh, and not His way, not wanting to do His will. From then on she would wear only dark colours to please Him because life had no meaning when people behaved like animals. One could only watch and pray, do good for one's neighbour, have pure thoughts and one day die with the grace of a happy death.

Mattie never kissed her again. She was sick of feeling left out as he flirted with every new girl in town, tired of that old feeling of being a worm when he hardly noticed her. So it ended up at all the social events down the years that she and Johnny would be left alone together at the end of the night, and Johnny would walk her home. In this time, maybe about two years in all, she told Johnny about her life in boarding school, even admitting her devotion to St Teresa. When he didn't laugh, she warmed to him a little, and then some more. He in his turn talked about the sheep and his plans for the farm when his father died.

Johnny was the one who had kept the farm on the go all these last years when his father had taken off to England to find work on the buildings again. He had seen the sheep safe, been out on the hills for the lambing, and had treated their ringworm and fluke. He confessed to Elizabeth that he hoped Mattie would go off to England for himself and find another circus or something, because he had no interest in the sheep and it wouldn't be fair really if he wanted a say in running the farm. Of course he would be entitled to half of it one day, but wouldn't it be better if it was making a few shillings and then there'd be something to have half of? Johnny was cute, in the Irish way, and knew how to do a deal.

So finally, when there was no word from England and no sign of his father coming back, Johnny turned to Elizabeth. 'How about it?' he said.

She stared her opaque stare, which gave back nothing. 'I'll think about it,' she answered, and she did. She thought about getting out of Glenview house, thought about crossing her own threshold into her own kitchen and shutting the door, thought about slamming it in her mother's face and smiling on the other side. She didn't think about what might happen in the night between sheets, couldn't imagine wanting tiny squealing pink creatures, like pigs, that kept coming out after the swelling and the tiredness.

For now, she pictured Gertrude's face and took pleasure in it. Mattie's too. Wouldn't he be astonished? She didn't think ahead about how this momentary caprice, this vagary, would last and last into the future until she was captured by it, imprisoned in her own life. She sought Johnny out the very next Sunday and said yes, smiling up at him her rare and brilliant smile.

Catherine's Diary

1 March 1985

I have to get out of the house. It's terrible being in there, thinking they're all looking at me. They don't know nothing, but I keep thinking they do – or that Mammy does. I think she's looking at me from behind her glasses but if I look at her she's looking the other way. She was always like that, her eyes aren't crossed but you never know if she's looking at you straight. It's hard to tell behind her glasses they're that thick.

Daddy is going on and on tonight. The news came on at nine o'clock talking about the Kerry girl again. They're saying now she had two babies and that she killed the both of them, one on the beach and the other in the field. They're all getting at her now, turning against her. In the beginning there was great sympathy for her after what happened the schoolgirl who died having her baby in the grotto.

Sure I remember the first time I seen her on the telly she was talking about the pains coming, and having the baby in the barn, praying to Our Lady. In the morning it was dead. That's what she said the first time.

Now they're saying she had twins. She put one in the ditch and then drove the other one away in a car to the beach where she stabbed it. It was thirty miles away. Could she drive herself I was wondering?

Anyhow, she'd know if she had two babies wouldn't she? But they're saying the babies had two different types of blood. That means two different fathers.

That has them flummoxed, so the police are now saying, to explain it, that she must have done it with two different men on the same day, in the same hour even. How could she?

That's pretty disgusting to be on the news at nine o'clock with families watching.

Anyway, this came on the telly tonight, and Daddy starts on at your woman as if she could hear him.

'Good enough for ye,' says he, 'carrying on with a married man. Was the once not enough for you, when you got caught before? Second-hand goods is all ye are. Isn't that right Missus?' he sneers at the telly.

Danny and Liamey pull up closer to Daddy, all interest now.

'Them brothers there will have to keep her locked up before she disgraces them again. They'll never get over the shame. Doing that to her family. No daughter of mine is going to go round like a bicycle.'

'What's that Da?' says Danny, all wide eyes pretending, just so he'd say it.

'A ride Danny, a good ride, ridden by everyone.'

And they laughed at their men's jokes.

Mammy got up then and jumped around the kitchen, first the plug on the kettle, then the cooker, then down behind the counter to the socket at the door, then over to touch the plug on the television.

Daddy roared.

'Sit down woman, you're not a window, I can't see through ye.'

The lads burst out laughing again.

Mammy said, blessing herself, 'John, I won't have bad language in this house. No bad language, no bad language, no bad language,' she continued as she went the rounds: first the kettle, then the cooker, then down beside the door, then the television all over again.

'Ah wouldya get out of it,' said Daddy, and he threw his cushion at her. It hit Mammy on the side of her face and knocked off her glasses.

'No bad language, no bad language,' she kept saying, crawling round the floor feeling for the glasses.

The boys went quiet. John Paul got them for her. That's when I slipped out and said I was going feeding the lamb in the shed.

He's a terrible tease is Daddy. I hate it. 'Little fatso' he used to say when I was twelve. Piggy fatso. I'm scared he's going to turn round and call me that again. I have the old shirt on still and my hair down loose.

It's very quiet up here in the shed. The calves munch away, then one gives out a big snort through his nose. It's nice when they breathe like that. I'm trying to breathe slowly myself, like them. My heart is going so fast it's pumping, like I'm after running a long way up the hill. It's pumping and pumping and I'm sitting here holding onto the hay, trying to breathe. My face is wet from sweating. I want to stay here snug in the corner and not come out. Just me and the calves and the baby lamb. He's lying beside me. The lamb. He's getting a little bit better but he's still very weak. His mother didn't want him so I'm feeding him his bottle. We brought him out here because the kitchen was smelly after him. Daddy said mind that lamb, he's worth a few shillings. So I took him in here with me where it's warm.

I can't go back in. I can't look at Daddy anymore. He'll know. One day he'll look at me and he'll know. It'll be terrible.

My heart is jumping again.

He'll kill me. He really will. He'll strike me and then he'll throw me out. I can hear him. 'You'll not bring shame on this family. There was no Mulhall ever born a bastard.'

And if I don't go running he'll go for me with his gun. That'd be better, I wouldn't feel it then.

I have my miraculous medal in my hand. I rub it all the time. It's in the pocket of my jeans. I rub it and ask Our Lady to help me. I'm here sitting in tight to the wall trying to breathe normal, and I say to Our Lady, please please you are the mother of God. You know what it's like. You were in a hayshed too. Take me now. Take me to your Son. I committed one sin, it's a mortal one, and they won't forgive me. Ever. Take me tonight. Intercede to your Son for me. Please. I beg you. I've no one to turn to. You took that girl in Longford, and her baby too, the night they died in the grotto. I've no grotto, I'm in a hay shed. Have pity on me. Have mercy. Take me to you now. Take me. Take it all away.

The tears are pouring down my face, pouring out of me in rivers, and I'm crying out loud and sobbing so I don't care anymore, only crying and saying take me please, please, please, and bawling, my nose is streaming too. Bawling I am with my face down in the hay beside the lamb. I don't care. I don't care. Just take me.

I'm no good anyway to anyone. Just second-hand goods. No man will ever want me. I heard Daddy. That's what happens. That's what men think. Even Simon. That I'm second-hand goods. Soiled. He'll never touch me again.

Thinking of Simon makes me ten times worse. The pain squeezes me so hard when I think of how it used to be, when we were young. Me and him up the field. When I was a girl, and untouched. Now I'm filth. My soul will go to hell. Our Lady help me please. Please.

I curl into a ball and shut my eyes tight until the tears stop. There's a river running down the straw and onto the floor, a flood rising to drown me. The lamb is all wet with me crying all over him. He's gone all quiet too. I blow my nose. There's a buzzing in my head but my heart has stopped jumping. I touch the lamb. He's stone dead.

Liamey comes calling.

'Catherine where are you?

I blow my nose again and climb down the stack.

'The lamb's dead,' I say, and we go inside.

3 March

They think I'm upset about the lamb. Well, I am. Daddy's upset too. He's very cross. I had big red eyes on me for two days and Danny said, 'Jays you're awful soft Catherine, it's only a lamb.'

Mammy's very agitated. She'll go to Knock in County Mayo soon, please God, she'll never get to Lourdes to say her novenas. I'll ask her to bring me back some Holy water. Helen's supposed to be coming at the weekend. I don't want to talk to her.

Mammy is on her rounds again, hopping and jerking around the kitchen.

'Mammy, sit down,' I say, 'please, you'll make yourself sick.'

'Sick?' she said, turning on me.

'Mammy, please.'

'All right, you're a good girl Catherine. Good girl.'

Then she starts to cry. And cry. I can't stop her.

'Mammy, what is it?'

'What am I doing here Catherine? How did I have all those kids?'

'Ah Mam, come on now, take it easy I say. It'll be all right.'

'I was going to be a nun or, oh I don't know,' she bawls.

5 March

Mammy's not well at all. Jumping, fidgeting and crying. Quiet all day then talking to me at night. When they're all gone to bed. She gets me then. Always the old days.

'I ended up going back to school that September, oh I know I said I wouldn't, it was after the summer of the circus and all. But Angela

O'Donnell, the nice girl, well, she didn't come back. Then the whispers started. Catherine Clarke told me first. "In trouble", she said.'

'Did she not do her Leaving Cert in England to go to that big university?'

'No she didn't. Catherine Clarke whispered in my ear that she'd got into trouble and told me that nobody else knew and not to tell anybody.'

Mammy blew her nose.

'That's the way with secrets, Catherine. Everybody saying nobody knows and everybody does, everybody whispering behind their backs and never saying it out.'

My heart was hammering when Mammy said this about getting into trouble. I thought she might say something to me. I swallowed and tried to stay still, but my face was roasting. Oh God.

'Catherine, do you know what happened then?'

She was snivelling into an old hanky, blowing and wiping the tears.

'Angela did come back. After Christmas. I got used to her being gone, and had met your Uncle Mattie by then, and your father, so I suppose my mind was taken off her. Then one day she was at Assembly. I saw the red gold hair a mile away. I couldn't believe it, my heart leaped up with the joy.

'And then at the end of the prayers I saw her turn to say hello to the bigger girls. They all turned away, one after the other, not saying a word, just looking at her. She stood still with the shock in the hall as the girls left like a wave going out. Angela alone with her head high. Her mouth was tight, she was trying not to shake.

'Then it was our turn to file out, with Reverend Mother looking down from the podium. We were in a straight line. I could feel her eyes on me as I went past. They burned into my cheeks and they had red spots on them from it. I was hot with shame.'

Mammy gave a big hiccup. I couldn't look at her.

'I didn't look at Angela, I didn't say hello. I scurried past with my head down, burning up so red was my face. When the line went past, I glanced around like, pretending to fix my hair. She would break your heart. Her face crumbling, her mouth tight and trembling. But with all those girls watching, how could I step out of the line? How could I? Oh I cried too that night. Cried for Angela. Why did she have to go and get into trouble?'

Mammy stopped, blew her nose, and looked straight at me. Jesus, I thought, this is it. My face burned. But no, she went on.

'I never saw her again. That was the last time. Never told her that I ... that I was her friend.'

Mammy sat back in her chair holding the hanky to her face. Her eyes were blood red. No wonder she's agitated. You'd think she'd be getting over the Master's death by now but it's only bringing back memories. At least she didn't say anything to me.

7 March

Today Simon came in his car, and who was with him only Helen. They came down from Dublin.

'What were you doing in Dublin?' says Danny.

I'm glad he asked because I was afraid to. They were surely arranging things for me.

'Oh I'm on a training course,' says Helen.

'Where are you staying?' says Daddy.

'I'm in a friend's house,' says Helen.

'Who?' says Daddy, 'is her mother there? Why didn't I hear about it?'

'Because it only came up yesterday – and it's Mary Murphy's cousin's house,' says Helen, looking daggers at Danny in case he says anything. He looks daggers at her back for saying anything at all. He's doing a line with Mary Murphy and Daddy doesn't know.

So Simon came in and I couldn't even look at him. I'm so fat. And ugly. And my hair is greasy. I wasn't expecting them or I'd have washed it. Ever since Daddy said that about the Kerry girl I'm worried sick. He thinks I'm dirt, that's what men think, and he'll never love me again. I'm not eating anything since the lamb died. Mammy tried to comfort me.

'It's only a lamb Catherine, they have no souls. Don't be upsetting yourself.'

'Does a baby have a soul?' asks John Paul.

'Yes,' says Mammy, 'even the ones that aren't born. They're angels waiting for a womb.'

'What's a womb?' asks John Paul.

'Oh,' says Mammy fidgeting, 'you know, blessed art thou amongst women and blessed is the fruit of thy womb Jesus.'

'I thought that was, die wound Jesus, the sore he got from the soldiers that hurted him,' says John Paul.

Then Liamey and he had a pretend sword fight so that was that.

I said to Mammy, 'it's not the lamb, I'm on a diet.'

'Too right she is,' says Danny, 'she's a piggy, oink-oink.'

Jes I blushed so much I would've swung for him, the little rip. How dare he. Does he notice? I'll show them. I'll stop eating now and be skinny again in no time.

Then after Simon went out Daddy started on his teasing.

'Little Mister Your Honour Sir. They should've called him James William Junior. He's just like his father. William then wee Jimmy James William, then Simon, they're all of a breed. I wonder was the Major called William too? Mammy, do you know?'

She couldn't remember.

Before Helen went off out in the car with Simon, she kept staring at me to come too, but I said 'no, I'm grand, I won't thanks.'

That's when Danny said again.

'Catherine's on a diet, she needs it doesn't she?'

I nearly vomited. Helen shut him up.

'I was going to ask you to come too, but I see you're still too infantile.'

As soon as the car turned in the yard Daddy said, 'did you hear that Mammy did you? Did you know Helen was above in Dublin?'

Then he started going on about what kind of flat Simon must have.

'Probably lives in Rathmines in one of them bedsits, or what am I saying, sure wouldn't he have an apartment, maybe Jimmy can rise to that with all his friends in the Four Courts.'

I don't know why he takes it out on Simon. Simon never done anything to him.

'He'll go away again now off up to kingdom come and we won't see the road for dust. What does he want with Helen, the poor relation?' says Daddy.

It's not Helen, I wanted to scream, it's me.

I found myself out in the shed again. With all the talk about Simon I was mithered. They're confusing me. I have to get away. Maybe I should've gone with them. 'Off up to see Granny Gertrude,' Helen shouted in the door as she left. Maybe he didn't hear. But it gave Mammy a shock. She did her rounds of the kitchen, fidgeting and tight in the face.

'Old Granny Gargoyle,' muttered Danny.

I have to get away. Have to. It doesn't matter where.

I'm sitting in my nest of hay in the shed when I see the can. It's in the corner with Valbazon All Purpose Wormer for Cows and Sheep written on it. That'll do, I says. I drink it all.

I'm lying halfway out of the shed, my face on the ground in a pool of sick. I feel like dirt, I'm a lump of vomit. Smelling horrible. It was all over me too. Helen finds me.

'Jaysus Catherine, what happened?' she says. 'Simon, come here and help.'

'No,' I groan trying to sit up, but he comes anyway.

'What's wrong?' he holds my head up.

'I feel sick.'

I puke again, over his shoe.

'Look what she's after doing,' says Helen, showing him the can.

'Christ did she ...?'

'Yes. She did. Should we get her stomach pumped?'

'Are you starkers? No, get her to drink loads of water, that'll fix her.'

You'd think he'd have given me more Valbazon, or Leo Yellow. That'd solve the problem for both of us. Wouldn't it Simon? The whole lot of us.

Anyway they drag me into the house. Lucky Daddy was gone out for his pint by then. Helen holds me over the toilet then puts me into bed with a basin. My stomach heaves and retches for the whole night. I don't mind. I want it to bring the other thing out.

I hear Mammy say to Helen, 'she's off her food lately, very upset since the lamb died.'

I better be careful. They told Daddy I had food poisoning. I stayed in bed for two days feeling a rumbling and a heaving like an earthquake in my belly. Besides a lot of wind, nothing else came out. I am so fed up. I have to get away.

12 March

They were gone for the day. Daddy brought Mammy off to Arklow in the car for her check-up and to get more tablets.

The kids were gone on the bus since half-eight. I took a sardine sandwich and milk with me that I made for their lunches. Nobody took any notice they were all so busy getting out in the rush. I had a notion I might go the back road to Moyne and on into Knockananna, to catch the bus for Dublin at half-two. I had plenty of time. I went up the field along the path to the wood. I saw some footprints from the deer. Then I heard a rustling in the woods in the old leaves. I stopped to watch. There were baby foxes playing, maybe four or five. They were tumbling and teasing each other rolling over and pretending to bite. One of them looked up and saw me. He froze for a second then took off like the clappers, letting out a squeal then a bark like a cough. They all followed him leaping over the leaves and dead branches, scooting off with their tails in the air.

I thought, don't go little foxes, it's only me, I won't hurt you, please come back. They were lovely playing there, like children. I wouldn't hurt a fly. I felt lonely after them. The forest was quiet, just the wind in the trees, sighing like the sea. I pulled my hood up against the wind and went on. At least I'd washed my hair and tied it back. It was great to be out walking up there as if I was free, with no family or anything. Just me and my legs walking. I had a bag with my sandwich in it and my purse. Only a few pounds in it. It felt good. High up on the track where the forest gets thin again I stopped and sat on a flat rock. I could see our house down below along the road that cuts the valley in two. There was no smoke. Across the way were the fields and lands belonging to Glenview, but the house itself was hidden on the side of the hill among the trees. Further up to my right was the old schoolhouse and high up above that again the avalanche mountain loomed dark and craggy. Down its side hidden in fir trees was the little hut.

From up here everything looked so small. Sometimes you'd wonder what all the fuss and worry and fighting is for.

I had to come down and cross below the schoolhouse before I'd go up the big hill towards Knockananna. By the time I got that far I was all out of breath. The wind had come up and the rain started pelting down so I had to run the last bit to the hut.

It was great to be in out of the rain, in shelter. It was very cosy in there, suddenly quiet with the rain beating outside. There were some log cuttings in the chimney so I lit a fire. I sat on the stone and folded my arms around myself.

I'm going to be a new slim Catherine, I said. They won't know me when I come back. But because it was raining so hard I said I'd stay put and get the bus to Dublin the next day. Wouldn't it be great to have my own little house I was thinking, where nobody'd be at me or giving out. I ate my sardine sandwich with a bottle of milk. It got dark quickly because of the clouds. The wind was cold under the door. It's hanging off anyway and the windows are all broken. Always were. Nobody seems to own the place or go near it. My feet got cold as my shoes were letting in water from running through puddles to get inside fast. Then my sandwich got stuck in my chest. It wouldn't go up or down. It was very sore. I ran out of Rennies. I thought I might go back before I'd be missed but then I thought of Daddy roaring and Mammy crying and so I thought what's the point.

I shut my eyes and thought about sunshine to try to keep warm.

Behind them was all red like in a film and I could see Simon. His big brown eyes and the way he looks just before he smiles when he's listening to you, and then he pushes back the lock of hair that's always in his eyes.

Oh God. I was wishing he'd just come knocking on the door, and I'd open it, and he'd look at me and open his arms wide and I'd run into them. And then we would melt and it would be all dark and swirling like the stars at night. But he probably wouldn't come running with his arms open. No, he'd just stand there and smile, and I'd get all shy and he'd have to do the talking. And I would feel so stupid trying to think of things to say, so I wouldn't talk at all. Or I would talk too much.

Like in the summer after the show. I just let him take my hand, it was the most natural thing in the world, and went with him down to the river. I showed him my favourite tree, the oak tree growing out over the water with its arms waving.

It waved down at the water trembling and shivering, and the water shimmered and tinkled rushing past saying hello, with the tree dancing in it. I said this to Simon and he didn't think it was stupid. He looked at me like we were the best of friends, like the time when we were seven and eight and used to play chase in the woods, or go down there on adventures.

But last summer he looked at me with those big eyes and I nearly fainted. I had a rush to the head.

So I turned away and kept on talking about the time he came after his Confirmation to visit us. I said, 'remember that Simon? And you with a good white jumper on you, and Aunty Linda fussing all over you and telling you not to get it dirty, and we went off to see the calves? It was strange that you stayed for your tea, just you and Aunty Linda, because we never normally saw you or Uncle Jimmy in our house. We only ever saw you at Christmas up at Master Cullen's house, or maybe

Easter. Mammy didn't mind Aunty Linda coming but she didn't talk to her own brother. Do you remember that Simon? Do you remember?'

He said, 'I do, Kitty, come here to me,' and he put his arm around me and gave me a hug. It felt so warm and I filled up I was so happy, just standing there, me and Simon looking at the river with the tree waving into it.

Then I said, 'do you remember Simon, the time you saved me from Mossie Dollard?'

'What was that?' he said, 'to tell you the truth I don't. What did I do?'

And his eyes were full of laughing.

'Oh,' I said, 'it was so embarrassing. I was mortified the way he was looking at me, like an old dog after a bitch in heat.'

'Kitty, that's a long time ago,' he said, 'you're a great one for yapping.'

'Oh, sorry,' says I. 'Am I talking too much?'

'Yes you are,' he said, and pulled me into his arms, with my head tight against him.

'But do you really not remember? My dress was so tight and my boobs were ...'

'Shush,' he said, and threw his cigarette butt into the river, catching my hand and pulling me down beside him on the grass.

'Show me those big breasts so,' he said in a real stern voice messing. He put his hand out and ran it very gently all over my chest. Oh my God it was gorgeous. Then we were kissing.

I can't think about it any more or I'll explode. It's all swimming behind my eyes. The tree river dance, wet earth in my nose, green smell of him.

Why can't he come?

I did, I imagined it all. Everything. I must have. He's right. I couldn't be pregnant. How? When I get to Dublin I'll be a new slim Catherine Mulhall.

I heard a tractor early the next morning. I was frozen stiff from the cold. It was Daddy. I got such a shock that I ran to the chimney and sat down in the corner hiding in my coat. He came in the door.

'Catherine, we were worried sick. What possessed you? Come on home now, good girl.'

His voice was the same that he uses for the calves.

'You'll catch cold. Your Mammy didn't sleep a wink all night.'

I couldn't say anything from the fright. So I didn't.

As we chugged along he said, 'we'll see about getting you a job, get you out of the house.'

'All right Daddy,' I said with my head down under my hair. I can't look at him anymore.

That's how they all agreed in the end that I should go and mind Granny.

15 March

There was a bit of a fight before I left.

Helen arrived down for the Saint Patrick's weekend. She had a few days off. There was a grand stretch in the evenings so she asked me to come for a walk with her. She was bubbling with excitement.

'I've a new boyfriend,' she said, 'but it's only in the early stages so I'm not telling anyone, no, not even you Kitty.'

I couldn't have cared less.

'Is Simon coming this weekend?' I asked, and she said he was, running and skipping ahead. She shouted back.

'Catherine, you've really got awful big.'

'I have not, what are you talking about?'

'Stop letting on, Kitty, I'm amazed no one has said anything to you. I think it's all organised, you're going to Granny's this weekend, on Sunday.'

'I'm going nowhere,' I said, 'and there's nothing wrong with me.'

I went into a sulk and didn't talk to her again, not until I had to, when Simon came.

We were having our dinner, chicken as it was Sunday, and they were all sitting there waiting for their ice cream and jelly while I cleared the table. We heard a car, and John Paul ran out all excited.

'How'ye Simon,' says he, like an old lad, 'come in and have a cup of tea for yourself.'

Simon comes in all dressed up in a tweed coat with leather gloves on him. If you didn't know him you'd swear he was city born and bred. He even talks like them ones on the news.

'Well,' he said, after the ice cream, 'are you lads going for a walk, or would you like to come for a spin?'

'Yippee,' said Liamey and John Paul, so in all the kerfuffle I went out to the shed and sat in my corner. Simon had to bring them all for a spin then. They skidded off out the gate. Daddy was inside watching the match and I left Helen to do the dishes.

Sometimes I hate him, Simon I mean. Then I want them all to disappear so I can just talk to him. I imagine if he came in and sat beside me. What I wouldn't give to have his arms around me, and to be lying beside him even on the hay. Just for him to look at me with those brown eyes like a spaniel. I'd melt then and do anything he says. Even this. What's going on now? Because now he comes quite often where he never came before. He seems to be a bit on our side now. One thing is sure, Granny Gertrude always loved him the best, obviously, because he's Jimmy's only child, and Jimmy was definitely her favourite, you could always tell, even if they hadn't all fallen out.

Maybe it was ten minutes or only five but I didn't hear them coming. So I'm sitting there dillydallying and I hear a cough, then a match being struck.

I jump up to slide down my haystack when I see Helen. My face drops. Simon is beside her with a lighter in his hand. He's about to light his cigarette after hers.

'Oh, there you are,' says Helen.

Simon said, 'hiya Kitty,' real nice like, and then says to Helen, 'would you mind if I talk to Catherine alone?'

I got a great kick out of that, Helen's face as she went in muttering. I was thrilled. He came to see me. I wanted to say nyah nyah nyah to her like when we were kids and she got everything first before me. I stood there smiling, with nothing to say, except something really stupid like, 'I'm afraid there's no calves today, they're up the field as the weather's so nice.'

He took my arm. 'That's OK. Is there anywhere we can talk?'

I lead him into my nest.

'You better not smoke in here, because of the hay.'

'OK. Catherine, I've talked to Grandmother, and she thinks it's a good idea.'

'What did you tell her?'

'Oh, don't worry, not that. I just said you wanted to get out of the house for a while and that you were in between jobs, and so you'd like to help her out with a bit of housework and chopping logs and things, you know.'

'Are you sure you didn't say anything else?' I said, looking him in the eye, 'because there isn't, you know Simon. I'm going to Dublin and I'll be slim soon, you won't recognise me.'

'Sure, Catherine, when it's all over. By the way I've made some arrangements.'

'Whatever they are I hope you've got me a flat, because I'm not going back home.'

'Er, yeah ...'

He really doesn't have a clue what I'm on about. He doesn't know what to say but I do.

'Don't worry,' I said. 'You were right about the other thing. I'm not.'

'You're not? But ... but, look at you.'

'Oh, that's just a bit of puppy fat I put on over the winter. I'll be slim for you in Dublin, I promise.'

'Catherine, this is serious. I'll help you all I can. First though you'll go to Grandmother's, won't you?'

'For what,' says I, 'why wait?'

Those brown eyes look at me for a minute. I have him, maybe. But he slithers out.

'Well it's like this. I went to talk to her and she's expecting you now. She'd be disappointed. She's looking forward to it.'

'Don't be cracked, that woman isn't interested in anyone but herself.'

I was bucking. They think I'm stupid. I know they want rid of me.

'That was what Mammy always said when she opened her mouth about Granny Gertrude.'

I had my lip sticking out. Screw him.

'Catherine, you can't stay here.' He's panicking. He takes my arm. I relent.

'You're right. Daddy's been watching me like a hawk since I went to the hut.'

'Yeah, Helen told me. That was dangerous you know, anything could have happened to you.'

He sounds truly concerned. His voice does it for me.

'I'm not afraid of ghosts or anything.'

'That's not what I mean. You've two months left by the looks of you.'

'Two months? I'm not staying two months with her.'

Simon took me in his arms then.

'I'm concerned about you.'

Well it wasn't exactly in his arms, but his two arms were out and holding on to mine, and he was looking very hard into my eyes.

'Catherine, trust me. We're friends aren't we? Friends, for always. Just do what I say now. It'll all be over soon. Grandmother is not the worst. I'll be there every weekend to visit. The time will go quickly, and then it'll be the summer.'

My eyes light up. I nearly burst.

'And I'll bring you to Dublin,' he says shushing me, to get away, because I nearly kiss him.

Well I am in heaven. Simon with me in my hay barn, in my arms, sort of. Making promises. I am nearly the happiest girl on earth. Nearly. We still had to tell Mammy and Daddy. 'For always,' he'd said. I'm mad about him.

Daddy went ballistic.

'A skivvy for her? Catherine may not be working at the minute but she has no need to go skivvying for her ladyship. Has she not enough to be doing here if it's more work she wants?'

'Daddy, it's only for a while,' said Helen. 'Granny needs someone, she's on her own, and she fell the other day. She could've broken her hip and would have been left there in the hall to die.'

Daddy muttered something. Mammy perked up suddenly with a glint in her eye.

'Good enough for her. I must get up there myself soon, see what state the house is in, when I'm feeling better. Catherine can keep a good eye on her in the meantime and tell us if she's up to anything.'

I was amazed Mammy said all those words. I think we all got a shock. Even Daddy stopped his ranting.

'Well, who's going to get me breakfast?' he said, grumpy like.

'I'll do it,' said Helen.

'You're never here, always off gallivanting,' he said.

'On the weekends,' said Helen.

You could see he was pleased.

So suddenly, somehow, I was in the back of Simon's car, jammed in beside Helen, with Mammy and Daddy and Danny and Liamey and John Paul waving at me, as if I was going on my holidays. Simon was talking all the time.

'Phew, that was close. You were great Helen.'

'I thought Daddy would freak out,' she giggled.

'No you stopped him, he has a soft spot for you all the same.'

And for me, I wanted to say, but then I remembered Simon's words. Always. So I was warm inside, because Helen doesn't know what we have, our secret.

Granny was out on the step. She was expecting us. 'Come in, come in,' she commanded, 'I'll make the tea.'

So we went in and it was like a visit on a Sunday afternoon to see an ordinary granny in an ordinary house, who has an ordinary family. I even began to feel we were ordinary, normal I mean. And then they left for Dublin.

I stayed. Granny showed me to my room. It used to be hers as a little girl, the box room over the hall at the top of the stairs.

'The toilet is down the landing, and here are some clean towels.'

I might have been staying in the best hotel in Dublin the way she was going on. What had Simon said to her?

Gertrude, 1961

For several weeks William came home when he chose, often far too late for dinner, and once or twice he didn't come at all. Gertrude stopped asking, feeling she had no right to do so; the pot calling the kettle black or something. He often reeked of alcohol but fortunately he was a pleasant drunk, incoherent but not aggressive. She would put him to bed and listen to his thunderous snores, lying awake beside him with only guilt lying heavily on her soul. For it was her fault, and this was her penance. During the days she would walk for hours on end, wide-eyed in a state of permanent alert, her mouth dry and she stiff with a tense waiting, for what she didn't know. Her roaming took her farther and farther away from Glenview, until one day she found herself well down the valley and out along the road to the woods, where one time long ago she had propelled herself in a transcendent trance late on a November night.

She was drawn by an unconscious curiosity, more perhaps, a need to connect, to the blacksmith's stone cottage with a thatched roof nestling under some large pine trees. It looked deserted. An old lace curtain hung askew in the grimy window set deep in the stone. Then she saw smoke rising up out of the chimney and curling into the overhanging pine branches. She almost panicked and rushed away, as if she'd been caught intruding. Her feet brought her quickly back to the corner by the creamery, and into the safety of the shop.

As she was buying the bread in Murphy's, she heard tell that old Mrs Mulhall wasn't well. Tommie had broken her heart leaving like that and she never recovered. Word had it that her daughter-in-law, Frances, had moved in to look after her, for she really wasn't able herself anymore. Gertrude perked up at the news. She had met Frances as a child, once or twice, but then her whole family had left for England. That's where she was nursing when Tommie met her, although Gertrude only heard this a long time after they married.

Maybe she would know her now, and maybe they could talk as women.

The next day while she was out on one of her marathon walks she slowed down a bit to look for berries and wild flowers to pick, not that there was much growing so late in the year. There was smoke curling out of the chimney right enough, and she could see a head moving back and forth through the window, but she couldn't be sure and she couldn't hang about and stare for too long either. What it was she was looking for she wasn't sure, it was something else, some primitive need for contact. She told herself that she might be useful to Frances, who wouldn't have a lot of money, might have trouble making ends meet. Yes, that was it, she could help her out, give her some of Jimmy's old clothes maybe, for her boys, if her pride wouldn't be offended.

So on yet another day she went out with a basket of buns, little tea scones she had baked herself. She set off with a sense of mission, until she reached the turn off to the woods. There she hesitated, feeling stupid, and certainly overdressed. Her boots seemed too highly polished for a muddy track.

Suddenly there was a rustle of leaves. Gertrude looked around to see two little boys come charging through the undergrowth, cracking twigs underfoot and crashing their way through a maze of brambles.

'Hey wait for me, I'm a Cheyenne.'

'No you're not, you're an Apache.'

The one in front stopped short when he saw her. The other one ducked and ran for cover. Gertrude flushed too, confused about the next move.

'Hello,' she said, 'are you playing cowboys and Indians?'

She sounded ridiculously posh, like a schoolteacher.

The boy just stared at her as if he didn't speak her language. And then Gertrude blushed some more, because staring back at her out of the child's face were two blue eyes, the same unmistakeable cornflower blue of Tommie Mulhall's eyes.

'What's your name?' she asked. But she knew.

The boy raised his eyes and then dipped them again quickly to mutter, 'Mathew Mulhall.'

'Mulhall,' she said. 'So you live over there in the cottage?'

'No we don't,' he said, 'we only came to mind our granny.'

'Mattie, oh Mattie, come on,' shrilled a boy's reedy voice.

'That's me brother Johnny,' he said, and made to run off.

'Wait a minute,' Gertrude called after him, 'would you like a bun?'

Mathew peered into the basket and like a flash reached in a hand that grabbed a bun and stuffed it into his mouth all in one go.

'You may have another,' Gertrude smiled. 'Would your brother like some?'

'I'll give him one so,' said the boy, grabbing two more, as he ran off.

Gertrude followed him on the dirt track to the cottage.

'Is your mother at home?' she called after him.

'Yep,' he tossed back over his shoulder.

Her step was surer now, and she was smiling as she reached the gate.

There was a chill in the air, the kind that insinuates itself into bones and gnaws and niggles there in the flat dead light of December. A woman was outside the cottage, gathering clods of turf from a pile and placing them in a bucket. She was tiny, very frail and thin. Her dress was a faded light cotton over which was a dark blue apron. It's a wonder she doesn't freeze to death, thought Gertrude. Must be old Mrs Mulhall, Tommie's mother. Then the figure turned, and the face was young. A thin once-pretty face, now worn with worry. It was Frances, Tommie's wife.

She started as she saw Gertrude, made to go into the house, then stopped, as recognition dawned slowly.

'Gertrude, is it yourself? I haven't seen you in years.' Her face warmed in welcome, her eyes creasing into a smile. 'Come in, come in, what brings you into this neck of the woods?'

'Oh, no I won't thanks, I was just passing. I was visiting a cousin of William's,' she lied.

'Who's that?' asked Frances, the way country people do, curious to know who's about, and if anybody is ill or dead.

'Ah you wouldn't know him,' said Gertrude quickly, sorry she had lied so readily.

'Here, have these, he wasn't there,' she said, pulling the tea towel full of buns out of the basket and pushing them into the woman's hands.

'So you're back home, are you?' she persevered.

'We are,' said Frances, 'sure his Mammy isn't well at all.' Her face dropped as she lowered her voice. 'She hasn't got long left, God love her.'

'Oh Frances, I'm sorry.'

'It's the Lord's way,' said the woman, brushing back a stray hair from her forehead. Her hair was grey and thin. Her nose jutted out in resolve.

'But I'm keeping her here, they won't take her into hospital. It's all we can do.'

Gertrude watched her eyes flare, and felt ashamed. What were her problems compared to illness and impending death, not to mention the woman's children and an absent husband?

'Will you not come in?'

'No, no, I've to get back to do the dinner,' she smiled. 'I was just passing.'

'You've a long way to go.'

'No no, it's not so bad, I like walking, sure it's good for me,' she smiled, feeling her joviality forced and out of place. They heard crashing in the trees again. Frances turned.

'Mattie, Johnnie, your tea's up, come in now,' she called.

'Them fellas,' she smiled fondly, 'they'll have me worn out.' But it was obvious she was full of love for them.

A hot flash of jealousy passed through Gertrude.

'It there's anything I can do to help?' she ventured hesitantly as she left. The words fell lamely into the limp light of the failing day. What could she do? What could anyone do? Except, like Frances, endure. Endure and go on. What else was there?

Of Tommie she dared not ask. Nor was there mention of his coming home to help out. It was always left to the women, she thought, suddenly angry as she hurried along the road home; angry at Frances, at Tommie, at whom?

Gertrude took to her bicycle and made her excursions almost daily down the valley to the woods. She didn't always stop, but would look in fondly as she passed, as if connecting in this way with another life, one that was so different to her own. One day, Jimmy, who was on a day off school, insisted on coming with her. He mounted William's old High Nellie, which was far too big for him, and pedalled off beside his mother.

'Giddy up Jimmy,' she cried as she pedalled furiously down the hillside. She felt as young and invigorated as if she were sixteen again.

Down the hill, around the bend by the river, on down past all the hedgerows and overhanging trees, over the bridge, past Murphy's shop, on and on into the village and out the other side heading towards the woods.

'Hey, wait for me,' yelled Jimmy, his breath catching on the wind. He arrived beside her, puffing heavily with cheeks on fire.

'Mum, did you have to go so fast? Are you training for the Olympics or what?'

She laughed, her face flushed with the effort. 'It'll keep your old mother fit. Aren't you lucky I'm still able?'

'Mum,' he protested, 'you're the youngest mother I've ever seen, not like most people's, they're old and fat.'

'Come on, let's walk for a bit.'

Jimmy let the bicycle drop to the ground and followed her along the track. A sound of laughter and children's high voices shrilled among the trees.

'What's that?' said Jimmy.

'A family lives here in the old cottage,' she explained, as the track opened out to reveal the house with smoke curling from its chimney. Some children ran outside, playing tig.

'Who are they, Mum?' he asked.

'They're the Mulhalls, I think,' she let on.

'Oh, them. They're new boys in my class, two of them. Always in trouble.'

'Do you want to call in?'

'No thanks.' He turned to go.

As they crunched their way on into the wood, Frances appeared at the door with a basin in her hand.

'Hello,' she called, and walked over to the fence in greeting.

'Hello Frances. How are things? This is James William.'

'Hello,' she said, 'you'd be our Mattie's age, wouldn't you? Come on in Gertrude, you'll have a cup of tea.'

Gertrude hesitated as she glimpsed Jimmy's stricken face.

'It's all right thanks,' she said.

'No no, you will, please,' Frances insisted.

Gertrude relented out of curiosity and followed Frances into the cottage.

'I'll wait out here Mum,' called Jimmy, hanging back by the gate.

'It was nice of you to call,' said Frances warmly as she filled a black pot with water from a barrel by the door. She pulled out a wooden stool from under the table and pushed it towards Gertrude, who sat gingerly as her eyes adjusted to the dark place. The kitchen, which was also the living room and everything else, was a small square, lit only by one window set deep in the stone wall. On the gable end was a chimney-breast with an open fire. Blackened fire irons still hung over the coals for cooking. There was also a two-ring gas cooker set on a block. There didn't seem to be any evidence of food in the house. Off this room was another, the bedroom Gertrude supposed. A makeshift wooden ladder led up to a loft, where most of the children would sleep.

Frances sat down and pulled a packet of cigarettes out of her apron pocket.

'It's nice to get a break for a chat,' she said. 'Thanks for coming.'

'Not at all, we were out for a cycle,' smiled Gertrude.

Frances' eyes sparkled when she smiled. Although her face was lined and thin, her voice rang with the lilting tones of south Wicklow. Gertrude flooded with warmth and pity for her, and at the same time she felt welcome and at home.

'How's your mother-in-law?' she continued.

'Ah, Mam? She's gone very weak, not well at all, not at all.' She pulled on her cigarette. 'I'll have to send word to Tommie and the others soon.'

Gertrude blushed bright red as if she had been caught doing something wrong, something a little embarrassing and inappropriate. What was she really doing here after all? Wasn't it for an opportunity just such as this?

'Oh,' she said, swallowing, 'and how's Tommie?' She hoped she sounded neutral, but concerned.

'Tommie's grand, doing well. Builds houses now,' she said. 'But it's still a struggle. That's why I said I'd come home to help his Mam.'

A silence followed. Gertrude sensed Frances was sensitive enough not to give too many details.

'So, he builds houses. That's hard work,' she offered.

'Work? That's nothing,' said Frances with a wave of her hand indicating her domain. She stubbed out her cigarette. 'Keeps him out of trouble,' she smiled.

Gertrude flushed red, with a kind of excited relief swarming through her. Tommie was still alive, at least.

'Frankie,' came a voice from the inner room. 'Frankie, who is it? Who's there?'

'What is it Mam?' Frances rose wearily to answer the call.

Gertrude heard mutterings from within, then Frances reappeared.

'Would you like to see her?' she asked, her eyes open and vulnerable, begging her to say yes.

'Oh, I wouldn't like to intrude.'

'Send her in,' came the voice.

Gertrude pushed open the door, to see a very old woman lying under a pink candlewick bedspread. Her nose was assailed by a strong smell of urine. She approached the bed, and with a smile extended her hand.

'Is that the Cullen girl?' said the old woman, screwing up her eyes, which peered through a milky haze into the gloom of the room.

'Yes, it is. Gertrude's my name.'

'Ah yes,' the voice trilled as she raised her head to peer more. 'Gertrude Cullen, the Master's daughter from Moyne. Is it yourself after all these years?'

Frances started and looked quizzically at Gertrude.

'Yes, yes, I remember, you were never in this house, but I used to see you out and about with Tommie, up the back there in the woods, chasing and playing.'

'Did you?' said Gertrude smiling. 'That was a long time ago so.' She patted Mrs Mulhall's hand.

'Ah yes,' said the old woman, grabbing Gertrude's hand to pull her closer until she could almost feel the papery skin against her own.

'Tommie was sweet on you, wasn't he, the poor lad. He shouldn't have left. He was very sensitive. I used worry about him but he's doing well for himself now.'

'And doesn't bother coming home much, the same Tommie,' interjected Frances, a little sharply.

'Ah well, sure he's busy. He'll be back to bury me,' she chuckled, and fell back on the bed with a smile on her face.

Gertrude looked at Frances shocked.

'Now now Mam, enough of that talk, there's no need for that.'

'You'll carry me out of here in a box, don't I know it,' the old lady smiled through closed eyelids. 'Sure that's all right, I'm praying the Lord will take me soon.' She opened one eye. 'God bless now,' she said to Gertrude, 'and thanks for calling.'

Gertrude bowed and murmured her goodbyes as she left.

She was glad to emerge into the open air outside the cottage and inhaled gratefully. 'Oh, I hope I didn't intrude.' She took Frances' arm. 'If there's anything I can do ... Jimmy, oh Jimmy,' she called, walking out the gate, 'we're going.'

Jimmy came running down the track and stopped breathless in front of her. His face was muddied and his jumper was torn at the collar.

'Those Mulhalls, they're right little brats, they took my bicycle and I had to chase them into the woods to get it back. They're terrible, I hate them and I'm not coming here anymore.'

The Mulhall boys appeared then, sauntering along the track. They pushed the old bicycle.

'Did you find your Nellie?' Mattie sneered, propelling the bike towards them.

Johnnie snorted and clapped his hands.

'Go home with your Mammy, Mammy's boy,' they jeered, as the bike tottered and crashed onto the path in a twisted heap. They turned and ran back into the woods.

'Mathew! John!' shouted Frances after them, turning to Gertrude in an agony of embarrassment.

'It's all right, it's fine, no harm done,' said Gertrude, gathering her bicycle and retrieving Jimmy's bike. 'Come on Jimmy, saddle up for home.'

She tried to be jovial as they cycled what seemed like endless miles up the hill for home. Jimmy complained a lot and she ran out of comforting things to say to egg him along, cajole him home. She cycled at first with a heady elation coursing through her veins. So Tommie married, and these are his sons, the image of him. Then she fell silent with a confusion of thoughts and memories crowding her brain. What on earth was she thinking of, bringing Jimmy to a place like that? She had no self-respect. As for old Mrs Mulhall, 'sweet on you', she really didn't need to hear that. Blast Tommie Mulhall anyway, blast him to hell. She pedalled determinedly pushing downwards hard on the pedals to blot out an image of long striding legs covered in brown serge, and a pair of tight buttocks.

'That's a smelly old place, I don't want to go there again,' announced Jimmy as he helped himself to more potatoes.

'Where's that son?' asked William, who was sitting in his usual seat near the range, having come home at the normal time.

'Ask Mum, she knows,' he said.

Gertrude flushed. She was lifting a pot of turnips to drain and so continued her actions at the sink in a cloud of steam. 'Oh you know the old cottage out the far side of town, on the road to Coolattin.'

'No, can't say I do.'

'Well we went out on the bikes today, that's all.'

'Yeah, and we met the Mulhalls, I hate them.'

'Tell Dad what happened his bicycle,' she interjected.

'What's that son?' William got up to join them at the table. 'What's going on?'

'Dad, I got up on your bike and Mummy went flying down the hill all the way through the village, and then we stopped at this house and Mum went in and I stayed outside.'

William looked at Gertrude questioningly.

'The old Mulhall place,' she explained, nodding for Jimmy to continue, not looking directly at William.

'Yeah, so these boys came along, they used to be in my class, and they tried to take your bike, so I held on to it, but they pushed and shoved so I had to let go, and then they ran off into the woods with it.'

William looked at Gertrude again. 'And where were you when this was going on?'

'She was having a cup of tea,' Jimmy accused.

'Is that right?' William stopped eating. 'Let me get this straight. You were in the Mulhall cottage while our son was being attacked by some gurriers.'

'They're the Mulhall boys, Frances Mulhall's kids.' She was flustered now, all this detail was unnecessary.

Her son rushed on. 'They're smelly brats, they really are, they started shoving me for no reason, but your bike was all right, really Daddy, I could ride it home again.'

'Show me your face son.'

Jimmy turned his face to show his father a graze on the side of his cheek.

'For God's sake Gertrude, can you not take more care.' William was angry. He got up, pushing his plate back and left the room.

'Keep your hair on, Will my boy,' shouted the Major after him.

Matilda made her usual attempt at smoothing things over. 'No harm done, only a slight graze, it will heal by the morning,' she chirped.

Gertrude remain seated and pushed a piece of turnip round her plate. Her cheeks burned. She felt she had been found out, doing something out of bounds, against the unwritten rules.

'Who are you talking about anyway,' persisted Matilda sweetly. 'A new neighbour?'

'No, an old family friend,' said Gertrude quietly. She swallowed. All this fuss about nothing; a cup of tea with a neighbour, an old family friend. Was she? Was Frances Mulhall, Tommie Mulhall's wife, an old family friend? She got up and tipped the remains of her dinner into the scraps. Such interrogation- was she to be a prisoner as well? As she busied herself with the after-dinner clear up, her heart rate calmed and she realised she was perhaps making too much of it. She was out for a cycle, it was a chance encounter, that's all. Needn't be mentioned again. She would cycle in the other direction next time. She knew all she needed to know. As if it helped anything.

So Gertrude resumed her afternoon walks but didn't always go so far down the valley. One day she bumped into Frances in Murphy's shop.

'Hello Gertrude,' said Frances warmly. 'We haven't seen you in a while?'

'Oh,' she said, and flushed. 'No, no, I seem to have become quite busy lately. I don't know where the time goes,' she laughed apologetically, feeling fraudulent.

'Oh, well, just to let you know his Mammy's been moved to hospital in Newcastle.'

'Really?'

'Yes, she's in a coma. We don't expect her to come out of it.'

'Oh dear,' said Gertrude helplessly. 'If there's anything ...' and she tailed off lamely, again.

'No, no, it's fine.' Frances' blue eyes were filled with sadness, and a hurt at the impossibility of everything, including friendship with Gertrude Cullen. 'I know what to expect,' she said.

'Please let me know, about the ...' Gertrude faltered, 'about the arrangements, if anything happens,' she continued quickly.

'I will,' said Frances, turning away.

'See you so,' said Gertrude and left.

A few days later Master Cullen drove up to Glenview in the morning with the news that Mrs Mulhall had passed away. It was understood that he would attend the removal and the funeral, as he always did when anyone in the parish died – he knew them all. Gertrude donned black the following evening and accompanied him to the church for the removal ceremony. She was taut in the expectation that Tommie would be there. Still, respects had to be paid, so she stood with her father in a pew near the back of the church. There was a moderate crowd, but apart from a few older men, she didn't see his tall frame in the front benches with the family. She skipped the funeral itself the next day; she had paid her respects. She had no stomach for family gatherings, especially other people's. Anyway, William had passed comment: 'You're being a bit excessive in your neighbourly duty, aren't you? I mean, these things go on for days, don't they? Just an excuse for the farmers to have a day out, get pissed, isn't it? Haven't you done enough playing Florence Nightingale to the peasants? They see through that you know.'

It hurt, hit home where it was meant to. Worse than anything Gertrude didn't want to lose face, or her dignity, so she bowed out and stayed away from the Mulhalls from then on.

It did mean that when she next saw Frances, the woman turned away in hurt, her back bent into a brace of sadness, the bitterness of being betrayed. She never found out that Gertrude had been there to pay her respects on the day before, just before Tommie arrived, and so this silence lasted for several years to come, until Frances fell into ill health herself, and worse had happened between the two families.

Catherine's Diary

17 March 1985, St Patrick's Day

Today was very, very cold. It was the most miserable St Patrick's Day I ever spent, and they can be very miserable indeed. It's always wet and cold with a wind that would cut you in half. I woke up early all set to get up and light the stove, and then I remembered where I was. There was no sound of the kids sneezing or playacting in their beds, and no one to call or tell to get dressed. So I was lying there staying under the covers where it was nice and warm. My nose was running from the cold, the only bit of me outside the blankets. It was so quiet. Then I heard a door creaking and my heart started to hammer, but she only called up the stairs.

'Catherine, do you want a cup of tea?'

Her voice hit off the walls and cracked against them it was so crisp, like a shot in the house. I nearly jumped out of me skin. It seemed to echo for ages before the house settled down again into silence. So quiet. I could hear the clock ticking down in the kitchen from up here in bed. I shouted back 'no thanks', for fear she'd come up here and I'd have to sit up in the bed. Not that she's said anything. She says nothing at all. But I knew then I'd better get up. I don't want to be any trouble, and anyway amn't I meant to be waiting on her, not her waiting on me. That'd be a good one all right.

So I got dressed. I end up always wearing the same things, my jeans and the big jumper. I brought hardly anything else with me. I can close the zip of my jeans a bit of the way, and leave it open at the top. I put an elastic band through the buttonhole and tie it round the button to keep them closed. You wouldn't know any different under the jumper. I keep my hair down all the time now so it hangs in front, with my shoulders a bit hunched, and my arms crossed when I sit. Daddy used to hate that. 'Straighten up', he'd say. 'Walk tall, walk straight, look the world right in the eye. You can always tell a fella is crooked when he's not looking you straight in the eye.' Daddy. I felt like crying. There was a lump in my gullet. I am so heavy. My boobs are so big they won't fit into my bra anymore. I feel like a cow.

Granny was sitting at the table in the kitchen with the tea. There was no range lit so I started to rake it out but she said to drink my tea first. I sat there with her looking at me and slopped it all over myself. She got up to put on the radio and there was Irish traditional music on.

'Oh I forgot, Saint Patrick's Day. Patriotic nonsense,' she said.

'When will we get Mass?' I asked.

'Mass? I suppose it's another Holy Day of Obligation is it? I forget.'

Well I couldn't believe it, imagine not knowing you had to go to Mass on Paddy's Day. Then I got into a fluster.

'Gran, we could go to the twelve o'clock up in Knockananna if you don't want to go to the village.'

'I'll tell you what Catherine,' says she, 'how about not going at all? We can offer it up for the repose of the souls.'

I was shocked. I think I said, 'not go to Mass?' with a kind of squeal.

'It's all right not to go if you're sick or infirm,' she reasoned. 'Well, I am old and infirm, and you are looking after me. I can't be left alone now can I?'

I don't understand. There's nothing wrong with her at all, for all the talk of the broken hip, or nearly broken hip. What could I do? She kind of smiled at me. I put my head down. I was red in the face. I felt stupid but I was feeling anxious about not going to Mass. What would Mammy say? Missing Mass is a mortal sin. I never missed it before. There was no use saying anything unless I was going to walk all the way by myself, and then who might I meet on the road? They didn't think of that with all their plotting and planning.

So I was all flustered and I cleaning out the stove, and I started dropping ashes everywhere. Then I had to clean that up, and by the time I got the fire going it was time to make the dinner.

'I have a leg of lamb,' she said, 'will that do you for St Patrick's Day?'

She was kind of smiling again, so what could I say? I didn't know I was going to be the fusspot around here. I peeled the potatoes.

'I can do that,' she said.

'Sure I always do it at home, what else would I be doing?'

Then when the saucepans were bubbling on the stove and the fire was going strong, I sat down in the chair by the fire. Just sat, waiting. She was going in and out with some clay for her bulbs on the window.

'Hyacinths. They'll come up soon, they smell beautiful.'

She seemed quite happy not to be talking, but it's nearly not normal she can stay so long without speaking. Even Mammy when she's sick is always muttering or jumping round, or Daddy, always talking back to the radio or television. Gran puts the radio off most of the time. I was never so quiet. I don't know what to be saying. I'm going to move very carefully because I always seem to be dropping things when she's there looking at me, so I'm going to go real slow, nice and easy. I do be dying to ask her about Grandad William. I mean they're married and all, but she hasn't said a word about him. Uncle Jimmy comes by with the groceries once a week on his way back from Arklow. That's the only person she sees in the week, apart from Aunty Linda now and then.

So there we were having our St Patrick's Day dinner of lamb and potatoes, with no mint sauce or green jelly or anything, not even gravy. It was a very dry dinner. Anyway I'm trying to get slim. But I do be starving sometimes. And the wind was howling and they were talking about the parade in Dublin on the radio, and that was that; just the two of us sitting looking at one another. She doesn't say a word about the other thing. I think she doesn't know. I'd say Simon didn't tell her, but then what does she think I'm doing here? Simon would be the only person I could talk about to her, but I'd be afraid I'd go red.

'How's Aunty Linda?' I tried.

'Oh she gets on with her life, don't we all,' she said, which is not what I expected her to say. I thought she'd have some gossip or stories, but she's just not interested.

'Do you miss the Master?'

She stopped and went still, looking at me real straight. 'Yes Catherine, I do. We don't appreciate people when they're here. Especially parents. When they're gone, it's like a roof gone off the world.'

If I thought Mammy was mad this one is half-cracked too.

'What was he like? I'd have liked to know him better.'

'A gentle soul, and a real gentleman.'

'He was a great teacher anyway by all accounts.'

'He was, he was. Daddy was so proud of his classroom, and he really cared about the children from around here, all of them, those who had and those who had not.'

'Daddy', she called him. I never heard the Master called that before. You wouldn't think of her as having a daddy.

'Sure weren't you going on for teaching yourself?'

'I was.' She went quiet, then sighed. 'But I got married and then life takes over and you don't get time to do everything,' she said very fast.

'What do you want to do Catherine?'

'I'd like to be a hairdresser, like Helen, only I didn't get called yet for a place on the course. It's quite hard to get in.'

'Well I hope you succeed,' she said. 'Every girl needs a career.'

Then we were cleaning the dishes and busy again. That's why I don't think she knows anything, the way she said about having a career. I was very surprised. She got married didn't she, and had Mammy, and never worked in teaching.

'Come on out for a walk,' she said. 'It'll do you good, some fresh air.'

So I had to put on an old coat of hers, which actually does fit me, and follow her up the hill into the woods. We took Jack the dog with us. He's nice, he runs ahead looking for rabbits. Granny walked faster than me, I was puffing and panting. She wanted to call into Doran's up above to borrow some more milk, but I said I didn't want to, I'd be too shy.

Tonight was the worst, the two of us just sitting there, the big radio crackling in the corner with the old Irish songs on it for Paddy's Day. I was still miserable. I miss Daddy believe it or not, the smell of him, his old woolly jumper with the hole in the sleeve and the raggy bits at the wrist where he wipes his nose. I missed his coughing and spitting and giving out, his greasy hair with the little curls. Oh Daddy, I'm sorry. I went up to bed quickly before she could see me crying. Oh Daddy, I'm so sorry, please love me again. I want to go home.

20 March

Easter is nearly upon us. I'm getting very worried. That's one thing Simon and Helen didn't think of. How am I going to get Mass on Easter Sunday? I have to talk to him soon. I can't get in touch with him, he said not to, and anyway how would I? There's no telephone here, and I can't be going down to the village because then I'd have to call in and see Mammy and the kids even if Daddy wasn't there, and that'd be too risky.

I wouldn't know what to be saying to them with all their questions about Granny. That leaves the post, but I'd be very embarrassed to give Granny a letter with Simon's name on it in case she'd be asking questions, and then I know I'd go red. I can't help it but I go so red, even when she asks me other things. I get all tongue tied and then my words don't come out. She's so posh, well not really, but her voice is so nice and clear and a bit English, like on the news at nine o'clock. So I keep my head down and try and mind my own business. It's not so easy when we're looking at each other all day every day. I start asking questions about the family and all, just so as I'll know all about my relations. We didn't see much of them up at the big house when I was small. Mammy wouldn't set foot in it so we only met them here at Christmas and Easter.

I suppose I could write to Helen. She'll come home for Easter anyway so I'll see her then. But it's Simon I want to see. He said to wait and he'd fix everything. But I'm not waiting much longer. I have to get up to Dublin. I have to ask him, did he get me a flat? I want him to put his arms around me again and tell me we're friends. His secret is safe with me. I have to tell him that again, in case he thinks I'd be talking to anybody. Well, who? I'm going demented here talking to the walls. I'll be for the birds soon.

24 March

I was out by the back door the other day talking to a robin. This little bird hopped onto the tree by the window, a little chap with a red breast, and he sang his heart out, piping away for me a beautiful tune. He was all lit up in the sun. I saw some yellow crocuses waving back at him. I wanted to whistle and sing back to him too. I did, in a low voice, in case herself would be listening and she'd think I'd gone cracked like Mammy. If you ask me she's the one who's not the full deck, after all of us being afraid of her and her airs and graces all those years up at the big house. I'm beginning to think it's strange myself she doesn't see Grandad William.

That was a nice day sitting on the back step. I took a bit of my hair and pulled it out away from my eyes. It was gold and shiny. Must be the sun. I spent ages playing with it.

Granny is all the time now up in the sitting room at the front. She's pushing and shoving the furniture and pulling out old photographs and piles of papers. Then she comes out covered in dust, coughing and puffing when she brings the papers out to the yard. I asked her if she wanted help but she said no, she had to sort them out herself. I sometimes see the old papers when she puts them in piles here out the back. They're so old, 1945, the end of the war, and talking about President de Valera and McBride and Cosgrove and them old fogies.

Out she comes and says, 'Daddy must have thought he'd miss something. He never threw anything out. It's very interesting you know Catherine, to look back. It reminds me of when I was young. You forget so much. The time goes so quickly. It could be only yesterday when I was sitting on the step here like you, playing with my hair.'

I looked at her funny, and she said, 'Yes, you know I did have hair like yours, I keep it all tied up now. You're lucky, you're so young, you've your life ahead of you.'

If only she knew. I don't think she has a clue. Not a breeze. Maybe she's half-blind and can't see. She wears glasses in the evening when she does be poring over the old photos.

'Here, do you know who this is?'

She hands me a tiny black and white photo of a man in a coat and hat.

'They all look the same, like in the films.'

'That's your grandfather, wasn't he very handsome.'

I feel like saying where is he so? Is he not so handsome anymore?

'And that's me at the show.'

Well. She looked so glamorous in a huge white hat.

'You looked lovely, Gran. Like a queen.'

'Hmmm,' is all she said. I was trying to be nice to her.

Then she goes quiet and looks for ages. I do think she's fallen asleep behind her glasses she's looking so long. She's muttering, 'I'm sure I have a photo of him somewhere, now where did that wedding picture get to?'

Then she lets a big gasp out of her and puts down the photos and takes off her glasses and just sits there.

'Live your own life, Catherine,' she said.

What does she think I'm doing? I don't have any choice, do I? She's a fruitcake. I can't believe she didn't go to Mass on St Patrick's Day. I'm afraid to ask her about Easter. You'd never know what she'd say or do. That'd be a real mortal sin, not to go to Mass when Jesus Christ is resurrected.

Live your life Catherine- how are you!

Gertrude, 1962

The countryside was luscious, its rolling hills and fields bathed in the spangled light of harvest air dense with hay dust. In the bowl of a hill bunting waved in the breeze and ripples of tattered music announced the great Annual August Show.

As the car approached Gertrude could see the lines of cars and trailers queuing at the entrance. Nearby rose the ferriswheel towering over the tombola and the coconut shy. A multi-coloured throng of women and children crowded the mouth of the tea tent. Further up the hill flapped the awning of the beer tent, with hay bales propped up outside as impromptu tables and chairs. At the summit the great paddock stretched out with its red and white fences erected in the jumping arena. It was here that the Grand Prix of the Inter-County Showjumping Championship would take place later in the day.

Gertrude sat in the front of the Ford alight with anticipation, tense with a powerful energy. She was not yet forty and was stridently beautiful. Her white linen dress fell stiffly, starched on her handsome frame. Crowning it was an immense white straw hat, allowing her to move with a regal sedateness. For today was the day she would bask in the reflected glory of Jimmy's triumph. Jimmy was to ride for the county team in a few hours' time, a team of four young accomplished riders, who so far this summer had managed to win all the heats in every show in six surrounding counties. James William Hawthorn Thwaite was the star of the team, the one who could almost every time be guaranteed to jump a clear round, especially under pressure in a jump-off, on his black and nimble pony Jessie. Jimmy and Jessie had made quite a handsome pair, a unity of stirrup and steed, as Gertrude had looked on proudly week after week. She had travelled to every county show all summer long to accompany Jimmy and his pals. Sometimes Elizabeth would come along too, dragging reluctantly behind, a heap of uncooperative teenage hormones and obduracy. She had no interest in horses and didn't see the point. Gertrude had to bribe her to come by promising to buy her more comics: the *Bunty* and *Judy* which came out on a Thursday, plus the *Summer Annual* with all the puzzles and free gift offers in it. Then Elizabeth would sit all day in the car, with her thick spectacles locked onto the page in front, as if no other world existed. Gertrude hardly knew what to be saying to her. This show was different though, and even Elizabeth knew it was to be the last and most important. She wore a belted shirt-dress that couldn't disguise her scrawny figure and flat chest, even at fifteen.

Now at the last and biggest of the county shows, in Tinahely in August 1962, the Hawthorn Thwaites were set to make a splash. Jimmy himself was business-like as he unlatched the back of the horsebox to lead Jessie down the ramp. The competition was due to begin in three hours so he would walk her for a bit and then keep her in the shade. The ground was looking good, nice and firm after a dry spell, perhaps a little too hard.

Jimmy was a tall handsome lad, his blonde curls cut back tight to his head, giving him a more manly appearance to counteract those full soft lips. He wore navy jodhpurs and riding boots, and later would don a show jacket and hat, with the colour of his team stripes.

'I'm off to see the prize cabbages. Anybody coming with me?' mocked Gertrude in a voice full of merriment.

'Mam,' sulked Elizabeth. 'Do we have to? I want to see the dogs.'

'I'll come, I love the roses,' piped up Matilda, who had bustled out of the car beside them. She was trim for a woman in her late sixties and dressed smartly in black and white.

'Come on Lizzie, we can catch the dog show later, we have all day.'

'Right so,' said William, rubbing his hands, 'we've to go off on a bit of business, isn't that right Pops?' He winked at his father the old Major as he clapped him on a tweedy shoulder to lead him away towards the beer tent. Gertrude raised her eyebrow slightly to catch William's eye and give him a look which said, 'remember the competition and don't be in a state by then please.'

Gertrude and Matilda tripped over the grass on high summer sandals, with Elizabeth sloping along two paces behind.

'Bye darling, we'll catch you in the tea tent at lunchtime perhaps?' she waved at Jimmy.

'I'm fine Mum, I'll see you later,' Jimmy said firmly, and went on unloading his saddle and tack.

The women went to the agricultural produce tent to marvel at the outsize vegetables. There were enormous cabbages, obscene carrots, giant onions, a tomato bigger than a turnip, all laid out on nests of lacy doilies, to show them off to their best advantage. There were also tables of brown bread, teacakes, apple tarts and fruit barm brack, lying in slices with their makers' names attached. The judges would pass by throughout the day to decide on first, second and third prizes in every category: the biggest, the tastiest, the most perfect. Then there were roses, indeed all specimens and varieties of flowers, arranged daintily in glass vases.

The smells and exuberant abundance pleased Gertrude. This truly was a wonderful time of year, when all the fruits of hard labour, the mysterious work of the seed in winter, came to light, there to be displayed in proud perfection. It gave Gertrude immense satisfaction to behold, even though she herself didn't enter such competitions. She wasn't blessed with green fingers for the vegetables, and wasn't a very active member of the Irish Country Woman's Association. She couldn't be bothered going to long meetings about the best way to make a feather-light sponge cake, by the finger action of kneading and rubbing such and such brand of margarine. She passed among the excited women, greeting one here, stopping to speak to another there, to compliment her on her achievements. It was one of those days when the world smiles with a quiet, sated satisfaction.

'Can we not see the dogs?' pouted Elizabeth. 'This is so boring.'

'All right Lizzie, off you go then, we'll catch you later.'

Matilda was discussing the merits of Royal Baking Powder with Mrs Greene when Gertrude felt a tap on her shoulder.

'Hello Gertrude, long time no see.'

'Oh hello Frances, how are you?' she smiled, flushing slightly, feeling the old guilt of pity rise up as Frances Mulhall stood before her in a light blue dress.

'Lovely show, isn't it?' said Frances.

'Yes, have you something in here?' asked Gertrude.

'Now where would I get the time?' smiled Frances, indicating a toddler hanging out of her arm.

'Yes indeed, so how are things?'

'Oh fine, did you ...?' queried Frances, indicating the buns in front of them on the trestle.

'Oh no, we're really here for the Grand Prix competition. Jimmy's on the team,' she added proudly.

'Really? Oh I must get up to watch that', said Frances. 'I think my pair are helping out up in the arena, building up the fences. The money's all right, keeps them out of mischief anyway.'

She laughed the thin laugh of the socially embarrassed, as the two women shuffled and nodded through the hiatus that teetered on silence.

'Right then,' said Gertrude, ending the exchange with a smile, 'see you later so,' and she melted back into the crowd, losing herself in the chatter of women. She found Elizabeth outside on the grass squatting beside a puppy.

'Can I keep him Mummy?' she asked. Her blue black eyes pleaded innocently as she looked up to catch her mother full in the eye, in a rare moment of naked asking.

'No you can't,' came the instant dismissal as Gertrude brushed past.

Elizabeth's eyes faded and dropped. Her face nuzzled into the dog's neck.

'We have enough dogs,' Gertrude tossed over her shoulder as an afterthought. Elizabeth's vulnerability disturbed her. It reminded her of Frances Mulhall. Helpless. Trying to be nice. Waiting for crumbs of affection. She felt burdened by them, their unspoken demands. Disgusted even. This was not a day to be marred by pity.

Glad to be alone once again she climbed the slope past the beer tent, to where the last fences were being erected for the jumping finals. It was not yet lunchtime. She leaned on the railings in the sunshine, adjusting her hat to protect her face from its rays. She had often come here as a girl, and once her eyes had strayed over to the ring where she had caught a glimpse of black curls. That time she had been rewarded by Tommie's devilishly blue grin and a cheeky wave. He used to get seasonal work at the show. It had been enough to keep her in high spirits all the day. She sighed a little, the sun warming her back, making her body tighten with youth. She shaded her eyes against the light, watching two boys heave and lift poles across the arena. One had curly black hair. She creased her eyes and stared hard. So like him. Must be one of Frances' boys, didn't she say they were working on the fences. One threw down a bale of hay from where they were building up a fence, placed one foot on it, took a cigarette from behind his ear, and lit up. The lad stood surveying the panorama before and below him, taking his ease. His head swivelled lazily around as he took in the jumping arena, and what was left to do. His brother still pulled and dragged the bales.

'Mattie, get a move on there,' shouted the one who still worked.

Mattie took one last pull on his cigarette, with a long slow look in Gertrude's direction. He may or may not have recognised her. What he would have seen was a woman dressed in summer white tilt her hat haughtily away.

Then it was four o'clock and time for the Grand Prix. A tannoy barked: 'Would all the competitors take their mounts, would all the competitors take their mounts please? Stewards stand by. Stewards stand by.'

A wave of people surged out over the field, to shove towards the arena. It flooded and eddied to settle along the fence until each side of the ring was fenced by people, standing three deep. Stewards ran along the barrier, pushing back small children who had slipped in under the fence onto the competition field. Gertrude had retrieved William from the beer tent and together they stood close to the finishing line, after the triple jump. William had a camera ready, a large brown Yashica on a tri-pod. It was to be a momentous occasion. The Major and Matilda had driven the car close behind, and were to watch from there. Elizabeth as usual couldn't be found.

'Oh blow,' thought Gertrude, 'I told her I wasn't waiting. Still with the dogs I suppose?'

Then the bell rang. A hush fell over the ring. The first rider entered the arena to reverent gazes as a thousand breaths were held. There were four teams of four riders each, the cream of every county. Every eye watched as the rider thundered into the first fence, to soar over it with ease and grace. Then the reining in, the turning, the urging, a loud 'yup', the groan of effort as the horse rose up again, quickly gathered itself in little steps to rise up for a double. A fence rattled, the bar tipped and then fell. A muffled groan rose from the crowd. Along the straight, heading flat out now for the water; a long long stretch of a jump. The animal's legs splayed behind and he cleared it, not a splash. A ripple of applause swirled around the ring. Then came the last fence, the big triple gate. The rider urged again, seemed to lift the horse between the fences with his promptings, a little kick here, a clip of the crop there, until 'hup', the final fence was cleared. The top bar of the last gate rat-tled but did not fall. The rider raced to the finishing line as the tannoy screeched, 'four faults, four faults', to thunderous applause. Inside the holding ring the rider dismounted to claps and pats of praise from his cheering team-mates. The bell clanged again for the next rider, and the crowd fell into a respectful hush, pregnant with waiting.

By five o'clock it was almost decided. The Glenview Giants would engage in a final jump-off with the Carlow Curlews. The other two teams were eliminated. They had eight faults each and would now jump it off against the clock. Jimmy had already jumped a clear round. He was chosen for the race against time, as Jessie was the swiftest of the team's ponies, nimble and sprightly on her feet.

Gertrude grabbed William's arm in a tight clench. 'Oh dear God, this is so exciting,' she breathed.

William patted her fondly. 'Steady on my girl, steady on.'

She hopped up and down in inelegant agony, but her eyes shone with joy and her cheeks flamed with excitement.

William put his arm around her shoulder and hugged her tight. 'Ah Gertie, these are the good moments,' he said, his voice full.

'Is the film loaded?' she asked, breaking from his embrace, her mind on other things.

'Yes, yes, stop fussing. I'll get the winning shot', he grinned. He turned the camera on her quickly. 'Smile!' The camera clicks.

'Would you stop it, silly,' she smiled.

The bell rang.

'Oh William I can hardly bear to look,' she whispered.

In the holding ring Jimmy strode up to Jessie, solemn and smart. He took the reins from a stable hand, swung his long leg up and over to land in the saddle. Jessie jumped forward.

'Whoa whoa,' he soothed.

She pranced again, but he reined her in and steered her towards the gate. The bell rang for the off.

'Come on girl,' he breathed.

He clicked her forward into a canter. After two paces she shied and bucked. The crowd stifled a moan. The clock was ticking audibly on the tower under the weathercock. Jimmy started to burn with determination.

'Jessie, come on girl,' he pleaded.

The horse shied again, wide-eyed with fear and bucked into the air behind her. Jimmy fell forward onto her neck as she landed. He grabbed her mane and shoved his rear end backwards. As he landed into the saddle the second time, she bucked even higher managing to unseat him completely. He toppled off onto the ground and lay still.

'Jimmy!' screamed Gertrude.

'Wait,' said William.

A groomsman rushed to Jimmy's side as another tried to catch the maddened horse.

'Oh my God,' wailed Gertrude. Her stomach had gone cold. She saw the linesman help Jimmy up. He stumbled but was conscious. He fought off the man and retrieved his hat, obviously intending to remount. He took Jessie's reins, soothing the horse, glanced at the clock as thirty seconds remained.

'He doesn't have to,' moaned Gertrude.

'He does,' snapped William.

'Jimmy!' a cry escaped her. 'Don't!'

A thin note sounded in the silence across a sea of tension. Jimmy turned in her direction, a black scowl on his cheeks already reddened by a deep humiliation. He glowered hate at that moment. 'Do not stop me,' his look said. He ran a hand quickly under Jessie's saddle, to see if by chance a burr or thorn had lodged there. There was none that he could find. Puzzled, his eyes scanned the arena. Then suddenly, decisively, he grabbed the reins, hopped on the stirrup, and swung into the air to remount. But on impact the horse pranced again, side stepped and shied. As he tried to steady and guide her, he pressed his heels into her sides to urge her forward. The horse sprang as if spiked, as a painful shock seemed to electrify her. She bucked high into the air. This time her rider landed with a dead thud on the flat of his back before she bolted round the ring, eyes white and neighing frantically.

The crowd broke apart in groans, heaved convulsively in consternation. Then there were cries and running as people flocked to the boy stretched still on the ground.

'William, do something,' Gertrude screamed. She clawed at him, frantic with fear.

'Show over,' the tannoy cackled. 'Stewards' decision. No winners.'

Gertrude was sick. She pushed and pulled her way through the crowd, her hat fallen backwards and crushed underfoot, to reach her boy. 'Jimmy, Jimmy, speak to me, wake up.'

Two attendants from the ambulance service were there before her.

'Will he be all right?' she cried desperately.

'He's probably just winded. We'll get Casualty to take a look at him,' said one.

'Stand back please,' said the other as they slid him carefully onto a stretcher and pulled a blanket up to his chin. Gertrude glimpsed Jimmy's face. It was white and closed.

'Is he going to be all right?' she whispered again, choking with terror. 'Is he? Please?'

They shrugged sympathetically as they lifted him up. 'Follow us if you like. We'll take him into Wexford General.'

The crowd parted. Gertrude stood stock still, tearing and pulling at the folds of her white dress. Ice in her stomach weighed her to the spot, leaving her unable to move. As William arrived to put an arm around her, she looked up. Over at the entrance to the arena, under the clock, she caught sight of a mass of dark curls, under which amused blue eyes stared out. She swallowed, shoot away the thought, disbelieving. Why? What had Jimmy ever done to deserve this? She hardened in hatred as William led her away.

The hospital corridor was white, too white. The sunbeams glancing off its shiny surfaces stabbed her eyes. It had been three sleepless nights since the show. Her footsteps clicked on tiles, the rat-a-tat reminding her she was mortal. A lump of lead sat in her stomach; she had been unable to dislodge it ever since Jimmy gave her that look, the look across the arena that twisted his burning humiliation into a baleful dagger, a reproach that was hellfire hot. Spots popped before her eyes in the sunlight. She'd have to sit soon, get something to drink, or she would faint. She pushed open the door of the ward.

Jimmy was propped up behind a *Boy's Own* magazine. His father sat beside him, as together they looked at pictures of cars. William rose to lead her to a seat.

'It's your mother, Jim my boy.' And then with a slight pressing on her forearm, 'How are you my dear, you look tired.'

She flashed him a mute warning. He should know how she hated to appear weak in front of their son. Wasn't once enough, indeed too much, already?

'Jimmy darling, how are you feeling?' she asked softly, touching his hair as she sat on the chair vacated by William at the head of the bed.

He shied away slightly, as a frown flitted across his forehead. 'Don't do that mother,' it said silently.

The movement seared her. She must continue. 'Elizabeth has arrived safely. All's well up in the convent. I hope that girl she likes is back, she doesn't seem to have many friends.'

Neither Jimmy nor William replied. She continued, forcing herself to be jolly. 'So, what cars are we planning to purchase, men?'

William leaned over to turn the pages of the magazine. She was grateful for this minor rescue.

'Ah, I see, a vintage, what is it? Daimler?'

'Yes, yes, no problem, a mere five thousand guineas to you, my dear,' William tried bravely to collude in her efforts.

She turned to Jimmy who stared downwards at the page, not moving.

'Which car do you fancy my love?'

'Don't "love" me mother,' he almost snarled.

'Jimmy.' She was stung to tears.

'Jees Mum, look, stop trying to make it better. We lost. It's over. QED. Finito.'

'No it's not,' said William hotly. 'Whoever did this is not going to get off lightly.'

'We know who did it,' said Jimmy in a voice which carried every ounce of sarcasm he could muster, 'but they'll never be caught, will they? No proof. Just a bad loser. Little Lord Fauntleroy Sissy Lips. I know what they're saying Dad, and I won't give them the satisfaction. I don't care,' he pronounced proudly, biting his lips.

But he does, Gertrude thought, he cares terribly. She felt hot pangs of remorse, for Jimmy, for herself, for them all. A minor riding accident. A horsey incident in County Wicklow. Ah but Jimmy might never ride again. He had chipped a vertebra in his lower back. With time it would heal, and he could slowly start to ride out again. But he didn't want to, ever. His jumping days were over. He had said so. Gertrude continued to look at him, his beloved face elongating into a young man's, the Adam's apple in his long neck rising and falling as he struggled with his inner turmoil. He obviously hated being in front of his parents, would rather have been left alone to howl like a baby.

Gertrude knew every line of his face, every muscle in his profile, every fine blonde hair on the perfectly rounded chin. She wanted to kiss it and weep, but a chasm had opened up and she dared not even put out a hand to touch him across the divide. Her shock and panic at his fall had settled into a wedge of pain in her heart and every flicker of an eye-lid from her son wounded her more. She was not to blame, they all knew that, but somehow Jimmy had caught sight of her before the fall, had heard her call out, and that image of a terrified mother flapping in a white hat had shamed him, made him burn with anguish. He could not dissociate his humiliation from her and her maternal reflexive action.

'Come on Gertie, time to go, the lad needs rest,' said William kindly, patting her shoulder.

'I'll be in again tomorrow afternoon. Is there anything you need? Some more grapes? Or Lucozade?' she asked Jimmy brightly in a brittle tone. She rose to lean forward, went to brush her lips against his velvety cheek. Again, a tiny shift away told her a membrane had grown up between them where before there had been none, only perfect unity. As one flesh. My flesh.

'I'll be fine Mum, thanks. I'm OK, really, stop worrying,' he said politely in a grown-up voice. So poised.

And so dismissed, Gertrude and William left the ward to click-clack back down the corridor out into the sunny day.

'I'll kill them, I really will,' said Gertrude between her teeth as William started the engine.

'Gertie, what's done is done. Jimmy will get over it. He might even ride again.'

'Those Mulhalls,' she spat venomously.

'Jimmy is right, we have no proof,' soothed her husband.

'I saw that boy smirking – he was happy. God almighty, Jimmy could have been killed.'

'Gertrude, a childish prank gone wrong. An unfortunate practical joke, the oldest one in the book, a burr under a horse's tail. That's all that happened.'

'I know all that William,' Gertrude interrupted crossly. She was irritable, her skin on fire, her head throbbing. 'I know what probably happened. I know it's only a county show. But how dare they pick on my son.' Her voice tapered off in a wail.

'What? Maybe there was no reason.'

William patted her hand, trying to placate her. Gertrude clenched her fist to her mouth.

Of course there was a motive, she seethed inwardly. It was vague and unformed, something to do with envy and social order and poverty. And Gertrude's little interlude, her few weak seconds of nostalgia in the empty arena before the show, leaning on a fence as she watched a mop of dark curls bend to its work, made her a conspirator, criminal by association. Oh yes, she was guilty, guilty of triggering a primitive jealously, a tempting of fate that had tipped the balance.

She was responsible for the fact that her one and only, her beloved son, had turned against her and left her bereft and alone. The disaster that had befallen Jimmy had come from her original sin, a punishment across time down through the decades. She burned now with a hatred of the current generation of Mulhalls so fierce that she vowed never again to allow their father's remembered image to intrude upon her consciousness, awake or asleep. It must remain unbidden, banished. The loss of her beloved son's affection was not worth the indulgence of nostalgia, not even for one second. The memory of Jimmy's poor pinched face, closed tight against her in that hospital bed made her wince in anguish.

'Hurry on home William, I'm tired,' is all she said to her husband in the quiet thin voice of defeat.

Catherine's Diary

25 March 1985

Granny tries to talk to me now. She has great chat out of her, about Jimmy when he was small, and her daddy, Master Cullen, and when she was a little girl how she played in the forest.

I said, 'and Mammy? What was she like as a little girl?'

'Oh, she was lovely with black curly hair and dark eyes.'

'You'd never think it now she's so grey.'

She laughed. 'Elizabeth could be difficult. Still it must have been hard on her going away to school so young.'

'Why? Why did you send her to boarding school?'

She stopped. 'I think I wasn't a very good mother. I was very young myself. It was done then, to get an education.'

'Did Jimmy go too?'

'No, no he didn't. He stayed at home. He was a lovely child, very sunny nature. Still is. A very good son to me.'

'Daddy doesn't think so. He says he was an awful little creep when he was young. Stuck up. Oh, I'm sorry, I shouldn't say that to you, you're his mother.'

I was mortified I'd said so much. But she only smiled.

'There was a falling out one time. I was sad about that.'

'Daddy says you didn't want Mammy to marry him.'

'No, I didn't.' She twisted her mouth. 'I had my reasons.'

'Did you know the Major's wife?' I said to change the subject. After all I shouldn't be telling her all our family's secrets, how we don't like them up at the big house. Daddy'd kill me if he knew I was so free with my tongue. 'Whatever you say, say nothing', he always says.

'You mean Matilda? I did,' she says.

'Wasn't she at the funeral in a wheelchair?'

'Yes, she came out of the home for the day. She's gone very forgetful.'

'Well Gran, to tell you nothing but the truth, she gave me the creeps, she was so old all covered in black, crouching in the chair with her two eyes looking out over the rug on her knees.'

'Poor Matilda. She was a great help to me when they were small. She did me a big favour once.'

'Or did she?' she said a few minutes later out of the blue. 'The National Maternity Hospital. Hah.'

I didn't know what she meant. That question seemed to put her into a trance because there wasn't another word out of her for ages. Later I asked about Grandad William Hawthorn Thwaite. I said it was a very funny name.

'I liked it,' she said. 'It made me feel important.'

'Are they really so snobby like Daddy says?'

'Your Daddy doesn't know everything. William wasn't a snob, no, I don't think so. If anyone was, it was me. He was born to it, the horses and the hounds, and was just doing his job to rear his family and keep me happy.'

She was rooting in the box of photos, whipping out the photo of her at the show in the white hat.

'Lady Muck, with notions. I hate that picture.'

She crushed it up into a ball and flung it over to the range, then laughed. 'Catherine, only you can make yourself happy. Don't expect anyone else to do it for you.'

She kept laughing and couldn't stop, like a horse snorting.

I know what would make me happy. Only I didn't dare say his name. Her grandson. My cousin. Oh, oh, if only. He'll never look at me again. I've got so huge. I'm a big cow.

In the end I couldn't resist.

'Where is Grandad? Why are you not living with him?'

'Ah, poor William is lost to the sauce.'

'Sauce?'

'The bottle.'

'Oh.'

'I let him down,' she said. 'He'd never say it, he's a gentleman, but he knows it deep down. It's really my fault he's so fond of it. We're a dying breed Catherine, the Hawthorn Thwaite name is almost extinct.'

She's rooting in a pile of photographs.

'Ah, here it is. Look, look at this.'

It was a tiny baby in Granny's arms, in a hospital bed, with William by her side.

'Look at it,' she said impatiently, nearly shaking the photo at me. 'Look. Your mother. When she was ... born.' She spat out the last word. 'This picture records one significant moment in a family's history, the official story, the one everyone has to learn as part of the tale it tells about itself.'

What's she on about? Jees but I broke out in a sweat. What does she know?

I stayed quiet for the rest of the evening in case I'd let something slip. Granny's all right really. But she doesn't know, she mustn't, or she wouldn't be so nice to me. She'll hate me when she finds out. She'll be disgusted. I feel disgusted with myself. How did this happen? I'm barely left school and was working hard trying to bring home the few bob to help Mammy. I might have got the hairdressing course like Helen. Then in a few years I'd get married and settle down with a few children. I'm not wild like Helen. I wasn't trying to get out as soon as I was fifteen, smoking and chatting up the fellas, talking about going to London. I'd be happy with my own little house and a few kids. And Simon.

If only he'd bring me to Dublin. Simon. Simon, that would be a dream come true. My best daydream was that he'd come back to the valley after his studies and marry me, and we'd build a house near the woods. I'd love that. And we'd walk for miles up the hill and talk like we used to, about the foxes and the leaves, all that sort of stuff. And the best part of the dream was when we'd stop at the hut way up the avalanche hill, and he'd hold my hand, and I'd look at him, and the birds would be singing and the sky would be burning blue, and my eyes would tell him how much I loved him. Then he'd kiss me and we'd melt away, one into the other, melt and sway as the trees would be sighing and swaying. I swell up just thinking of him. Simon, where are you?

That's what it was going to be like. Before this. I want to get away, just to disappear. Then come back, a new slim Catherine Mulhall. No baby. Nothing. There's ways of doing it. Ways to make it all go away. Then we'll all get back to normal, me and Simon. I'll go to Dublin and clean the flat and make his dinners so he can study. He'll love me too, he will. Then in time Daddy will be grand about it all. He'll come round, and think it's not the worst to marry your cousin. Jesus, is that allowed? I think maybe the Church has a rule against it, in case the children would be born disabled, but maybe there are ways round it. It's not that part that Daddy would mind, no, it's the Hawthorn Thwaite part.

'Simon will carry on the Hawthorn Thwaite name,' Gran said before going to bed.

I went puce. Can she know? Jees what would Uncle Jimmy think? What would Daddy think of that? The Hawthorn Thwaite name. He'd hate it even more.

26 March

I'm nearly sure I saw Daddy this morning early. He was on the tractor behind the house on the headland. He'd never be up there normally. I was out the back but I ducked in again for fear he'd see me. I got an awful fright. Funny, but at the same time I'd love him to have seen me, and for him to wave at me and smile.

So now I'm back in the kitchen shaking like a rabbit, imagining how his eyes would fire up had he seen me, and his face would change. Oh, I couldn't bear that.

Granny says, 'What's wrong Catherine? You look as if you've seen a ghost.'

'Nothing,' I say real fast. After a few minutes my heart slows down again and I say, 'But you sometimes see ghosts, don't you Granny? Or so Mammy says.'

'Me?' she laughs. 'Why do you say that?'

'Well, the night of the funeral. You went white as a sheet and then fainted.'

'Yes,' she says, 'I did.'

'Was it a ghost?'

'No, no.' She gets busy around the kitchen. 'It's not true, I don't see ghosts.'

'What was it then? The stranger coming in?'

'Ah Catherine, he's no stranger.'

'Sure I know, wasn't it Tommie Mulhall who works on the buildings in England? He gave Uncle Mattie a job too, so he did.'

'Oh, father and son, thick as thieves no doubt.' She is smiling.

'And there was great singing out of them after.'

'I didn't stay. William brought me home to Glenview that night. It was all too much, the funeral and everything.'

'They were at it for three days. Mammy kept going back and forth up there with sandwiches for them and Daddy had to go on the tractor into Black Tom's to get more drink. That's funerals for you ... and you didn't come back again?'

'No.'

Just that. That's all she said. That's how I knew it was the end of our chat. Still, I had to ask her for Mammy's sake. So a while later I said, 'Granny, what about the Master's house?'

'What about it?'

'Is there a will?'

She looks very surprised. 'Well, Catherine, if you must know, and you can tell your mother, there is no will.' She frowns. 'By rights it all goes to me, but it's in probate so that means it could take a long time, up to a year.'

'Mammy's sure the Master made a will.' I am being a bit stubborn.

'Catherine,' she says sharply, 'there is nothing hidden in this house. Why should there be a will? I'm his direct heir. Anyway, there's not much left is there? Who wants a tumbledown house and some old papers?'

Mammy, I almost said, but didn't. I'm beginning to know when to stop with her. She'll tell me in her own time.

Gertrude, 1963

'Are you coming along tomorrow night?' Gertrude asked cheerfully.

There was to be a New Year's Eve ball in Hunter's Hotel in Arklow, and William's partner in the practice, Mr Jones, had invited them to share a table at the dinner dance. The question was addressed to two heads slouched over a game of Monopoly on the rug by the fire. She got no reply. Elizabeth raised her dark head. Her eyes, out of focus behind her glasses, swam in puzzlement. Jimmy just swung his blonde head slowly from side to side as if to figure out the gamble of buying more houses on his Monopoly site.

'Your Dad's practice is paying for us all to go. We could dress up ...' she tried again, forcing herself to be cheerful. Her tone all over Christmas had been relentless. 'Let's all have a good time, it's the season of goodwill,' she had chirped before every outing, whether to Mass on Christmas Eve or to visit the Master, Grandad Cullen. Even the cake sale in the school hall and the Christmas carols on the Saturday had been guided by the obligatory smiles. But there was no getting away from it. Jimmy had changed. The four intervening months back at school since the summer show had not brought any give in the barrier of reticence that now surrounded him. For once, he and Elizabeth shared prolonged and sympathetic silences. Gertrude's cheerful resoluteness intensified as flutters of panic clawed more and more at her insides. Cheerful she would be, and keep this family jolly together.

The door creaked open as William entered. Both teenagers' heads came up in a grunted greeting.

'Look here Jimmy, I have acquired for you ...' and William pulled out a brown paper bag which crinkled noisily, 'a completely authentic tuxedo. Here, try it on, your very own dress suit.'

Jimmy rose sheepishly, embarrassed at his father's frivolity.

'Dad,' he protested, as William slipped the black jacket around his shoulders. But his expression softened and he preened himself in the mirror over the mantelpiece with some pleasure.

'Jimmy, you look smashing,' enthused Gertrude. Elizabeth scowled. Gertrude picked up the cue. 'Darling, I have just the thing for you: a white broderie anglaise gown, the first one I ever had. It might only need taking up.'

Somehow then, with a little cajoling and persuasion, Gertrude managed to get her family together at the hotel in Arklow for the New Year's Eve ball of 1962.

The room was sumptuous with red drapes everywhere under millions of crystal chandeliers. Two dance floors competed for dancers, one with a regular dance band playing all the waltzes and quick-steps familiar on these occasions, the other with a group of four young lads who crashed their way through the new sounds of Elvis Presley and Buddy Holly, on old and badly tuned electric guitars and a cheap drumkit. The adults gave this room a wide berth. Jimmy watched enthralled and hung around the doorway to listen, long and graceful in the black dress suit. His frame had begun to have manly edges. Angles protruded through the jacket at his shoulder blades, hip bones showed sharp through the serge as he walked in an unconscious swagger. If to his mother he was suddenly achingly handsome, he was completely unaware of it himself. He had the charm and beauty of a fawn growing fast into a young buck. His rounded baby cheeks had all but receded into a long bony face, still sporting those too red lips. 'He would melt my heart if I were that age again', thought Gertrude watching him.

The gong went for dinner and everyone filed into the dining room. Course after course arrived on large silver trays. The speeches and tributes were interminable; people waxing lyrical as they do when the old year ends. Elizabeth's face wore her mask of impenetrable boredom, even though she did look, if not pretty, at least original, like an eighteenth-century miniature in the virginal white dress. No matter how often well-meaning questions were aimed her way by William's colleagues' wives, Gertrude squirmed, and many the time almost prodded her, as Elizabeth remained tongue-tied. Then, thankfully, they were released from the table. Jimmy took off again to the rock and roll room, to take up a position by the door. The room was filling up with younger couples, twisting and jiving, or dancing the hucklebuck. The lights had

dimmed and the band even had two spotlights on the makeshift plat-
form with blue and red gels which blinked on and off.

Jimmy found his foot tapping in time to the rhythm. His eyes caught
sight of a blonde girl who gyrated and twirled with a girlfriend not far
away in the centre of the floor. She wore a wide skirt pulled in tight at
the waist, with very high heels. Her blonde hair was cut tight in a fash-
ionable bob, and her feet moved very fast in time to the music. Jimmy
was mesmerised. She smiled from under her hair, and began to dance
even faster, wiggling her hips. He was filled with a strange emotion,
thrilling him like fear or laughter.

When the music stopped the girl looked towards him, then picked
up her handbag and went to join her friends – all girls, he found himself
checking. For another hour or so Jimmy slinked around the hall
between numbers, always keeping an eye on the golden head. Suddenly
he couldn't see it anymore in the crowd. He stumbled blindly towards
the door in case she had gone home. As he emerged into the hotel corridor, like a diver surfacing for air, he bumped into someone lounging
behind the door against the wall. It was she.

'Oh,' he said, and swallowed.

'Hi,' she said.

If he had wanted to speak he could think of nothing to say. His heart
had risen to thump in his throat.

'Are you dancing?' she said simply, swinging round to open the door
to the dance floor. He followed dumbly, a sleepwalker bewitched. Then
he was swallowed up in the heat and noise, blood pounding in his head,
as he found himself on the dance floor face to face with her. He
attempted a shuffle from side to side in what he hoped was an imitation
of modern dance. The girl laughed out loud, showing rows of large
white teeth. He laughed too.

'I'm Linda,' she said.

'I'm Jim,' he said, deciding the monosyllable sounded more sophisti-
cated.

Linda was fun, she was warm, and she was gorgeous. Jimmy followed
her example, doing rhumbas and cha-chas until he learned to let himself
go, allowing himself to be guided by her, even daring to grab her waist
in a burst of exuberance. Then the music slowed down. She looked at
him, her eyes a wide appeal. Jimmy gingerly placed his hands on her
shoulders. She felt fragile, breakable under her silky jumper. He pulled
her closer and she turned her mouth upwards to kiss him. Jimmy

exploded with joy and his mouth flooded, as did other parts of his body. When midnight came with a sudden loud announcement in the adjoining hall, Jimmy came to, groggy with infatuation.

The New Year countdown commenced: Ten ... nine ... eight ... seven ... The crowd gathered in a circle, faces joyously awaiting the final roar of midnight. Just then someone touched his shoulder. It was Gertrude, alight with excitement.

'Quick Jimmy, we're all together over here.' She grabbed his arm and yanked him to one side to join the family circle.

'Six, five, four, three, two, one, midnight!' roared the microphone.

'Happy New Year!' yelled the crowd.

'Happy New Year!' Gertrude sang, flinging her arms around Jimmy in a suffocating embrace. 'Happy New Year darling.' She kissed him plumply on both cheeks.

Jimmy wrenched himself out of her arms and tore blindly around the room, bumbling through the thickening throng of merrymakers, frantic to find Linda. Gertrude stood, arms outstretched in shock, as Elizabeth waited with a silly smile for the next embrace.

So it was that on New Year's Eve 1962 the love story of Jimmy Hawthorn Thwaite and Linda Scott the doctor's daughter from Arklow began. For the remainder of that school holiday, and indeed every subsequent one, Easter into summer and again the following year, for several years, Linda was a frequent visitor to Glenview House. In fact she practically lived with them, only leaving when William got the car out to drive her home to Arklow in the evenings.

At first, Gertrude found Linda brassy, with a cheeky confidence quite unknown in the valley. Jimmy's attention to Linda was whole and undivided so that she, his mother, was totally eclipsed. She would find herself seized suddenly as a twinge of jealousy darted through her, running up her spine. Yet, over time, she relaxed and warmed to the girl, relieved to see the light shine in her son's eyes, his body alive with energy once again.

In that summer he mounted Jessie for the first time since the fall, and with Linda on a pony from the riding school, they hacked up the mountain trails under the avalanche hill, their laughter echoing like Sunday bells against the granite.

Gertrude was genuinely happy at this transformation in her son. Never mind that Linda was a Protestant, they would sort something out later. Eventually, after a long teenage courtship, Jimmy would announce that he had asked Linda to marry him.

Before this should come to pass however, Gertrude's heart was broken with seventeen year-old Elizabeth. When Elizabeth began to hang around with the Mulhall boys she at first had pursed her lips in disapproval, thinking it a passing phase and they mere acquaintances. Even when she came home from school for the Christmas holidays and insisted on hanging around the circus encampment up at the big house, Gertrude tried not to show her anxiety. Then another year passed in which very little reference was made to them, and Gertrude relaxed. Now it was summer 1963, and Elizabeth had left school for good. She had become very strong-willed in that intractable way she had, offering no excuses and even less remorse. The night before had been a humdinger, a row where Gertrude had lost her temper and her dignity. She didn't like losing control, especially as nothing seemed to impinge on Elizabeth in any way. She was left shaking and ashamed afterwards when Elizabeth had gone to bed. She could not understand what the attraction to the Mulhall boys was, or if she were honest, theirs to her daughter. They knew she was a Hawthorn Thwaite and there was no love lost between the Mulhall brothers and Jimmy, who simply avoided them where possible, and then ignored them when forced to come into social contact. Was it a perverse kind of revolt on Elizabeth's part? It was a mystery. Elizabeth would manage to leave the house, even under curfew, and make her way to Arklow by bus or lift, to hang around the Mulhalls and their crowd on a Saturday night. She didn't even take a drink, whereas Gertrude knew the older boy, Mathew Mulhall, was certainly fond of a drink, which was a charitable way of saying he took up to eight pints of beer at one sitting, no trouble to him.

Johnny, the younger one by hardly a year, was probably as bad, but he always faded into his brother's shadow, being smaller and more mousy in colouring. And so Elizabeth, from some strange unshakeable loyalty, hung around them week after week despite her parents' pleas and threats of near imprisonment at home. She had to be near them, had to be out, had to hang around with that crowd. And she did so alone, without a girlfriend to tag along with for moral support.

Elizabeth's dress code was still prim and strict, like a nun's. Her only concession to the 1960s was a fur coat stolen from Gertrude's wardrobe. She let her hair hang about her face in a wild bush, so at odds with her thin girlish body. She still wore her glasses, those non-reflective barriers through which she could see out, but no one could see in. So disguised, or maybe armoured, she went blindly into the infested waters of a small town social scene. Ostrich-like she was, willing herself to be there in a semblance of belonging, despite being an obvious social oddity, a misfit fresh from the convent. As part of fitting in she didn't even try to smoke, maintaining her fastidious purity and religious zeal. What need drove her? Gertrude couldn't guess. Perhaps it was a hopeless unrequited love for one of the brothers? Gertrude hoped they would have more sense than to fall for her, because Elizabeth didn't. And so the rows went on every week, Saturday after Saturday, until Gertrude was worn into a state of near collapse, her nerves shot to bits.

'Lizzie, please for my sake don't go.'

'Why?' was the short reply.

'Look, those lads are no good. Please tell me, what do you see in them?'

'You wouldn't understand.'

Gertrude continued, forcing her voice to be mild and mollifying. 'Lizzie, I know you need friends and to get out and enjoy yourself. I'm not stopping you. But can't you see they're not your sort?'

'You're a snob, mother.'

Gertrude swallowed hard. Beads of sweat prickled on her forehead. 'Maybe they are nice lads. Frances did her best with them I'm sure. It's not their fault with the hard life they've had, it hasn't been easy for them.'

'They're not your friends. What would you know anyway?' said Elizabeth.

At this point Gertrude's voice frayed, her tone grating on her tonsils. She broke through the restraint. 'Elizabeth, I don't want you seeing them. That's all there is to it.'

Elizabeth stared in silence, her look more dead-end than defiant.

'Remember what those boys did to your brother!' Gertrude blurted out in exasperation.

'Prove it,' came the insolent reply.

'Oh for God's sake Elizabeth, see sense. You know quite well they've no interest in you. They're probably laughing at you behind your back the way they mocked Jimmy.'

'They are not.' Eyes down. Foot jiggling. Lip out below in a pout. Fingers flicking at a thread on her cardigan.

'Oh Elizabeth, you're hopeless. Pathetic, making such a fool of yourself – and the family.'

'Ashamed of me, are you Mummy?' Low. Sullen.

'No no, of course not. Look,' Gertrude came to sit in front of her now, begging, 'couldn't you mix with some of the girls from school? I'm sure they have nice brothers, a nice crowd to hang around with.'

'I only had one friend in school. And she went and got into trouble. I don't care about the rest of them. Or you.' A shot of hatred darted from Elizabeth's eyes as she rose. 'It's my life mother.'

Gertrude shouted weakly then sagged back down into the sofa as the door shut firmly. She had lost again. Why did she feel so much the loser in each encounter? Elizabeth was an emblem of betrayal, a travesty of all she, Gertrude, stood for.

Something lurking deep in her bowels stirred, coiled like a snake, releasing poison into her blood. It was oozing now, hissing up through the cracks. Nothing must come out. Ever. Let it fester.

Catherine's Diary

30 March 1985

I was up this morning early. I can't get comfortable lying down; my back is at me and I'm in and out to the toilet all night. So I was sitting in the kitchen before five when it was still dark. Jack is an old dote. I rub his head and he licks my hand. I'd swear he'd talk to you if he could. He has big brown eyes that are so kind, and he's not afraid to look at you. Just big open eyes. I look back at him too. 'Yeah Jack,' I said, 'just you and me in the whole world, only you to talk to.'

Then there was great kicking and punching in my stomach. I put my hand there and rubbed it round and round. 'Hey, stop that now would you?' But in a nice voice because Jack wagged his tail and it was thumping on the mat. 'Hey you in there, stop that now, go to sleep,' I said, smiling and winking at Jack. 'Shush,' I says to him, 'she'll really think me gone in the head now.'

So just tickling him under the chin we watched and waited for the light to fade in at the windows. Granny came down at seven.

'Oh, it's you,' she squeals. 'You gave me a fright.' She puts her hand to her throat. 'Could you not sleep?'

'Ah no, I'm all right, wasn't tired,' I mumble.

Then she opens the curtains and the sun streams in, with the birds singing like mad outside.

'Do you know what Catherine? We could do with a big long walk this morning, just the two of us.'

'Well there is no one else Granny.'

She smiles.

'Gertie.'

'What?'

'Gertie. That's my name. Enough of the Granny.'

'Oh my God, no I couldn't. I always say mister and missus to people, and aunty and uncle to all my relatives.'

'As you like,' she says, very friendly.

We set off after breakfast and do you know where she was headed? Across the field down to the river. There was my oak tree looking very sorry for itself with no sun on him this time of year, and the water sneaking past a sluggish brown. I missed the sparkles. The tree looked heavy and old. Did I imagine the whole thing? Make it all up? The riverbank was brown and spongy, old leaves rotting in the muck. No bed of roses.

Out of nowhere a tear trickles down my face. I sniff.

'Catherine, hurry on you'll catch a cold,' she says.

I follow her on up the side of the avalanche hill, up the dirt track by the fir trees on the edge of the forest. All the while I sniff and cough. A lump had come up in my throat and wouldn't go away, blocking my nose, making me weep.

'Stop it Catherine,' I say to myself. 'You're a big girl now. It's of no help anyway blubbering like a babby.'

Somehow I know where we are off to. Granny is ahead with her coat swishing long behind her, her boots squishing and sucking in the mud. She's strong and tall when you see her out walking like that. From the back you'd never think she was old, not at all, she looks really young with her blondey hair. It starts to fall out of its clasp and down in wisps around her face. When she turns round on the forest track her eyes are glowing and she has a big smile on her face from cheek to cheek. I stop. She is so full of life. And so happy. I have never seen her like that. She isn't a granny anymore. So I say it. Suddenly.

'Gertie! Oh you look lovely.' And then, 'Oh I'm sorry Granny, I didn't mean ...'

'Catherine, don't be sorry.' She steps forward holding her hand out to take mine. It is warm. She lifts the hair back off my face so I'd look at her. 'And thank you for the compliment.'

I laugh out loud suddenly.

'That's better,' she says. 'I haven't heard you laugh yet.'

'I never heard you laugh either,' I say, and put my head down and start to giggle.

Then she roars laughing and that sets me off again, and we are roaring and laughing at nothing at all there in the forest, giggling like two lunatics.

Do you know it made me feel great? It was mad but there we were falling around and slapping our knees and holding each other with the tears rolling down our faces. The laughing was ringing out in the forest cracking against the branches and shooting up into the sky.

When we stop we are exhausted. Then a great silence comes around us, like after communion. It is quiet as a church when we tiptoe along to the hut, as if not to disturb someone sleeping inside it.

Granny goes first. She looks at me seriously and then shoves open the door. It creaks loudly and some twigs fall down in a rattley cloud of dirt. Inside is shadowy with dusty cobwebs hanging from the rafters. There is a faint smell of cold ashes, and a smell of tar: resin from the woodcutters' planks left lying around on the floor. My foot kicks a bottle. It makes an awful clatter.

'Oh!' I say in fright.

'What?' says Gran, concerned.

Wasn't it the old bottle of milk I brought with me that day?

'That's mine,' I blush. 'From not long ago. I came here. I like to sit here in peace,' I blurt out.

'Me too,' she says.

'You do? Oh.'

She sits in the corner on the big stone by the fire, where I had sat.

'I like it too,' she says softly. 'It's homely.'

'Yeah, cosy isn't it?' I say, which sounded stupid because there was nothing there at all, just cold stone and the wind sighing. 'I do think of the avalanche,' I continue.

She shivers and gets up, starts flapping her arms around her to keep warm. 'Yes, those old stories.' She lets out a big breath.

'But the avalanche happened.'

'Oh yes it did, it did. The mighty snow toppling and thundering, slipping and sliding downwards in a deluge, rushing to oblivion.'

Granny's voice seems to separate from her body to soar against the walls, circling us in an echo from afar.

'The aftermath. Frosty wastelands. White nothingness. Ice seeping into the bones. Frozen terror. Like Pompeii. Fire locked in forever. No thaw possible. An icy mantle, hard as diamonds. What tragedy.'

She sounds like a schoolteacher reciting a poem, just standing in the middle of the space, her eyes very wide and blue. She goes quiet, so quiet I can hear our hearts beat. Her face falls down as if all the care of sixty years has melted away, leaving no marks. A child's face, unsure, frightened even. The heartbeats go on in the silence. The stillness so quiet, like prayer. I look to see if her lips are moving. They are open slightly, as if she is seeing something. Her eyes stare beyond me, she forgets I am there. So young. So troubled. The silence comes around us like the hush of snow that time, white cold and so so still.

I can see an angel baby swirling in the sunshine.

I gasp.

She comes to.

'It's so sad.'

Her eyes are full of pain. She sighs a long long sigh.

'Yes.'

I don't mention the baby. But somehow that's what was there. Sadness. Babies.

A blackbird hops in the doorway in front of us and sings a long clear note of lament. His song bears our hearts out of the hut and up the mountain cleansing them like water. We walk quickly back down the track, comfort in our footsteps trudging firm and fast. We chat an odd time like two old ones out for a morning walk. I feel like a woman.

On the way back up to the schoolhouse I see a lilac bush.

'Hey!' I run over in delight to smell it because I love lilac in the spring. I break off a sprig and run after her. 'Here, it's for you.'

She steps back in shock, as if I've given her a snake.

'Here, it's lilac, for you Gertie.'

'Take it away,' she snaps.

'I'm sorry Catherine. I don't like the smell. It makes me sick.'

She leaves me with my hand stretched out, the sprig of lilac flopping and my jaw down to my knees. I smell it once more, filling my nose with the purpley petals, then throw it away. She is Granny after all. I feel hurt.

Later I am very quiet. She is rummaging again at the kitchen table.

'Aha. Found it,' she says, waving an old letter in the air. She opens the envelope. It rustles and nearly falls apart.

'Dear Daddy, I'm having a nice time in Roscrea.' She turns over the envelope. 'April 1945, Easter. What a lie. Such deception. That innocent hand, perfectly executed in ink, and operated in lucidity: so adult for one so young. Who was that person? I hardly recognise her.'

'What do you mean? Show me.'

'Oh Catherine, I wasn't there at all. In Roscrea.' She stops, her face young again, bare. 'But there are some things you would never understand. You have so much goodness in you.'

She looks at me with her wide eyes, such a look that I put my head down. I am embarrassed. Me? Good?

To break the silence I say, 'Gran do you mind me asking, but why don't you like lilac?'

'Oh. That.' She swallows. 'It's the smell. It makes me gag. Like disinfectant.'

'Well ... ?'

'Oh, I got ill once during my exams. It was in First Year so I couldn't finish the exam paper.'

'Is that all?'

'The lie goes on,' she mutters.

'So I ended up not going back at all. The end of that chapter in my life.'

'Oh, I see.' But I hadn't a clue what she was on about.

'Nurse Rooney was arrested, did time. An English lady. They got her. Imprisoned for criminal acts. I was shocked when I heard. I never realised it was criminal; a sin, yes, but a secret. She was providing a service with her chloroform and needles.'

She isn't talking to me at all, for she says suddenly.

'Hah. Do you know that being a mother is not a self-evident skill? "Look Mrs Hawthorn Thwaite, here's your baby".' She turns to me savagely. 'You saw the photo. Do you know what it does to your body? The pain, the bleeding, the after-effects? Nobody tells you. The indignity. The shock.'

She begins to laugh, a bit hysterically I think.

'It's all a question of timing isn't it? Being on the right side of the blanket: one side happy families, the other side, exile. Where was my compassion? For myself?'

She was almost wailing, and sniffles a bit.

'Oh, forgive me Catherine, it's not fair on you.'

What does she know about me that she's not telling, I think frantically. She calms down a bit and looks at me very seriously.

'I must write a story for you Catherine, a true story. It will begin at the beginning. "My grandmother was born under the avalanche".'

Gertrude, 1966

Gertrude was tense with excitement. She slipped into the drawing-room lightly touching the tray of savoury crackers with her fingertips, and admired the display of crystal glasses set out on a side table, flanking a bottle of wine. She caught sight of herself in the mantel mirror and paused to admire the woman looking back. Light auburn hair puffed up on top, blow-dried to flick out all around the bottom just above her shoulders, a little knitted black two-piece suit hugging her trim figure. Her eyes stared back large and serious. She smiled. Not bad, not bad at all, for the mother of the groom to be. Tonight was the night of Jimmy and Linda's engagement party and she was hosting a reception, a drinks party so the two families could meet a good month before the wedding. Flames crackled in the grate. The doorbell rang musically making her jump.

Gertrude pouted at the mirror to check her lipstick, patted her hair held stiffly in place by lots of hairspray, and went to answer the door. The guests were few, only family: Linda, her parents, and two brothers, her best friend and bridesmaid; and the Hawthorn Thwaites themselves, Gertrude and William, the Major and Matilda, old Master Cullen and Bridie to help out. Oh, and Elizabeth. She set her face with a welcome smile as she pulled open the front door. On the doorstep was a young farmer in a shabby coat with a tweed cap. Gertrude's pleasure soured. On his arm was Elizabeth, her head resting on his shoulder.

'Hello Mummy, this is Johnny. Johnny Mulhall.' Elizabeth held on tight to his arm, ready to march him in. 'He's coming to the party too. After all, it is a family affair, isn't it?'

Elizabeth smiled brightly, baring her teeth. An uncomfortable Johnny shuffled past her into the hall, mumbling greetings and touching his cap.

'Oh,' said Gertrude. 'Well, you're the first.' She took a deep breath. 'Come in, I'll take your coat.'

She extended her hand, and Johnny the farmer slipped off his coat, muttering. 'Thanks very much. Sorry to disturb you ma'am. Thank you, that's grand.'

He handed over his coat, which Gertrude took on the end of two fingers. It smelled of sheep manure.

'Would you like to bring your friend down to the kitchen for a cup of tea? You're a bit early,' suggested Gertrude anxiously.

'No no, it's fine Mummy, we'll just stay in here,' said Elizabeth, opening the door to the drawing-room with an impudent confidence Gertrude had not seen before.

Elizabeth led Johnny to the fire and shoved him down into the sofa. If she hadn't known her daughter better, Gertrude could have sworn she had been drinking. Elizabeth's eyes shone with elation, her cheeks aflame.

'Make yourselves comfortable, but don't eat all the snacks,' Gertrude managed to say before hastening to the bathroom. Her composure was rattled. Dear God, she hadn't expected this, of all nights. What was Elizabeth thinking?'

Then the bell went again. Gertrude descended into the hallway to find it alive with guests and greetings. Jimmy had let them in himself, having driven in a convoy from Arklow. There was much exclamation and handshaking as coats were taken.

And so the evening started. Gertrude began to relax. The drawing-room was warm and welcoming, and she felt proud of their home and her achievements. William was a charming host, making sure glasses were filled quickly and refilled. Jimmy and Linda were in sparkling form; a mere glance would set off an explosion of some private joke. It had been a long time since the drawing-room at Glenview had been filled with such liveliness.

The Major was trying hard to make Johnny Mulhall feel welcome and had got him into a serious discussion about hoggets and mart prices for sheep. Elizabeth, sitting near the fire with her Grandad Cullen, seemed to gleam with pleasure, the firelight flickering and dancing in the thick glass of her spectacles. Suddenly she bounced out after her mother down the hall into the kitchen, when she saw her leaving to start the tea.

'I think I'm in love,' announced Elizabeth.

'What would you know about it?' Gertrude's response was instant, a whip crack of disdain.

She was perhaps too fired by terror to see the hurt in Elizabeth's eyes. They swam for a moment behind her glasses, the pupils opening in surprise, a fish-eyed vulnerability, quickly clouding over to close against her mother.

'Well, we're engaged. That's all there is to it,' she stated again.

'Engaged?' Gertrude was apoplectic. 'Engaged? To Johnny Mulhall? Elizabeth, are you out of your mind? Anyway, I thought it was that other renegade Mattie you were sweet on.'

'Yeah well, I'm engaged to Johnny now. What's wrong with that? Jimmy's engaged, and he's younger than me,' said Elizabeth defiantly.

'That's different.' Gertrude dismissed the argument, her brain spinning in turmoil.

'Yes, I know. It was always different for Jimmy.' Elizabeth's voice was low and threatening.

Gertrude stopped. A dark cloud hung on the outskirts of her vision, threatening to pour all over her. She almost wanted it to. It would be easier to drown than live to witness this. Her eyes popped and swam. She sat down suddenly, her skin ice-cold.

'Mum, a wedding I said, not a funeral. You look as if you've seen a ghost.' For once Elizabeth was concerned, her tone suddenly kindly. 'I didn't mean to shock you. Here, I'll get you a glass of water.'

Gertrude was dizzy, her insides wanting to spill out in protest. 'It's just not a good idea Elizabeth,' she said weakly.

'Why? Why Mum?'

Gertrude shook her head from side to side. Her eyes were stricken and clouded.

'Mam, I have a right to a life too, a home of my own, children, just like Jimmy. I'm almost twenty-one. It's about time.'

Gertrude seemed to come to. She looked her daughter full in the eyes, pain catching in her voice. 'Do you really want a life back down in the valley in a cottage full of crying children, just like Frances Mulhall?'

Elizabeth got up off her knees and said slowly, deliberately, disappointment freezing her voice. 'You are a snob. You look down on everybody. I hate you.'

'I'm warning you Elizabeth, don't do this. You will not see me at your wedding.'

'Don't worry, you won't be invited,' said Elizabeth, rage catching her breath as she left.

'Elizabeth, don't spoil Jimmy's evening,' she called out to her daughter's departing back.

Elizabeth slammed the kitchen door. Gertrude heard a commotion up in the front hall, then the door banged shut. She got up. Her palms were sweating, her throat tight with fear. The black deluge was about to pour all over her. She took a deep breath. Voices called. She stood up, patted her hair, armed herself with a large teapot, and coughed to clear her throat as she faced into the crowded room. Her teeth ached but her smile was bright.

The chatter had recommenced from where it had obviously stopped for a few seconds in stunned silence at Elizabeth's exit. Gertrude began to pour tea, her voice at its most lilting and charming. She avoided William's raised questioning eyebrows. Her smile continued to close him out.

'Great party, Mrs Hawthorn Thwaite,' said Linda brightly, as she came over to fill her plate with tea-scones. 'Thank you so much for having us,' she went on warmly.

'Yes, a great occasion,' said Gertrude, her teeth set in determination. 'Excuse me, will you dear?'

Gertrude glided over to William, tugged at his arm. 'Let's have a few words to mark the occasion, shall we?'

William's brows knitted further but he took his cue and clinked two glasses together accordingly.

In the far corner of the room, where he had been put sitting away from the fire which had become too hot, the old Master Cullen raised his eyes to watch his daughter. He saw a woman in her prime, splendid, powerful, a bright light, basking in the convivial warmth, flitting and fluttering like a butterfly, all things to all people on this night. But he also saw her eyes in between conversations cloud shut, her jaw tense, the little muscle in her cheek twitching. He had seen what had happened: Elizabeth had come back into the room too quickly, her face a grimace of pain, he seen her grab Johnny by the shoulder, Johnny who had risen stupidly and had simply followed her out of the room through the crowd, not saying goodbye. The Master had heard the front door bang. What was it all about? He watched the tapestry that was spread out before him, the living tapestry woven from all the children he had once taught in the valley school, their intermingling and intermarriages, and then the little versions of themselves that were their offspring. He tried to place this Mulhall boy, but he could only see the brother Mathew, the bold one with the curly hair – or was that Tommie? Now when was that exactly? All the faces swam before him. 'I'm a confused old man', he thought. His blue eyes blurred, but he caught Gertrude's hand as she rushed past.

'What is it Daddy? More tea?' she asked.

'Ah Gertie, take it easy love. Take a minute to slow down. Yes, yes, I'll have the tea.'

As she poured, he asked gently, 'What's wrong with Elizabeth?'

'Oh that one Daddy,' she said crossly, 'what will I do with her?'

'Herself and the Mulhall chap? Be gentle with her Gertie, sure it mightn't come to that.'

'No,' she said, flinty and determined, 'no it won't. Of course not.'

There was a pause as she stared into the middle distance. He took a chance.

'Try to love her,' said the Master.

Gertrude looked askance at her father.

'As your poor mother used to say, "you don't have to love the sin to love the sinner".'

Gertrude started out of her reverie. 'Sure nothing has happened yet, nothing at all. No, no, she's young yet.'

'Same age as you when you got married,' he reminded her.

Gertrude flushed. 'That was different Daddy.' She was crimson now. Hot. She rubbed the back of her hand across her forehead.

'Well, I can't tell you what to do. But I tried to love you all anyway, no matter what. That's what your mother taught me. We're all family in the end.' Gertrude looked stricken, as if she would cry. The Master continued, 'That's what counts. Blood is thicker than water.'

Gertrude coughed, rushed to pick up the teapot. 'I never knew what that meant.' She laughed him off, tut-tutting, shaking her head. 'Now Daddy, drink up your tea there, William is going to make a speech.'

But something had risen in her throat, something that threatened to spill out, her heart going to burst. She swallowed hard, patted her father's hand. 'Now Daddy, this is Jimmy's day, enough of your old palaver.'

There was a hush, a clearing of throats.

'Now, may I have your attention everybody please?'

A warm air of expectancy swelled in the room as a merry William launched into a fond remembrance of Jimmy's escapades as a boy. As his voice droned on, in the heat of that room, the Master's vision clouded, and sadness weighed heavily upon him. He watched Gertrude smile on and on, laughing loudly at the humorous bits, leading the applause at the end. Those little lines, hardening around her mouth. The telltale strain. The effort. She was formidable. She wouldn't, couldn't, stop. Nor thaw out. She kept going, brilliant, glittering, and he reluctantly had to admit, glassily hard. One day perhaps the ice would melt. He hoped so, for Elizabeth's sake.

Catherine's Diary

8 April 1985

Thanks be to God. Simon came. By himself. I nearly fell running out to the car to meet him.

'Hi,' says he, real cheery, then he looks up at the house. 'How's it going with the old bat?'

He laughs. He isn't looking at me straight. I try to give him a hug but he kind of shies away, like a horse. To tell you the truth there's a bit of a bump now in the way.

'Simon,' I says, 'it's great to see you. How's it going up in Dublin?'

'Oh, you know, all work and no play. Lots of exams coming up, I can't stay long.'

Then Granny came out and was fussing all over him, and we went in and she made tea. I was sitting there dying to talk to him but with her there I didn't say a word.

'When are your exams?' she asks.

'They start in May.'

'You're very good to come down at all,' she says.

'Well, it's most probably the last time. Until they're over.'

He didn't look at me. I got a shock. In May. Oh God. That's only a few weeks. Does he not realise? So we went outside.

'Simon, I've something to show you.'

He looks at me and I can see he isn't coming, so I say, 'Come on,' and take his arm.

'Hey, where are we going?'

I run and run pulling him up the hill at the back. When I look at him I have tears in my voice and am breathing hard from the climb.

'Simon, take me with you.'

'Ah Kitty, you know the score.'

'Simon, she won't be going to Mass for Easter.'

'Jesus,' he says, and he snorts snot all over himself, and into his hanky. 'Jesus, is that what you're worried about Kitty?'

'I am,' I said. 'I am so. She's cracked. She doesn't go to Mass. It's bad enough I missed the last few Sundays but Mammy and Daddy will be wondering.'

'I'll tell them you're fine up here. And that she's going to Mass up in Moyne with Father.'

'But that's not true.'

'No, it's not,' he agrees. 'It's not the truth.'

'Look Simon,' says I, 'I don't want to be any trouble but it's not so easy you know.'

He doesn't say a word. Sometimes he's like one of the kids.

'I'm not complaining but I was dying to see you. I know you're awful busy with your study, but I was wondering when I'll be able to leave and come to Dublin with you. Have you got me a flat yet?'

Simon stops and says something I can't hear.

'Catherine,' he says, 'look, you know we all care for you, but until, until, you know, well ... you've got to stay here.'

'Why? Granny doesn't know.'

'What? She hasn't said anything?'

'No, she hasn't, not at all. She hasn't a clue. She's cracked too, I told you.'

'Are you sure?'

And he looks at me, swinging me around.

'Catherine, maybe you should say something.'

'Me?' says I. 'Sure you're the one that's doing all the arranging. Anyway I told you I'm coming to Dublin. You won't know me, I'll be so thin.'

He takes my two arms and looks into my face.

'Catherine, you're having a baby.'

I'm not a child, I think to myself.

'You have to stay here.'

'Simon.'

I am nearly crying.

'You said you were making arrangements. So did Helen. Now I have decided I'm not staying here anymore.'

'Look,' he says, 'you can phone me any time. I'll give you a number. But remember our secret. Promise me again. You're not to say anything, ever, OK?'

'Simon, you know I'd do anything for you, you know that.' I am in tears now. 'Only don't leave me here on my own, it's so long since you came.'

'Helen will be down in a few days for Easter. Don't worry, she'll help you.'

I look terrible, my eyes are smarting. He can't stand it.

'I'm sure she'll bring you to Mass.'

He fumbles in his pocket for a fag.

'Simon, I can't stay here. Granny will find out. Then she won't talk to me anymore. I can't. And then, then what will we do?'

His voice is kind again, and very strong. Oh God.

'Don't worry, Kitty, I'll look after everything.'

He kisses me on the forehead and turns and marches off down the path, his coat flapping behind him.

'Oh, Simon.'

A wail. I sit down on the grass and hug my knees.

His car starts.

Simon. My cheeks are wet. I just want to get away from here. Before Daddy sees me like this. Or the kids. They'd be disgusted. Please help me God please. I'll get to Mass on Easter. Somehow.

9 April

Granny knows. Last night she said, 'Come into my room. We'll have to get you some clothes to wear, I'm sick of looking at you in that old jumper, and it could do with a wash.'

'Ah no, it's all right thanks.'

'Nonsense, come on, I won't bite.'

My mouth went dry. I was mortified. She took things out of the Master's wardrobe that she must have had at my age, long flowery dresses and things.

I said, 'no really, it's not that I don't like them it's just I never wear dresses anymore, they just get in the way when you have to work around the place.'

I tried every excuse, I really did.

'I don't understand you, you'd look lovely,' she said. 'They'd suit you too, we have the same colouring.'

So I took the dresses and went back to my room to strip and closed the door. I sat on the bed. What could I do? She was sure to notice. I picked up a blue dress with yellow flowers and held it to me. It matched my eyes. There was only a small mirror on the dressing table so then I tried it on. It did fit me, only I left it loose at the waist. There was a belt but I didn't close it. She knocked and I jumped out of my skin, pulling my old shirt up to cover me.

'Well? Is that nice on?' She was smiling. 'You look lovely.'

My face was puce. I sat back down again and was shaking.

'Catherine, oh Catherine,' she said, just standing there looking at me.

'I'm sorry Granny,' I said, and burst out crying. She came and sat on the bed. She didn't say anything for ages. I couldn't stop crying. I was blowing my nose and feeling really stupid.

'Don't tell Daddy,' I said.

'We won't, there there, I'll make you some cocoa.'

That's what I mean she's odd. She didn't say another word, not 'you hoor, you stupid little slut, how could you do that to your father?' Or even 'may God forgive you.' She just went on down and didn't say another word. In the kitchen I was looking at her to see if she would but she didn't. I feel peculiar, I mean she never says what you think she will. I hope she keeps her word and doesn't tell Daddy.

So tonight I'm watching her like a hawk to see if she'll say anything else. The clock ticks loudly and I can't wait for it to be ten.

'Goodnight Granny.'

'Oh you're going up?'

I scuttle across the room saying goodnight again.

Suddenly she says, 'It's Simon isn't it?'

I stop dead in the doorway. I can't look around. My face burns. I don't say a word. I promised him. I promised him and he can trust me. My lips are tight.

'Ah Catherine, I know you probably love him too.'

She sounds kind. I start to shake, and have to hold myself against the door.

'I'm going to bed,' I mumble, still not looking.

She comes and stands behind me and strokes my hair.

'Catherine, it's not a crime to fall in love. Believe me. I know. Maybe you can't imagine your grandmother, but I was madly in love once too, here in this valley. It made me feel like singing all the time, dreaming of him and how he would touch me.'

I turn around. She is smiling.

'Yes, that too. That too.'

I am so shocked. I put my head down, hotter than ever.

'In the hut,' she says.

Oh my God that's disgusting, and her an old married woman.

I run up the stairs wanting to get sick. Now what'll I do? I'm so confused.

10 April

Helen showed up yesterday. Her hair is orange now, I don't know how Daddy doesn't kill her. She was all chat and I was dying to know about Simon but couldn't let on.

'Won't be long now, Kitty,' she says. 'How many weeks? Four more?'

'I don't know,' I say, 'I never count.'

'Ah now look at you Kitty, sure you're huge. Sorry, I didn't mean it. You don't see a thing from the back. Here, I got you a pressie.'

She gives me a bag from Dunnes Stores with a jumper in it, a big pink thing.

'It'll do the job, it's nearly down to your knees.'

'Helen, will you stop going on about it. When can I go to Dublin?'

'Aren't you all right here for now?'

She lights her fag.

'What about the arrangements?'

'Don't worry, Simon has it all organised.'

'What? Where am I going to have it?'

'God, I don't know.'

She sounds surprised.

'Simon said something about a mother and baby home run by the nuns. Sure he'd know all about it with his medical contacts.'

'It better be soon,' I say. 'Anyway you're wrong, he's getting me a flat with him in Dublin.'

'He's what? Come off it Kitty. You're better off here I'm telling you. Getting you a flat? I don't think so.'

'He is. He is. I'm not staying here.'

'Ah Gran's not the worst. You're better off here. Has she said anything?'

'She doesn't know, I'm telling you. I'm going to Dublin. He promised.'

'Cop on, Kitty,' she said. 'Mammy's not very well, she's missing you something terrible.'

Jesus. That did put a stop to my gallop.

'Why? What's Mammy doing?'

'You know yourself, up at the crack of dawn some days, wandering.'

That upset me. Poor Mammy. She was certainly very ropey before I left. I wonder how she's getting on without me? When I seen her sitting there, her eyes flicking and darting behind her glasses, I was worried. I miss her. I'd love to tell her not to worry. She has such a frown on her face, a big line deep down the middle of her forehead to the top of her nose, right between her glasses. Her face is papery looking, with lines around her mouth and bags under her eyes. She looks plain miserable all the time, and there's nothing I can do, could do, even when I was there.

John Paul used to be able to make her laugh with his silly jokes, or Liamey with playacting, but that wasn't working either. Liamey would snap his fingers, put out his tongue, pulling his eyes back and cross them, and there'd be not a gig out of her. Not a gig. Not even pretending to smile. Liamey would look at me, or go over and kick the bin, topple it over for badness. Not a stir. They usually all went out. No one likes staying around her. That left me and Mam. I didn't know what to do with her. Then she might perk up and get notions.

'I'll take the bus to Arklow today Catherine, I have some legal business to sort out. Where's my coat?'

And she'll rummage in her handbag, take out lipstick, open the powder compact and smear her lips.

'Is that straight Catherine, is it?'

Next she'll tie a headscarf on, and pull it tight under her chin.

'Do I look nice, do I Catherine?'

She'll stand there with her coat on, puckering her mouth to show me.

'Is there lipstick?'

She pulls back her lips for me to check her teeth.

'That's grand Mammy. But you forgot ...'

'What?' she says, her face snapping shut.

'Your slippers Mam.'

'Oops, you're right Catherine. What would I do without you? Bye now.'

And she'll head for the door, down the lane, walking quickly away, with the slippers still on.

I gave up trying to go after her, or stop her, for she'll always come back, slowly, very tired, saying the bus was full when I know only too well there was no bus, for she was only gone ten minutes at the most. She'll sit back into her chair with her coat on letting out a big tired sigh. 'Oh well. The business will have to wait until tomorrow.' And she'll take up the handbag, and rearrange her purse and her compact and lipstick and all the other things that jingle in there: a nail file, knitting needles, a scissors, dirty big hankies, a hairbrush. 'All present and accounted for,' she says. She closes the bag, sets it down under the chair, settles back, and you mightn't get a word out of her for the rest of the day until the boys come home at five.

Oh Mammy, what are we going to do with you? Sure I can't do anything now, can I? It'll be all over soon, I promise Mammy, and you'll never know a thing about it. I'll be good Mammy, I will. Good and pure. You were right.

I'm crying now like a babby. Can it be christened? Will I say an Our Father in its ear first?

14 April, Easter Sunday

Granny got Uncle Jimmy to give us a lift. We went up to the chapel in Moyne where I don't know many people. At least I got Communion. I wonder if that's a sin? To be taking the Body of Christ if there's a mortal sin on your soul. But how am I supposed to make it better, make reparation? I am sorry, Oh Lord, I am. I didn't mean it. I really didn't mean it. I wish I was ten again.

I kept my head down and didn't look at anybody in the church. I had another coat of Granny's on, she wouldn't let me wear the old anorak. She gave me a tweedy thing instead, with black buttons. I left it open. I washed my hair and put on the new jumper Helen gave me. Even I thought I looked quite nice, and slim. The jumper is long and swings at the front.

So when we were getting ready for Mass she says, 'Happy Easter Catherine', and comes in with this tweed coat. When Uncle Jimmy comes with the car she says, 'May I take your arm dear?' and lets me help her out and into the car.

She did all the talking so I wouldn't have to say anything. She said to Jimmy, 'Catherine is a great help to me you know,' and on the way back, 'doesn't she look nice?' I nearly fell over.

Uncle Jimmy said, 'Very nice,' and then looked at her like he was raising an eyebrow, but she looked straight ahead out of the front seat of the car and talked about the lambs and the daffodils. Her coat was nice and warm on me.

Gertrude, 1967

On a snowy morning in January, the inhabitants of Glenview House awoke to the stillness of death: Major Hawthorn Thwaite had died quietly in his sleep overnight. He had been having little turns since Christmas, and had gone to bed early the night before, suffering from indigestion. When Matilda stirred in the morning to get up and make his tea, he was stone cold in the bed beside her. She arrived trembling at Gertrude's bedside, her teeth chattering and almost incoherent.

'Father, your father,' she managed to squeeze out between gasps.

William jumped up with a great cry and ran to see for himself. When Gertrude came into the Major's bedroom, she saw mother and son sobbing silently in each others' arms. It was Gertrude who had to take charge, calling the doctor and the priest. Gertrude rang her own father who came immediately with old Bridie who always knew what to do. Bridie summoned Nurse Mahoney the district nurse, and together they washed the body and laid it out, shooing the family away off to get dressed.

'William, please have some breakfast,' Gertrude said, taking him firmly by the arm.

He looked at her, a sleepwalker, stricken, and followed her obediently down the back hall to the kitchen. Then he sat down suddenly on a stool. His face creased and collapsed as he shook with a series of strange sounds. For Gertrude it was terrible to hear. She busied herself after breakfast, making lists and talking to the undertaker. She couldn't remember who had done all this when her mother had died. It felt like a rehearsal for when the Master's turn would come, and how would she feel then? Hearing her husband's dry retches shook her to the core, wringing her with pity. She was saddened herself, but not desolate like William at the loss of a parent; those blood ties, thicker than ever in death. She had always assumed William to be so even-tempered, she hadn't credited him with deep feelings, pits and places where he could store and hide his hurts.

William informed the office of his father's death in a taut voice. Jennifer on the other end of the phone was unbearably kind. He collapsed again. Gertrude had to lead him upstairs to wash and dress.

She called Jimmy, who said he would come as soon as he could get away with Linda. And Elizabeth was there, sitting in the corner of the kitchen looking on, owlish and dry-eyed. She didn't appear to sense other peoples' distress, her eyes turned inward to herself and her own concerns. Mostly Gertrude was worried about Matilda. The woman's chirping ceased for good on that day, and a vacant stare replaced the light in her beady eyes.

However, on this day, the ordering and the organising, the informing and the preparing, took over. The body was finally dressed and laid out, awaiting its removal to the church. The women were kept busy in the kitchen, and neighbours called in to help make sandwiches and apple tarts. Jimmy was dispatched to replenish the stocks of whiskey. On his return he took his mother aside.

'Mum, Linda and I were discussing this. I think we had better postpone the wedding until later. It wouldn't be right. Dad seems to be taking it badly. Let's give him a chance to recover. We don't mind.'

Gertrude hugged her son gratefully. He returned it with some of the old warmth.

'Oh Jimmy, that's a good idea. Thank you.'

Her eyes stung with tears. She was grateful she still had him, and that the grieving was not for him. She didn't know how she'd cope if anything happened to one of her own. She knew there was a well of grief bubbling underground ever since her mother had passed away. She was glad to be spared this now.

'Fine darling, we'll think about a summer wedding instead.'

The funeral two days later was swift and small. In the immediate aftermath of the Major's death Glenview House was a changed place. William's grief was tangible. It weighed down the air whenever he was in the room, making light conversation or any attempt at levity impossible. In spite of feeling awfully sorry for him, and really trying to cherish and hold him, Gertrude found her husband unreachable. Whatever rift had begun to emerge now yawned like a soundless chasm between them.

In this atmosphere, Matilda's behaviour of sudden starts and erratic movements was unsettling. She would come hastily into a room, stop in the doorway, stare around, eyes wide but unseeing, and leave again, as if she had forgotten what she was doing there. She would cry out loud exclamations or greetings, start a sentence, and stop, so that the words would hang unfinished, echo and taper out, to fall back onto her chest and fade away. Gertrude began to get jumpy as she was startled in this way several times a day. What scared her most was the phrase, 'tell her the truth'. She tried to ignore it, shake it off as the ravings of an old woman, but she knew deep down what Matilda was trying to say. She meant Elizabeth, and she referred to a cold night a long time ago that Gertrude would rather forget. Tell her the truth. 'Never', thought Gertrude, 'I'll bring it with me to my grave. It is of no consequence. To anyone.'

The Angelus bells chimed on the radio. It was six o'clock. Gertrude automatically blessed herself while lifting the lid on the pot of potatoes simmering on the range. Time to get Matilda from the drawing-room. William would be home soon with Elizabeth, who was halfway through a secretarial and bookkeeping course in Arklow, and took a lift with her father morning and evening. Gertrude wondered what William and Elizabeth spoke about on those trips. She couldn't imagine great confidences or warm chats. The chill that had set in since Jimmy's engagement party had grown into an icy wasteland, although it was a cold war directed mainly at her mother. Elizabeth was not inclined to give much away and William had stopped his efforts to be hale and hearty since his father's death. He had become very subdued, getting through his day's work with assiduous attention to detail, blindly following a routine. He managed better that way.

Gertrude clattered along the tiles up to the hall and entered the drawing-room. Matilda sat in the semi-darkness, gazing at a display of photographs on the wall.

'Come on Mumsy, time for dinner. The others will be home soon.'

She forced herself to be cheerful. Matilda started, and swivelled her head towards Gertrude with blank, unseeing eyes.

'You must be hungry, come on then,' she cajoled.

Headlights swept the room.

'Ah, here they are,' Matilda piped up suddenly with some of her old cheerfulness as they went to eat.

In the clatter of the daily dinner routine it was some minutes before any talk could start.

'How was your course today?' Gertrude inquired politely of Elizabeth.

Elizabeth kept her eyes focused downwards on her food.

'Same as every day mother,' she said with a full mouth.

Gertrude glanced at William. He was of no help. Matilda pushed her food around her plate and didn't come to the rescue as she used to with her chirping interventions.

'Jimmy rang today,' Gertrude offered. Jimmy was still studying in Dublin.

'Oh. How is he?' asked William getting busy with his chop.

'Fine. He'll be getting a placement in a solicitor's office for three months.'

'Where? In Dublin?'

'Yes. But fortunately he'll be finished in time for the wedding.'

'That's good.'

Matilda stopped eating and stared down the table at Elizabeth.

'And when is your wedding dear?'

Elizabeth started, her eyes darting round the table. The subject had not been broached since the night of the party two months earlier.

'Johnny has booked the Arklow Bay Hotel,' she muttered, flushing.

'Really?' said William, sounding surprised. 'You never said. So it's going ahead?'

Gertrude was tight-lipped. 'She's very good at keeping secrets, isn't she?' she flashed at Elizabeth.

'But you didn't get engaged, did you my dear?' Matilda said, not noticing.

'Oh we're not getting engaged. I mean, I'll get a ring, that will do me. I don't like fuss,' said Elizabeth.

'You could let us in on these things,' said Gertrude, accusing, sarcastic.

'I didn't think you ... You didn't want to know,' said Elizabeth, her voice hurt and defiant.

'Girls, ladies,' said William wearily, 'please stop the bickering.' He addressed his wife firmly, 'Gertrude, Elizabeth is obviously set on marrying this Mulhall fellow. So, let it be now, and give me some peace.'

Gertrude looked astonished, bile rising in her throat. 'William, you can't be serious. Just letting her. I just don't know how you can stand by and watch your only daughter ...'

'Yes mother?' Elizabeth challenged.

'Oh you know,' said Gertrude faltering, 'make a fool of herself, make a mess of her life.'

Elizabeth's voice rose an octave. 'Mess?' she squeaked. 'You'll see.'

She got up, lifted her dinner plate and dropped it into the sink with a clatter.

'Elizabeth!' commanded William. 'Sit down. I'm fed up with this atmosphere between you. Come back and talk to your mother.'

'Ask her to talk to me for a change then,' sulked Elizabeth.

'Oh dear,' moaned Matilda. 'Oh dear.' Her eyes darted between them like swallows.

William looked daggers at Gertrude to silence her. Then, addressing his mother to soothe her. 'It's all right Mumsy. Sorry for raising my voice.'

But his look flashed a warning to Gertrude. He turned to the sink. 'Now Elizabeth, come here. Sit down and finish your dinner.'

'I'm not hungry, thank you,' was the sullen reply as she sloped into her seat.

'Anyway,' said William, attempting some of his old joviality, 'when is the big day?' He pushed back his chair, smiling at his daughter.

'June Sixteenth. It's a Saturday I think.' Elizabeth added by way of apology, 'and a good time for Johnny before the harvest, before he gets busy.'

Gertrude stared hard. 'But you can't. That's the same day as Jimmy's, the new date he and Linda have set.'

'Oh dear, a bit of a mix up,' said William.

'Let him change it then,' said Elizabeth. 'We booked ours ages ago. That's not my fault, for once. We're not moving.'

She was adamant.

'Elizabeth, you can't do this,' protested Gertrude.

'Why not?' said Elizabeth.

'Because Linda's relatives are coming home from Canada. They've booked their flights already.'

'Ah for God's sake that's three months away,' William complained. 'First you don't want her married, then you tell her what day to pick. Would you leave her alone,' he finished on a roar.

'William!' Gertrude was shocked but still she turned to her daughter. 'Elizabeth, this is just ridiculous, the two of you cannot get married on the same day.'

Elizabeth raised her eyes to her mother, her pupils magnified.

'You don't want me to get married at all, that's it, isn't it?'

Gertrude opened and closed her mouth.

'Elizabeth,' she rose to her feet, her cheeks pink blobs. 'I have made myself perfectly clear. I do not approve, no I don't.'

'I thought you'd get over it,' said Elizabeth in a voice small with disappointment. 'I thought you'd want me to be happy.' Her voice cracked. 'But you never do, do you? I hate you.' She gave a great sniff as she rushed from the room, blinded by tears.

William looked at Gertrude, his look accusing. 'Jesus, can there be no peace in this house?' He slammed his hand onto the table and stood up. 'Out of respect for my father at least.'

Matilda's teeth started to chatter.

William glared at his wife.

'All right, calm down, I'll go to her,' said Gertrude leaving the kitchen.

She climbed the cold stairs into the box room where Elizabeth slept, and pushed the door open quietly.

Elizabeth sat on the bed, clasping a black haired doll, rocking slowly back and forth. 'It's all right, it's all right, it's going to be all right,' she whispered in short breaths, her lips strained with pain. 'It'll be all right.' Tears gathered and fell slowly out through her eyelids to spill down her cheeks.

Gertrude coughed.

Elizabeth looked up, her eyes gleaming and wet. At the sight of her mother, her chin trembled. She threw down the doll and rushed at the door.

'Get out. Get out. I hate you mother.'

The door slammed in Gertrude's face.

'Elizabeth.' She knocked on the door. 'Elizabeth, please, let's talk.'

'About what? About how you disapprove of me and everything I do and everyone I love? No thanks. Go on, get away.'

'I'm your mother,' Gertrude persisted, 'I care about you.'

'Care? Care? You care all right.' Elizabeth opened the door a little, her face crumpled and red. 'As long as I'm out of your sight and out of your hair.'

She slammed the door shut again.

'Elizabeth, please, for the last time, open the door. I am your mother.'

'Just get away. Get away. I can't stand it. I can't stand you. Leave me alone.' The last was muffled through the wooden barrier.

Gertrude stared hard at the blank unyielding door. Inside, there was a banging and pulling and pushing of drawers being opened and shut.

'Elizabeth. We'll work something out. You can get married, I just ask you to wait a few years.'

Elizabeth yanked open the door. 'It's too late. I'm going.' She had a schoolbag under her arm stuffed with underwear. 'I'm going to Grandad's.'

'You're what? Elizabeth, this is going too far.'

Elizabeth pushed past her down the stairs. 'I'm going to Grandad. Master Cullen always had room for me in his house. He loves me.'

The last words were uttered in a cry that echoed in the air. The unfinished remainder, 'and you don't', hung accusingly between them.

Gertrude followed her daughter heavily down the stairs. Voices were raised in the kitchen. William was arguing with her. 'You can't go out now in the dark. It's too far. And it's freezing.'

'Bring me there Daddy,' urged Elizabeth, 'it's the least you can do. Get me away from her.'

As Gertrude came back Elizabeth glanced at her with a look of pure vitriol. She turned back pleading to her father. 'She never wanted me. Well now she can be rid of me for good.'

She marched out, pulled open the back door. William followed her, slipping on his coat and shrugging. He patted Elizabeth's shoulders.

'Things might look better in the morning Lizzie love. But if that's what you want I'll bring you to Grandad's. Should we ask him first?'

'No,' screamed Elizabeth. 'Just get me out of here.'

She was shaking, her voice rising again, near hysterical.

Matilda looked on aghast, then looked straight at Gertrude as they left. 'Tell her the truth,' she whispered.

Gertrude stared back at her for a good few seconds. Then her eyes clouded over and she turned and swept out of the room. The car engine started outside.

In the darkness of the hall Gertrude's heart hammered in her chest. She placed her palms one after the other on the wooden banisters and mounted the stairs slowly, each step like a mountain. Her legs were lead, weighed down by sorrow. She reached the door of Elizabeth's room, with its bed dishevelled, clothes spilling out from drawers onto the floor. Then her legs gave way. She sank down, holding onto the side of the bed. Her breath came in short gasps. She couldn't cry. Her head was a jumble, a thick stew of thoughts racing and bumping. She retched but couldn't vomit. She keeled over, kneeling with her forehead on the floor, the cold perspiration drizzling down her back. She retched again. Her head swam. She clutched the bed. As she tried to calm her breathing, her eye caught sight of a small china bootee. Dolly was lying under the bed, abandoned or forgotten where she had fallen. Gertrude reached out, pulled the porcelain legs towards her, picked up the doll and clasped it to herself. A sob clutched her throat and tears started to stream down her cheeks. She hugged the hard china head into her shoulder, stroked the silky synthetic hair, rocking back and forth, back and forth. Her breath sobbed and caught. Dolly's eyes stared glassily blue over Gertrude's shoulder, the plastic eyelids clicking softly up and down, up and down, as the mechanical eyes opened and closed with the rocking movement. Then, as Gertrude calmed and came to, she placed Dolly gently in a box, laid her down and closed her eyes.

Catherine's Diary

15 April 1985

'So the wedding went ahead and you didn't go?'

Granny stirs out of one of her memory trances and looks at me. We are looking at photos again. She hands me a big glossy photograph of Uncle Jimmy's wedding. There they all are in full colour, Gertrude and William flanking the smiling bride and bridegroom, then Linda's parents, and Matilda, tiny in a wheelchair at the edge. Some of Linda's brothers stand behind in their dickey bows. But no Elizabeth.

'Do you know I can't even find a picture of her wedding,' she says crossly.

I cough. 'I think Mammy has it at home.'

'I was sure there was one here. Daddy kept it always on the mantelpiece. The poor man had to choose, so he went to Elizabeth's ceremony, then came to Jimmy's reception to share a glass with us after the meal. What stress to be putting on an old man. And he kept smiling, always a gentleman.'

I cough to make her go on.

'Ah yes. Your question. No, no I didn't go to your Mammy's wedding. Although I was sore tempted when I heard he was due to come back ...'

'Who?'

She jumps and looks at me. 'Oh, of course, I didn't tell you, did I?'

'What?'

'Who I was in love with.'

It struck me like lightning. 'Tommie? Tommie Mulhall?'

'Yes. Tommie. For a split second my heart leaped and the old feelings came rushing up. But I clamped them down firmly.'

'But why? You told me he made you feel like singing ...'

'Yes yes,' she says impatiently. 'But that was before ... when I was Gertrude Cullen the schoolmaster's daughter from Moyne.'

Then I ask her the one question that has me burning up too.

'Gran, did you faint because of him that night at the funeral? Did you really love him all along?'

She draws her breath in sharply, then lets out a long sigh.

'Dear Catherine, what can I say now after forty-something years? Am I the girl I was then? Do we grow up and into someone else? I don't know. I can't answer you that. You ask me what is love, and that is the biggest mystery of all.'

She stares off into the middle of the room, her voice rising clearly.

'When I was fourteen and more, Tommie was like a part of me, like the air in the valley when I ran over the fields to the forest. I was free, free as a bird sailing on the breeze. Completely free, and at the same time truly and utterly myself. Tommie was part of the air I breathed, part of the wind whistling through the treetops, or rushing full blast into my face.

'He was everywhere even when he wasn't with me. He was in the sky and in the smell of the pine needles in the forest, in the sway of the trees and in the bark of the fox. He was me, then.

'And later, at eighteen or so, we had the hut. Our palace. Do you know the sonnet? "We made of that little room an everywhere."

'As you saw Catherine, that place is special. It makes you feel things, life stripped raw, as if newborn, bare.

'And I was naked there too,' she laughs. And laughs. Ringing in my ears. I blush scarlet.

'I mean my soul,' she goes on. 'I was so exposed and vulnerable. I don't know. The weight of the mountain, the cold of the snow. Our passion, fire and ice. Which is the stronger? Fire fans the flames, they leap to their death. Ice from so fragile beginnings, survives: cold crystals coalesce slowly, slowly, hardening to a sinister sheen. They clink in the heart. And afterwards, the consequences. Shards of secrecy silently stabbing you from the inside. They shrink the possibility of love.'

She is in that trance again, like in the hut. Words tumbling out of her. I can't keep up, I don't know what she means but I feel her, her feelings so strong, flooding out.

Gertrude turns to me wide-eyed. Her eyes shine and her mouth trembles.

'I loved him. Yes I did. But I never told him, not really. I let him think he didn't matter. Because he came from the wrong end of the valley.'

Her eyes fill up.

'I never had the courage even to tell myself.'

She slapped a hand suddenly hard on the table, making me jump.

'Look at that poor girl in Kerry. What is her crime, really? Trial by television, everyone holier than thou. "Let he who is without sin cast the first stone".'

She is fierce as she says this.

'Ah. We've too many of them lining up already. What is her sin? To have loved, like Mary Magdalene. Or to have been caught? That's Irish all right. I didn't get caught.'

Her voice is low.

'But there is always a price. Consequences. And of course I couldn't blame anyone else, just myself.'

She's completely lost me now. Not a clue what's she's on about.

'I was very hard on myself Catherine. Driven always to be perfect. To make it work. Because you see, it all had to work. And it did.'

She sits back quietly.

'Who paid the price? Oh God I'm not sure I want to answer that one.'

'Who do you mean?' I ask.

But she is still going on to herself.

'I glittered Catherine. I made my choice, by my lights at that time, and was captured in it. But you can be free.'

She gets up, eyes blazing.

'Tell your story Catherine. And I will write you mine. I must. The truth? All the way to Jimmy's wedding I sat up in the front of the car with my hat on, dolled up to the nines, watching like a hawk as we rolled through the village for a glimpse of him, anywhere, perhaps ducking into Byrne's hotel for a quick scoop, as they put it, or crossing the road to go up the hill to the chapel. God how shameful!'

'Ah well Granny you hadn't seen him in all those years ...' I bumble in, trying to make her stop.

'No, I mean when you think about it, it wasn't Elizabeth I was looking out for, not thinking of her at all. She's right. I am a bad mother. Didn't look out for my own daughter on her wedding day.'

'Ah no, don't say that. Did you ever try to patch things up with Mammy?'

'Yes, once in a way. For the Master's sake, for my Daddy's sake. He asked me to.'

Gertrude, 1968

When the wedding was over life began to get back to normal. Jimmy and Linda went to Dublin to live in the flat he was renting while still studying, until such time as they could come back and take up residence in Glenview House, as had William and Gertrude before them. They always came home for the weekend. Gertrude encouraged them to use the drawing-room and the old dining room as their quarters as much as possible, leaving the kitchen as her domain.

They were gone for most of the week and the house was deathly quiet. Jimmy had attended secondary school in Carlow so on weekdays the house had always been silent, but at least it was full of his presence: boots kicked off in the hall, a sweater thrown over an armchair, posters on the walls of his room. Now he had truly grown up and moved out. The house echoed with emptiness. Gertrude found herself wandering aimlessly from room to room, tears rolling down her cheeks. Stop it silly, she would blow into her handkerchief, stop it. And then her eyes would fill up again, and the tears roll down her cheeks, and roll and roll, onto her collar and the top of her blouse. She would stand and gaze out of the window, watch a blackbird call in the fir tree. Feel as grey as the sky.

All through that summer and autumn and well into the end of the year, after both weddings, and the Major's death, Gertrude slipped into a decline of grief and loss. She was not grieving for the Major. She grieved for Jimmy, for her son, for her child, for her baby. The joy he had brought her. The closeness. Filling her up. Then a pang would shoot through her for her father, the Master, living alone in the schoolhouse still. Then the old guilty secrets would threaten to surface. No. She just felt miserable, there was nothing left to do. She was forty-two, and felt as ancient as time. What was there left to do? Who in the end did she really care about in the valley? Oh yes, neighbours came and went, William was always there at the end of the day, Matilda hobbled about getting lost going from one room to another, haunting her with those beady eyes. 'Don't let her', she had said, 'tell her the truth.' But Gertrude had ignored her, pretending not to hear, and continued to look the other way. Now she felt those eyes pursue her from room to room, accusing her. But there was nowhere to run, no one she could tell. Somehow Gertrude had cut herself off over the years, didn't belong to the local valley community, didn't even belong in Glenview House. She didn't belong anywhere, to anyone, or even to herself.

They were bad days, stalled in the doldrums. Her hair fell out of its clips, uncombed, uncared for. She wore the same skirt for days, an old one, long and soft. She wished she had it all over again, wanted to curl up on the sofa as at seventeen and read Tolstoy. But she was an old woman whose life was over.

The real reason for her lack of life force (more than the empty nest left by Jimmy) was that she had lost the struggle with Elizabeth. She had no more battles to fight, no more young ones to protect. What do you do when your own daughter sleeps with the enemy?

Linda and Jimmy arrived one weekend bursting with something to tell her. She knew it by the way they fidgeted and fussed around the kitchen, or laughed out loud suddenly.

'Come on, what is it you two? You're up to something.'

Jimmy came over and put his arm around her shoulder. 'Mum, I hate to do this to you ...'

He looked at her very seriously, so that for a moment she thought the worst.

'... but you're going to be a grandmother.'

'What?' She looked at Linda in bewilderment, 'You're ...?'

'Yes Mum, Linda is pregnant.'

Linda added, 'isn't that amazing, I'm going to have a baby.'

Gertrude smiled kindly at her daughter-in-law.

'That's great news Linda.' She looked at Jimmy, her brows knitting. 'So soon? I mean, when are you due?'

'Oh it's early days. Not until spring, around the end of February,' said Linda laughing.

'Oh. I'm ... I don't know what to say. I'm overcome, I suppose.'

'Come on Mum, give us your blessing,' Jimmy said.

'Oh I do, I do. It's just that ... I wasn't expecting it, so soon,' Gertrude tapered off.

'This is supposed to be what happens when you get married,' teased Jimmy.

'Or don't,' said Linda quickly, and they both snorted in great guffaws.

'Mum we're married, it's legal,' Jimmy reassured her.

'Oh I know, I know.' Gertrude sat down at the kitchen table, wiping her hands on her apron. 'I'm just a little flustered.'

She looked at Jimmy, then at Linda. 'Of course it's wonderful news, and you must mind yourself Linda. You take good care of her, son.'

Gertrude's eyes filled with tears and her lips trembled. If she spoke another word she would gush forth a torrent of tears. What was it? A kind of helplessness, a sadness, envy, betrayal even? She couldn't decipher. She was pulp inside.

'Mum, it's not the end of the world. We thought you'd be pleased.'

'Oh I am, I am,' she said, as a gulp escaped her, midway between a sob and a laugh. 'Here Jimmy, has anyone a hanky please?'

They all laughed and Gertrude blew her nose hard. What mixed feelings a baby can bring!

Later she told William they were to become grandparents.

'Well, it can happen,' said William, a proud grin on his face as he lit up a big cigar to celebrate. 'Come on Gertie, you look tragic. The world isn't about to fall in. And, at least they are married!'

He winked at her, but she rushed into his arms and held him very tightly.

'Hey Gertie girl, hey, come on granny.'

He lifted her chin to smile into her eyes. All he saw were the wide eyes of a frightened child; Gertrude, vulnerable as she had never been.

'What? What is it?'

His voice was puzzled concern.

'Oh William.' She hugged him tight again. 'I'm so mixed up. I should be happy for them, but my baby, my Jimmy, a father, already? I can't believe it.'

'Gertrude, he's married, and twenty years old. I grant you that is young. But we weren't much older, now were we?'

'It seems so young,' wailed Gertrude.

'I suppose it is. It is. But we survived.'

She looked at him then, her pale blue eyes wet and glowing.

'I suppose we did William, I suppose we did.'

Then the tears came. Gertrude sobbed in her husband's arms for many minutes, joy and sorrow flowing through her in some sort of atonement.

After this evening Gertrude took out the knitting needles. She sent for patterns from Clery's of Dublin and started to knit tiny white bootees, frilly bonnets, little cardigans in white, not pink or blue, just to be on the safe side. She put satin ribbons through the bootees, sewed tiny pearl buttons onto the cardigans. She ordered the best soft wool blankets and nappies for the layette. Often as she knitted she cried. The bootees were so small, how was any human being once ever so small and defenceless?

Her womb ached. She wanted it to swell up again, longed for a baby. The feeling grew into a pain which throbbed intensely in her lower abdomen. She would look at the patterns, see the bonny babies in the magazine pictures, and her womb would flip over. They were so beautiful. How had she not had more of them when she had the chance? Then she knew what to do. A baby would be the answer to everything. It would bring her and William closer than ever, and bring healing and hope. A new baby. New life. It wasn't too late.

For about three weeks William was greeted by a new Gertrude whenever he came home. She was dressed elegantly, her make-up perfect, her hair shining. But more than that, she was soft, pliant almost. She would curl around him, curve her body towards him, even as she made the simplest of gestures. Pouring tea she would place a hand on his neck, stroke his hair, let a finger slip under his collar. She would press his head against her bosom, which was soft and perfumed. While he enjoyed the attention, he wondered what was coming next. He knew Gertrude only too well of old.

Evenings by the fire, when Matilda had been put to bed, she would stretch herself languorously, or take off a shoe and rub a shapely foot under its arch, then run a palm up along her calf muscle. She was sensuous and cat-like. On the third evening, as William watched her lift her skirt to continue massaging her thigh, he caved in. He slipped his hand up alongside hers, lifted his other hand to brush over her breasts oh so gently, then pulled her head to his, to kiss her full on the mouth. Their fluids merged and melted that night. William took her, his beautiful compliant wife, and he loved her more than ever, almost as much as on that first night by the fire long ago. She felt the sticky wetness and lay back, sighing in satisfaction. They continued like this every other evening for almost three weeks. Gertrude felt better than she had in years. Her appearance glowed, her manner was kind and warm.

When the full moon had waned to a tiny sickle cold and sharp in the sky, Gertrude's body let trickle forth the first signs. The deep red clots left Gertrude in no doubt – she had not conceived. Her dismay was absolute. She couldn't believe it. It threw her into a pit of even greater despair, where she was given to wild fits of weeping. She lost all appetite and sank into hopelessness. That was it. She was old. Barren. She would not be blessed, now when she wanted it more than ever. Her womb would never carry a beautiful little baby. It was her fault, she had damaged it herself.

A son was born to Jimmy and Linda and he was called Simon. Linda had a terrible time during labour, had shrieked obscenities at Jimmy never to come near her again, and decided she would never have another child. Gertrude pounced on the little baby in delight and awe, her tears flowing freely. She would look after this precious creature for them. She would help out in whatever way she could. In the midst of their joy, on the second day after Simon's birth, Master Cullen arrived to visit his great-grandson. He brought with him disturbing news: Elizabeth was also with child and would bear a child six months hence.

Into the euphoria and light surrounding the new birth sounded a gong of warning. Gertrude felt the clang in her stomach but decided for the moment to ignore it. She must visit Elizabeth, to see how she was keeping. She hadn't seen her since the weddings. She had heard that Johnny was building a new bungalow for them not far from the school-master's house in the valley, on the road that fell away under the avalanche hill. He had sheep grazing there on commonage, and had bought some extra acres of mountain bog. So although Elizabeth was busy settling into her new life, and setting up home, she hadn't seen or spoken to her mother. Now that she was expecting, Gertrude decided to break the ice. The birth might change everything.

She set off one day from Glenview, through the cold of early spring, to walk down the valley. She heard a tock-tock-tock of brick upon brick, and came across the shell of a house, in a gash hewn out of the side of a hill. Two men were bent over in the task of setting and laying blocks to build up the four walls of a house. Gertrude stopped short. The men looked up. One was Johnny Mulhall. He stared at her from under his cap, then turned back to what he was doing. The other man, who was unknown to her, grunted a greeting. It was useless to inquire further. She supposed that Elizabeth for the moment was back at the Mulhall homeplace, in that little cottage under the fir trees. Frances, his mother, had passed away some years previously from the cancer that gnawed her for the longest time. Tommie had no reason to come any more. At least Mattie had gone off to England.

Gertrude turned back and mounted the hill for home. She only hoped that the baby would go easy on Elizabeth, especially in that cold little cottage.

'Tell Elizabeth I called,' she shouted down at Johnny's bent back.

Somehow Gertrude never found time to visit again. Linda had come to stay for a while at Glenview, so that now she had her hands full. She could spend all day carrying baby Simon around, cooing and playing with him. And so the time went by.

The Master would call for his tea every Sunday. William would go and pick him up for he was too frail now to drive himself. He still seemed to manage though, with the help of the ancient Bridie. He brought news of Elizabeth, and how their new house was nearly finished.

He would look at Gertrude pointedly and say, 'Elizabeth is blooming. She's looking better than I have seen her in years,' and wait for a response.

Gertrude would smile brightly back, cooing all the while at the baby, and say, 'I'm glad for her.'

When he was leaving, her father's face would furrow. 'Gertie, will you do me a favour? Go and see her when the baby is born, see if she needs any help.'

'I will, Daddy, I will,' she promised, kissing him warmly.

She closed the door with a wave and leaned back against it in relief. Why did she feel such guilt? It was Elizabeth's stubbornness that had meant Gertrude couldn't attend her wedding. The dates couldn't be changed, and that was that. Gertrude had a facility for forgetting – forgetting the words that had flown between herself and her daughter, flashing arrows thrown at each other to wound, changing the course of history. Gertrude had lost. She convinced herself that she had tried, that

Elizabeth had always been difficult and she had never understood her. Now she was married to one of those Mulhalls.

Oh well, Gertrude couldn't do anymore. Of course I'll go and see her, she had reassured her father. But deep down below all the words and self-justifying thoughts, a bell had sounded and was clanging sonorously, sending out waves of warning. Deep in her soul, Gertrude was frozen in terror at what Elizabeth might bring forth. A monstrous child, punishment for her sin? No. She avoided those bleak staring eyes, Matilda blackly watching her throughout the day. 'Tell her', they said. Tell her. What was the use? What was done was done. The past was nobody's business.

On a summer's night some months later they got word that Elizabeth had had the baby. A girl. 'Is it all right?' was the first cry that escaped Gertrude on hearing the news. 'Oh thank God,' she wept, on receiving a reply that affirmed the child seemed healthy. Oh thank God.

As a form of thanksgiving, she resolved to visit Elizabeth. Now she could show her goodwill, and in this gesture let bygones be bygones. Her relief was immense, and she was filled with gratitude, to God, the universe, and to the secret for staying put.

Gertrude quickly knitted a pink romper suit in the finest softest baby wool, wrapped it in tissue paper with pink ribbons. When she heard Elizabeth had come home from the nursing home in Dublin, she asked William to drop her over to the new house.

'It's all right, it's better if I go in by myself, this is between me and Elizabeth,' she patted William to dismiss him. However she asked him to park a little bit away but not to leave altogether. Then she arranged her coat and hat as she picked her way over the unfinished path to the front door. She rapped with her knuckles as there was as yet no doorbell. From inside came a baby's cry. The door eased open slowly. Johnny stood there, his shirt loose about his neck, his beard unshaven.

'Hello Johnny, how are you all?' Gertrude piped up cheerfully.

He looked at her, rubbed his eyes in disbelief.

'Who is it Johnny?' called Elizabeth from within.

Johnny stayed silent, so shocked he just stood back to let Gertrude pass through.

'I've brought a present for the baby,' Gertrude ventured, about to step in. Just then Elizabeth came walking out through a door at the end of the hall, a baby swaddled on her shoulder. She looked haggard, her eyes black-rimmed from sleepless nights, her hair standing out in a wild bush. She stopped.

'You!' she accused. Her eyes were balls of fire. 'Get out. Get out and never set foot in my house again.'

Johnny shuffled and mumbled, 'ah come on now Lizzie. She's your mother. Let her see the child.'

'The child's name is Catherine. And you will have nothing to do with her. Ever.'

The baby let out a squawk, the insistent squeal of a newborn infant who is hungry and cannot wait. Elizabeth turned on her heel, walked back down the hall and shut the door.

Gertrude pushed the present into Johnny's hands. Its crinkling was the only sound in the vacuum that had rushed in to swamp them. Gertrude's head spun and she held the wall to face out into the road. As she left, the tissue paper fell open and tumbled softly to the floor in a sigh of pink ribbons.

Catherine's Diary

19 April 1985

I've been thinking a lot about Granny's story. She's not the worst, she had her reasons. And she did try to make it up, but Mammy just hated her by then.

Then this afternoon I got the biggest shock. I was going up the stairs after dinner when who should I see coming up the path but Mammy. I couldn't believe it. Mammy never goes out by herself, and she never visits Granny, said she wasn't talking to her ever again. Mammy, walking up the drive in the Easter hat with her gloves on all by herself.

Oh my Jesus, what am I going to do? I run down, I run up again, my heart hammering. I call Gran, but I don't know if she hears me before the bell rings. Then Gran is pulling the door open and I am halfway down the stairs.

'Elizabeth,' says Granny. 'Oh. What a surprise.'

Mammy just comes in the door without saying a word, sort of pushing Granny away and coming into the hall. She stops and looks all around, then heads for the kitchen. Granny looks up and makes a sign for me to go back upstairs, so I do. But I can hear them, I hear everything.

'Elizabeth,' says Granny again in her loud clear voice, 'it's nice to see you. Can I get you tea?'

She follows Mammy down into the kitchen.

'Where's Catherine?' says Mammy.

'Upstairs having a rest. Do you want to sit down and wait for her?'

'You have the house nice,' says Mammy. 'Better than I expected. I suppose you have Catherine killed with all the work.'

'She's a good girl,' says Granny.

'You two weren't at Mass on Sunday. People were asking after her.'

'No, well we were actually. Up in Moyne. Jimmy dropped us up.'

'Jimmy,' sneers Mammy. 'How is he?'

'Getting on as usual. Linda's always running around. Simon's up in Dublin doing medicine.'

'I know. Sure doesn't he call to see us,' says Mammy.

'Good,' says Gran.

Then they say nothing for a long time. I hear Mammy walking around the kitchen. I hope she isn't feeling the plugs.

'So will Catherine be long?' says Mammy. 'We want her to come home for her tea, for Easter. Her Daddy misses her.'

'I'll wet the tea,' says Granny.

'No, I won't have any,' says Mammy.

'Ah do. You might as well. Just while I go up and see if Catherine's awake.'

'That's not like her,' says Mammy. 'Lady Muck now, is she? I'll go up. About time I saw the state of the house for myself.'

'Elizabeth,' says Gertrude. 'It's all right, I'll go.'

I am listening on the stairs. When I hear that I run up and into the toilet. Oh my God, home for tea. I'm going to be sick. If I sit on the toilet and talk to her through the door she won't see me.

'Catherine,' calls Granny.

'Kitty,' calls Mammy. The two footsteps come up together.

'I'm in the toilet,' I say.

'That's all right,' says Granny. 'Take your time.'

'I haven't got all day,' snaps Mammy.

'I might be a while, I'm feeling sick,' I say.

'So,' says Mammy, 'what are you doing with all his things?'

'Oh, I'm busy clearing out wardrobes and drawers at the moment. The accumulations of a lifetime,' says Granny.

'I want to see it. I don't want his things thrown out with no respect for the dead.'

'I am his daughter, next of kin.' Granny's voice is steady.

'We're all family,' says Mammy. 'But you forgot that a long time ago.'

'Elizabeth, did you come here to complain?' Granny's voice is tetchy.

'No, mother,' she says, 'I want my daughter back. And I'd like to know what you are going to do with this house.'

'The will is in probate, Elizabeth. You'll be kept informed. Now if that's all you've come to say, you've said it,' says Gran, starting back down the stairs.

'I'll wait here for Catherine,' says Mammy.

I was stuck. I flushed the toilet, pulled the swing jumper down over my stomach, and held my breath. My hair was hanging in front when I opened the door. I think I was trying not to smile.

'Well Catherine,' says she, 'how're you getting on here?'

Her eyes were gleaming through her glasses.

'Fine Mammy,' I says, leaning against the door. I know my face was red.

Then the glasses frost over. Her lips go tight.

'Oh. Oh. You dirty girl,' she says with her mouth closed, and turns and goes down the stairs with loud steps. She runs into the kitchen to find Granny.

'You knew about this you conniving witch.'

Her voice is high.

'Dear God and his Holy Mother, what are people going to say?' she wails. 'Catherine,' she shouts up the stairs, 'this will kill your father.'

And she throws a cup or something because there's a smashing sound and thumping coming from downstairs. When I hear that I run down in case she'd be going for Granny.

'Stop, stop it, it's all my fault, and anyway I'm going to Dublin and that'll be the end of it,' I say.

Mammy was standing in the middle of the kitchen with a teapot in her hand.

'I'll, I'll ... God help us what'll become of us?'

She's waving the teapot as if she's trying to break it on the table. She sees me at the door.

'Did I not teach you about the importance of purity? Oh Catherine, your soul, your immortal soul.'

She looks at me as if she's going to cry. She's rubbing the teapot and twisting it in her hands.

'Oh the shame. What will your father say?'

She lets the teapot down on the table. There's no bang.

She runs out of the house. Granny goes to the door and shouts after her, but she was gone running back down the valley.

I'm so scared she'll tell Daddy and he'll be up here next shouting and roaring. I'm shaking for ages as Gran wets the tea.

'Calm down love,' she says. 'It'll be all right.'

I stare at her. I feel like a mad woman.

'Catherine, there is something I didn't tell you. That time after the funeral? I did meet Tommie, just the once, and very briefly.'

'In the hut?' I ask.

'Almost.' She smiles. 'I was out walking with Jack. I came over from Glenview across the fields to check the schoolhouse. It must've been the fourth day, because they were all gone, except for the mess. Anyhow, there he was, at the bend below the road at the river, just at the path to the forest. I couldn't mistake him, the tall strong cut of him, in a brown Crombie hat. He was gazing up the hill, rubbing his hands together against the cold. Handsome. He turned and his eyes crinkled into a smile, as if it were only yesterday. Sunshine.

'"Ah Gertie, it's yourself."

'And I stood beside him, two old people, side by side.

'"Yes it is myself, at last Tommie." I smiled at him. It was easy between us. We had both come home.'

'Is that all Gran?' I asked her.

She gave a big sigh. 'And that's life. No happy endings.'

I could see she was very sad. I went to put out my hand when she grabbed mine hard.

'Don't be afraid Catherine,' she said suddenly. 'I'm here for you. I know what it's like to be pregnant and ashamed. I know.'

I hate it when she goes all emotional. I'm not used to it. That makes it all worse, she won't want more shame in the family. Maybe she'll help me get rid of it, maybe she knows how.

But she has me all mithered. Does that mean she wasn't a virgin when she got married? Is that what she's telling me? Imagine that, in those days. What did she say? She had a baby? If she did, where is it? Oh my God, I don't want her to tell me more, I can't cope with all this, it's too much, my head is bursting. I want to die. It would be better to leave the baby on a beach. Like in Kerry.

23 April

The house is very quiet. Granny is saying very little. I didn't sleep the last two nights so I'm nodding off in the chair during the day. When Jack barks, I wake up, and then I don't know where I am for a minute. That's when the pain comes back across my stomach. It's a heavy feeling and I want to be sick. It's Daddy there in my tummy as if he'd hit me. I squeeze up inside imagining his face. Then my heart goes again, hammering and running like the clappers. I can't stand up because I'm afraid I'll faint. When Gran starts to talk, I get a fright and look at her as if I didn't know she was there. She says, 'there there child, it's only me, you were dozing.' I can't eat. I don't want to. I sit in the chair by the range until it's time to go upstairs to bed. Sometimes I say to Gran I'm going up now, and it's only two o'clock in the day. I lie down and pull the blankets up and want it to be dark. I lie on my side. I don't feel so heavy then, with the ball hanging out the side. A big ball. My tummy is hard now, stretched. I feel stretched down there too, like I want to push to go to the toilet. I'm often wet. I have terrible dreams. About water rushing down and spilling all over me, about rocks falling down on my head crushing me under an avalanche. I'm trying to come up for air and I can't, and I'm pushing and fighting and this big stone is holding me back. Then Simon comes in my dream, and gives me a hand, and helps me up out of the hole, and kisses me. A big flood gushes through me and for a minute the roar of the water stops and it's sunny and peaceful and still. When I wake up my face is wet from crying. The sheets are soaked from sweat.

Then I have to get up because there's something pushing down on my bladder and I have to pee all the time. My body is so heavy I can hardly walk. My back hurts. I would really like to stay asleep, go back to my dream where it was sunny and warm but I can't. I ache all over from the stones crushing me. I'm black and blue but I don't see any bruises. I'm afraid to sleep and more afraid to stay awake.

When I go back to the kitchen for my tea I jump every time the kettle hisses on the stove. The clock ticks. It's very loud. I want the sun to go down and the day to be over. Once the doorbell rang. I stood up and went white.

'I'll go Catherine,' said Granny.

My hands were sweaty. I was terrified. I was sure it was Daddy. It was only Jimmy with the groceries on his way home. I sat in my chair behind my hair and didn't look at him. I feel so dirty. Everyone hates me. Why wouldn't they? I hate myself.

I know what Daddy will say when he comes. He'll say, 'you little hoor, who did it to you?' Then he'll drag me out home by the hair like he does when he loses his temper with me, and he'll say, 'where's the bastard 'til I beat the living daylights out of him?' As for the baby, what will he say? 'No Mulhall was ever born a bastard. There'll be no bastards born in this house.' Then he'll show me the door, or he'll wait and then drown it, like the puppies. Then he'll kill me or never talk to me again. How will I look him in the eye in the mornings?

I swallow when I think of all this, and go cold inside. I think I'll drown it myself. No one will ask me then, we'll just go on like before, normally. No one will talk about it. Nobody really knows. I haven't said it. I can just say I put on a bit of weight and that my body has a lot of fluids sometimes when I get me periods. No one can say otherwise. No one will ever see a baby, because they won't find it. I have a knife and a stocking.

30 April

The last few days passed very slowly. Me and Gran are sitting in the kitchen again and night begins to fall, except it is long drawn-out on account of the stretch in the evenings. The fire dies down gradually in the range, the embers slide and creak.

Granny says in a kind voice, 'Dinnertime soon Catherine, would you like a hot chocolate to keep you going?'

'Thanks Gran, that'd be lovely.'

I've been very quiet recently. There has been no news from Dublin. Helen has been up the once. She is at home now keeping house, but she hasn't seen Simon she said.

Granny was smiling as she gave me the steaming cup.

'So, do you mind me asking what you are thinking of doing?'

I go red.

'Simon said he'd help me get to Dublin.'

'Simon?'

I drop my eyes.

'He's making arrangements,' she mutters.

'Ah,' says Gran, 'then I should talk to him.'

'No, no Gran don't. It's OK, it's fine really.'

I get up too quickly spilling the cocoa.

'I think he should hear from me then,' she says.

Some hours later there is a knock. Gran comes back into the kitchen followed by Simon. He is wearing his fine tweed coat, looking like a handsome young medical student. His hair is dark and curls over his collar. His eyes are deep almond but he shies away from my gaze as he says hi.

Gran seats him at the kitchen table. She gets straight to the point.

'Catherine says you have made arrangements. I'd like to know what they are. You know her time is running out?'

Simon's voice is cocky. 'Oh yes, there's a mother and baby home on the Navan Road. They'll take her.'

I jump.

Gran looks at me.

'Are you sure that's what Catherine wants?' she asks him.

'Well, she doesn't want to stay here, with her father and all,' he says.

'Catherine?' Gran asks gently, looking at me.

'I ...' I try to make Simon look at me.

'I told you, Simon, I'll come to Dublin.'

He's still not catching my eye.

Gran takes over.

'Simon, Catherine is going to have a baby. There may be another way to handle all of this.'

'No no, it's fine this way, the arrangements are made. I know some-body with a sister working there. She's a nun. They get them adopted.'

I get very confused suddenly.

'I don't want all this,' I say.

Gran is brisk.

'Then I want to know what's going on. I'll go to the post office in the morning and call the home.'

'No,' Simon protests, 'it'll be OK, really.'

'And how is Catherine going to get there?'

'I'll bring her as soon as my exams are over.'

'And what happens if it's sooner?'

'Then Helen is just down the road. She'll bring her.'

I hang my head and fiddle with my medal. This is the most embar-rassing moment of my life.

'I don't want to be any trouble,' I look over at him. 'But ... a home? Is that all Simon?' I whisper.

'Yes,' he says. 'It's got a good reputation, they take in girls, sometimes they keep them for a few months until they can show their faces at home again. Or if they can't find families straight away they have facilities to keep the babies.'

'An orphanage you mean?'

I don't believe this is happening.

'I suppose so. The women are well looked after. If they stay there long enough they can go to school, and then work in the home later.'

My stomach sinks.

'A tiny baby, surrounded by others in a big ward? All alone without its mother for three months or even longer.'

Gran's voice is high. 'No I won't have it. The poor baby, who knows what damage will be done to it? That's not on.'

She seems to choke and swallow, then turns to me.

'Catherine, we'll work something out. Don't worry.'

Simon shifts in his chair, making noises about hitting the road.

'You can stay here,' says Gran.

He wriggles a little but she holds his gaze. He can't escape.

'All right, but I have to leave very early in the morning, I've lectures at ten.'

'Anyone for a drink?' he says brightly, still determined to escape for a few hours.

'No thanks,' I mumble. I feel like getting sick.

'But Helen's at home, minding Mammy,' I offer, to get rid of him.

'Yeah, thanks,' says Simon as he leaves.

I couldn't wait to get up to bed and stuff my face into the pillow. I don't want to see any of them. I don't want this to be happening. I hate it.

I fall asleep. Some hours later a car pulls up. I hear Simon get out, followed by a girl giggling.

'Come on in for the one, they're all asleep,' he says.

'Jesus, do you think we should? Granny's house?' she says. It's Helen.

'I'm sleeping on the sofa. She sleeps at the back.'

I hear a match striking as they lift the latch, then something falling against the hall table. The sitting room door creaks open.

Now I'm really awake. I strain my ears for a few minutes, to listen to the sounds of shushing and murmuring. I need to talk to Simon, on my own. I wait for ages and ages, maybe twenty minutes or so, but hear nothing. My heart starts to beat very fast. I have to see him. I pull on my dressing gown, the old candlewick that Gran lent me, and creep down the stairs.

I stop at the door, hearing a moan. Then I push it open. Oh dear Jesus.

Helen is sitting on top of Simon, her breasts bare.

'Helen,' I call out, Helen!'

'Catherine,' they both say, as they come apart and jump up to get some clothes.

I can't believe my eyes. I'm breathing hard through my nose.

'Simon?' is all I can say.

He's half naked too.

'Listen, Catherine,' he says.

'I ... Simon? ... Helen, you cow.'

'Ah now Kitty, I was going to tell you, calm down now, you'll do yourself damage.'

'Damage. I think the damage has been done the way I'm looking at it.'

I'm in a daze.

'Simon, what are you ... what's going on?'

I start to cry.

'Kitty, I told you I had a new boyfriend didn't I? Well, it's Simon. That's all,' says Helen brightly.

'I would have told you Catherine,' says Simon too.

'But Simon, the flat. Our future?'

I'm choking with the tears.

'I can still take care of that.'

'Simon, don't tease her, she's not well, look at the state of her,' says Helen.

'But I was going to come to Dublin after ...' I sob helplessly. My tears are falling like heavy rain.

'Come on, Simon, tell her we're getting engaged.'

'Wait now, Helen, not yet, I didn't say yet.'

'Married? You're getting married? Simon, what about our baby?'

My voice was in a high squeal.

'What's she on about Simon?' Helen snaps.

'Jesus girls calm down. Let there be no crisis. It's all arranged.'

'What Simon?' screams Helen, 'what's all arranged? Tell me what she's on about.'

'The baby Helen, our baby. It's his. He done it.'

'Don't listen to her raving Helen. That's nonsense,' says Simon quickly, like a boss.

'Your baby. You're the one?' roars Helen. 'You did it with her? Jesus Mary and Joseph you're disgusting.'

Helen's face twists. She can't believe it either.

'She's lying. Why do you believe her and not me, Helen?'

Simon sounds so smooth. And hollow.

'Kitty did you? Did he? With him?'

Helen turns to me now. She's distraught too.

'Helen I never went with Mossie Dollard or any other chap. Why would I? I love him.'

I point to Simon and then my knees give way.

Helen holds me up.

'I believe her. I'll never trust you again as far as I can throw you, you scheming little runt.'

'Helen calm down, she's making it up.'

Simon's voice rises.

Helen looks at me. I see her all blurry through the tears, like a broken mirror. Jesus I hurt. She believes me.

'So it is your baby? Poor Catherine.'

She turns on Simon.

'Well you can do as you promised and help her get rid of it. Get rid of it Simon, take it away. We don't want it. She doesn't want a baby.'

Helen's voice is thick. She's disgusted with him.

'I was going to bring it to Dublin like I said, there are homes ...'

Helen is cold. 'Look at the trouble you've caused.'

'Simon, please.' I'm crying and begging him. 'Simon, our plans. Oh Simon Simon Simon. Jesus Helen don't tell Daddy.'

I'm gasping from shock. The pain winds me.

'I won't, shush now.'

Helen turns again on Simon. 'Help her then, go on, like you promised, with all your palaver.'

Simon steps into the hall to be near the door. 'I've got to go,' he mumbles.

'I can't fucking believe it. You and Catherine. What's she going to do now?'

Helen follows him to the door.

I'm gasping for breath and wailing, 'Go on, get out of here you two, get out get out get out get out and leave me alone. I hate you, I hate you Helen, I'll never speak to you as long as I live.'

Helen comes back in. 'Stay here and don't move Kitty. Sit down, sit down, there, there.'

'I hate you. Take your hands off me.'

I push her away but it's no good, I'm so feeble.

'Simon, come back,' commands Helen.

He's halfway out the front door.

'Simon,' Helen calls and runs out of the house after him. 'How are you going to live with this on your conscience, Doctor Hawthorn Thwaite?'

'Ah Helen lay off, give us a break.'

'You thought you'd get away with it, didn't you? You shithead, you big fat piece of pig shit. How could you? Catherine. Catherine, of all people.'

Helen starts hitting him. She's raging.

'Ah Helen calm down. Come on now, get into the car,' he says.

'Go with you? You're unbelievable. Go on. Run away, go back to Dublin and don't show your face down here again. Go on run rabbit run. You bollocks!'

Helen slams the door on the way back in.

'Come on Catherine, go on back up to bed.'

'I can't. Leave me alone. There is no baby. No baby do you hear me? There won't be a baby. I don't want it.'

I am sobbing now, my face down in the old sofa.

'You're not to tell anyone. Nobody. Ever. There is no baby. Oh Jesus help me, help.'

I was in some dark place for hours until a hand touched my shoulder. I think it was Granny who put me to bed.

1 May

Day dawns on the valley. Mist on the avalanche mountain blocks the sun. Loud knocking wakes me up. It booms all over the house.

Gran rushes to answer it. The door opens. I hear Mammy.

'Well,' says Gran. 'You're in a hurry. What do you want at this hour?'

'The slut, the little hoor.'

'Elizabeth.'

'No, no I won't be stopped. Daddy knows now and there's no two ways about it, there'll be no Mulhall bastard born in this valley. He's going after whoever did this to her. I'll take care of the baby. Where is she anyway?'

'Elizabeth, now come in and sit down. We can sort something out.' Gran leads Mammy to the kitchen. 'It's hard on her, you know, It's not her fault.'

'She's a dirty girl. I sent her to Mass every Sunday washed clean after her bath on a Saturday night. She used to be a good girl.'

'She is. She's only expecting a baby. It's not a crime.'

'You're a right one all right. It's a crying shame and a mortal sin so it is. She's not married. Daddy's going to find him whoever he is and he'll have to do the decent thing and marry her.'

'Elizabeth, it's not so simple.'

'Oh yes it is now please do not try to interfere. You're aiding and abetting her in all of this.'

'Well I am surely not the culprit. I didn't cause it if that's what you mean.'

'Don't mock me. Where is she?' snaps Elizabeth.

'I'll get her. Catherine!' Gran calls up the stairs. 'She must be still asleep. Why don't you just sit down. There's tea in the pot.'

'It's not right, it's not right, it's not right. It is not.'

'No no, it isn't, but it's Catherine I feel sorry for now. Her time has come.'

'So I'm too late. Or am I?'

Mammy jumps up. I hear her bag snap open, then a loud clang.

'I came prepared.'

'Put those scissors away. There's no need.'

Mammy's bag doesn't snap shut.

'Catherine,' calls Granny, then mounts the stairs.

She opens my door.

I'm in the cubbyhole under the stairs. My pains have started. Footsteps clack outside.

'Bitch. The little bitch. Where is she?'

'Elizabeth, calm down right now. We have to find her, and help her.'

'Why should I? What has she done only bring shame?'

'She's your daughter, that's why. As a Christian.'

'Holy now are we? A bastard. Catherine's bastard. Daddy will beat the life out of her and she'll not do it again. He'll drown it.'

'Elizabeth.' Gran is appalled. 'I think now she needs the both of us. This is no time for fighting.'

'You took her from me. Like you took Grandad in the end, and now the house. You take everything don't you? You think you deserve it.'

'What's all this about, Elizabeth? You're my daughter. Help me find Catherine. Help your girl. You're her mother.'

'Mother – ha! You don't know the meaning of the word. Motherly love was it, sending me away.'

'Elizabeth we can talk later. Let's find Catherine. Please.'

'Then you couldn't even show your face at my wedding. Your own daughter's wedding. You always hated Johnny Mulhall, and what did he ever do to you?'

'Elizabeth I ask you one last time. Be compassionate.'

'Why should I? She's shamed us all. Shamed. Were you ashamed of me mother, were you, that you tried to stop me getting married, telling me I wasn't in love, that I didn't know the meaning of the word. Were you, were you, ashamed of me? Why should I help her?'

'Because I know what she's going through,' Gran says quietly, steadily. 'I got pregnant before I was married.'

I open the front door, half asleep. I wear an old anorak and some large woollen things, like a bag lady. I move quickly forward and turn the corner of the house to walk down the hill in front.

I walk as briskly as I can, and cross the ditch under a hawthorn tree to go over the field below. There is birdsong. I imagine so anyway, as no one else has stirred yet, for it must be only seven o'clock. I stop in the middle of the next field, bend down to a sheep trough and lift up some hay. I hold the bundle, as much as my arms can take, tightly to me, and continue on. I make my way down to the river and then up the track into the woods, to the old hut.

I go inside. In the dampness I prepare my bed in the corner by the chimney. I try to sit down but I have no peace. I get up to walk in circles, round and round the room, trying to shake off the cramping down low in my tummy. It grips me and will not let go, like a mad dog.

I hold on to the wooden mantel above the chimney and hang there for relief. I kneel to arch my back and stretch like a cat. I moan. I go outside to search the mountains for a sign.

'Holy Mother of God, angel baby help me.'

I lie on the hay in my anorak and fall asleep.

I am woken by a pain so severe it frightens me. The sweat pours off me and I want to cry. There is no one to hear.

'Won't be long now, angel, and you'll be with your Mammy, your angel Mammy, in heaven.'

I sit up and then lie on my side again, the pain is so strong.

Suddenly I hear a rustling. Twigs crack outside.

Ah no. Go away. I could cry. I pull the anorak tighter around myself and squeeze into my corner by the chimney.

Luckily I have barred the door.

'Catherine, Mammy's here,' says Helen.

'Go away,' I scream, 'you two-faced bitch.'

Granny says, 'Catherine we're here to help you, me and your mother and Helen.'

'Get her out of my sight. Her, send her away.'

Gran says, 'Run up to the house and bring back some blankets there's a good girl.'

Helen obeys like a child.

'Catherine, Catherine, it's me, Gertrude. We want to help you. Let us in.'

'Not her,' I scream again.

'Helen's gone,' Gran says, 'look out the window.'

So I do.

Mammy sees me and says to Gran. 'You are in cahoots with her. She's gone mad.'

I must look terrible. My eyes are all blotchy from crying all night and there's hay in my hair.

'Elizabeth, she's having a child. Now help me get in to her, she needs us.'

Mammy starts her prayers, mumbling and swaying.

'My own mother tells me she had a bastard too, well my God, Holy Mary Mother of God, what am I to make of that? Where is it now then?'

Gran takes over.

'Elizabeth, now is not the time.'

'Tell me then, where is it?'

Gran's face contorts.

'She was a lovely baby girl.'

She looks at Elizabeth. Then Mammy understands.

It's herself.

She was Gertrude's baby, born too early.

Mammy pulls at Gran's coat.

'Oh Holy God. Liar. It's not true, you lying vixen. You're telling lies. Dear Jesus, what have you gone and done to me?'

Gran is brief. She is trying to open the door of the hut.

'William is not your father.'

'Liar. I am Elizabeth Hawthorn Thwaite.'

'Yes, yes of course you are.'

The door begins to give way under her shoulder.

'I was in love with ...' Gran can't say the words. 'And I had his baby before my time. I'm sorry Elizabeth.'

Mammy stands there, shouts at her mother's back.

'Some other man is my father? Now she tells me, now she tells me I'm a bastard. The nerve of it, and would you mind telling me where he is now.'

Gran pushes and shoves against the door.

'He went to England. He never knew because I never told him. I married William.'

Mammy stands square, a petulant child, on the verge of a massive tantrum.

'You lying deceiving bitch. I hate you. I hated you before but now I really hate you and all you've done to this family.'

Inside the hut I cry out in pain.

There is a lull as this all sinks in. Even I sit up in the middle of all the spasms.

Granny had a baby. I can't think.

'But Daddy, William, did he know?' snaps Mammy.

'No, not until later,' says Gran quietly.

'Ooowwww,' I cry out, 'ooowwww, Holy God have mercy on me. Help help help!'

The last word rises in a squeal of anguish. Gran turns to Elizabeth. Her eyes are pleading, conciliatory, on the edge of desperation.

'Yes Lizzie I have sinned too. You can hate me later. But help us now. Please.'

She turns back to her task.

'Catherine, Catherine love, let us in.'

Her voice almost breaks. The door opens.

I stand there, tears rolling down my face.

'He doesn't love me Granny.' I lay my head on Gran's shoulder. 'He doesn't love me, he doesn't love me, what'll I do? He said he'd get a flat in Dublin, it was going to be all right.'

I sob and heave until Gran has to hold me up.

'I want to die.'

'Catherine, Catherine, there there, it's all right, come here to me, lie down now and hold my hand. There there, calm down love, rest against me, yes, cry, cry it out. You poor child.'

'Who? Who is he?' demands Mammy. 'Who, where is he?'

Does she mean her unknown father, or the father of my child?'

'Simon,' I blurt out and fall into another fit of sobbing. 'Simon, Simon, oh I love him so much.'

'Simon,' says Mammy, cold and sharp. 'A Hawthorn Thwaite. Wouldn't you know. That'd sicken you.'

'Yes Mammy, he said we'd be friends for always, always, and now he's with her.'

'Who?'

'Helen. I hate her I hate her I hate her. Gran, I'll never speak to her again.'

'Oh dear, what a mess,' sighs Gran.

I arch and buck as a spasm of pain shoots through me.

'Easy now,' says Gran. 'Easy. Breathe out.'

'So it's a Hawthorn Thwaite is it? A true blue Hawthorn Thwaite. Better for it that it's buried before it breathes.' Mammy's voice is poisonous.

'Elizabeth,' said Granny sharply. 'This is a baby.'

'A baby? A baby. So what did you do with me then?'

Gran winces.

'What is she on about Gran?'

Gran sighs heavily.

'I fell in the family way once Catherine. Like you. Some months before I married William. So it was a secret, and had to be kept quiet until the child should have been born. Your mother was put in a home for three months.'

'So you were ashamed of me, were you mother?' Mammy attempts sarcasm, but her voice cracks. 'Hid me away did you, even then?'

'I was young. I didn't know any better.'

I'm breathing fast, in great big gasps. I manage to ask.

'So Granny, you got into trouble too?'

'Yes Catherine, I got into trouble. I know what you're going through. Here hold my hand.'

'Gran, does that make Mammy illegitimate?'

I gasp and blow out the pain.

'Does that mean ... can my baby be baptised? I promised the angel baby I'd baptise it before ...'

I fall back, the sweat is pouring off me.

'Before what Catherine?'

Gran wraps her cardigan into a cushion, puts it under my head and holds my hand.

I look at Gran, searching for trust, and whisper. 'I was going to give it back to the angel baby, here in the hut.'

'Yes Catherine, hush hush love there there,' Gran soothes.

Mammy starts walking, hopping, her gait stop-start and staccato. She runs on a track of her own, raving to catch her runaway thoughts. They race ahead of her. She walks faster to catch up.

'Illegitimate. Bastard you mean. She's made a bastard of me. Ruined my life that's for sure. Wait until Daddy hears what she's after doing now. He always said there was bad blood there with all her airs and graces. And now I find out there's not a drop of Hawthorn Thwaite blood in me. Isn't that a good one? He'll be happy about that anyway – I'm not one of them. So who was my father, mother?'

Mammy screams.

'Who is he? Tell me that will you, after all the lies – where is my father? Who is he, who was he? The man you did it with? Oh Holy God to think of it, my own mother. Dear sweet Jesus what did I ever do – and Grandad, the poor Master Cullen. Butter wouldn't melt in his mouth as far as you were concerned, did he know, did he? Did he? Did he?

'Tell me mother, tell me mother, or I'll kill this little babba here and now. There'll be no Mulhall born a bastard, there'll be no Mulhall born a bastard, no bastard no bastard no bastard, in this house.'

She is spent. She crumples into a heap on the ground, shoulders heaving soundlessly.

'Shush now Elizabeth,' says Granny gently.

I sit up, turn to her with tears in my eyes.

'Help me Mammy, help me please.'

Mammy gets up. 'Stop it stop it stop it. I told you stop it, oh no, we won't stop it, no we won't, and there'll be more shame, more shame and people talking and oh what'll your father say. Oh dear Lord Jesus have mercy on us.'

She opens her handbag. Something glints sharp in the dimness. A scissors.

'Mother, who is he?'

She stands to menace Gran.

'Elizabeth. Not now. It's not the time now.'

Gran sits behind me, holding my shoulders, puffing and blowing with me. We concentrate on the task in hand. Mammy takes a step.

'There was never a time was there? Was there? Tell me now or I'll … I will I will.'

Gran looks up in horror.

'Put the scissors away.'

'Daddy doesn't want it.'

Gran lays me gently down, and stands up.

'I want it. I'll look after it. I'll take the shame if that's what you call it.'

I whimper.

'Shush Catherine, it's all right. She won't hurt you, or your baby.'

I call out. Pain takes my voice higher.

'I don't want it Gran, she can have it. Take it, take it away, he doesn't love me, what'll I do?'

'Shush shush,' Gran soothes.

Another spasm shoots through me. Mammy's eyes flicker and dart, she twists the scissors in her hands.

'I tell you what you'll do. You tell me my father's name. If we're talking about shame, tell me, let it all come out into the open, come on fill me with more shame, what does it matter anymore it's all over anyway. I'll never hold my head up again, maybe I'll take the scissors to me, that's what I'll do, I'm no good anyway so I amn't.'

'Elizabeth.' Gran commands. 'Elizabeth. Stop that now. Stop it. Stop it.'

It echoes round the hut like an ancient command.

She stops still, frozen in her gesture of threat, or plea.

'Elizabeth,' Gran says. 'You are my daughter, my only daughter, and I love you, yes I do. I may not have been a good mother but I do love you. So help us now, help your daughter. She needs you. I need you.'

Mammy's face crumples. She says in a low voice, a voice you can barely hear, in real pain.

'Just tell me who he is.'

In between the mountains of pain that topple down on me, I already know the answer.

Granny breathes out very softly. 'Tommie Mulhall,' she says.

There is a long moment. Granny looks into Mammy's eyes, a faint blush on her cheeks, her secret uttered after forty years.

Mammy starts walking again, marching round and round.

'Ah. Ah. I don't believe it. Johnny's ...? Tommie's baby?'

I gasp looking at Gran. 'You had his baby, but I thought ...'

I turn to Mam. 'Mammy, he's your father.'

'Oh sweet mother of divine, that makes Daddy my half-brother. And you let me marry him and have all those children?'

'I did try to stop you.'

Mammy is stock-still in the middle, staring.

'My father,' she whispers.

Granny is too busy with me to say more. In the meantime, Helen has come back, has crept in quietly with the blankets. I'm crying out every two minutes now.

'My half-brother,' Mammy says. 'Thank God they're all right, the children. That's a sin you know, a sin.'

She's laughing, but it sounds like crying, or crying that sounds like laughing, in big sobbing hiccups, her thin frame shaking.

'So are you happy Mother? You've made a sinner and a bastard out of me. Are you happy now?'

'No, Lizzie, I'm not.'

Granny is panting with exertion too, labouring with me.

'Help us now, please Elizabeth, we all need you.'

Gran gestures swiftly to Helen to take my other hand, and points Mammy to take her place at my shoulders. She gets up to go to my feet. She sees the baby's head.

Those moments are infinite, the straining and heaving bigger than huge boulders rolling down through me.

'Push now, Catherine, there's a good girl,' she orders. 'Here it comes, now, go on, now.'

There is an endless shout, like an echo down the side of a mountain, followed by a great gush of fluids, as I deliver myself of the baby.

A hush. Time stops.

'Look,' breathes Granny. 'A beautiful baby.'

'What?' we call out together.

'It's a girl.'

'A girl?'

I just roll over, dig my face into the hay. I will not look. 'Take it away, give it to the angel, I said I'd leave it down by the river.'

'Ah yes,' says Granny, 'the angel.'

She lifts up the child, and says softly.

'The angel baby. Let her be called Angela.'

'Angela? Angela?'

It was at this point that Mammy started to cry, and cry and cry and cry, and she took the little baby and wrapped her up in a towel, while Gran cleaned up and washed me. Mammy cried all over the baby, but the baby never cried, just looked up at her, looked up at us all.

'Show me,' I said suddenly, and Mammy took her and put her on my tummy, and the baby started nuzzling and looking for the teat and I gave it to her. She started to suck and it was the most natural thing in the world, and the most beautiful.

A silence descended in the room then, in that little hut under the avalanche hill, a silence and a peace broken only by the sounds of sucking, and if you could hear smiling then the place was singing too with the happiest of smiles on all four of us women. It was like the sun, and although outside there had been no sun, suddenly the room was lit up with a radiant white light. I'm sure I could hear an angel singing; a quiet delighted humming that filled us up until we were brimming over with joy. Laughter filled the room and spilled out over the threshold and out along the valley, rippling all around the forest, rising up into the sky to fly over the avalanche mountain. Like a spell broken, the mountain lit up in the sunlight and twinkled and gleamed, smiling back at us too.

When Daddy came trundling down later with murder in his heart, he heard the sounds of manic mirth, which stopped him in his tracks. When he got there Mammy just said to him, 'Go home now Johnny, I'll talk to you later, we've women's business to attend to.'

Mammy opened her mouth and sang the purest note, a long long sound rising higher and higher into the sky until Granny wiped a tear from her eye. Hallelujah. Thanksgiving.

I was crying and smiling too. 'I'd like Daddy to see my daughter,' I said.

'There'll be time for all that, he'll come round, the baby will work her magic on him too,' said Gran.

And so we did live happily ever after, sort of, for a while. I think myself that the spirit of the tiny baby that was killed in the avalanche long ago came back to live in my baby, because Angela is the best thing that ever happened to us.

Now to where my story started, with my grandmother.

Gran let me and the baby come and live with her, and then she left the schoolhouse to me when she died, which was much later. Gran also gave Simon a roasting and made him pay me an allowance until Angela was eighteen. He can well afford it. He's an eye surgeon in London now.

The kids are great uncles to Angela, it's a wonder she isn't spoilt rotten, but I have to say she was always a sunny and happy child; angelic is right, what with all the love being showered on her from all sides, sure she basked in it. Can you imagine that even Uncle Jimmy and Aunty Linda, Simon's parents, recognised her as a grandchild. So she has all her grandparents close by.

Simon used to visit at Christmas in the beginning, and always sent her a present on her birthday. He's married now himself with two kids. I wonder does he ever miss her?

As for Simon and me, well, I got over it. I gave him the cold shoulder for a while but what's the point, sure he has nothing to do with our lives now.

Daddy was put rightly in his place and became a doting grandfather, I'd say especially because he got the better of the Hawthorn Thwaites, what with one of theirs now living among us down in the valley. He was of course more than delighted that Mammy wasn't really one of them, after all.

As for poor Grandad William, and Gertrude's secret, he said he had always had his suspicions, but he preferred everything to be kept under wraps. He actually forgave her in the end. I think he really loved her. Imagine that, or was it the angel baby working her magic again? Gran even moved back to Glenview House after a while, until William died five years later.

I did eventually speak to Helen again. I guess I was really distraught for most of that time. And I did hate her then. Now she's the best aunty in the world, I even showed her my old diaries when I started to write the story. The rest I got from Granny and all her old papers and photographs. And from Mammy too. Mammy's never been the same since, that is, she's been so well she's never had to go back into hospital, and she's forgotten all about the plugs and stuff. She just takes her tablets, and dotes on Angela.

I suppose I wish she could have been a nicer Mammy to me and Helen, but I have to forgive her that because we all have our histories and our stories and hers was untold. It's better now that everything is out in the open and not hidden anymore, so that you don't know who you'll be offending or hurting.

And best of all, Tommie Mulhall came home from England on a visit. Mammy wanted to meet her father after all those years. Frances was long dead and buried along with his mother. Gertrude met him too and they got on like a house on fire, if you can judge by the light in her eyes. She's like a young girl again.

I can safely say that the valley is no longer a place of shadows and sadness, because when you look up at the hill now it seems always to be sunny and twinkling, as if it had melted.

I like it better living in the light.

Designed, typeset, printed and bound in Ireland by

The Book Producers Ltd.
www.thebookproducers.ie

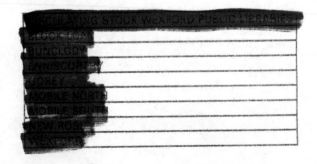